Unholy Spirit

BOOK THREE
THE NECROMANCER'S DAUGHTER

GENEVRA BLACK

CHAPTER ONE

ADAM EINAN HAD SPENT a lot of time and effort trying to forget his past. Unfortunately, despite two decades of running, his past wasn't as keen to forget him.

Even before he'd run away at seventeen, he'd known there was something inside him, huge and destructive and trying to claw its way out. It wasn't until he'd started squatting in Alphabet City that it had bloomed into anything more than a feeling.

What it was, exactly, was hard to describe. A strange, cold energy; an odd feeling of comfort and healing in darkness. Sometimes he could make things happen just by thinking about them—make the air around him cold, dim the lights, force someone to blush. For a brief period, it had seemed like a gift … something that set him apart from others, protected him almost.

Twenty-five years, and he'd long since learned it was the opposite.

He wasn't sure what else he was capable of. He wasn't even certain if any of it was real or if he was crazy—and he wasn't anxious to find out. You didn't play chicken with a curse.

After that honeymoon period, he'd covered it up as best he could. Brushed it off. Ignored it. Making his apartment in C-Squat livable had almost been a full-time job, and everyone was high off their asses anyway, so people didn't notice if something wasn't quite right. New York City's underground punk rock scene had kept him safe from himself; with all the pills and shows, he'd only had to endure a few vaguely lucid years before Death Benefits had sold out to a record label. *Like bitches*, most of his ex-friends would certainly add.

They could talk about art and *keeping it real* all they wanted, but to a twenty-year-old with no family and no future, the dollar was king. Or, at least, what he could get with the dollar was. K-holing every night made it easy to forget and compartmentalize the unexplained incidents that had plagued him since his teens.

But the drugs were gone now. The money from DB's tours and albums was pretty much dried up. Adam was getting older, and it was getting harder and harder to deny his nature its due attention.

The band's breakup had sucked, but Mikey's overdose had been devastating. That whole night was a blur of trauma, and after it, the dark feelings had gotten exponentially worse. Music still helped a little. It always had. Even strumming his guitar idly on his bed, as Adam was doing now, calmed the waves of power beating against his skin.

The all-black Ibanez Genesis RG521 had been a gift from his stepdaughter, a tribute to the original RG550 he'd played with Death Benefits. Before the Genesis, he'd never understood what musicians were talking about when they went off about their One Instrument; he had always just picked up whatever was available and played. Now, he understood. As soon as the Genesis was in his hands, two became one.

And dabbling in songwriting was a good break from his work, though it didn't make him much money. He glanced at his desk, where his pro tablet monitor was still open to a work in progress. After a torturous stint as a cubicle drone and a failed marriage, he'd finally quit to fulfill his new dream of becoming a digital artist. It hadn't made him rich, and he'd had to suffer freelance clients and plenty of nights eating cheap noodles, but his webcomic now had a decent fan base and made pretty good money.

He'd worked so hard, and he'd managed to carve out a tenuous little bit of happiness in an unforgiving world. The thought of whatever was coming to the surface washing it all away shook him to the core.

As the years flew by, he became more and more frightened of his own thoughts and reactions to things. The doctors said it was OCD. He wasn't sure.

Adam brushed a bit of hair behind his ear and tried to focus on the melody he was creating. It would sound like a real song if he could find a good time to plug in without incurring the wrath of his downstairs neighbor. When worked, the Genesis was an angry lady, but she could be gentle, too. How something could be so loud, clear, and soft all at once was like magic. He leaned to the side to wake up his laptop, then erased the last line of notes in MuseScore and replaced it with something lower to show off the guitar's tone.

As he did, the distinct sound of the front door opening stopped his heart for a split second, a reaction he still hadn't shaken after over two decades out of his father's house. The rational part of his brain reminded him of reality a beat later: his stepdaughter was home from hanging with her friends.

Elle was now over half his own age but still in dire need of parenting. Her mom's bizarre blend of strict but arbitrary moral codes and several subsequent marriages had bred an exuberant, attention-seeking kid. When Adam had first met her, she'd done everything she could to needle him into resenting her, but he'd persisted. Slowly but surely, they had formed a rapport.

He must have done something right, at least, because she'd chosen to keep visiting him after the divorce—and she was spending the summer here, not at her mom's. She still acted out, but against all odds, she was alive and in college and *sober*.

She was a good kid. Maybe he was especially equipped to see through her silly facade, even if her wounds weren't as visible as his. Unconsciously, he touched the scar that sliced through his right eyebrow and disappeared into his hairline.

Out of force of habit, Adam slung his guitar over one shoulder before he went out to greet her, so that it was resting upside down against his back. He entered the kitchen just as she tottered by, head tipped back with a hand over her nose.

"Ready for Madison Square Garden, dweeb?" she teased good-naturedly as she leaned over the trash can. When she removed her hand to paper-towel her nose, he could see blood dripping from her nostrils.

He frowned. "Another nosebleed?"

Elle shook her short, wavy blond hair out of her face. "The air is really dry out there."

Adam glanced at the kitchen window, his heart sinking when he saw how hard it was snowing. It was almost August, for god's sake. When he'd read that a blizzard was about to hit NYC, he hadn't really believed it. A rare light snow in summer was one thing, but this . . .

"I've got a humidifier you can put in your room," he said, tearing his eyes away to focus on her. Though he kept his tone even, concern gripped him, and not just because of the weather. Elle's recent trend of unexplained nosebleeds could very well be something serious. "You should really go to the doctor."

She trashed her bloody paper towels and groaned. "If I find out something's wrong with me, it'll be something expensive to fix." After a pause, she added wistfully, "I can't wait till we live in the *Mad Max* world. All the downsides of our current society with the upside of it being socially acceptable to shoot a bazooka from my wasteland tank."

As she mimed aiming various heavy weapons at him, he deadpanned, "Or you could just go because your mom's insurance covers it."

"Karen doesn't want me using her stuff," Elle said, setting her bag down and leaning against the kitchen counter with a pout. "You know I'm right."

"I really don't think that's true. Promise me you'll go?"

It took a moment of earnest staring, but finally, she caved. "Fine. I'll call tomorrow..."

With a smirk, Adam went to the sink and turned on the hot water to soak the dishes there, mumbling, "I should have done these earlier..." If only his OCD was the kind that made him sterilize everything. At least then he'd get a clean house out of it.

Before he could fall down that rabbit hole, Elle approached, rolling up one sleeve preemptively. "I can help. Or," she added quickly, as if he'd blindly approve of her suggestion if she said it fast enough, "we could get takeout and watch *Sailor Moon* until 3 a.m. again."

Adam laughed and handed her a sponge. "I already thawed chicken. If you wash up, I'll cook."

With a long-suffering sigh, she manned her station in front of the sink.

He didn't bother taking off the Genesis. If you could jump around a dark stage coated in fake blood with an electric guitar strapped to your back, you could do just about anything. He barely even remembered it was there as he moved to the fridge and fetched ingredients for an uninspired dinner of chicken, veggies, and rice.

Enough soy sauce and he might even cover up the taste of freezer burn. He might be a good dad, but he was still a disaster of a human being.

"So," Elle said from the sink, already elbows deep in suds, "what'd you do today?"

Adam grabbed a knife from the block and started to trim the chicken. "Worked on a commission in the morning. I usually wouldn't, but some indie game dev offered me a shitload of cash for some pretty promo art."

"How's the comic coming? You know people are going to kill you if you don't get Part 5 out soon."

He cracked a smile and answered coyly, "I'll get to it."

"Considering you left Prince Argon stuck in Spiritstorm Cairn, you better."

"I'm done working for the day, slave driver."

Elle glanced over her shoulder and smiled. "We can still watch *Sailor Moon*. The original? Or we could co-op *Stardew Valley*. Or I could destroy you in *Mario Kart* as usual."

"Sure, whatever you want."

His heart warmed as he walked up beside her to begin chopping veggies. Between her and Karen, their little "family" was small and unconventional and broken, but it was the only one he found worthy of the word. Like music, caring for Elle soothed him, made him feel grounded. Almost normal.

Sometimes, it felt like Fate had brought them together. Though hopefully not for any higher purpose, considering most of their time was spent eating dumplings and playing video games.

Adam oiled up a pan and threw the chicken in, but when he went to throw away the packaging, it barely fit in the trash. With a sigh, he turned back to Elle. "Hey, do you mind taking this out?"

She looked over her shoulder, whining when she saw he meant the trash. "But I'm washing dishes! My hands are all wet!"

"It'll just be a second, and I need to start on the veggies."

"But—"

Unmoved, he tied the bag and hoisted it up, offering it to her with a quirked brow. She huffed but nevertheless dried her hands, took the bag, and went to the back door. Their fire escape was more like stairs, and it led right to the dumpster out back. She slipped on her shoes, wedged the doorstop in place, and stepped onto the landing.

Adam had already turned back toward the chicken when he heard her cry of pain. When he spun to face her again, Elle was teetering on the edge of the landing; the trash bag had fallen at her side, and she clutched her head with both hands. Blood dribbled from her nostrils, down her chin.

He knew what she would do before she did it, and before he had time to stop it. On instinct, she dropped to her knees … but there was no floor to catch her. Instead, she went tumbling headfirst down the icy steps.

Adam barely registered that he had moved toward the back door; the next thing he knew, he was on the landing, watching just as she reached the cement at the bottom of the fire escape with a final *thud*.

"Elle! Ellie!" His feet carried him over the ice with preternatural haste, the Genesis thumping against his back each time he descended a step, matching the tattoo of his heartbeat.

When he reached her body, he sank to his knees and cupped her rapidly paling face.

As he did, a shiver rushed up his arms. Somehow, he could still feel a spark of life within her, and his energy—that part of him he usually tried so hard to keep under wraps—reached out to it. This wasn't the first time he'd felt the life of a dying person.

Just like Mikey, Elle was hurt bad, but there was still hope.

Trying not to succumb to panic, Adam leaned in, desperate to bring her spark of life closer. Somehow, he knew if he could figure out how to hold onto her light, he could keep her alive long enough to call for help.

But he struggled, trying to move his energy into the right shape. It couldn't find purchase on anything, couldn't find any layers to crawl under. And the slower her heart beat, the faster his breath came, the more panicked his thoughts—the harder it was to hold onto her.

Finally, he was able to latch on, but the light was growing smaller by the second. The full force of his power was almost too much, her soul like a tiny flame, fed by oxygen but snuffed out by a harsh wind. He pulled back and tried again, and again couldn't quite figure out how to get a hold of the even fainter spark.

Hold on to her, idiot. Save her. **Do what you were too weak to do last time.**

And then, without warning, the spark was gone. As Elle's body went limp, a final breath of air left her lungs, and their tenuous happiness left along with it.

Too late. Not strong enough. Just like with Mikey.

Before Adam could react, every nerve in his body came alive, like someone had plugged him into an amp. Every hair stood on end as energy rushed through him like a river, and the senses that were usually content to lie low sprang to attention. Fluttering shadows and tremulous whispers clouded his head; a sickeningly familiar coldness spiraled through him and burst from his back like a lance of ice. Darkness enveloped him for a moment, his eyes open but unseeing as insubstantial gray figures rushed past and through him.

When he finally came to, everything was just as it had been. The warm little spark of life that had been nestled in Elle's chest was dormant as a dead coal.

Pain hit him like a train, rending him under its wheels. He let out one inhuman wail and cradled her body as eddies of snow whirled around them. Shaking hard, he buried his face in her shoulder and let tears, boiling against his freezing skin, flow.

"Adam?"

A frantic voice just over his shoulder dried the tears at once. Sorrow was replaced with terror. The voice, abrupt and stark in the silence, was unmistakable.

Elle.

Adam pulled away and looked down at her lifeless body. It remained completely still. Dead. But then where—?

He looked over his shoulder and inhaled sharply at what he saw.

CHAPTER TWO

FOUR DAYS EARLIER

THE SNOW in Anster had slowed down in the past couple days, with only dingy little piles remaining on the sidewalks, but the air was still unseasonably wintry as Edie took a deep breath and closed her eyes.

As if stoked by the cold, magic thrummed through her body, rendering even the darkness behind her eyelids busy and anxious. She clenched her fists around her vibrating fingertips, shoved them in her pockets, and opened her eyes again to look at the unfamiliar street in front of her.

Edie felt older, she realized. Much older than her twenty-three years. And though her powers were slowly but surely coming more naturally—and they had saved her more than once since her escape from Indriði's dungeon—she felt powerless to stop whatever tragedies were yet to come.

So much had changed since Astrid's death that it felt like it had been two years instead of two weeks. Without the valkyrie's guidance, the Reach was adrift, and those left to pick up the pieces were unsure how to restore a faction they hadn't been alive to witness.

Still, they weren't destroyed, and they certainly weren't ready to give up.

And, as far as she knew, they still expected her to lead.

Why Astrid had chosen Edie to be the Reacher in the first place was still a mystery. The fact that her father had tried to revive it once? The belief that a powerful hellerune would be feared and respected?

Whatever the case, ready or not, the responsibility had been dropped in her lap, and it was too late to run away.

Her friends were adjusting well to their new situation, especially considering some of them were juggling the death of a beloved friend at the same time. Since the battle at the Temple of the Rising Divine, their ragtag group had stuck together while their trip to New York City was arranged.

Matilda had been hosting everyone save for Sissel and her father, though the Inuutsutoqs were around more often than not. Tilda's generosity was much to the chagrin of Cal, who avoided her, preferring to spend his time running errands or patrolling the city. Edie tried to be extra gracious to make up for him, but the vampire's sad, passive acceptance was unwavering.

As Edie walked the street, she looked around. Worn-down buildings surrounded her on every side with only the thinnest thoroughfares for traffic, a warren of a neighborhood. Dark windows glared down at her from all angles. A few streets away, police sirens wailed, and nearby, a cat screeched. Glass crunching under her feet made her look down, eyes traveling over the snow-edged sidewalk.

It had been snowing a little bit every day, and freezing at night. The chilly air caused the stubborn piles to stick instead of melt. Edie had stopped posting on social media months ago, but she checked her feed for news and had seen that it was even worse in other places. Anster wasn't known for its gentle winters, so that was new. A circulating map had promised that they'd probably be driving into New York in the middle of a blizzard.

But blizzard or not, New York would be better than here. The Aurora were so shaken by Radiant Eirik's betrayal and the huge loss of vivids that their support against the New Gloaming had come to a screeching halt. According to Cal and other contacts, Watcher patrols had diminished, but they'd been replaced by New Gloaming reveling in their newfound invulnerability.

Some were content to walk around in broad daylight, brazenly unglamoured; others were practically walking riots, causing destruction to humans as they saw fit. The fact that neither the governor nor the president had sent the National Guard to help made Edie dread just how far up the Wounded's influence went.

Personally, it was too dangerous for Edie to go outside anymore without covering up—which was why, when Klein had asked to meet up, the two had agreed on the quietest bar in the most unfamiliar neighborhood they could think of.

Edie lingered on the sidewalk and waited for a barhopper to stagger through the door first, following him close to slip in unnoticed. Inside, it was dark enough—with only neon signs and the muted colors of an old jukebox illuminating the room—that she felt comfortable pulling down her scarf and taking off her sunglasses.

While she tried to discreetly search the bar for a familiar face, she ordered the first draft beer she saw. The bartender handed her a bottle instead.

It took a few moments of looking to find Klein sitting in the backmost booth. Edie could see at a glance that the vampire had done their best to conceal their striking appearance. Hair that was usually platinum blond and straight down their back had been cut, dyed dark brown, and pulled messily into a ponytail. They wore no makeup or jewelry and had donned a pair of thick-rimmed glasses that somehow changed their whole face. On the wooden table in front of them sat an untouched cocktail.

In the couple years the two had worked together at Nocturnem, a goth club downtown, Edie had gotten used to seeing them every shift. Too bad Nocturnem's owner, Scarlet, had turned out to be not only a

Gloaming loyalist but a friend of Zaedicus Oldine and crony to Sárr, the Wounded Lord.

Edie approached with her "draft" and sat down unceremoniously. "You don't even look like the same person."

"Good," Klein replied with a snort. "Unfortunately, that's the goal."

"Are you okay? What exactly happened?"

Klein heaved a long sigh. "I *was* okay, for a while ... but Scarlet must have suspected something, because she checked Nocturnem's security footage. Must have seen me talking to you and realized I told you she'd kidnapped Cal."

"Shit."

"Yeah. I'm not sure how I escaped with my un-life, honestly, but here I am." They sighed again. "I know I don't have to worry as much as someone like you, but it's been rough. You know how Scarlet is, with her legendary grudges. It's getting harder and harder to hide. Those stupid Watchers seem to follow me everywhere I go."

Edie rubbed her forehead. If Scarlet was ordering the Watchers around, she must play a bigger role than just Zaedicus's pet human-wight. It figured. "Christ. I'm sorry."

"Not your fault," they replied with shrug.

"It kind of is. I was the one who dragged you into this. I can't help but feel at least a little responsible."

"I get it." Klein smiled wearily. "Maybe it was for the best, though. What kind of asshole would I be if I kept working for her? Even if it was just as a bartender."

Edie fiddled with the label on her beer. "It being for the best doesn't change the fact that you're lucky to be alive. Just ... let me know if there's anything I can do, okay? Before that luck runs out."

"Actually ... there might be something you can do." The vampire leaned back and crossed their arms, searching Edie's face. Their own expression seemed to be asking an earnest question. "Man, I died in the early eighties. I don't know shit about the Reach. I've always been neutral."

"Why not join when my father tried to revive it? The Reach *is* a neutral faction."

"I don't trust factions. They always turn into something horrible, over time."

Edie sighed. "That's fair."

Though Indriði had obviously had an ulterior motive, her critical words about the Reach had piqued Edie's interest, and she'd done a little research. Although the old Reach had had a reputation as arbiters and harborers of refugees, Edie had been reminded soon enough that, when it came to the status quo, *neutral* had meant something different several centuries ago. Slavery in many different forms, among other things, had been overlooked.

According to Satara, her ancestors on Mare Isle had been one of the first groups to splinter, and Astrid had been one of their first advocates. From there, internal conflict, faction wars, and the growing popularity of the Aurora and Gloaming had ultimately been its demise. So, really, Klein was right.

"I just never thought about it," they continued. "I was safe enough. But I don't have to tell *you* things have changed. I'm not sure how much longer I can do this on my own."

"Yeah." Edie was quiet for a moment, before she finally put into words what she'd been thinking for the past two weeks. "The old Reach is gone, and it isn't coming back. I think my dad was trying to resurrect something that just doesn't exist anymore. *Can't* exist."

"Typical necromancer. Sooooo, I guess you start over, then?"

"I guess we don't have a choice."

Klein shrugged. "Choice is an illusion anyway. So what are you guys doing now?"

"An old, uh, friend of Cal's, Matilda Ardelean, joined up right away. She managed to recruit some of her rich buddies, and they've been helping set up safe houses and funds for displaced people." Edie finally took a thoughtful sip of her beer, trying to recall Tilda's recent updates. "They've got beds, food, transportation. She and Satara negotiated for a bunch of in- and out-World mercenary groups to come guard the operations and stuff."

Klein raised their brows.

"Yeah, I know. The mercs are almost one hundred percent armed and ready to fend off any Gloaming raids. I can send you some info if you want"—Edie shifted to take her phone from her back pocket—"but I'll be in New York soon, so I won't be around to check up on you."

At the mention of New York, Klein lit up. "Like the city? How come?"

She hesitated. She trusted Klein not to go blabbing to the Gloaming, but what if the Gloaming wouldn't take no for an answer? Edie didn't want anyone to have to withstand torture to keep her secrets safe. "It's … complicated."

"Wait," they said, "where the hell are you staying in NYC? I thought you were broke."

Edie opened her mouth to reply but quickly stopped herself. Right. She *wasn't* broke anymore. It was hard to get used to the fact that she now had a substantial inheritance—newly acquired, thanks (and no thanks) to Cal—at her disposal. The full nearly nine million, too, after Tilda had insisted on paying off her and Mercy's medical debt. Bless that woman.

When Edie didn't answer right away, Klein leaned forward. "Come on, Edith, you don't have to keep things from little ol' me."

"No, I'm not! I mean, I *was* broke. It's just—" She shook her head. "I'm just realizing how much work Tilda has been doing these past couple weeks. She's putting us up at her apartment in Manhattan. I guess she has someone managing it, like an Airbnb thing, and they'll meet us there."

"Well, okay, listen," Klein replied, glancing around the bar. "I need to get out of this city, like, yesterday. And since you keep insisting you owe me one…" They smiled hopefully. "Maybe you could bring me with you?"

"Well—"

"I'd stay out of the way. Let you do your Reach business or whatever. I just need to get somewhere less *batshit*, know what I mean?"

Edie considered the request. She couldn't see any reason why bringing Klein would be a problem, but probably best to ask anyway. "I'll talk to Tilda and the others."

"Great. Awesome! If it pans out, text me when and where I should meet you, I guess." After a pause, Klein peered at her. "Wait, what do you mean you *were* broke, Miss Starving Artist? You come into some money recently or something?"

Some. A half-mad laugh escaped from Edie. "You could say that."

With a grunt, Edie lifted the last of her bags into Ghost's trunk, then stepped back to survey her work. She'd been tasked with jigsawing everything to fit into the snug space, and she'd done a pretty good job. Thank the gods for all those hours of *Tetris*.

Cal, leaning against Ghost's side, gave the '63 Eldorado a pat, and the trunk closed seemingly of its own volition. One of the many perks of owning a haunted muscle car.

Edie turned to look at the small group gathered in the parking garage of Tilda's building. Apart from the vampire wight herself and the group going to NYC, Sissel stood with her hands in the pockets of her bomber jacket. Beside her was Fisk in all his naked, slimy glory. Finally, next to him sat Mercy, her shoulders slumped forlornly.

Mercy's medium brown skin was a couple shades grayer than normal, and there were dark bags under her chocolate-colored eyes. Since they were still rooming together at Tilda's, Edie knew that her best friend hadn't slept; her tossing and turning had kept Edie up all night, too.

The worry wasn't doing anything to help her usual fatigue either. An unexpected battle at Gloaming Lord Zaedicus's party three months ago had left her permanently disabled, and though she'd regained some use of her legs through medicine and therapy, she was using a wheelchair today. Her not even bothering with her crutches or cane was a telltale sign she was in a lot of pain.

"You have to text me every day," Mercy said seriously before immediately yawning.

"No," Sissel cut in, "call us! I want to know everything you do!"

"I'll remind her," Satara promised as she came closer to hug Mercy goodbye. Dressed warmly in a turtleneck and puffy vest, the shieldmaiden kept glancing anxiously at Ghost, probably eager to get on the road. She had already locked Astrid's shop up—maybe for good—and arranged to have her cats looked after. Like Edie, she'd packed all she could from her apartment into boxes that now resided in Tilda's storage unit.

It had been Satara's idea to follow Indriði to New York City. At first, defeating the Gloaming had seemed like an abstract concept, and they'd all been rolling with the punches. Now, it was personal. Indriði had obliterated Astrid, and her death had caused Satara to become a fledgling valkyrie. If they didn't figure out how to transition her into a true valkyrie soon, she would die.

To add insult to injury, Indriði had also taken Astrid's ancient shield and spear as trophies. Satara intended to get them back.

Edie had been wary of the plan at first, but there was too much at stake to sit around and hold down the fort; they had to go confront the people trying to turn the world to chaos. The letters Cal had stolen from Indriði claimed there was not only a Reach presence—something Astrid had led them to believe didn't exist—but a hellerune hidden in New York. Another person like her. Aside from her and her dad, she hadn't so much as *heard* of another one before.

As the others continued saying their goodbyes, Edie turned to look at the one person who hadn't spoken all morning.

To be fair, Marius hadn't spoken much at *all* these past couple weeks. Though Tilda had kindly let him stay with the rest of their group in her penthouse—and gifted him new clothes, to boot—Edie could tell he was still troubled by what had happened when they'd faced off with the Aurora. Not knowing if his father was still alive or not was hard enough; when Marius had run from the Aurora, he'd left behind the only support, the only family, he had ever had. He'd left behind his life.

When Edie thought about it, she was surprised he was doing as well as he seemed to be. She guessed he was trying to keep his head down and focus on the task at hand.

"You ready?" she asked him quietly.

He glanced at her, awkwardly shoving his hands in the pockets of his lightweight jacket, then looked over her shoulder at the daylight pouring in from the garage entrance. "As ready as I'll ever be."

Their exchange was interrupted by Sissel, who left the rest of the chatting group to give Edie a firm handshake. The teenager—now officially sixteen—had been enduring hugs for a few minutes, but no longer, it seemed. "Augustus will miss you," she said, dark eyes crinkling into crescents.

"Promise you'll take care of him." Edie smiled back. "And stay safe, and listen to your dad."

These days, Tilda and Nils's independent study curriculum occupied most of Sissel's time. She still studied literature and math, but there was now a bigger focus on the magical world around them and the history of it, and she seemed to enjoy it more than the online classes she'd been taking previously.

Still, finding ways to get into trouble was Sissel's specialty, and the adolescent Venomgut drake she'd hijacked from Indriði only encouraged her. Edie figured teenagers were the same no matter their species.

"Don't do anything I wouldn't do," Sissel said, releasing her hand.

Edie snorted. "That seems like a curse on my safety."

Without warning, she felt something cold wrap around her and lift her off the pavement. She tensed, gasping, but relaxed once she realized it was just Fisk.

"Strength, speed, and well-wishes to you, skald Edie!" The towering sea spirit nuzzled the side of her head, dampening it. He still insisted on referring to her as a skald despite the fact that she hadn't so much as *picked up* her guitar in almost two months. She'd packed it and her portable amp into the trunk on a whim but would probably be too busy getting her ass kicked to use it.

"Thanks." She wiggled to look over her shoulder at him. "Is this a hug?"

"Yes." He squeezed tighter. "Mercy says I am getting better at them."

"The first hug he gave me nearly broke my back," Mercy confirmed from a few feet away.

Fisk set Edie down carefully and nodded to Satara and Marius as well. "Safe travels, my friends. May the gods watch over you." Then he turned to Cal and deadpanned, "I do not care if you perish."

"Love you, too, Shamu," the revenant grumbled around a newly lit cigarette. He was already on his second pack of the day, by Edie's count. But she didn't have to monitor his smoking to know he was stressed about leaving Anster—even with the walls he put up so she couldn't get inside his head, their connection was taut with anxiety.

Finally, it was Tilda's turn, and she hugged Satara and an awkward Marius as she spoke: "My caretaker, Yuval, is expecting you, so everything should be set up for when you get there. Don't worry, I am absolutely certain you'll love her." When she hugged Edie, she lingered, tilting her head to whisper in her ear. "Please be safe. Please, *please* don't let them get into trouble."

Since Edie was far from the most responsible one in their party—and everyone knew it—Tilda probably meant *Don't let Cal get into trouble.* Their reunion at the Gloaming party had been the first time Tilda had seen Cal since he'd abandoned her and skipped town, and she clearly still had feelings for him. Not that Cal had done much to deserve it. He was like family to Edie, but when it came to Tilda, he acted like an ass. That was shitty enough on its own, considering how friendly she was, but especially bad after everything she was doing for them.

The wight released Edie from her embrace and looked at Cal, black eyes shining. She was usually more inscrutable, but when it came to the revenant, Tilda wore her heart on her sleeve. "Good luck, Cal," she said hesitantly. "Take care of Edie. And Ghost, too."

Cal was stiff, looking at the car instead of her. "Yep."

Stubborn bastard.

Edie looked forward as Mercy, who had finished saying goodbye the others, came to a stop in front of her once again. She ran a hand through her bubblegum-pink mane, brows drawn. "When will you be back?"

"It shouldn't be more than a couple weeks," Edie promised, though she couldn't be certain. She wasn't *planning* on being gone for more than a couple weeks, but best-laid plans and all that.

If she was honest, there was a chance she wouldn't be coming back at all. Not alive, anyway. They both knew it without having to say anything.

"Are you all packed?" Mercy asked, taking her friend's hands and pulling her into a tight embrace.

Edie hugged her back. "Yeah."

"Are you sure? You have everything?"

"Yep. It's all there."

Reluctantly, Mercy pulled back from the hug. But as she did, she grabbed Edie's forearms, keeping her from pulling away. "Stay safe," she said quietly, staring into her eyes.

Edie swallowed. "You, too. Don't take risks. And get your parents out of here as soon as you can."

"I know," Mercy responded with a nod. "They're already back in the Cape. With a little extra protection, thanks to the Reach."

There was a moment of silence, and the two embraced one last time, tighter and longer. When Edie finally pulled away, she couldn't look at her friend's face. Leaving Mercy went against every one of her instincts, but it just wasn't safe to bring her along. Thank god for Tilda and Fisk.

It wasn't until Edie had walked to Ghost that she glanced back at the people they were leaving behind. *Please keep them alive*, she prayed, to no one in particular. Whoever was willing to listen, at this point.

The next thing she knew, she was sitting in the backseat, watching out the rear window as they emerged from the parking garage.

Beside her, Marius was looking forward. But he caught her eye when she turned, and tilted his head. "They're safer staying than we are going."

She swallowed the lump in her throat. "I know."

That was part of what was scaring her.

Freezing rain was beating on the car by the time the group reached the safe house Klein had ended up going to. Klein stood just outside the doorway, scanning the street cautiously. On either side of them, men in dark tactical armor stood, keeping silent watch. The new Reach mercenaries, Edie guessed, finally in position. And it seemed like no one was giving them trouble yet.

Ever since the New Gloaming had appeared, seeing people battle-ready with armor and weapons had become an everyday thing. The human police didn't even bother to intervene anymore—they simply cleaned up the mess when the fighting was over. In fact, it seemed to Edie that most unattuned governing bodies were *withdrawing* from the city rather than buckling down and militarizing like she'd expected them to.

She didn't know which option was more terrifying. There were still unattuned humans living here, and the force she and her friends were trying to build wasn't yet big enough to contend with the full power of the Gloaming. They couldn't protect them all. It made her physically ill to think about.

A knock on her tiny window startled her, but she was relieved to look up and see Klein waving. Beside them stood one of the mercs. Cal climbed out of the front seat and chatted with him while Edie scooted to make room for Klein.

"Hello, fellow sardines," the wight said as they climbed behind the driver's seat and into the back.

Edie waved, squirming a bit. The middle seat wasn't the most comfortable place to be in an old Cadillac, especially considering there was no security, but Cal had made it abundantly clear that they were lucky to have seat belts in even the standard areas. It also meant she was now snuggled up to Marius. His thigh was tense against hers.

"This thing is a fucking yacht!" Klein remarked as they settled in, gazing around the car's interior. "How the hell do you even find anywhere to park it?"

Ghost growled rather sharply, and Klein raised a brow.

"Her name is Ghost," Satara said from the front seat, looking up from her book with a small smirk. "She can hear you."

Klein's mouth turned into a little O, and they drew their hands away from the leather seat they had been caressing. "Sorry, ma'am." Then they looked down at Edie's lap and squinted behind their glasses. "Do you all wanna switch places? Musical chairs sucks, but I don't really need the seat belt, on account of the deathlessness."

"It's fine," Marius answered quickly.

Edie looked at him and smiled. It was nice to see him being polite to *creatures of darkness* or whatever. He smiled back uncertainly.

The car rocked as Cal settled back in, and Satara traded her book for her cell phone, into which she plugged the address of Tilda's apartment. Edie took a deep breath and one last look at Anster as they sped toward the interstate.

It was time to go after Indriði, stop the Gloaming, and find the other hellerune. Sink or swim.

CHAPTER THREE

As Scarlet stepped out of Indriði's limousine and into the noise of Midtown Manhattan, her spirits lifted. After spending a week underground, helping her new boss store the contents of her raided townhouse and formulating plans for her Watchers, she was eager to see the place where they would actually be living while here. She took a deep breath of night air and looked up at the glittering shafts of the Baccarat Hotel's crystal windows.

"Home sweet home," Indriði said from in front of her, having stepped out first. "For now." Bedecked in sapphire jewelry and a dress of soft white leather, the Norn looked like a natural fixture outside of this grand building. She smiled at Scarlet and gestured for her to follow her past the chic outdoor fireplace and through the main entryway.

A dark vestibule of slate and marble enveloped them. To one side, an art piece made of crystal glasses was illuminated by a spotlight, twinkling in the dim room. After a short elevator ride up to the second floor, they bypassed the front desk without a glance, though Scarlet could feel the concierge watching them. There was no doubt that they were expected.

As they entered the grand salon, Scarlet tried not to stare in awe like some kind of rube, but it was difficult. Every inch of the place shone bright and clean, from the silk-covered walls stretching over twenty feet above them to the polished parquet floors. Large globes of red roses dotted the space, breaking up the white like vibrant rubies. Within the intimate nooks of the salons, a few guests—all dressed to the nines despite the late hour—shared nightcaps. Even the furniture looked cliquish, gathered into little groups. And all this dripping with millions of dollars' worth of French crystal.

Such excess was considered almost profane in New England; the people *here* made it seem natural.

The clicking of Indriði's heels against the parquet called Scarlet to attention again, and she walked faster to keep up with her boss. She liked Indriði. She didn't want the Norn to think less of her because the lavishness didn't yet come as naturally as it should. She was used to being excessive, of course ... just not like this.

Although she looked forward to being like these people, truth be told, she found herself almost hiding behind Indriði as they passed through the grand salon. But that was fine—in any case, she was relieved to be free of Zaedicus and his leering. If he thought he was being subtle with his attraction, or obsession, or whatever it was, he was even more foolish than he acted.

He had thrown an unholy hissy fit before she'd left, but really, *he* should be the one who was relieved. Treating Scarlet like a pet had been the last mistake of many a male wight, high and human both. And her patience for Zaedicus in particular had been wearing deadly thin.

He was old and arrogant, and hopefully, someone would end him soon. Perhaps the Wounded would regret the decision to make him Gloaming Lord and get rid of him. Scarlet felt a jolt of glee go through her at the thought of Zaedicus's body hanging from the spire of his own manor.

As she and Indriði entered the adjacent room, the lighting and the mood of their setting changed, darker once again. This must be the famous Baccarat bar, though it looked different from the pictures she'd seen—the lights were mostly off, and it was curiously empty, with only one bartender at his station. The merlot walls arched into a high ceiling and gave the illusion of walking into the heart of some great beast.

It was beautiful. It dawned on her that this was what Nocturnem was *trying* to be. Not even the Ash Wyrm Club could hold a candle to the style brimming in this comparatively small room.

Scarlet scanned the dim area, and quickly, her gaze caught on the only other people there. Two tall figures in crimson coats and hoods stood nearly shoulder to shoulder about twenty feet from them, guarding one of the small tables. Their faces were sheet-white and gaunt, and for a moment, Scarlet thought that they were undead—but no, they were just wearing masks. Skull masks that seemed to have the detail and texture of real bone, with bold silver filigree on the jaw, under the cheekbones, and crawling up the temples.

Scarlet approached, following Indriði. Walking across the checkerboard floor made her feel like a chess piece. Which piece she was, exactly, remained to be seen.

Closer now, she could smell that the masked guards were human. She couldn't even sense any magic on them. Odd. Conviction and fear and hatred rolled from them in waves—not a bad snack, but strange nonetheless. The men glared but parted to let the Norn and vampire pass.

The woman sitting at the table behind them was not what Scarlet had expected at all, considering who she was. She had peachy white skin with a healthful complexion, long, carefully maintained waves of blond hair, and greenish hazel eyes. She was pretty but rather nondescript and wore carefully applied daytime makeup. Her finely tailored blue dress spoke of an elegance that far exceeded her years—barely thirty, Scarlet guessed.

When Indriði approached, the woman stood and hugged her warmly, like one might hug a mother. They exchanged words under their breath, then Indriði turned and gestured to Scarlet.

"Daschla, Scarlet."

The vampire hesitated before holding a hand out to shake and was surprised to find the young woman's grip quite strong. Now that she looked again, she noticed that her dress carefully concealed what were probably muscular shoulders.

The three slid into the sumptuous white leather chairs surrounding the small table. Something about the way Daschla kept glancing at her impassively made Scarlet squirm in her painted-on leather pants and cropped feather coat. The young woman exuded an air of harsh judgment, and the fact that she was almost exclusively addressing Indriði didn't escape Scarlet's notice.

"It's been too long since I saw you in person," she said. Her voice was soft, almost girlish. "What exactly happened in Anster? He only gave me some of the story."

Indriði groaned. "Some losers calling themselves the Reach decided to raid my home. They ran off like rabbits, but it was just better I pull out, you know? Figured the Aurora would be right behind them. I did everything I needed to do in Anster, anyway."

"I heard about Astrid." Daschla smiled. "Good. It was a long time coming."

"That it was, my dear, that it was."

Without any of them asking, one of the masked guards appeared with three espresso cups, comically small in his hands. As he leaned over Scarlet, he whispered in a breath, "Enjoy, beautiful," and she felt her hackles rise.

Hanging from the spire. Just imagine him hanging from the spire.

"And these are your Blood Eagles, I assume?" Indriði asked, raising her espresso cup to her lips.

"Two of them." Daschla gestured with her chin, addressing them. "I'll be fine from here. Go wait at the door."

The men bowed their heads, turned in unison, and stalked away.

Scarlet raised her brows. Eating out of the palm of her hand, they were. She looked back at Daschla, feeling a sudden yearning for the much younger woman's favor. "They're rather well trained," she said, finally breaking her silence.

"Oh, I didn't train them to do all that. They just like the drama."

Indriði looked from the men to Daschla. "How are things going?"

"Well, we've been largely unchallenged. A few protests here and there, but the unattuned police keep them at bay."

"That's fascinating," Indriði remarked genuinely.

"It's definitely helpful. So nothing has really happened to us at demonstrations beyond a few fistfights."

Scarlet quickly found herself lost in the conversation. Her briefing had been incomplete—the Gloaming were protective of their secrets, and she'd been assured everything would be explained once she was on-site. She spoke up again, drawing a long-suffering glance from Daschla that made her heart twinge. "What are you demonstrating? It can't be safe to recruit people to the Gloaming right out in the open."

"Officially, I'm not," Daschla replied. "The Blood Eagles are a human organization. A little project I've been working on for a couple of years now. A lot of them don't even know the Gloaming exists. Yet."

"I thought they were going to be foot soldiers." Scarlet frowned. "Shouldn't we induct them as soon as possible, so they can start doing work for us?"

"Oh, they *are* doing work for us." The young woman looked at her pointedly now. "They're helping your Watchers more than you'd think."

Scarlet schooled her expression and abandoned her espresso, pushing it away from her. The china squealed against the table.

"I'll induct them eventually," Daschla continued, "and I'm sure most of them will be all for it."

"If they're part of the operation, I need to know their movements. I can't coordinate patrols if I don't know where our people are at any given time."

Daschla laughed, but frustration crept into her voice. "That's the thing; I don't know where they are at any given time. Most of them have families and jobs occupying their life."

There was a pause as Scarlet digested this. Finally, she spat, "What kind of soldiers participate *in their free time?*"

"They're not soldiers," Daschla replied. Her voice hadn't raised a bit, but it dripped with a condescension that made Scarlet's head spin. "Well, some of them were military once. They're just ... private citizens with certain ... concerns. They're unsatisfied with current affairs, and we're offering them something big to be a part of."

Indriði laughed. "You give them a lot of credit. You remember the chickens, babe?"

Daschla nodded solemnly. "I remember, don't worry."

Scarlet had no idea what the Norn was talking about, but she was slowly beginning to realize just what was happening here—what these Blood Eagles were. She glanced behind her at the crimson-clad pair guarding the door, the wheels in her head spinning a hundred miles an hour. In their attempts to gain power, the Gloaming had aligned themselves with nefarious human forces before, but...

"Are we sure this is a good idea?" she asked Indriði as she turned back, holding the Norn's gaze.

Indriði smiled. "Don't worry about it, sweetie. They're just a tiny stepping stone. And not going to be involved in making decisions, obviously. I mean, come on, they're *human*."

Scarlet looked back at the Eagles. What did she care? Even if they were involved, was it really a problem? A bit uncomfortable, perhaps, but she'd subjected herself to plenty of discomfort before to get ahead. The benefits always eventually outweighed whatever minor objection she had. This was no different.

She turned back and relaxed in her seat. The other two had already resumed their conversation.

"How are you coping with the transition?" Indriði asked.

"It was ... I can't describe it." Daschla's expression became even more serious. "All I can say is that securing Astrid's warhorn should have been our first priority."

Indriði sat back, considering this. "It's not too late. She and the Izem girl took it back, but that doesn't mean we can't go after it again. I'll see what I can get arranged." She paused before adding, "Is the change really that profound?"

"Yes. And it would be even more so for the fledgling ... considering my circumstances."

Scarlet watched Daschla's jaw clench—so tight that it was a wonder she didn't shatter her teeth—but the vampire had lost the thread of the conversation. Whatever they were talking about now, she had no knowledge of it, and it made her blood boil. Had she really left Zaedicus's one-man show for more of this bullshit?

"Have you predicted whether or not the Reach will follow you from Anster?" Daschla asked.

"I'm sure they will." The Norn sighed. "We'll have to get to the other hellerune before they realize he's here. Which will be annoying."

"But it also means they've left their friends, and a defensible position," the younger woman responded. Her lips curved in a smile. "They're divided. Now, we conquer."

CHAPTER FOUR

The first half of the drive to New York went relatively smoothly.

While Edie and Klein caught up, Marius listened to music on Edie's smartphone. He finally had the opportunity to listen to the '80s and '90s bands he seemed strangely familiar with, and was clearly pleased. Edie hadn't yet asked exactly *how* he was familiar with them, but it was pretty adorable nonetheless. Up front, Satara was trying painstakingly to explain the plot of *Inception* to Cal, but he was more focused on the merits of Cillian Murphy's androgynous good looks.

Then the snow started to fall.

Edie's prediction came true—they hadn't missed the blizzard that was supposed to hit the city but were driving *through* it, and even with Ghost's preternatural grace on the road, they had to slow down to a snail's pace. Marius took out his headphones; Cal and Satara stopped talking. They all watched silently out the windows, horror mounting as the blizzard in July whited out the road.

When all was said and done, the last half of the trip took three hours instead of an hour and a half.

When Edie and the others finally drove into the Sutton Place neighborhood of Manhattan, they were road-weary, and shivering despite Ghost's heaters blasting. Anster had had some strange snowfall, but it hadn't been *cold* like it was here.

Edie was surprised to see that the city dwellers were much more prepared than she was—most of the people walking along the sidewalks wore coats and boots and bored expressions, like this was the most natural thing in the world. Typical New Yorkers.

But it *wasn't* natural. What the hell was happening?

Satara scrolled through her texts and directed Cal to the parking garage of Tilda's NYC building. Once she punched in the code, the gate lifted, and Ghost purred into the darkness, fitting herself neatly into the apartment's assigned space.

The moment Edie stepped out of the car, she could feel that there was something … different about this city. It was like something was calling to her, just out of reach—a strange, almost electrical buzzing. Similar to the feeling of Cal's presence, but *busy*, not soothing. She tried to shake it off but remained distracted as the others unloaded the car.

Cal was mumbling as he stashed his Bear Claw in the trunk locker, where he kept most of his weapons and a portion of the Holloway inheritance. The rest of the money was god only knew where. Edie hadn't asked and almost didn't want to know. That much money made her nervous.

"What's wrong?" Satara asked the revenant as she pulled her suitcase from the trunk.

"I don't have an open carry permit for this dumbass city," he grumbled in response, though Edie couldn't help but notice he was equipping one SOB and two shoulder holsters. His trusty Colt and two similar revolvers slid into their new concealed homes.

"But concealed carry, you have?" the shieldmaiden asked skeptically.

"Well"—he coughed—"they won't find it if it's *concealed*, right?"

Klein was watching with big eyes. "Maybe don't march into a nice stranger's house armed to the nipples, yeah?"

"I'm not gonna shoot *her*."

"It's more than a little threatening!" Klein looked at Edie. "Does he forget he's a six-four white dude with muscles the size of your head?"

Edie shrugged. Most of the time, she forgot what Cal looked like to people who couldn't see through his glamour. *She* wasn't scared of him anymore. With a sigh, she looked back at Cal. "How about you just leave them in the car for now and we'll come back if we need them?"

He bitched and moaned the whole way but pared it down to just the SOB holster before the group finished unloading and finally stepped into the garage's elevator lobby. The elevator was nice, obviously well kept, and Edie was reminded once again of just how loaded Tilda must be.

"I wonder how long she's had an apartment here," she said to no one in particular.

"You said she was practically ancient, didn't you? Who knows?" Klein was staring at the digital floor counter and nearly bouncing, not quite the cool-as-a-cucumber attitude Edie had come to expect from them. "I hope the caretaker's nice."

"You've always been the caretaker, Mr. Torrence," Cal mumbled to Satara, drawing a chuckle from her.

When the elevator finally opened, their small crowd eased out, and Edie was relieved to finally have some personal space after hours of being squished in the car. The apartment hallway was spacious, with clean cream walls and handsome wood floors. She always forgot how crappy her old apartment back in Anster was until she stepped into a place like this. She felt the same way staying at Tilda's.

Apartment 11A waited for them toward the end of the hall, and Klein, with their long stride and quick pace, was the first to reach it. By the time the rest of the group caught up, the wight had already rapped on the door several times. Anxious to get settled in, it seemed.

There was a call Edie couldn't quite make out and some shuffling before the door opened. Standing before them was a woman of medium height and soft build, with amber skin, tightly wavy dark hair, and large brown eyes. Her elegant nose, dappled with light freckles, swept from her brow into a soft point. As she took the party before her in, her full, top-heavy lips spread into a grin. Something about her reminded Edie of Mercy, and it made her heart ache. She already missed her.

"Hello! You must be Matilda's group," the woman said, greeting the two people closest to her—Klein and Satara—with hugs like they were old friends.

"Oh, hi." Klein grinned and patted her back. "That's us."

"Great!" Once the woman pulled away, she gestured, still smiling, toward the others. "I'm Yuval. Come— Oh." She stuttered for a moment, and then grimaced. "Sorry, I forgot. Tilda actually wanted me to ask you to video call her when you arrived. For security?"

Edie wasn't surprised. Tilda was so conscientious when it came to stuff like this that she wondered if she'd been a spy in one of her past lives. It only took her a second to pull up their chat and press the Video Call button; then she handed the phone to Satara, who was standing in front of her.

Tilda answered almost right away, looking flawless as usual, and smiled when she saw the group. "Is everything all right?" she asked quickly. "Did you arrive safely?"

"We're here," Satara confirmed, turning the camera so that it was facing Yuval.

The wight gasped when she saw her. Her accented voice was strident through the phone speakers as she cried out, "My love, look at you!"

Yuval seemed equally happy to see her, waving with both hands. "Matilda, hi! So these *are* your friends!"

"That's right, darling."

"I'm sorry." Yuval gestured with open hands, still grinning, toward the others. "I don't usually shriek. Please, come in! Let me help you carry stuff."

"She means it," Tilda said with a laugh. "The thought of a guest lifting a finger will weigh on her more than the suitcases will."

"Well, I want to be a good host!"

Klein snorted as they slipped inside. "Can't relate. My wight nature dictates I should curse you if you enter my barrow."

After quick goodbyes, Tilda hung up, and Edie retrieved her phone, pocketing it. She walked into the apartment after Satara, with Marius and Cal behind, each of them slipping out of their shoes—even Cal, much to his discomfort. Thankfully, he was wearing socks today.

It was clean and bright in the small entryway, with a wall of pictures —most of Yuval's family vacations, it looked like—immediately to their right. The smell of some richly spiced food wafted through the air, mingling with the soothing scent of vanilla.

"I'm Yuval. Again. Sorry about that." Their hostess laughed as she extended her hand to Edie, then shook everyone's hand in turn, exchanging names. "Make yourselves at home. I would usually have come down to help with your bags, but ... you know, security." She waved them further into the house.

The group followed her into a spacious, naturally lit living room that looked like it had just been peeled off the cover of a *Better Homes and Gardens* magazine. Modern white furniture was punctuated with orange and dark blue accents, and personal items were expertly placed and tucked to make the space feel less like a soulless hotel suite and more like a friend's apartment—which, to them, it was.

There seemed to be more of Yuval's influence than Tilda's, however. On the far window hung a colorful hamsa suncatcher with a Star of David in the center; elegantly printed blessings and affirmations were framed in various places around the room. Looking through an archway, Edie could see a laptop and an easel set up in the dining area, looking out onto the city.

Yuval led them through the house, briefly checking on whatever was cooking in the kitchen before showing them the bedrooms. "There are four to choose from," she said as she opened the curtains of the master. "Tilda said that would be enough, since some of you don't sleep."

"Two of us don't, but that's it." Edie looked back at her two undead companions. Klein was taking in their surroundings with an approving eye while Cal lingered in the hallway uncertainly.

Yuval smiled at both of them in turn, her hands on her hips. "Well, you're free to take the extra room if you want, regardless. Rest is still important, right?"

Cal mumbled a thanks. Probably still grumpy about having to take his boots off, and that he'd have to go outside in the snow if he wanted to smoke, Edie thought. And definitely unsure of how to respond to hospitality.

After the humans had chosen their bedrooms and left their bags, Yuval led them back out into the living area. As they walked, Klein mused, "I'll probably find somewhere else to hang my hat. Not that this place isn't great. But the deal was you'd bring me to New York, and that's all taken care of."

Yuval looked at them with concern and said, "Oh, I'm sure you don't need to run off right away, with the blizzard and everything. And you're always welcome to stay with me and my girlfriend, Miri, any of you. We live around the block."

"Is that so?" Klein smiled, apparently already warming up to her. "It's an intriguing offer. I don't wanna get stuck hanging out with these losers all day." They winked playfully at the group.

"It's probably safer if you stay somewhere else, anyway," Marius said as they settled into the living room. Their hostess brought a pitcher of what looked like pomegranate juice. "Both you and Yuval. If someone comes for us, you won't be stuck in the middle."

"I can take care of myself if worse comes to worst," Yuval said, setting six glasses on the table. She didn't elaborate—at least, not verbally. With a flick of her wrist, the juice jumped out of the pitcher in a long, thick rope, whipping its tail like a claret snake. She splayed her fingers, and the rope separated into six parts, flowing weightlessly into the cups. Each pillar of liquid rippled before settling.

"Oh, juice powers," Klein said as they picked up their glass. "That'd be useful for a bartender."

"Ha." With a good-natured smirk, Yuval flicked her fingers in Klein's direction. Seemingly from thin air, clear droplets sprayed outward and hit the vampire with a gentle splatter.

Water powers. Edie sat forward attentively, reminded of Fisk's claimed mastery over the element. Yuval's seemed more genuine. "Okay, now I see what you mean. How is it for, you know, protection?"

"I do well, if pressed! I've dealt with one or two creeps in my day, *believe* me." She coaxed a tiny globe of juice from her cup and slurped it up. "Thankfully, it's always proved completely nonlethal. People usually stop trying to fight you once they're wrinkly and dehydrated. One sec."

She left briefly to get whatever she was cooking, so Edie checked her phone.

[Mercy Cedeno]: Text me once you make it there safely !! And tell me when there's a good time to video call. Love u <3

Edie smiled and texted back.

[Edith Holloway]: We're here and in one piece. I'll text you again later tonight. I love you!!!

As soon as Edie shoved her phone back in her pocket, Yuval came back with a skillet of what looked like eggs in tomato sauce, garnished with fresh herbs and chunks of feta. It smelled amazing, and Edie could feel her mouth start to water. She had been too nervous to eat any of the snacks she'd packed for the trip.

"I wasn't sure which of you, uh, ate, either," Yuval said, placing the skillet down on a ceramic trivet in the center of the coffee table. "I hope this is okay."

"Is that shakshouka?" Satara asked, brightening and inching closer.

Yuval smiled over her shoulder as she went to get more stuff from the kitchen, speaking as she went. "Yep! And I don't usually cook this much at once, so I hope it turned out all right."

Marius jumped up to help in the kitchen, and the pair of them quickly brought out a stack of small plates, silverware, a dish of bread, and a small bowl of green sauce.

"Careful," Yuval said of the green sauce, addressing Edie specifically. "It's very spicy!"

"You're not a vættr, are you?" Edie asked as everyone began filling their plates. "That's probably a stupid question, but the only hydromancers I've met so far are vættir."

"Nope, I'm human. It's just..." Yuval shrugged. "A gift. I never studied it; it just came."

"Juice powers," Klein said again, nodding sagely.

Their hostess looked between Klein and Cal, her tone suddenly less certain than it had been. "You two will ... be able to sort everything out, right? When it comes to, you know. Eating? Tilda said I wouldn't have to worry, but—"

"It's fine," Cal grunted, arms crossed uncomfortably. "I don't need anything."

"And I probably won't have to feed for a while," Klein added.

"Can't you just call it *eating*, for Christ's sake?"

"Sure," they said, "but it's not as cool."

The food settled surprisingly well considering Edie's nervous stomach, and now that she'd had something to eat, she felt a bit more focused. "How did you and Tilda meet, anyway?" she asked between bites of bread.

"Oh." Yuval wiped her hands on a napkin, smiling brightly once more. "We met around six years ago. Tilda obviously spends most of her time in New England, but—well, you know, she's got a few places here and overseas. She usually has someone taking care of each one when she's not there."

Cal snorted and said, "She must be cutting down. One too many chateaus and she might not have enough money to build a rocket."

Edie elbowed him, and Yuval glanced uncertainly in his direction before continuing. "The last caretaker of this place was renting the apartment out without Tilda's knowledge and pocketing the money.

Rental prices around here are insanely high anyway, but he was raising it for attuned folks and extorting people once they arrived, and it was a huge mess. She obviously fired him on the spot.

"We actually ran into each other by chance just after, at a friend's party. We got to talking, and when she found out I was studying to go into the hospitality industry, she asked me right away if I was interested in helping her." Yuval smiled brightly. "She paid off all my student debt and hired me right away. It was like a dream come true."

"If she's paying you to take care of this place, why turn it into a ... what was it?" Marius asked softly.

"Airbnb," answered Satara.

"Oh!" Yuval jerked her thumb toward the door. "The building is actually a co-op, so we have to pay a pretty high maintenance fee every month. It covers that plus a little extra for my expenses. What Tilda pays me covers my own rent and stuff."

Cal wrinkled his nose. "Then where the hell does that leave her?"

"Well, I always offer the cut she's entitled to, but she always turns it down." Yuval peered at him. "You joked about her cutting down, but ... she hardly ever visits, she doesn't really turn a profit—I don't think she really considers this place hers anymore."

"And what about you?" Klein asked, swirling their glass.

"Well, I set prices and book in a way that will cover our expenses, but...." She smiled. "I went into hospitality for a reason. I *want* to make people comfortable. My dad always had extra room for friends, or even strangers. Even when we were barely making ends meet. If I know someone's struggling or in transition, I'll put 'em up, and it's not a big deal. And," she added, "if I someday change my mind about hospitality or it somehow falls through, hey, I have a rent-free Manhattan apartment to live in. Even if it's a little big for me and Miri and the occasional visiting sister."

"Wow." Edie couldn't imagine *wanting* to take care of hotel guests, but then, she could barely take care of herself some days. Leave it to Tilda to have a bunch of friends just as generous as she was.

The conversation flowed, so to speak, as they continued to make small talk. Yuval was good at bringing her guests into the conversation, so much so that she even got a few smiles out of Marius when describing her vacation to Iran—where, Edie learned along with the rest of them, his maternal grandmother had been born—and a chuckle or two from Cal.

Eventually, Yuval broached the topic of their stay itself. "So, why are y'all in NYC on such short notice?"

"The fabulous weather, o' course," Cal said, nodding at the snowdrifts outside the window.

"Tilda said that it was something about the Reach." Yuval's thick brows drew. "I didn't know there *was* a Reach."

Edie wasn't keen to give too much information, but considering Yuval was risking not only her livelihood but her life to help them out, she deserved to know what was going on. "There wasn't—not a proper one. We're trying to fix that."

"Giving people not welcome in the Aurora safe harbor from the Gloaming is our top priority," Satara added, pulling her knees to her chest. "It's been getting exponentially more difficult since the Rising Aurora in Anster have retreated."

"The Rising Aurora *retreated*?" Yuval gaped. "Oh my…"

"They're licking their wounds," Marius mumbled, moving food around on his tiny plate. "We revealed that their Radiant was being blackmailed by the Gloaming somehow."

Edie couldn't help but notice that he failed to mention the Radiant had also been his father. She glanced sideways at him but said nothing.

"I don't like them—the Aurora." Yuval frowned. "I was still unattuned when the last Radiant was in charge, but people have told me she was okay. She let people be, kept the Gloaming in their stalemate, and didn't let them harass anyone. The new one is awful. He's a religious fanatic, and he only cares when the Gloaming threatens the Aurora's temples, no one else's."

Marius looked up. "Radiant Oddfreyr?"

"That's him. His obsession with serving the Aurora has actually made the Gloaming problem even worse. I don't trust him *at* all."

Marius blinked a second too long, then bowed his head. "I don't either."

Yuval sighed, looking around uncertainly. "I don't know much about the Reach, but they're neutral, right? I'm honestly not sure neutrality will do us any favors at the moment. Especially with the way things are going here..."

"We've kind of been talking about that." Edie glanced at Klein, then the others. "We haven't worked any specifics out yet; we're still kind of treading water. But think of it more like ... an alternative faction than Switzerland."

"New Gloaming, new Reach. And not Dick Holloway's *new Reach*, either." Cal bounced his leg, fingering what was probably a pack of cigarettes in his jacket pocket. In a grumble, he added, "Hopefully."

Satara looked at Yuval earnestly. "What did you mean when you said 'especially the way things are going here'?"

"There are some ... bad people around here," she replied with a sour expression. "They just showed up a few weeks ago out of nowhere. They'd apparently been a thing for a while, but I'd never seen them in public, I guess."

"Yeah, we had to deal with the Watchers back in Anster, too," Edie said, assuming that was what Yuval meant.

But their hostess shook her head. "No, not Watchers. I saw stuff on Facebook about those, and I heard there were sightings here—but they're different. As far as I know, these guys are human. They call themselves the Blood Eagles."

"Blood Eagles..." Edie looked to the others. "Where have I heard that before?"

Satara sighed, resting her chin on her knees. "A blood eagle was supposedly a form of torture, or execution, used by the Vikings. It involves severing someone's ribs from their spine and ripping them out through their back. Splaying them like bloodied wings. Some people claim it was a ritual sacrifice to Odin."

"It's a myth," Marius added. "A Christian mistranslation of kennings for the dead on battlefields, picked apart by carrion birds. That hasn't stopped some from adopting the idea, however."

Yuval crossed her arms, looking a little paler for the graphic description. "That makes sense. It definitely sounds like something they would romanticize."

"Who are they?" Klein asked, their tone serious for once.

"They're some kind of white supremacist group, or alt-right, or whatever they're calling it these days. There have been a few incidents. Protests and counterprotests, and some of it gets out of hand. I just wanted you guys to be aware, so you can avoid them."

Edie wasn't surprised. It seemed like every city had the same problems lately. Someone, somewhere was always rioting or protesting something—and in many cases, if her punk soul had actually been free to live life anymore, she'd have been right there along with them. But the Blood Eagles and their ilk weren't oppressed people demanding rights.

"Thanks for the heads-up," she said with a nod. Even if the Blood Eagles were just a group of humans, it was good to know they were a threat.

Still, it seemed weird that a group with a pseudo-Viking name would pop up in New York around the same time the Gloaming did. There was a chance it was a coincidence, of course. Lots of hate groups had latched on to Norse imagery without the Gloaming's interference before. But Edie's gut told her there was a connection.

Yuval seemed eager to change the subject. As she finished off the last of her juice, she asked, "Do you guys know how long you're staying here?"

"Can't be too sure," said Cal, who was sitting with his ankle resting on his knee, now looking a bit more comfortable. "A week? Whatever it ends up being, we'll pay you. Name a price and it's yours."

She shook her head. "No, I couldn't take anything. This is Tilda's place, and you're her friends—"

"Please," Klein groaned, "let them pay you!"

"Tilda already—"

"Having us here is dangerous," Satara reminded her gently.

"Yeah. Think of it as ... insurance, in case shit goes south." Cal sat forward, and Edie nodded in agreement. "We've got whatever you need. In cash."

Yuval's eyes flew wide. "Please, it's not necessary. And that much money in *cash*, I couldn't—"

"It's fine!"

"It's really not a big deal."

"What you got against free money?"

"Let the people pay you, I'm begging!"

The chorus of voices made her cringe and laugh a bit, waving her hands. "Okay, okay! We'll think of it as a *deposit*—and if *nothing* happens, I'm giving it back." After a moment, she settled down again, but Edie could see the wheels in her head turning. "I'm going to have to make you guys more food. Do you like mousse? I'm weirdly great at making mousse."

Cal pulled a face. "The hairspray or the animal?"

CHAPTER FIVE

Yuval and Klein left within a couple hours, leaving the group with four bedrooms and only three people who needed to sleep. All the rooms seemed to be the same size, albeit with varying bathroom dimensions, so none of them ended up choosing the master. Cal, with an aversion to rest as always, was just leaving to scope out the neighborhood when the others began getting ready for bed.

When Edie walked into her chosen room, which was decorated in sandy tans and subtle purples, she noted something she had overlooked when she'd dropped her bag off. On the bed, soft towels, robes, and washcloths were neatly rolled up next to some kind of gift basket. A little card was attached to the basket handle.

> *Enjoy your stay! Help yourself to any of these treats and feel free to take them home. Please text me personally—or run over to my place to see me!—if there's anything I can add to make your stay better.*
> *—Yuval.*

Edie sorted through the soaps and lotions, candy, and other amenities curiously. The places she usually stayed, the most they ever left was clean linens and a mint on your pillow.

She didn't bother to unpack her bag yet. Exhaustion was starting to shut her down, and she just wanted to enjoy a few hours of solitude before whatever lay ahead of them tomorrow. She made her way to the bathroom, hoping to freshen up after the long drive. It was spotless, nice-smelling, and painted a calming lavender.

Shutting and locking the door released tension she hadn't even known she was holding. Finally, she was alone.

She shed her clothes before taking her hair down. The sight of herself in the mirror made her cringe. She was waxy and looked half-dead from exhaustion, and there was a reason she usually kept her hair up anyway—long, loose hair didn't suit her at all. With a sigh, she opened the cabinet mirror so she couldn't see herself anymore and started the shower.

A full half hour later, she emerged, with only enough energy to struggle into a T-shirt and pajama bottoms before collapsing into the big, soft bed.

Branches scraped Edie's skin as she moved through the thick wood, their fingers leaving tiny razor-thin cuts that stung when the eerily uncold snow touched them. It took her a moment to realize what was happening, considering this dream usually began with her waking in the small white clearing.

She got the strange sense that the familiar sequence of events had already started without her—that the wolf had already howled, that the forest was already awake and aware of her presence. Sure enough, it was only a few moments before the river began to murmur, and a moment later, the crow appeared, soaring past her head to wait for her in the trees beyond.

She was going father than usual again. The last time her dream had proceeded like this, she had actually seen the wolf. She had been able to call her powers up for the first time and use them to defend herself, and it had carried into the waking world. With that in mind, she now followed the crow eagerly, wondering what she might learn this time around.

But her eagerness was rewarded only with a strong sense of dread that built and built the closer she came to the river. By the time she breached the treeline, every hair was standing on end, her stomach doing nervous flips. Was she sensing the wolf about to pounce from the bushes?

But it never appeared, and the feeling intensified the longer she stood there. As she looked forward, she couldn't help but think that whatever was causing this unrest was somewhere in front of her.

And yet, everything looked the same. The footbridge was the same as last time, with the crow resting on the pilaster, watching her just as it had before.

None of her logical observation made any difference, of course; the dread persisted, and Edie was compelled to approach the river. Despite her mind begging her to turn around and go back the way she'd come, her body seemed intent on seeing the dream through.

Two steps closer. Three. As she crept up to the riverbank, the water finally came into her line of sight.

And it wasn't water.

A slow-moving, almost viscous substance flowed where dark water should have been, cloudy with cobwebby forms pulled and stretched through it. Horrified, Edie peered closer, able to make out bodies and faces—some with eyes closed as if asleep; some with mouths open in distant screams, fingers clawing upward, searching in vain for a way to the surface. The loud whispering around her, which she usually interpreted as the rushing of water, had never sounded as much like human voices as it did now.

The sight wasn't anywhere near the worst thing she'd seen, and yet it filled her with immense terror. She balked inwardly, but her body didn't move an inch, her toes touching the very edge of the bank. Only in a nightmare would she be transfixed like this. She could do nothing except look into the river of trapped souls as their prayers and pleas and screams enveloped her.

Next to her, the crow cawed. Edie managed to tear her eyes away from the river's soft glow to look up at it, frowning. It felt almost as though the bird had said something she hadn't quite understood. "What?" she uttered, turning slightly with the intent to approach its perch on the bridge.

Suddenly, cold licked her ankle, and she lost her balance, almost going down onto one knee in the snow.

It took her a moment to realize what had happened. Panic paralyzed her briefly, and then she began kicking her leg, trying to free herself of whatever was holding on—*clutching* her.

When she looked back, she screamed. The sound cut through the snowy forest.

A pale purplish face and a skeletal upper body scrambled behind Edie, trying to use its grip on her to pull itself up the steep riverbank. She kicked and kicked, but the thing's grip was unnaturally steady, like it had its clutches around something more than her body.

She bent at the middle and lashed out, clawing and pulling at the ice-cold hand as whispers and the sounds of swarming crows clouded her mind. Black wings obscured all vision, and—

Not black wings. It was darkness, and there was silence save for her thrashing and whimpers.

Darkness. Her first thought was that she must still be in Indriði's dungeon. Not another dungeon dream...

Then ... sirens. Traffic. Somewhere close by, there was a street, lots of city noise. Lucidity rushed back in as her hand flew to her throat. Her heart was thundering as if she'd just sprinted a mile, and her ears rang with her own shrieks. Had she screamed out loud?

She sat up for a moment, trying to catch her breath. That damn nightmare. She almost missed when it had been predictable, as unsettling as reoccurring nightmares were. What, she didn't get traumatized and attacked by bad guys enough when she was awake?

It took a few moments for her heart rate to settle, and she resolved to get up and go to the bathroom. She filled a tiny glass with water from the tap and drank it like she'd been trekking through the desert for a day, then splashed water on her face and patted it dry. With a deep breath, she braved a glance at her half-dead appearance in the mirror again.

As she did, something gave her pause. That strange electric feeling she'd felt in the parking garage suddenly surged, and she swore that she saw her dark gray irises pulse a faint blue—the color Satara said they turned when she commanded large amounts of death magic.

She frowned and leaned closer to the mirror, watching closely ... but the moment seemed to have passed. Leaning back, she took one last look at herself before exiting the bathroom—

—and slamming right into someone's chest.

The past few weeks had been harder for Marius than any other time in his life. There was no path for him from here that didn't end in alienation and strife, and though he'd never admit it out loud, that fact was slowly and steadily breaking him down.

The Aurora, the only home and family he had ever known, had left him in the dust. Rejected him. They had dismissed his fears. They had tried to cover up their own crimes. They had threatened the truth with punishment.

Out of fear for his own life, he'd had to run from them, and running from the Aurora made you a fugitive forever.

It was all because of what had happened with the Radiant—or former Radiant, now. Going from trusting his father implicitly, to thinking he was an evil traitor, to being unsure of the truth at all had been ... difficult, putting it lightly. What was worse, the truth that was beginning to reveal itself now told a story that implicated Marius, too. According to Tara, the last surviving witness of his father's deal with Indriði, Radiant Eirik had only agreed to the Norn's terms when she'd threatened to tell Marius's "secret."

What that secret was, Marius still had no idea. He'd never kept a secret worth breaking a holy oath.

And it haunted him. He had been ready to kill his father when he and the Reach had infiltrated the Temple of the Rising Divine. Now, Marius couldn't find it in his heart to hate him. He was hurt and confused, but he couldn't hate him.

In the end, the Aurora had turned out to be no more noble. In the end, it seemed this had all been Eirik's misguided attempt to protect his only son. And now he was gone. Gods only knew where.

Had all this betrayal been Marius's fault, at its core?

He had been chewing on the question for weeks, and now that they were in Radiant Oddfreyr's territory, it wouldn't leave him in peace. Even the pleasant company and the big comfy bed he had claimed weren't enough to calm him. As he tried to sleep, he kept flipping over and looking out the window, watching the snow fall and build up.

This snow. Another hellerune. A secret branch of the Reach. Not one but two dangerous groups roaming the city. Even beyond the scope of his own personal dilemma, there was too much to think about.

So he knew he wasn't dreaming when a yelp from the next room cut the frustrated silence, causing him to jump to his feet. He recognized the voice as Edie's.

For a split second, his mind raced, wondering if someone had snuck in and attacked her—but he had been living with her and the others for a couple weeks, now, and had quickly learned that night terrors were common among the guests in Matilda's home.

Marius settled on the edge of his bed, conflicted. Should he go to her? Was that too much? She had been kind to him so far, but *kind* didn't mean *I want you to enter my bedroom at night.*

Then again, what if there was a chance she was truly in trouble? If something had come through the window in the night and incapacitated her, she would need help even if she couldn't shout for it. Especially if she couldn't shout for it.

Best to be safe. For the sake of the group, if nothing else.

He quickly pulled a shirt on and stepped into the hall, walking the ten feet that separated his and Edie's rooms before knocking on her door. There was no response. After a handful more seconds and another unanswered knock, Marius took a deep breath, braced himself, and entered.

The room was empty, and a sense of dread turned his stomach until he noticed a light shining through the crack under the bathroom door. He exhaled in relief and took a few steps closer, approaching to knock there as well.

Just as he was reaching out, however, the door opened, and a shorter figure collided with him.

It was Edie, as became apparent when she stepped back with a surprised gasp. Marius froze, taking her in.

He had only seen her in her nightclothes a couple times now, and it was still shocking every time. He was used to taking cues from appearance—who was important, who was not to be trifled with—and however compassionate she had turned out to be, her usual black, spiky attire suggested the opposite. It was almost as if, like him, she wore armor. To see her unmakeupped and dressed plainly was still jarring for him.

And, against his better judgment ... exciting. She was dressed as modestly as one could ever imagine, in a T-shirt and flannel pants, but it wasn't the amount of skin shown that transfixed Marius.

"Jesus!" she breathed, putting a hand to her chest. "You scared me."

He refocused quickly. "My apologies. You were, um, screaming."

She blinked, and he could have sworn he saw a shimmer of magic trace a circle around her dilated pupils. "Oh. Sorry."

"I wanted to make sure you weren't being attacked," he added in haste.

"I'm okay. I just had—" She paused in a way that concerned Marius, but simply shook her head, sitting on the edge of her bed. "I just had a nightmare. Pretty standard these days."

Marius nodded, standing stiffly for a moment. Did she want to be left alone? Should he go? He was about to take his leave when she bent herself in half and buried her face in her hands, groaning.

His shoulders sank. No, he couldn't just leave her like this. After another pause, he sat down next to her. "Is there anything I can do to help?"

"I don't know." She sat up again and looked ahead blearily. "I don't think I can go back to sleep."

Marius glanced out the window. The orange haze of light pollution had shifted. It was probably around an hour to sunrise. "We could always go into one of the common areas. There's no point in sitting in the dark for hours."

Edie quirked a brow at him but nodded. "Yeah ... that sounds good."

She grabbed the throw blanket from the end of her bed and wrapped it tightly around her shoulders as they made their way out into the living room. Marius flicked on a lamp, and they sat on opposite ends of the couch, her curling up and him resting his head sleepily back against the cushions.

After a minute or so of silence, he noticed her smiling at him. His brows drew together. "What?"

"It's, uh ... I dunno. Nice to see your hair down and curly." She looked uncertain, like she wasn't sure if she should be saying it. "It's almost always slicked within an inch of its life."

"I just don't like it in my face," he mumbled.

"I feel that." She reached back and patted her bun. Her hair wasn't quite long enough for it to be a proper messy bun, so the ends just stuck up in the back like spikes. It reminded him of a blackbird's plumage. A second later, something seemed to dawn on her, and she looked around the room with concern. "Cal's not back yet?"

"Maybe he's in the master bedroom?"

"Nah. He probably won't touch it. He's ... weird about hospitality."

"I've noticed." Marius huffed. How could he not notice, the way Cal treated Matilda—*Tilda*, he corrected himself. She wanted him to call her what everyone else did. "He goes off on his own a lot, doesn't he?"

Edie snorted. "Yes. And not always at the best times, either."

"But you don't control him."

"He's his own person." She looked at him, frowning. "Why, would you?"

Marius considered it for only a second. "No. But I'm not a...." The words died in his throat, and he pursed his lips tightly.

"But you're not a hellerune," she finished flatly, and sighed.

He looked over at her. Was she ... upset? When they'd first met, she had seemed indignant to any suggestion that she was evil by nature, but now was different. She looked tired and sad.

Marius sat up a little straighter. "Necromancers usually raise the dead, and most wouldn't do so without the intent to control them. That's all I meant."

"Yeah." She scrubbed the side of her face.

He could tell his explanation hadn't been enough. And, if they were getting technical, it was only the creation of a *revenant* that stole raw, pure life energy—husks were typically soulless, driven on by magic instead of sentience or a compulsion to follow orders. Edie hadn't done anything like that since accidentally raising her hamster from the dead, as far as he knew. Guilt settled in his stomach at the look on her face.

He was trying to find the words to apologize when she continued on without waiting: "I hope the hellerune here isn't like that. But with our luck, he'll be, like, a murderer or something."

Marius peered at her. "Can you feel him?"

"I don't know. I feel *something*, but I'm not sure what it is."

"What is it like?"

"It's like ... electricity." Edie peered over at him. "Can you feel it?"

Marius shook his head.

"I guess it must be him, then," she concluded with a sigh. She scrubbed her face again. "Or something having to do with the Reach, maybe."

"It seems more likely that a hellerune would be able to sense another hellerune." Marius sat up straighter, tucking one leg under himself so he could turn toward her. "Do you think you'd be able to locate him if we set you loose?"

She chuckled, smiling, and Marius gritted his teeth as his heart thudded. But her lightened mood only lasted a few seconds before she answered solemnly, "Yeah, I think I could. If we can get around through all this snow."

"We'll figure out a way. We're going to have to if we want to find him before Indriði does."

They sat on the couch for well over an hour, chatting and falling into silence at intervals. The sun eventually rose, but it barely filtered through the steely clouds lording over the city, filling the living room with thin morning light. Marius laid his head back briefly and must have drifted off, because the next thing he knew, Edie was presenting him with a plate of fried eggs and plain toast.

"Sorry I'm not much of a cook," she said sheepishly, looking down at her own plate. Her toast was completely blackened. "I'm surprised I didn't wake you with the smell."

"It's fine," he said, taking the plate. "Thank you."

He glanced out the window at the sun and felt a twinge of guilt when he realized he hadn't said rising prayers.

Beside him, Edie was already wolfing her food down, burned toast be damned. She dipped her charcoal into the yolk of her egg and said between bites, "I never got to ask you what you thought of the music you were listening to on the drive down. It, uh, looked like you were enjoying it."

Marius smiled, happy to have a distraction. "It was better than I thought it would be ... but also different."

"What kind of music do you usually listen to?"

"Traditional music, I suppose." He shrugged. "I like it well enough. It's not *bad*. And our people do still live in the world, of course, so I'll occasionally listen to some pop music."

"Really? I find it hard to imagine you jamming out to some Taylor Swift."

Marius snorted. "I'm not sure who that is, but you never know. I never left the temple long enough to discover my music taste, and it's not as though there were many avenues for me to discover it otherwise. No internet access."

"But you..." Edie began, and then paused, shaking her head.

"I what?"

She glanced at him uncertainly, her cheeks turning a shade pinker. "When we ... ran into each other at the party, I told a joke about the Cure, and you laughed. So you knew my kind of music even before hearing it."

Oh, Tyr. How was he supposed to explain that he'd had an issue of *Rolling Stone* hidden under his bed like a dirty magazine for the past five years? That he'd read it from cover to cover nearly a hundred times? Furthermore, how was he supposed to explain that he still had it—with him now, in fact, packed in his bag? If he told Edie that, she'd laugh at him.

He cleared his throat and simply answered, "It's a long story." That would have to suffice for now.

She looked like she wanted to ask him more questions, but her attention was turned elsewhere when a figure entered the living room doorway. Marius followed her gaze, polishing off the last of his eggs.

Satara stood there, already dressed cozily but looking as exhausted as Marius felt. *Exhausted* seemed to be all their default states of late, but her most of all, with bloodshot eyes and shaking hands. Folded protectively around her shoulders were the shadowy wings of a fledgling valkyrie, the ones she had revealed to him and Edie a fortnight ago in Astrid's home.

Marius's heart sank when, with a deep breath and a grimace, she spread them. They shuddered with what must be immense pain. The last time he had seen them, they'd been feathery and healthful looking, albeit not quite opaque in all places. Now, they almost sagged under their own weight, the incorporeal feathers sparse in one or two places as though she was molting. The very tips of them almost seemed to weep, like bleeding ink on a painter's canvas.

How could things have changed so drastically in just two weeks?

"Are you okay?" Edie asked in a hushed tone, standing and going to her at once.

Satara kept her body drawn inward, but she relaxed when Edie touched her arm. Her voice was thick. "I— I just hope we can figure things out soon. It gets more painful every day."

"But ... I thought we had more time."

The shieldmaiden took another deep breath. "There's never enough time."

Edie was quiet, her gaze drifting to the floor thoughtfully. Marius looked at Satara, and the heartbreak in her face made it hard for him to stay where he was. They didn't know each other very well yet, and he wasn't sure how he could comfort her, but the urge was almost overwhelming.

After a moment of silence, Edie looked back up and asked, "D'you want me to make you breakfast? There's plenty of eggs and bread and other stuff in the kitchen."

Satara cast a subtle glance in Marius's direction, and he shook his head.

"I'm fine," she said, taking a step away. "I can make my own food. But thank you."

Edie seemed disappointed but didn't argue. As Satara entered the kitchen, the necromancer drifted back to the couch and curled up again, staring at her black-painted toenails. Marius could tell she was deep in thought, so he left her to it, instead going to stand by the window.

In the distance, the East River flowed almost like ink under the darkened sky, and the peaks of the Queensboro Bridge were covered in white. The blizzard had cleared, but the city still wore a mantle of snow, with eddies drifting here and there in the chilly winds. Climate patterns hadn't been as predictable as they should be of late, but a blizzard in July? It was more than concerning. If he didn't know any better—

Satara reentered the living room, and Marius turned away from the window to keep an eye on her. Her wings were hidden from sight as she settled in the middle of the couch, and he couldn't help but envy her avocado toast and omelet with hot sauce, even as she listlessly pushed it around on the plate. At least she was eating. He'd noticed her struggle with that, too.

"I wonder if there's someone around here who can help," Edie said suddenly. "Help us figure out how to transition you. We have to do something, I mean, there's no other choice."

Marius considered this as he sank into a nearby armchair. He still cursed himself for never finding more information in his father's library —he'd become completely sidetracked when the letter from Tara had suddenly arrived. "The secret Reach may be able to help." He frowned. "If we believe the theory that they've set up a network to protect the other hellerune from the Gloaming, they *must* have more resources than we do."

"And once we find the hellerune," Edie continued, "he'll be able to bring us to whatever books or scrolls or ... I don't know ... wax tablets they have."

Satara sighed, cutting up her omelet but not eating it. "There's a huge chance that whatever ritual I'm supposed to complete for my investiture is *secret*. That it's *never* been written down, it's supposed to pass from valkyrie to shieldmaiden." She held her forehead with one hand. "There's a good chance that I'll never be able to find it."

"Maybe we could ask a valkyrie." Edie shrugged. "There has to be someone around here who knows *something*. We can't just give up."

The shieldmaiden looked at her seriously. "I'm not giving up. I'm being realistic. The sooner I come to terms with the fact that I could very well die, the better, Edie."

"But what about Indriði?"

"If the last thing I ever do is go up against a Norn, at least I won't have died sitting and waiting for it to happen." Satara stared at her food, then set it aside to rub her temples. "I ... I still hope you're right. I hope someone here can tell me how to fix this."

Edie nodded and said gently, "No time like the present. I guess we start looking today."

"Perhaps you could scry," Marius suggested.

"I'm not sure. Considering what happened last time..."

He quirked a brow in silent question. They had all been living together for a couple weeks, but he still sometimes had to be filled in on what the Reach had been doing in all the time before.

"Last time we scried, I'm pretty sure we saw Indriði. Or I did, anyway."

"She's extremely powerful," Satara said. "However powerful you think she is, take it and multiply it by nine. We opened a mirror to look at her, and she turned it into a window."

"So it will only give away our position." Marius sighed and shifted to cross his legs under him. "I suppose that's out, then."

"But I think..." Edie began, then paused. "I think I'm getting a pull toward the other hellerune, so ... if I can follow the pull, maybe we can do it without scrying or divining or anything."

The shieldmaiden considered for a moment before nodding. "If you think you can follow it, we may as well try."

After making sure Satara ate at least a little food, Marius and Edie left to get ready for the day. Marius showered quickly, moisturized, and decided not to *slick his hair within an inch of its life*, as the necromancer had so eloquently put it. Figuring there wasn't much chance of battle, he threw on regular street clothes before emerging into the common area again.

Satara was reading, and Marius went to the window so as not to bother her. A few minutes later, Edie came out, too, in the process of putting her wet hair up into a careless bun. As she did, she looked around the room, brow furrowing. "Where—"

Before the question could even leave her lips, the *click* of the door unlocking startled them all. A second later, Cal came barreling into the entryway, blue eyes wide.

Three variations of "What's the matter?" came from his captive audience, and in response, he spat out a breath.

"Couple blocks from here. Shit. You guys gotta see this."

CHAPTER SIX

WHEN EDIE STEPPED out of the apartment building and onto the sidewalk, she expected to see Ghost waiting for them—but to her surprise, the haunted Cadillac was nowhere to be seen.

Cal was already walking briskly toward the corner, and she and the others were forced to keep up with him as she asked, "Where's Ghost? I thought we were going somewhere."

"No Ghost," he answered, waving around at the city in frustration. "This fucking traffic is demented; finding my way through was a bitch 'n' a half. The damn street's blocked off, anyway."

"What street?"

He didn't answer. Edie simply exchanged glances with Marius and Satara before picking up speed to keep pace with the frustrated revenant. As they hurried along, icy rain came down, so Edie was careful on the pavement. The last thing she needed was to slip and break her arm on top of everything else.

It wasn't long before she understood what Cal had been talking about. A few blocks down, they turned a corner and were immediately faced with a crowd of people in the middle of the road. Police cars were parked on either side of the street, with a cruiser idling diagonally across the median, and officers seemed to be corralling the shouting crowd—smallish, some holding signs.

In front of the crowd, they had set up metal barriers, and beyond them, Edie could see another, even bigger crowd. They were clustered around a platform, holding signs of their own and chanting, though she couldn't make out exactly what they were saying. A few people were attempting to erect a large awning for them to stand under, and one above the platform as well. A rally?

"What a shitshow," Cal mumbled before plunging into the smaller crowd of people.

Edie and the others had little choice but to follow him, doing their best to shield themselves from the rain as they did. As they pushed through the crowd, signs were waved above them, familiar words and phrases shouted—but Edie was more focused on following Cal and didn't fully register what was going on around her.

She, Satara, and Marius finally came to a stop next to Cal at the forefront of the smaller crowd, the swell of people pressing them up against the barrier.

She squinted through the rain at the rally before them, trying to make out what was happening. But they were too far away for her to read their signs, and the shouting of the crowd around them made it hard to hear the chanting.

"What is this, exactly?" Satara called over the noise, looking at Cal.

"I dunno what it is *exactly*, but—"

Marius touched Edie's arm, grabbing her attention. "Didn't Yuval say something about the recent protests in the city?"

She nodded in reply. "Yeah, but who's protesting?" After a pause, she said, "I'm going in deeper."

"Edie—" Cal began.

"I'll be two seconds. Wait here!"

Before anyone could stop her, she was scooting along the edge of the barrier, trying to find a break in it. The only way they were going to get a straight answer was if she melted into the crowd and had a quick look herself; she'd be in and out in a minute or so.

It took a bit of looking, but she finally found an in. The barriers the police had lined up didn't quite span the width of the street, and they had tried to make up for it by blocking the tiny gap with the front half of a cruiser. With a cursory glance, Edie saw that no one was watching the area, all much more focused on the crowd they were trying to keep out. She leapt over the hood of the cruiser unceremoniously and slithered into the bigger crowd.

From the other end of their connection, she could feel Cal watching her movements closely. She continued worming her way carefully toward the rally's epicenter, but it wasn't long until she could feel him tug the thread between them, the volume of his emotions rising. Edie looked back and managed to catch a glimpse of him through the crowd. He must have lost sight of her, because he was leaning forward and squinting into the rain with a hand shading his eyes.

Shit. She should signal him before he decided she wasn't safe and came running in after her. She stood on her tiptoes to try to get a clear look at him, head bobbing over the shoulders of the ... mostly male crowd, she was now realizing. But the realization was only a twinge in the back of her mind as she raised her arms as high as she could, waving wildly in Cal's direction so he could find her again.

"Hey, lady," said a voice beside her.

Edie barely glanced at the speaker as she shifted to the side, assuming he wanted her to scoot over.

But instead, he followed her the step she had taken, continuing to speak: "I like your tattoos!"

For some reason, that statement stopped her dead in her tracks. Tattoos ... there was something wrong with the way he'd said it. Why did that sound *wrong*?

She lowered her arms. Stretching them up that high and waving them had caused the sleeves of her leather jacket to ride up, exposing her wrists. Her gaze touched the runes tattooed there, ingwaz and ehwaz, and then flew to the man who'd spoken to her.

When she saw him, things started to come together. Dread filled her.

He was a little older than her, probably in his late twenties, wearing wraparound sunglasses and sporting a high ponytail with an undercut. His beard was separated into three awkward braids, and he held a giant poster board. The stark red paint was starting to run, but the images were still clear: three ornate interlocking triangles framed by a pair of wings, and the words ODINIST PRIDE WORLDWIDE.

Oh, shit. How had she not realized it earlier? These were, without a doubt, the people Yuval had warned them about.

Blood Eagles.

Edie had no response for the man. She stared, wide-eyed, backing up as far as she could before bumping into someone else. The man in front of her as well as a few others watched her, confusion and an agitated kind of nervousness radiating from them.

For the first time since arriving on the scene, she really looked around her. Styles of dress ran the gamut from tactical vests and helmets to polos and khakis; there were men in baseball caps and men with dark sunglasses and scarves covering their mouths. All around her, signs similar to the one the man was holding glared with big block letters and stark, angular symbols, the sight of which turned her stomach. Others held homemade shields, or waved flags.

She already knew that by not responding to the compliment, she had outed herself as an interloper. Without a second glance, she turned away and began shouldering her way through the crowd once more.

Only shouts of abuse followed her, and she was able to slip past the cop car and behind the barricade again. Within a minute, she was standing next to Cal. Tension rolled off him, Marius, and Satara in waves, and Edie inserted herself into the small circle they had formed near the front of the smaller crowd—counterprotesters, she realized now.

"Those are Blood Eagles."

"Yeah," Cal said, "we can see that now. How about not runnin' off and separatin' us? Some bad bullshit always happens when you do."

Edie cut him a look. "Yes, because *I'm* always the one who runs off."

"So what do we do?" Satara asked through clenched teeth. "Just stand here and watch them?"

"We could try to get somewhere we can get a better vantage point, so we're not in the thick of it." Edie looked around, but the street was completely blocked off, and she wasn't about drag Satara and Marius through that crowd. At least in her case, the Blood Eagles had assumed she was one of them. She glanced at the markings on her wrist again and felt heat rising up her neck. "If we could—"

Cal raised a hand, shushing her wordlessly, his gaze focused straight ahead. When she followed it, she realized that a woman had ascended the platform and was readying to speak. She was too far away for Edie to see in great detail, but she was young, thin, blond, wearing high heels and a raincoat with the hood pulled up.

The microphone on the podium squealed, and the woman began to speak over the rain, thanking the crown around the platform for coming. As she launched into the rest of her speech, however, the counterprotest around them erupted in a chant: "*Say it loud, say it clear, Nazis are not welcome here! Say it loud, say it clear, Nazis are not welcome here!*"

Edie had to strain to hear the woman's words but was able to pick up a few, interspersed with the sounds of her crowd cheering and clapping: "Collective interest ... your heritage ... victory ... European warriors ... sense of honor..."

Beside her, Satara's noise of disgust was audible despite the cacophony. She looked at the others and said in a tone that brooked no argument, "Let's get out of here."

Marius and Edie nodded in unison, and they began pushing their way through the counterprotesters, back toward where they'd come. They didn't stop until they stood at the mouth of an alleyway, far enough that the rally and chanting were only a dull roar.

They stood in a circle, all arms crossed. Edie looked at the snow to avoid looking at her friends, mind swimming with indignation and shame. When she finally raised her head to search Marius and Satara's faces, the anger and hurt there were unmistakable. Satara shifted from foot to foot, and Marius stood still as a stone, staring in the direction of the rally.

Edie couldn't help her protective impulse. With nowhere to vent her frustration, she turned to Cal. "You should have told us what was going on before asking us to follow you."

"We should have done something," Marius murmured. "We should have said something."

"And paint targets on our backs?" Satara returned, turning more fully toward him.

"I— Look, I'm sorry!" Cal grimaced and shoved his hands in his pockets. "I thought it might be the Gloaming. Y'know, the people we're after, here?"

"Yes, Cal, I get it. I just— I don't—" Satara took a breath and wiped the air with both hands. "I don't want to talk about it anymore."

Marius took a small step toward Cal. "So, was it? The Gloaming?"

"Well..." He took his hands from his pockets, placing them on his hips with a sigh. "She's older than when I last saw her, but no doubt the bitch giving the speech was Daschla."

"Astrid's old shieldmaiden." Satara's eyes shone with hope as well as anger. "That means—"

Something seemed to catch her eye, and she cut herself off, looking back toward where they had come. When Edie turned, she noticed that a group of people were approaching them, dressed like those she'd been surrounded by at the rally and carrying baseball bats. In a matter of seconds, her heart was thundering against her rib cage, and she could feel the whisper of magic skimming her arms. She'd rot them right there in the middle of the street if she had to.

"Five of them," Marius said, his voice ice. "Armed. Should we engage?"

"We can't," Satara replied, looking at him like he'd just grown an extra head. "The police are right there."

Cal took a step forward and spat, reaching for his gun. "We can take five humans. Easy."

"You're not listening to me." The shieldmaiden grabbed his arm, drawing his attention to her face. "Absolutely *not*."

They were about twenty feet away, now, and Edie was starting to realize ... something was different about these people. Their formation—four men circling one taller woman—struck her as familiar, but it wasn't until one of them summoned fire in his hands that she understood what they truly were.

Not Blood Eagles. Watchers.

Satara took a step back. "We need to go."

Beside her, Cal nodded and readied himself. "Run. I'll see if I can't put a dent in their little plan."

The group took off, but Edie lagged behind to watch Cal over her shoulder. One of the Watchers was charging up a fireball that would no doubt overtake the revenant and surge down the alley after the others. With inhuman strength, Cal grabbed a full Dumpster to his left and dragged it until it was mostly blocking their retreat, then took off running after her.

As they ran, the rain began to come down harder. The already snow-covered pavement became even slicker, and Edie nearly lost her footing a few times as she tried to cut through the impossible crowds on the city streets. Not only were the civilians getting in the way, they were in danger and they didn't even know it.

Satara led them from up ahead, and it seemed she'd had the same thought; she quickly switched direction, driving their retreat toward a nearby stretch of green—Central Park, Edie assumed. There was a chorus of honking as they cut across five lanes of traffic and pushed into the park.

Edie glanced back. Behind her, Cal was bringing up the rear but gaining on her. On the other side of the street, the Watchers lingered for a moment before following after them, cars be damned. She watched in horror as the tallest one jumped on top of a taxi and hopped the cars' hoods like stepping stones.

Adrenaline surged through Edie's veins. She turned back around to focus on picking up speed. Their group wove between trees, heading for the more densely wooded areas of the park, but no matter what they did to try and shake them, the Watchers' dogged persistence won out.

It was starting to look like they wouldn't have any choice but to fight them. Either that or draw attention to themselves by running through all of Manhattan—and that was sure to attract more police attention.

"Ahead! The arch!" Satara called back to them, her voice barely loud enough to be comprehensible.

Edie raised her head and squinted through the rain. Sure enough, up ahead of them was a stone arch, its opening barely big enough for two people to pass through side by side. Massive stones flanked it on either side, creating a blind spot just within the entrance.

She gasped, suddenly understanding Satara's plan. Ambush.

Pumping her legs harder, she was able to catch up with Satara and Marius quickly, Cal close behind.

And then she slipped.

A patch of black ice that she had been certain was a puddle brought her to the ground in an instant. The force of it knocked the air out of her lungs so hard she couldn't even scream.

Propelled by momentum, Cal sailed right past her. He and the others were already through the arch by the time they realized what had happened.

Go! Go! she thought, wishing they would just leave her behind and go through with the plan. But Satara and Marius stopped, lingering as Cal doubled back sharply. He rushed toward her with an arm out for her to grab.

Hiss. A biting frost kissed Edie's face as something whizzed over her head and thudded into Cal's chest with a sound like breaking glass. She watched in terror as an icy sheen spread over him, his movements becoming jerky and labored. When she whipped her head around to see what had happened, she spotted the Watchers barely twenty feet away from her.

And then, another unexpected noise. Scarcely audible over the rain and her pounding heart, the sound of fabric rustling in the wind reached her ears.

Before she could even wonder where it was coming from, a figure touched down in front of her, having apparently been crouched atop the stone arch.

Edie couldn't make out much about this person in the thin light and rain, but she thought they were a man, of average height and build. Staring at the back of his head, she could see that his hair was short and snow white. He wore shiny dress shoes and what looked like a black robe.

The stranger turned his head as though to glance over his shoulder at her. As he did, a strange pale light flashed. The next thing she knew, she was looking not at the face of a man but at a sun-bleached, empty-eyed skull.

The Watchers were already upon him, and he raised his hands—completely skeletonized, with no flesh or tendons between the bones. He grabbed two Watchers by the napes and knocked their heads together in one swift motion, then reached without hesitation for the larger woman. Using her almost as a shield against the remaining combatants, he clutched her throat, digging his fingers into her skin. The flesh withered under his hand, and rot was climbing up her face by the time he threw her aside.

Two more men—a kick, a knee to the groin—and then he turned on the original two, shoving a blade that Edie hadn't seen a second ago into their abdomens one at a time.

Behind her, she could hear the familiar hum of Marius summoning his solar weapons, but the skeleton remained focused. He slashed a throat and summoned another blast of death magic, and the Watchers were lying at his feet, barely alive.

Just when Edie thought the battle was over, the skeleton adjusted his stance. He stood straighter and let his arms fall to his sides, palms turned upwards. As he slowly began to raise them, a strange, almost windy sound filled the area. Indeed, shortly after, a strange wind picked up, whisking Edie's hair all around her head and the stranger's robe around his ankles.

The bodies at his feet trembled, like they were writhing at ten times the speed of their normal motion. Edie watched as a pale periwinkle film, like a mask, appeared over their faces. The wind tugged the film. With the Watchers' features mirrored perfectly by it, it almost looked like the skeleton was peeling their skin off. As the wind blew harder, the purplish image began separating from the rest of their bodies, too, until a translucent copy of them shivered just slightly above their forms.

Suddenly, Edie realized where she'd seen such a thing before. The translucent, almost viscous forms; the agonized faces of once-living men. Like in the unquiet river in her dream, she was seeing a soul. A spirit.

And the skeleton seemed to be ... sucking them into himself.

The spirits swirled, distant screams joining the harsh sound of wind as they wheeled around him. He stretched his arms out as if to welcome them, and one by one, they collided with and sank into his chest, causing a bright white spark of energy each time.

For a moment, the robed form glowed, just as the spirits had. He bent at the waist with his hands on his knees, like he'd just run a marathon, and Edie could have sworn she heard him panting. The wind died down, the normal rainy weather returning. With it went his odd glow—as well as his skeletal appearance.

Behind her, Cal had unfrozen completely, coming to stand next to her. The others lingered close by, watching warily. Was this strange man a savior, or was he an even bigger threat than the Watchers?

The stranger stood up straight again, took a deep breath, and finally turned.

He was an older man, light-complected and probably in his late sixties or early seventies. His square jaw, long, straight nose, and heavy brow gave him the look of a bird of prey, blue eyes intense behind a pair of tortoiseshell glasses. Now that he was turned toward them, Edie could see that it wasn't a robe he was wearing but an old-fashioned Catholic priest's outfit, white collar and all.

Thin mouth drawn, the stranger looked at each of them in turn, studying them. And then, he broke into a dazzling grin.

"I was wondering when you'd show up. Let's find somewhere we can talk."

CHAPTER SEVEN

THE PRIEST'S apartment was relatively austere, with white walls and neutral carpeting, but was by no means shabby. Though, if Edie was honest, the giant stone coffee table—about six feet long, nearly black, and clearly very heavy—was a bit out of place, the only statement piece in a room decorated with nondescript furniture.

She and the others sat awkwardly in the living room, with Marius in an armchair and the rest of them squeezed onto the couch. In the adjacent kitchen, the priest whistled as he banged around—presumably getting them all tea, since he'd mentioned he wanted some.

Beside her, she could feel how tense Satara was, and she wasn't in a much more relaxed state herself. The priest's sudden appearance had been fortunate in that they hadn't had to battle the Watchers, but none of them had any idea what to expect from him. Only his promise that he was on their side had brought them to his home.

Before too long, a kettle's screech cut the silence, causing Edie to jump. A handful of seconds later, the priest exited the kitchen carrying only one mug.

Okay, apparently only tea for him, Edie thought, frowning. She could have used some, considering she'd fallen into an ice-cold puddle, but whatever.

The priest sat in a vacant armchair and propped his feet up on the stone coffee table nonchalantly, stirring his tea all the while. With a sigh, he spoke first: "It took you people long enough to get here. I could've used you earlier, to be honest." When there was no response, he added, "Before the blizzard, ideally. What the hell was the holdup?"

Aside from a priest cursing, this situation seemed ... odd, to say the least. He'd been waiting for them? How had he known they were on their way, let alone that they exited at all?

Edie tilted her head as she responded, "We, uh ... we didn't realize you were expecting us."

"I wasn't expecting *you*"—he gestured with his free hand, observing her over the rim of his glasses—"that's for damn sure. But I was expecting *somebody*. It's been awhile since we got some new blood down here."

New blood? Edie glanced at Satara. Could this be related to the "Reach problem" Indriði's contact had spoken of? Astrid had led them to believe that she was all there was left of the Reach, but clearly, that wasn't true. This man must be one of them. And given the powers he had...

"You're him," she said quietly, shifting to sit on the edge of her seat. "The other hellerune."

The priest leaned back to laugh. "Ha! No."

"Oh."

"Why, are you looking for one?" He pursed his lips and examined her again. After a loud slurp of tea, he mumbled, "Ah, okay, I get it. You're a Holloway."

"I'm Edie," she responded pointedly. "This is Satara, Cal, and Marius."

"All right..."

Satara nodded in greeting. "With all due respect, if you're not a hellerune, what are you? That was ... a very impressive display of magic in the park."

The priest sighed deeply, then took another sip of tea before setting it on the stone slab. "Well, first of all, my name is Basile. Basile Bolet. I'm a priest. Although, uh, not a priest of who you'd expect." He leaned back again and waved a hand. "Go ahead, play your Twenty Questions. I know it's coming."

Marius was regarding him warily, and Satara didn't seem overjoyed to be in his presence either. Edie had to keep reminding herself that her Norse companions weren't exactly at ease with Christians. She wasn't remotely religious herself, but for someone who'd grown up unattuned—and in Boston, no less—seeing priests walking around wasn't anything strange.

"Who *are* you a priest of, then?" Marius asked.

"Odin, of course."

Satara's brow furrowed. "If you're a priest of Odin, why moonlight as a Catholic?"

"It's the best way for me to keep my ear to the ground," he replied with a shrug. "I can go almost anywhere in the city and make up some excuse, which some rando would never be able to do. And it gives me the quickest access to people I might be able to help along the way, attuned and unattuned both."

Cal crossed his arms. "Well, ain't you just a regular Mother Teresa. That's nice, but what about the soul flaying, pal?"

"Hmm … one dead guy to another"—Basile cut Cal a withering stare—"you might want to watch your attitude."

"Dead?" the revenant returned, in that dumbfounded tone he reserved for when he was truly confused.

"I guess, unless— Can you be dead if you were never alive?" the priest asked, drumming his fingers on his mouth. "Questions, questions…"

Edie squinted. "You can't be a revenant."

"Ding, ding, ding, we have a winner. I'm *not* a revenant, young lady." He spread his hands. "I'm a draugborn."

Edie looked at the others for guidance but was surprised to find that they all looked just as confused as she was. Even Satara—whom Cal and

Marius had also turned to—seemed at a loss. The shieldmaiden shifted uncomfortably where she sat before saying, "I ... I don't know what that is."

"Not surprised." Basile picked his mug up again. "We aren't exactly widespread, thank the High One, or this world would be deeper in crap than it already is. Draugborn are children who die in the womb when they are cursed to be sál-skálpar."

"Soul scabbards?" Marius whispered.

"What is a ... that?"

Satara could answer this one: "A sál-skálpr, or skálpr for short, is the vessel in which a lich keeps their soul. But..." She frowned, staring at Basile. "I had no idea *people* could be skálpar."

"Not all the time," he replied. "Not already-living ones. But the unborn are a gray area, and so..." Basile gestured to himself. "A ritual was performed, and I was emptied, prepared to become a vessel! How nice for me. Eventually, I was born, and the lich's soul was inserted."

"But if you ... *died* before you were even born," Edie began slowly, not wanting to offend him, "how are you ... you know, older?"

"Nice try, but I realize you just called me old," he scoffed. "Draugborn don't have heartbeats or souls, but we do grow up, despite being technically dead. We age a hell of a lot slower than normal humans, but even when we *do*, it doesn't affect us the same way." He took a sip of his tea. "I'm over three hundred years old, if you can believe it. After a while, my flesh just ... withered away and left bone. Somehow, I'm still kickin'."

"That's why I saw you as a skeleton," Edie said, thinking back to the fight in the park.

"Yup. Dropping my glamour helps me focus when flaying and eating souls."

She bit her lip. "Can everyone who uses death magic *eat* souls? I've never seen that."

"Me either," Cal added gruffly. "Use the energy as a source of power, maybe, but..."

Basile sighed. "Because I don't have a soul, I have ... hmm ... room, I guess, to house as much spiritual energy as I want. Draugborn tend to be experts at exorcising spirits and obliterating them, or taking their power into themselves, but there's a risk."

"Risk?" Satara leaned forward as the priest lectured them.

He seemed amused that she was so rapt, and began speaking directly to her. "Heh. Well, you know how if you overeat, you stretch your stomach? It's a bit like that, but with souls. They say that if we consume too many, the space where our own souls are supposed to be becomes bigger and emptier. Draugborn who exorcise and consume a lot of spirits, even over a long period of time, supposedly become hungry and evil." He waved his hand uncertainly. "It's not usually a problem, because their liches keep them close by—and if they go feral, so what? As long as they're physically intact, they're serving their purpose."

Edie looked around the room, suddenly on edge. Any lich who would make one of these draugborn was not someone she wanted to be friends with. "But ... where's yours? Do we have to worry...?"

"Nope." Basile grinned and leaned back a little further in his chair, so that his legs were properly elevated. "A few centuries ago, I sealed my creator up in a big stone sarcophagus. She won't be bothering anyone now."

Almost all at the same time, the group looked down at the stone coffee table. Edie's stomach turned when she realized that it wasn't really a coffee table at all.

"Someone is *in there?*" she squeaked.

"Correct!"

"What about your—" Marius paused and cleared this throat, starting again: "It wouldn't be that hard for a lich to make a skálpr from an object. Why take the extra steps and hurt your mother in the process?"

"Oh, hell," Basile chuckled, "the lich didn't *hurt* my mother, kid. She *was* my mother."

The room fell into silence.

After a moment, Basile leaned forward and slapped his hand down on the stone, patting a few times. His tone remained conversational. "I mean, I get it. There's a *laundry* list of upsides to having your vessel able to walk around and follow orders. Makes them easier to keep track of; they can learn to defend themselves against anyone who might try to destroy them; and no one sees it coming, anyway, because it's such a rare, involved process.

"But I obviously couldn't let it continue. I knew that the second I understood what was going on. She wasn't just some lich—she was a lich *queen*, ruling over a swath of wasted land and taking whatever she wanted from the people who lived there. Just a real bitch. So ... I made it so she couldn't hurt anyone ever again."

"But," Satara said slowly, "you couldn't kill her because you're her skálpr; she *can't* be killed permanently unless you're destroyed. So you sealed her away instead."

Basile shot her a finger gun. "Bullseye. You're sharp."

"You being her vessel won't cause any problems, will it?" Marius asked grimly. "Her soul hasn't corrupted you?"

"Well, I haven't had any issues yet." The priest seemed less than pleased with that particular line of questioning, smiling coolly. "I am technically a vessel for her soul, yeah, but I only *facilitate* a resurrection. My *existence* makes it possible for her to come back, even if her body is completely destroyed. But she has no power over me. Especially not in the box." He added pointedly, "*I* am my own person."

So, Edie thought with a sigh, *he understands that he's not his mother, but I'm just "a Holloway."*

Cal grunted and said, "You're useful in a pinch, I'll give ya that."

"No kidding, cowboy. Do you people always get into so much trouble?"

Satara sighed, rubbing her forehead. "Occasionally. But for once, it wasn't our doing. It was the *rally* that was the trouble."

"Rally, eh?"

"Do you think they were all Gloaming?" Edie asked.

"That's unlikely." Marius shoved his hand in the pocket of his jacket.

"Almost all the people gathered there were regular humans in silly costumes. Humans with full-time jobs and things like that, most likely. The Gloaming doesn't think much of humans, and certainly not ones that haven't dedicated themselves fully to the cause."

Cal grunted. "How much more dedicated do you want the bastards to be, exactly?"

"Maybe the Gloaming don't want humans in positions of power," returned Satara, "but as foot soldiers? Why not, if they have the zeal? They need fresh waves of fighters, and we *still* don't know how the Wounded amassed the force that struck Zaedicus's party." She hugged herself and added grimly, "If they aren't Gloaming now, they will be soon."

Marius shook his head. "I disagree. The Gloaming has had the opportunity to work with groups like the Blood Eagles in the past, and they never did. Whether it was because they were too proud or actually have limits to their depravity, I don't know."

"Since when did you suddenly get all pro-Gloaming, Sunshine?" Cal asked, wrinkling what was left of his nose.

"I'm not," the vivid said firmly, "I'm simply looking at the facts, the patterns."

"Times are changing." Basile finished his tea and reclined again, latticing his fingers over his abdomen. "Clearly, things have really been going down up north. I'm almost jealous! You're gonna have to fill me in."

"Likewise," Marius mumbled.

Edie was still trying to wrap her head around the whole ordeal. "I just ... I can't even understand it. Those men, all their Norse imagery..." She looked at Satara. "They don't even know that you're a shieldmaiden! To a *real-life* valkyrie! And Marius is a Blade of Tyr, an *exalted warrior.* Maybe I'm naive, but Christ."

"It doesn't matter who I am," Satara said with a sigh. "Even if we weren't those things..." She trailed off, closing her eyes.

Basile lurched out of his seat suddenly, as if an invisible boot had kicked him, and began to pace the room. "Let's get an exchange of information going, then. I know who Zaedicus and the Wounded are, but I could always use more context, and since you all are such good friends with them, well..."

"Fine." Cal crossed his arms. "And you tell us about what all's happening down here."

"Sure." The priest stood straight, one hand behind his back, the other palm up. "I guess I'll start at the beginning."

He began to pace again as he relayed his information.

"I guess it was about a month ago that the Blood Eagles started getting noticed, but I did some research, and they've existed for a lot longer. A year and a half or so. They began as a small social media group. One of those pages you can join, or whatever it is humans do on the internet. They expanded into an online forum full of 'Odinists,' they call themselves, or 'folkish heathens.' Basically, people who worship the Old Gods but believe it should be an Anglo-only affair.

"You'd be surprised by how many different groups of these people there are, but this one is particularly ... tedious? Troubling? Not only are they depraved, but they're militaristic, into grand gestures and manifestos, idolizing mass murderers—" He swiped the air with a hand. "The works. Really up their own backsides. I guess that's probably what caught the eye of the Gloaming, or whomever is responsible. And since they were picked up, they've started having an actual physical presence in the city, an actual leadership ... Daschla Hyltir came out of nowhere and has pretty quickly turned into a symbol for them. She's—"

"Oh," Satara said, "we're familiar with Daschla."

"Is that so?"

"She was Astrid Fengrave's shieldmaiden a decade ago," Edie explained. "Satara was her replacement."

"Huh." Basile lifted his chin and studied Satara for a moment before continuing. "Well, ever since she turned up, things have been going downhill." His tone became increasingly exasperated. "And they've just been growing exponentially! *One month*! Their forum traffic has skyrocketed, their page likes have soared, they've been collecting new members like flypaper..." He came back to his armchair and slouched into it. "And I didn't even see it coming ... which is kind of my job, as an agent of Odin. So you can imagine the trouble I'm in."

"At least they aren't trying to murder ya," Cal mumbled from the side of his mouth.

Basile didn't seem to hear him, gesturing instead to Marius. "He's right, though. I mean, I've been doing this for centuries. I *know* the Gloaming are terrible. But they're usually terrible in their own special way ... they don't tend to ally with groups like this—or any groups, for that matter. Especially ones run by humans, like you said."

"But that doesn't matter," Satara insisted, rubbing her knuckles anxiously. "This is the *New* Gloaming. There is no precedent for what they'll do, and they've already proven that."

The priest pinched the bridge of his nose. "Ugh ... New Gloaming, new Reach. Hey, maybe we'll get lucky and get a New Aurora. Now with blackjack and strippers!"

Edie's gaze darted toward Marius in time to see him cast his eyes down without a word. In that moment, she wished she could go over there, though she wasn't completely sure what she could do to comfort him. She was still so uncertain of where they stood ... if he still thought she was an abomination. It seemed like his opinion changed every time it was brought up. For now, she simply kept an eye on him.

"Well, new or not," Basile continued, "I'm just glad there's more Reach here now. For a while there, I thought I was the only one up north."

Edie balked a bit. "The only one? What about the hellerune?"

Satara seemed confused for a moment as well; then her expression turned crestfallen. "The papers Cal stole said there was a 'Reach problem.' We ... thought there would be more than one of you. A network."

" 'Fraid not," he said with a sigh, crossing his arms. "Just one very powerful draugborn. But turns out even I'm not powerful enough to keep up with everything going on around here, let alone fix it by myself.

When Odin told me I'd be getting some extra hands, it was a relief, but frankly ... I expected more people."

"We— Wait." Cal sat forward in his seat, squinting at the priest. "Roll it back a sec. Odin *told* you?"

"Are you saying you have a direct line of contact with ... Odin?" Satara asked. "The Allfather?"

Basile shrugged. "Sure, why not? I mean, you work for a guy for three centuries ... I don't always speak to him *directly*, but I answer to him personally. He's kind of a micromanager like that."

Edie sat back in her seat, processing this new information. So far, she'd met elves, vampires, and even a lesser Norn. Most of the people she spent time with talked about the gods nonchalantly, like their existence was a given. But Basile was the first person she'd met who regularly spoke with a god on a personal basis. Her family had never been religious —as far as she had known, anyway. Contending with the fact that rulers of the universe actually existed wasn't really something she was comfortable with. And it ultimately raised more questions than it answered.

Cal, Satara, and Marius were more used to the concept of the Pantheons being real, but finding out that Basile knew Odin personally still seemed to come as a shock. There was a pause before Marius broke the silence. "You're a priest of Odin, you're one of his agents, and you commune with him ... is that right?"

Basile hummed affirmatively, squinting at him. "This is a lead-in to a weird question, I can tell."

"Odin is Lord of the Valkyir," Marius continued. "Freyja had her hand in creating them, and she leads them, she's their Mother—but in the end, they answer to Odin."

"Most things do," the priest said with a sigh.

Marius gestured to Satara, his tone growing firmer. "Like Edie said, Satara was Astrid Fengrave's shieldmaiden. But Astrid was obliterated by a lesser Norn named Indriði, and she never prepared Satara to take her place as the laws dictate. We've been searching for instruction on how to continue with her investiture, to no avail."

Edie felt Satara tense beside her, but it was clear where Marius was going with his spiel—clear enough that the priest was able to finish his thought for him: "And you want me to tell you what to do next, is that it?"

He sounded weary and put-upon, and the tone made Edie's blood boil. "If we can't figure out how to turn her into a valkyrie," she said, enunciating each word, "Satara will *die*."

A subtle turn of Satara's head silenced her, and the shieldmaiden spoke up. "My fledgling wings appeared pretty soon after she died, and they've been rotting quicker than I thought they would," she said, her voice soft though she looked Basile in the eye. "I'm not sure how much time I have left. If you can point me in the right direction, I'll be in your debt."

The priest considered her for an extended moment, crossing his arms and tucking one hand up to his chin. Eventually, he pushed his glasses up his nose a bit and said, "I'll do it. But I need your help first."

Their mouths opened, but before they could say anything, he held up a hand.

"First, you need to do what you came here for, whether you knew you were coming here for it or not. We need to take down the Blood Eagles, or whatever force is behind them. I don't care how; we need to put a stop to it.

"Second"—he pointed at Edie—"you're looking for a hellerune, correct? Well, I got one. I've been watching over him for a long time, using magic to cover his scent so no one ever found him. But it's been getting a hell of a lot harder recently, with all the Gloaming crawling around here. A latent magical signature, I can hide just fine. When someone's looking specifically for *him*? Well. So he needs protection."

Cal threw up a hand. "You want us to bring down a whole faction before you help us? Motherfucker, I don't know if you heard what the lady said, but this is kinda *time-sensitive*. Shit's *rotting*." He scoffed. "What kinda priest're you?"

Basile shot him a look, equal parts befuddled and unimpressed. "Yeah, I got that. But plenty's time-sensitive, bub, including what's going on here. I wouldn't expect you to understand; you haven't been here." He considered Satara. "Besides, I'm not going to let you die. We need to get this out of the way as soon as possible, and I'll work on getting you hooked up, all right? You just have to trust me."

The shieldmaiden watched him warily for a second, and Edie felt a shiver go up her legs. Nonetheless, she nodded. "We'll do it your way for now. But I'll die without your help, and the dead make poor allies."

Cal huffed. "I resent that!"

"I'll keep my end of the bargain," Basile said, pacing a fist over his heart. "You have my oath that I will help you."

Well, that was a good sign. Edie had learned pretty quickly that oaths weren't something the Norse took lightly. In fact, according to Marius, breaking an oath was considered tantamount to murder.

And in this case, if Basile broke his oath, it really *would* be murder. When the rot in Satara's wings entered her bloodstream, she'd die and have to spend eternity as a twisted demon fledgling in a castle made of snake venom or whatever the hell it was.

When the oath was given, Satara relaxed a little. But she remained wary, rubbing her hands together anxiously. "I guess we should start with the hellerune, then."

"We were looking for him anyway," Marius said. "Hoping to find him before the Gloaming did. Indriði's papers spoke of him, too, but there were no specifics."

Basile snorted. "Finally, some good news. At least I've done that aspect of my job right. Where do I even start with him...?" He walked around his armchair and finally sat back down. "Well, first of all, his name is Adam, and he ... doesn't exactly *know* he's a hellerune."

"Great." Cal put his head in one hand. "More ass-blastingly lethal mages just walkin' around like bozos at a clown convention."

"*Odin* determined it'd be best to just let him live his life," Basile continued pointedly. "His powers have been active for a long time, but I've managed to hide his energy with a regimen of suppression and cloaking spells. Like I said, though, since the Gloaming are focusing on finding *my* hellerune specifically, the regimen has had to become more convoluted. Harder and harder to maintain."

"But where do we come in?" Edie asked.

"Hmm ... I need some muscle should the Gloaming show up and try to kidnap him, to begin with. But ... truth is, it's just not practical to keep him in the dark any longer." Basile spread his hands. "He needs to be told the truth, brought into the circle so we can protect him properly. And he's, um..."

"He's ... what?"

"He's kind of ... precarious. You know, in the mental health department. And I'm not sure if you've noticed, but I'm not the warmest creature who ever walked the earth."

Cal raised a brow. "Say it ain't so."

"I put on a good show for the humans, but that's pretty much it. Now that you're here, though," the priest continued, "I can delegate the touchy-feely part to you."

Edie ran a hand through her ponytail, considering this. Telling another hellerune about his powers wouldn't be easy, but it certainly wasn't the worst job in the world. She didn't consider her mental health particularly *precarious*, but she had gone through the same thing recently—finding out about her lineage, about the hidden world around her. If anyone could help, it was her, with Cal backing her up.

"Uh ... one thing, though," Basile began, and Edie could already tell she wasn't going to like whatever he had to say next. "I kind of haven't checked in on him for a couple days. I've been busier than a one-armed house painter. But ... I have the sneaking suspicion that something went ... *wrong*."

"Wrong?" Marius wrinkled his nose. "Wrong how?"

"Well, call it what you will, but I have this awful feeling that Adam has been using his powers. You know, the powers he's not supposed to know he has."

Cal shot Edie a look. "That's not good news."

"Tell me about it," Basile mumbled. He sighed and reached for his empty mug, peering into it. "I'm gonna have to switch to gin."

CHAPTER EIGHT

DESPITE THE FACT that a blizzard in July had landed not even a full twenty-four hours ago, New York City carried on almost like nothing had happened. The rain had helped wash the worst of the snow away from the roads, and traffic and the subway system ran as normal. Still, as the group walked to the nearest subway station, they had to keep an eye out for ice; in the nearby park, a tree had come down, and a few streets over, some utility vehicles worked on a collapsed scaffold.

Edie, relieved to be of some help, happily took point when it came to navigating the subway. Cal had spent the last decade in Las Vegas, Satara had grown up in small towns, and as for Marius, it turned out when you could summon a horse made of sunlight at will, you didn't get much use out of the metro system. A long ride later, they arrived at the Church Av Station in Flatbush, Brooklyn.

The apartment building was old, brick, with an imposing stoop out front. The group forewent the front entrance, though—Basile had been very insistent that they use the apartment's back door so as not to draw attention to themselves, though what a New York City apartment was doing with a back door, Edie wasn't quite sure.

After a quick inspection of the alley leading to the rear of the building, she understood. A fenced gate separated them from a tiny back garden, with just enough space to put a couple of plastic chairs and a birdbath, both now heavy with snow. The garden apartment had a back door, as expected, but the apartment a floor above it did, too, with a fire escape leading down into the garden area.

"That must be what he was talking about," Edie mumbled, turning to the side slightly and pointing it out to the others. "He said something about us taking the fire escape up there."

Hooded by the fire escapes further up, the stairs were still mostly covered by a layer of fluffy snow. Things were stacked on the steps and the landing in front of the back door, but Edie couldn't make out what they were from this angle, this far away.

She looked down at the gate, which was fastened with a shiny combo padlock. When they had infiltrated the Temple of the Rising Divine, she'd used her death magic to rust a giant metal construct, but she wasn't sure if the same rules applied to a completely inanimate object. Best not to take chances and make herself look like an idiot when Marius could get them in guaranteed.

Cal seemed to have the same idea. "Hey, Sparky, you wanna do the honors?"

Marius paused for a moment before coming forward with a shrug and taking the padlock in his hand. The metal quickly turned a glowing white-gold in his palm, and within a few seconds, he was able to twist it off the latch and discard it.

He stepped through first, with Edie following close behind. Hopefully, whoever owned the garden apartment wouldn't notice someone had just broken into their yard.

As they approached the fire escape, Edie was finally able to make out what the strange shapes sitting on the steps were. She slowed, letting her eyes touch each one with growing confusion. A gallon of milk, a couple juice cartons, margarine, yogurt and pudding cups, various takeout containers ... shoved into a corner of the landing, two crisper drawers were stacked on top of each other, one of vegetables and the other of cheese and deli meat, covered in a snowy crust.

"Oookay," Cal said under his breath. "Any reason this guy's got his entire fridge on his back steps?"

"Maybe his power went out during the blizzard?" Satara suggested.

Edie left the others behind, avoiding the food as she crept up the fire escape herself. There was a window next to the back door, and though the blinds were closed, she could see light coming from the room beyond. "No, look—the lights are on. His fridge must be working."

She eyed the window for a moment before looking at the door. This was it; the moment of truth for whomever was on the other side of this thing. She was about to do what had been done for her when Cal had shown up in her apartment that first night—confirm the impossible. Change someone's life with just a few words.

In all honesty, she wasn't sure how to feel about it.

Focused so intently on the door, she felt rather than saw Satara come up and stand on the landing beside her. The shieldmaiden sighed, touching Edie's elbow briefly. "If the state of this fire escape is any indication, I think he's probably ... in distress."

Those words conjured images in Edie's mind of her own struggle coming into her powers. She had thought she was losing her mind. She'd have done anything to relieve herself of that feeling, to get an explanation. This was difficult, but necessary.

With new resolve, she took a deep breath and knocked on the door.

Nothing changed for a few long seconds. Then, Edie nearly jumped as one of the slats in the nearby window's blinds snapped open, then closed again before she could see who was there. She could hear things moving around inside the apartment, then another period of silence.

Finally, he opened the door.

It was only a bit. Only enough for her to see him, not into the apartment. Standing before her was a man in maybe his early forties with dark brown chin-length hair, pale skin, and an angular face with high cheekbones. His

V-neck shirt revealed a labyrinth of black-ink tattoos that climbed down his neck and disappeared under the fabric, then reemerged on slightly muscular upper arms, the only remotely built part of his thin frame. The tattoos continued all the way down to his wrists, where he wore leather bands. As his eyes darted nervously from her to Satara, Edie noticed they were a peculiar shade of light hazel brown, with almost amethyst undertones.

She paused, certain that she knew his face from somewhere. But he wasn't in any state that she recognized. His red-and-purple-ringed eyes and pink nose led her to believe he'd been crying recently. Patchy stubble and a slouched posture spoke of a long night with little sleep. Loose strands of dark hair had sprung from his widow's peak, sticking to a waxy forehead.

Stronger than ever, that agitated, electric energy she'd been feeling since their arrival in New York vibrated across her skin and under her feet. Strange sense that she already knew this man aside, there was no denying that this was the hellerune they'd come here to meet.

He gave no indication that he recognized her, though she noticed his gaze lingering on her face and the hairs on his arms standing up. He frowned anxiously, a scar on his forehead deepening as he finally spoke. His soft voice was scratchy with stress. "Can I ... help you?"

His other hand shook as he braced it against the doorway, leaning slightly to get a better look at the people on the steps. When he saw Cal, he turned even paler—something Edie wouldn't have thought possible—and closed the door slightly. Only a couple centimeters, but it didn't escape her notice. Something had scared him, but he couldn't possibly be seeing through Cal's glamour, could he?

Probably not, considering he looked more anxious than horrified. Edie wasn't sure what was going on, exactly, but Basile had been right. Something bad had happened.

"Hi," she finally said, trying to keep her tone light. "Um, I'm Edie, and this is Satara, and Cal and Marius. You're ... Adam, right?"

The man shuffled from foot to foot like he was ready to run at any moment. "Yeah … can I help you?" he repeated, even softer than the first time.

How did she put this, exactly? Her own wake-up call hadn't been gentle, so she was working from scratch here. "I, uh … my friends and I are part of a … group—"

Much to her relief, Satara cut in. But there was no getting around the truth, which sounded bonkers coming out of anyone. "We're part of a group advocating for people with preternatural abilities. Supernatural beings. One of our agents advised us that there was someone here who needed our help, so we came to check up on you."

Unsurprisingly, Adam simply stared at her, speechless.

"I know it sounds insane," the shieldmaiden continued, squinting at him. "But I suspect it doesn't sound as insane to you as it should. Am I right?"

After a pause, he shifted apprehensively. "I'm— Sorry, but I have no idea what you're talking about..."

"It's okay. We're here to help." Edie tried to look as open as possible. "Something happened, didn't it?"

Adam blanched again and moved to close the door.

Edie's pulse quickened, and she reached out, stopping him with a firm hand. "Please, I get it. But you're in danger. We're here to protect you."

That gave him pause; she could practically hear his thoughts just by watching his face. She'd had a lot of the same thoughts herself only a few months ago. He didn't quite believe them—what normal person would?—but he didn't have much of a choice at this point. He must know something unnatural was going on. If he was going through anything like she had gone through, he'd take any help he could get.

He searched her eyes like he might be able to read her mind, and a surge of energy passed between them. For a moment, with the intensity of his gaze, she wondered if he actually *was* reading her mind.

Finally, he sighed, his face crumpling. He turned away and, as he did, managed to choke out, "Come in."

He disappeared into the apartment, leaving the door open behind him. Edie entered and found herself in an open kitchen-dining room combo with a hall directly to her right and a small living room on the far left, beyond the kitchen counters. There were more windows than she had expected, but all the blinds were shut. Something about the air wasn't quite right either. Oppressive.

A chill went through her. This apartment felt like a tomb, dark and cold and silent.

Adam crossed to the little dining table, his back to Edie, and she couldn't help but notice how the kitchen lights dimmed the closer he got to them. As the others filed into the kitchen, he seemed to take a moment to pull himself together, running his hands down his face and through his hair.

By the time they were all in, Cal shutting the door behind them, he had turned around. "Okay," he said, voice a little less shaky now. "I let you in ... but you're going to have to explain what's going on, because I ... I have *no* idea."

It was a pressing request, but Edie found it hard to focus on. She couldn't shake the feeling that she knew this man's face, his voice. As she observed her surroundings, her gaze caught on something framed in the hall—a big poster featuring a stylized illustration of a man with patchwork skin, playing a horned electric guitar. The words DEATH BENEFITS were plastered across the poster in messy white writing.

With that, the pieces finally clicked together.

"DB..." she mumbled to herself. "*Adam*. Oh my *god*." As realization bloomed in her chest, she looked back at him. "You're Adam Frankenstein. The lead singer of Death Benefits."

She was aware that she sounded like a dork, but she wasn't sure what else to say. Along with the Dead Kennedys, the Misfits, Hüsker Dü, Siouxsie and the Banshees, and Skinny Puppy, Death Benefits had been in Richard Holloway's frequent rotation, and Edie had inherited his taste.

Even though it had been over ten years since the band had split up, DB always had a place in her Top Songs on Spotify. When she'd still been on social media, she'd even casually followed their lead singer's new career as a digital artist. He had always seemed really cool, even if he talked more about comic books and *Dungeons & Dragons* nowadays.

And now he was standing in front of her, trying not to weep.

To his credit, he seemed more perplexed than anything when she recognized him. A second later, he smiled uncertainly. "It's just Einan, now, really. I haven't been Frankenstein in a long time."

"What ... are you two talking about?" Marius asked, arms crossed uncomfortably.

"Death Benefits. They're— Well, they *were* a punk band. A little industrial..." Edie caught sight of another poster and drifted closer to get a better look. It was a picture of the band all together, autographed in silver marker under each of their faces. She leaned in and read the names, heart beating fast. "Mikey Mausoleum, Clottia Cumshot, Brian Brain Damage, Dead Thing— Oh my *god*." She turned to Adam. "My dad would've—"

"Holloway," Cal cut in sharply. "You can fangirl on your own time. We're on the clock here."

Adam flinched. "No ... no, it's okay. I just wasn't expecting one of you to recognize me." He cast a nervous look around the room, forcing a chuckle. "What are the odds?"

"I know, I can't believe it." Edie managed to refrain from going on, although her whole body tingled with excitement. She had no idea what to say to a person she admired so much, let alone someone who had turned out to be a hellerune like her. Maybe there was too much to say.

Her excitement slowly fizzled out, however. Beyond Basile's vague prediction that Adam had used the powers he wasn't supposed to know he had, something about this whole situation was *off*. For one thing, the apartment radiated death.

"Do you live all alone here?" she asked, peering around the kitchen.

Adam's breath caught, drawing her gaze back to him. He swallowed convulsively, and it took a moment before he could choke out, "Uh, yeah."

A lie, and a pretty blatant one at that. As Edie scanned the room, she noticed a backpack near the front door: holographic pink, covered in pastel patches, with the word *Crybaby* on the front panel.

Something told her it didn't belong to Adam. She looked back at him, trying to keep her tone gentle. "You don't have to lie to us. We're not here to get you in trouble. We wanna help, but ... we can't unless you tell us what happened."

Those words seemed to strike a nerve. Her words hung in the air for a moment before he took a few dazed steps backward and collapsed into one of the dining chairs, face buried in his hands.

Muffled sobs filled the kitchen a second later, so sudden and violent that Edie was stunned into silence. Above his head, the already-dim kitchen light flickered before extinguishing completely.

Edie exchanged a look with the others before going to crouch in front of Adam. "Hey ... it's okay. Whatever happened, we can try and fix it. All right?"

From behind his hands, Adam loosed another sob. "You can't fix it. I couldn't. I killed her. Fuck me, I killed her..."

Who? If she remembered correctly, he had a daughter, although she knew absolutely nothing about her. That must be who the backpack belonged to. Dread crept up her back. "Don't worry about that right now. You need to calm down and tell us what happened, okay?"

Satara and Marius crept closer, the shieldmaiden pulling a chair up next to Adam. Marius lingered on his other side, looking up at the kitchen light. With a gesture, he replaced it with a ball of golden energy.

At length, Adam seemed to calm down, at least enough to form a coherent sentence.

"Elle. Ellie ... my stepdaughter. She— she's been having these headaches and nosebleeds lately, and she.... I don't know what happened. I made her take the trash out. There's a dumpster around the side of the building, so she usually uses the fire escape. She got dizzy or something ... it was icy. She— I— She fell. I went outside after her, and, and I tried to help her, but she..." His voice broke again, and he rubbed the butt of his palm against his forehead.

"It's okay." Edie took his free hand and squeezed. She had never seen a man older than her in such distress. If she was honest, it was kind of hard to watch. And even worse was the thought that, if his experience was anything like hers, he may have turned his own daughter into a revenant.

But if that was the case, where was she?

"How did you try to help her?"

"I ... I don't know. It's so fucking weird."

"I know."

He inhaled sharply. "I felt like ... like I could keep her from dying, if I tried. But I did it wrong. I couldn't save her. I made her take the trash out," he repeated miserably. "It was my fault."

"No one is to blame," Satara said softly from beside him.

"What happened next?" Cal pressed, shuffling from foot to foot. Along their connection, Edie could feel how uncomfortable he was with this whole situation. Something about the way Adam was acting bothered him, but she couldn't decipher what. It couldn't be that he was crying—Cal wasn't a big fan of emotion, but he wasn't a monster.

The revenant's voice seemed to reach Adam well enough, though. He glanced nervously at Cal before bowing his head and continuing his story. "She ... she told me to keep her cold. In the fridge."

Silence. The lot of them turned their heads to look at the fridge, which hummed innocently behind Cal. A shiver went through Edie. So *that* was why it felt like a tomb in here.

"I— I didn't know what else to do! I just ... panicked and did what she said!" Adam's voice grew unsteady, on the verge of hysterics as he looked into each of their faces, expression begging for their understanding. "What else could I do? It was an accident; I'm not a murderer! I'd never hurt her, ever!"

"Wait," Marius said, brow furrowed. "What do you mean, she *told* you to put her body in the fridge? Did she not die?"

Adam tensed up at once, and Edie felt a faint pulse of energy pass through his hand and into hers. He swallowed, eyes wide, like he'd said something he hadn't meant to let slip. "I..."

Edie was as confused as Marius. Had whatever happened when Elle had died been so traumatic that he'd lost touch with reality, or what?

Thankfully, Satara seemed to pick up on what was going on. She tapped his elbow to draw his attention. "We don't doubt you heard her voice, Adam. But we need to know where it came from. Was her body speaking to you? Was she animated?"

"No," he said softly. "She was ... dead."

"Did she move?"

"No. God, no."

He hadn't raised her from the dead, then. Good thing, too, since he'd have to leech someone else's life force to create a revenant. They didn't need another dead body on their hands. But then what the hell *was* going on?

"Okay," Satara said slowly. "Where do you hear her voice? Where does it come from?"

He sighed heavily, holding his forehead. "You're not going to believe me. It's ... batshit insane."

"Try me."

Without warning, he rose from his seat, stepping around Edie and into the nearby darkened hallway. By the time she was standing, too, he had already come back from one of the bedrooms, an electric guitar in hand.

Although she was more familiar with basses, right away, she recognized it as the one on the poster she'd spotted on her way in—black, with big, sharp horns and an angular head. Except ... it wasn't the same guitar, not exactly. The frets were slightly different, and the neck was slimmer. *Super wizard*, she was pretty sure the style was called. It must be an Ibanez, but she couldn't be sure beyond that.

"My Genesis. It was a gift from her and my ex-wife. I had it strapped to my back while I was trying to save her." He looked down at the guitar with equal parts awe and horror. "I *felt* her die, but ... then I heard her voice behind me, and..."

Adam held the guitar up, and a strange periwinkle mist streaked from the head to the pickups, stroking the strings with a barely audible *zing*. The guitar shook, and he held it tighter, closer, like he was trying to wrangle a small child.

"I'm trying!" he whispered heatedly. To the guitar. "They said they'd help!"

Edie eyed him for a moment before she realized what must be happening. The energy coming off the guitar as it glowed and "talked" was undeniable.

"I know, just wait a second," Adam mumbled, then looked up apologetically. "Sorry about her."

"Can you ... understand what it's saying?" Marius asked.

"Not *it*. She. I can hear her; it's *Elle's* voice. She's ... I don't know." The guitar protested again, and Adam shivered. "She says she's trapped."

"In your guitar," Satara murmured, slowly standing. She crossed the room and held her hands out. "Can she hear us? Can I hold you, Elle?"

The guitar whined again. Adam sighed. "She said, 'Yes, please.'"

Satara took the guitar gingerly from a reluctant Adam, eyes following the pale mist as it pulsed and skimmed along the instrument's surface. "If she says she's trapped, then she is *not* possessing this guitar. A possession is purposeful, a choice the spirit makes. Like Ghost."

"Ghost is not *possessed*." Cal rolled his eyes. "You make her sound like some cheesy B-movie shit! She's just *haunted*."

"A spirit attached to an object is not the same as a spirit living *within* an object, manipulating it. Ghost is possessed." Satara raised a brow at Cal, then looked back at the guitar. "But this is not a possession, and it isn't a haunting either."

"Can she feel where she is?" Marius asked. "Can she confirm she's in the guitar?"

Edie felt the dead girl's next answer rather than heard it—a crawling sort of feeling at the base of her skull, like a subsonic noise. Adam translated: "She said she's inside it. She can feel it."

Satara looked the Genesis over one last time before handing it back. "When her spirit left her body, you must have been able to store it in the guitar somehow."

"Can hellerunan do that?" Edie asked, looking Adam over before glancing down at her own hands.

He echoed the word in confusion. "Hellerunan?"

"You typically have domain over death, or a transferal of life energy, rather than souls themselves, but..." Satara spread her hands. "These kinds of things are possible. Liches do something similar with their own souls when they create skálpar."

Marius shook his head. "But I've only ever heard of spirits being trapped in items specifically *designed* for trapping spirits, not everyday objects."

"There are probably a lot of things hellerunan can do that are just ... lost to history at this point. They were almost all wiped out, after all. Maybe this was one of those things."

"Maybe," Cal said, rubbing his chin. "Maybe it's kinda like what your dad used to do, E. 'Member I told you? When he used to store spells in items. No one else was able to do it like that ... and o' course the bastard never told his secrets. But that don't mean he's the only one who could figure it out. Even by accident." The revenant gestured to the guitar. "Woulda never guessed it could be done with human souls, though."

Adam slung the guitar across his back again and grimaced, clearly struggling to keep his head above water. His voice cracked as he spoke. "What ... what the hell is going on?" Then, quieter, "What the hell am I?"

It took a moment for Edie to realize that everyone was looking at *her*. She supposed it made sense, considering she was the only other hellerune, but she wasn't used to being an authority on anything.

She cleared her throat. "You're something called a hellerune. A long time ago, the goddess Hel gave some of her followers mastery over the, um, 'ebon' magics: blood, death, shadow, and ... plague, I think. They were really powerful, but eventually, people started seeing those kinds of magics as evil and decided to hunt them down. Which is not good news for the descendants of those original followers, since we don't exactly get to decide whether we're hellerunan or not..."

Adam stared at her. "It's genetic?"

"Yeah, why?"

From his back, the guitar sung faintly. He shook his head, glancing to the side. "It must be skipping generations. My father didn't need dark magic to be a monster, but ... I would've known if he had it."

"You don't have to be a monster," Edie said. "Actually, I strongly encourage you not to be. Being a hellerune is, you know, what you make of it."

Cal looked up at the kitchen light, hands on his hips. "Well, at least we know you're not all plugged up like Edie. The magic seems to be comin' to ya pretty easily."

"I— I guess so." It was Adam's turn to look at his hands, whispering, "This ... has to be some crazy-ass dream. This can't actually be happening."

But when he met Edie's gaze again, she could see a familiar light in his eyes. He didn't want to believe it, sure, but what she was telling him was answering questions he'd probably had for a long time.

No wonder he was so *precarious*, as Basile had put it.

"We can explain more later," Cal said, taking a cigarette from his back pocket and clamping it between his teeth. "Lord knows there's plenty shit to wade through. Let's work on fixing the girl right now."

Adam glanced at the revenant nervously but conceded with a nod.

"How old is she?"

Tears welled in his eyes. "She's twenty-two."

"What about her body? What's the condition?"

"Um ... well, she's intact. Nothing broken, I don't think. But— but I couldn't tell you anything else." Adam gestured toward the fridge hopelessly. "I haven't opened it to check on her. I ... I didn't want to see."

Cal sighed, gnawing on the filter of his cig. "Probably for the best. Means you kept the cold in."

"It's good that you put her in the fridge," Satara said, taking her seat again. "The dead should be kept somewhere cool, but freezing her would have damaged her cells. At this point, her body is probably relatively pristine."

Adam touched the guitar strap across his chest. "It was her idea."

"Smart girl." Cal huffed. "Being in a well-preserved body is probably a lot nicer than being in a rotted one. Ask me how I fuckin' know."

"H-How do you know?" Adam returned weakly.

Edie reached out and stopped Cal before he could weaken his glamour. This poor guy had been through enough in the past twenty-four hours without seeing a rotten corpse in his kitchen. "We'll explain later. Like you said, Cal."

"Hmph. In any case," the revenant continued grumpily, "magic isn't really my wheelhouse, but I know what I need to know. A couple anti-decay spells and I think I can keep her fresh for as long as we need."

Adam frowned. "Wait, what do you mean?" It took a moment for him to connect the dots. Slowly, his face brightened. "You think you can put her back in."

"Worth a try," Cal said with a shrug.

Marius had begun to pace up and down the kitchen. "Would she be a revenant, then?"

"Nah. It's that 'transferal of life energy' thing Satara was talkin' about earlier. Revenants are made with energy taken from a sacrifice, not your own soul." He jabbed himself in the chest with a frown. "Me, Cal, now—that's not who this body belonged to before. I got no idea what will happen. Satara?"

"I'm not sure either. If we can connect body and soul properly, maybe we really can bring her back to life, fully."

"It's unorthodox," Marius said. "In the old stories, you can never truly return someone to life in that way unless you get their soul from Hel, or whomever is holding it." He glanced at Adam, then Satara. "But since we have her soul here, perhaps…"

"We won't know until we find out."

The guitar on Adam's back twanged, and he touched the chest strap again. "Even if there's some way you can do that, she's still trapped … she's still stuck inside the Genesis."

He was right. They needed to get her out of the guitar first. If Elle's soul was stored in the Genesis the way Dad had stored spells, there had to be a way to take her out. If it *was* the same principle, there was no point in storing something you couldn't retrieve later. There had to be a way.

They just needed someone who could separate her soul from the guitar.

"Don't worry, Adam," Edie said with a smile. "We know a good exorcist."

CHAPTER NINE

THE GRAY LIGHT filtering through the Baccarat condo's huge windows was cold and drab, and it made Indriði long for her house in Anster.

It was useless to get homesick now, of course. The weather here was disgusting, but it would certainly be no better in Massachusetts, and she couldn't go back there when she had so much to do elsewhere. In New York, she was surrounded by culture, art. Still, she missed the quaint charm of her little New England city and the honeylocust trees that had shrouded her lounge.

At the very least, she had escaped the lower Baccarat's silks and crystal. The hotel was nice and all, and certainly an appropriate display of wealth and power, but a bit too old-fashioned Parisian for Indriði's tastes. Having a residency on the upper floors had its perks, and one was decorating it however she pleased. This new lounge showcased the furniture she'd been able to move from Anster—as well as some new pieces—adequately enough. Sleek, clean, modern. She'd even managed to find a fitting place for her harp, right next to the baby grand piano.

And, for now, she had found a fitting place for herself: reclining on the sectional while her new steward fixed her a cosmopolitan.

When word of Roggvi's death had spread, a light elf noble had generously gifted her a servant from their household. At first, Indriði had been grateful ... but it wasn't long until she'd realized the "gift" had been more of an underhanded slight than anything.

Ilphas Miravn hadn't yet lived away from Alfheim long enough to lose any of his elven features and resembled a locust; tall, thin, all awkward limbs and bony elbows and knees. The elf was absolutely ravenous to do things for her and yet too incompetent to do any of them right.

Kindly put, he didn't measure up to Roggvi. But then, the old dwarf had been with her for centuries. There was a chance Ilphas would become less tedious. Not a good chance, but a chance nonetheless.

As the elf fumbled around in the kitchen, he tried to make some limp conversation, despite being out of her line of sight. "Such strange weather we're having, isn't it?"

"Mmm. You have no idea. It's supposed to be summer here."

"Summer, ma'am?" *Clang, crash.*

What he was doing with the pots and pans when he was supposed to be making a cocktail, Indriði had no idea. She tipped her face toward the ceiling and closed her eyes. "Summer. The Midgardian season."

"Oh, yes, the season. Of course. The weather in Alfheim scarcely changes."

"Mm-hmm."

"Except sometimes during the afternoon—a warm rain to encourage rest and breeding." *Clang.*

Indriði simply kept her eyes closed, willing him not to speak further. The Lord of the Elves, Yngvi-Freyr, also happened to be the god of virility. If Ilphas launched into a tangent about *breeding*, she'd have to freeze him in time and make her own damn drink.

He couldn't let the silence go unbroken—*of course*—and the limp conversation made a comeback. "And your day, ma'am?"

"It'd be better if I had a cosmo, Ilphas..."

A hurried wave of banging and clinking issued from behind her, but at least the blessed sound of ice in the shaker accompanied it. She desperately needed to have her bar moved in here. "I've heard word that Miss Daschla's work is going well, what with the rallies and the red cloaks and the— Is ... is it the orange liqueur or the raspberry? Bugger."

Indriði sighed. "Yep. She's doing great."

"And what of your other endeavors, ma'am?"

She opened her eyes, mulling the question over. The projects she'd set in motion here were developing well. Progress on finding the new hellerune was moving briskly forward, and Scarlet's Watchers were falling in line. Thankfully. For a second there, she had wondered if Scarlet would go running back to Zaedicus. She hadn't expected the human-wight to be so apprehensive when it came to the Blood Eagles— after all, she'd had no reservations before this point, and they had an important job to do here.

"Ma'am?" Ilphas's voice came from in front of her this time, and she opened her eyes to see him holding her finished cosmo in one spindly hand. His skin was pinkish, tinged with green at the joints; spines climbed from his wrists to his elbows, and his deep brown irises were so large his eyes had hardly any whites. As she took the glass, he drew himself up again, smoothing back his oil slick hair and small antennae.

Indriði took a rejuvenating sip of her drink. "Roggv— Ilphas. Why are humans so ... weird?"

Ears that looked like locusts' wings, diaphanous and speckled, flicked outward in confusion. He blinked. "Ma'am?"

"You think you understand a human and then they spring these random convictions on you ... ones that don't even make any damn sense. They change their minds so arbitrarily. Why is that?"

"I don't follow, my lady." He sat on a nearby footrest, long legs folded close to his chest.

"You should have seen how Scarlet balked when she realized what the Blood Eagles were. You would've thought she hadn't been working for the New Gloaming for years."

Ilphas bared his fangs awkwardly. "I confess I know very little about humans, much less why they do what they do..."

"Humans have mistreated each other for eons. For Web's sake, Scarlet herself has been commanding the Watchers for months now. She takes pleasure in it. She's *killed*. The Watchers wiped out an entire homeless camp a few weeks ago." Indriði took another deep sip. A little heavy on the vodka, but maybe she needed it right now. "But Nazis are too far? A bunch of rallies and a couple fistfights, that's what makes her squeamish?"

"Well—"

"Granted," she continued, "the Blood Eagles are absolute idiots. Practically useless at the moment, let's be honest with ourselves."

"Perhaps she—"

"But they're not here to make decisions. Good lord, can you imagine? I've told her *that*." Indriði rubbed her forehead. "And she won't have to think about it for very much longer, if everything goes according to plan. All she needs to do is turn her head and look the other way."

Ilphas opened his mouth to say something else but was cut off by a loud *whoosh* from the kitchen, like the sound of a whirlpool. Both he and Indriði were on their feet in a second, though once she understood what was happening, she was frankly more interested in her drink.

A flash of crimson filled the kitchen archway, and a few moments later, two figures clad in silver masks and raven feathers stepped into the lounge, their hands already resting on the hilts of their sheathed weapons.

Just as she'd suspected, the Wounded himself wasn't far behind. He strode into the room, scanning his surroundings with a look that could only be described as disgust. As he turned toward the window to take in the Manhattan skyline, the claymore strapped to his back whacked against a jeweled ewer resting on a table and sent it spinning toward the floor.

Ilphas gave a strangled noise and dove for it, but the Wounded turned and caught it in one hand without missing a beat. As he slid it gently back into place, he looked at Indriði.

"Such excess."

The last time she was face to face with Lord Sárr, he had looked a little worse for wear, but he was even more ashen now—exhausted. His hair had grown slightly longer, a startling silver against his black leather armor, and his gray eyes were ringed with dark circles.

At once, Ilphas was beside himself. He fell to his pointy knees before the Wounded Lord and bowed his head, ears pinned back.

But for Indriði's part, Sárr didn't scare so much as annoy her. He hadn't even sent word ahead that he'd be showing up. She crossed her arms, lifting her glass to her lips. "What do you want, kid?"

The only reaction her jab elicited was a brief glance toward the ceiling. "I knew that you and Daschla would disappoint me here somehow, Norn, but I never thought it would be so soon."

"I see." She sighed. "And what, exactly, have we done to evoke your awesome rage?"

Rather than answering, he glanced around the apartment. "Where is Scarlet?"

"She's out. She'll be back later. So. What is your problem?"

Sárr's guards stayed put as he stalked across the lounge, past a quivering Ilphas. Once he reached the windows, he folded his hands behind his back and half-turned to her. "My agents have reported back to me about something called the 'Blood Eagles.' And how fortunate, for I heard nothing about them from *you*."

"Don't you have people who can bring you up to speed on this? I'm kind of busy, Sárr."

"I understand the cause they serve," he continued firmly. "But I have yet to understand what it has to do with the New Gloaming. With your commitment to me. To our master."

Indriði sighed. "Don't tell me you're about to get all missish on me, too."

"This has little to do with my *feelings*, Norn. They aren't needed, they aren't wanted; focusing on them is taking up resources. We already have plenty of skilled fighters at our disposal."

That was certainly true. She glanced at the silver-and-black-clad guards across the room. It didn't please her to admit that she wasn't one hundred percent sure where those fighters *came* from, but they just kept coming—when one fell, another was always right behind to take their place. She had her suspicions and theories, but Sárr was keeping this one close to the chest.

"Not only are the Blood Eagles rabid dogs," he went on, "they have little tactical value. No power. One Auroran vivid could cut a swath through them. My own warriors, too, would make short work of them."

"Oh, for the love of the gods. I'm not trying to raise an army against you, if that's what you think. The Watchers are still out there; I'm still looking for the hellerune. It's just ... a personal project of Daschla's." Indriði finished her drink and spread her hands. "What, you never had a rainy day craft box as a kid?"

Sárr turned more fully toward her, brow wrinkled furiously. "We agreed that *personal projects* would not obstruct the path of twilight. You lied to me, weaver, both of you. I was never asked permission."

"Ugh!" The Norn threw up her hands and collapsed on her sectional again. *Typical.* "May I remind you, honey, that I'm not the only one who's been lying?" She pointed to the window with a perfectly manicured finger. "You never told me the snow would come so soon. That would have been kind of good to know, don'tcha think? You didn't consider that that might put a kink in some of *my* plans?"

"Plans," Sárr scoffed. "If the winter is going to ruin your plans, you may want to rethink them." He took a few steps closer and looked at Ilphas, who was still practically prostrate on the floor. "Watchman's teeth, elf, you shame yourself."

With a mumbled apology, Ilphas rose to his feet, though he kept his gaze down.

The Wounded looked back at Indriði. "Enlighten me. What is the purpose of an army that cannot fight?"

After a moment of silence, she rose from her seat, smoothing her dress out. "That's just the thing: they're not an army. Not exactly. Not yet."

She could see the bewilderment and frustration on his face. Little as she liked interacting with him, his confusion wasn't unprecedented; their plan wasn't immediately obvious.

It only took a little farm wisdom for the pieces to slide into place.

"Let me tell you a story about chickens."

Marius had insisted on being the one to fetch Basile and had left as soon as possible. Armed with a MetroCard and Cal's smartphone, the group had agreed he would probably be okay for a quick round trip—thankfully, he'd paid painstaking attention to Edie's lecture on how to navigate the subway. Still, she couldn't help but worry about him. Everywhere they went, it seemed, they attracted dangerous attention.

Then again, maybe she should worry more about herself than the highly trained warrior with solar energy weapons.

With him on his way, it was time for the rest to face whatever they would find in Adam's refrigerator. More accurately, it was time for Edie and Cal to face it; Satara had noticed a signed *The Crow* poster and had expertly lured Adam into the living room to ask questions about it.

"Ya know," Cal said, pulling a face as he took the cigarette from his mouth, "these things aren't nearly as satisfying when you can't light 'em."

"I'm sure Adam wouldn't care if you took a smoke break out back."

The revenant huffed. "I'm gonna need one after this."

He tucked the cig behind a torn ear and reached to pull open the fridge. Edie held her breath.

There were some things she'd seen in the past couple months that she would never forget. No matter how hard she tried, the images were burned into her brain as crisply as if they were still in front of her: the carnage of battle, the grasping void of a brush with death.

Somehow, the sight of Elle's body rivaled them both. She was a big girl, curvy, but she seemed so incredibly small curled up. She leaned against one wall, knees to her chest and head bowed, looking more like she was sleeping than dead. Her skin was the color of the fridge around her, bleached white, and a chin-length mane of honey-blond waves obscured her face.

Beside Edie, Cal's breath caught. He was frozen for a moment, then reached out to scoop the body up, careful not to disturb the pink sheet she was wrapped in.

"Damn," he mumbled. "She's like a fucking statue. Can you get her other end?"

His words shook Edie to the core, but there was no time for squeamishness. Rigor mortis had set in, clenching the body up tight like a ball; all she could do was heft her back end up and avert her eyes as they transferred her to her bedroom.

Once they deposited Elle on her bed, Edie glanced around the room. The majority of it was decorated in shades of pink, ranging from soft to eye-burning. Fairy lights hung along the walls, casting a soft glow over the room; a laptop and a heap of shimmery cosmetics sat on a desk shaped like a cloud; the twin daybed against the far wall was filled with stuffed animals and fluffy pillows. Mercy liked pastels, but she was still goth and edgy—it seemed Elle was the girliest girl there ever was.

Edie looked back at Cal, who had brushed the dead girl's hair from her face and was trying fruitlessly to get her muscles to relax. "Are you good here or do you want me to stay?"

"Nah, I'm fine." He tossed his head back. "Better get back to Frankenstein there. Seems like comforting him is gonna be a two-person job."

"I dunno ... I think he's doing all right. Considering in the past twenty-four hours he's witnessed his daughter fall down the stairs and die, sucked her soul into a guitar, been told magic exists, and found out he's part of a dying breed of mages with innate death magic." She shrugged. "But maybe that's just me."

"I guess. When he's not busy flinching every time I move."

"Yeah. What's with that?"

"Fucked if I know." Cal abandoned his effort to loosen up Elle's limbs.

He pulled her computer chair forward and took her hand, squeezing his eyes shut to concentrate.

Edie waited for a moment before slipping back into the hall. Best to let him focus on the preservation spells. She didn't even want to know what would happen if he screwed them up.

When she walked back into the kitchen, Adam and Satara were still sitting together in the living room, chatting. Adam seemed to be wrapped up in whatever he was saying, so she took the opportunity to properly examine the posters she'd been eyeing earlier.

There were only a few having to do with Death Benefits, though. The rest affirmed Adam's other loves: *Akira, Sandman, Eraserhead, Half-Life*. She slipped past the living room couch and noted the amount of gaming consoles, old and new, stored under and around the TV. On nearby bookshelves, she found figurines and action figures, game manuals, manga, and what must be every *World of Warcraft* novel ever written. *Dungeons & Dragons* books, maps, and minis dominated the remaining space.

Edie crouched in front of one of the bookcases and thumbed through his collection of graphic novels. It only took her a moment to find the one Adam himself had published last year, an omnibus of his long-running webcomic. She hadn't read it beyond a few pages here and there, but she knew the gist of the series: a saga following High Prince Argon, who used shadows to warp through worlds. She thought she remembered there being some element of his birthright being stolen but couldn't quite remember. Now that she was looking at the cover, she couldn't help but notice how eerily alike Argon and Adam looked.

Jesus Christ.

She looked over her shoulder just in time to catch Adam's eye. He was sitting on the couch next to Satara, turned pointedly away from the kitchen. The guitar was still strapped to his back, and though he was making polite conversation, his muscles were almost as tense as Elle's.

He anxiously ran his fingers over one tattooed forearm as he asked, "Did everything go all right? Is she ... okay?"

"She looks fine," Edie said, putting the Argon comic back where she'd found it, right next to something called *Legion of Superheroes*. "I left Cal alone to do his thing."

Something changed in Adam's energy suddenly. She didn't know if it was because their powers connected them somehow or if he was always such an open book, but she could feel his mood shift. And had the living room always been so dark? "Maybe— maybe I should go watch after her."

Satara frowned. "I don't know if that's a good idea. You said you didn't want to see."

"There are some things you can't unsee," Edie agreed, standing. "Her body isn't gross or anything, but it's ... listen, she's in good hands."

"I just—" He lowered his voice. "I don't want to ... leave her all alone, you know?"

"You didn't mind a second ago when I was helping Cal move—" And it finally clicked. "You don't want her to be alone with Cal."

Adam rubbed his arm again, tone becoming a bit defensive. "He's a stranger, and he's all alone in there with her."

"She's *dead*," Edie returned, sounding pretty defensive herself. "And he's doing you a favor, so maybe you could try giving him the benefit of the doubt."

"It's my job to keep her safe. I don't want to fail her again."

"I know, but seriously, it's *fine*."

She couldn't quite figure out what she could say to put him at ease. He was casting aspersions on Cal, not her, but it felt like a personal attack. What a specific concern—and aimed solely at Cal, a man whom he'd never met before in his life.

At least Elle seemed to agree with her, groaning loudly from the Genesis.

Satara glanced at her, then turned toward Adam on the couch. "It's all right. Cal has a bit of a gruff exterior, but he's a good man. He wouldn't do anything to hurt her."

Adam didn't look completely convinced, but he seemed to have warmed up to Satara a bit. "I'm sorry. I probably sound like an idiot."

"It's all right," she repeated, standing. "If it'll make you feel better, I'll go supervise. Hopefully me being there won't break his concentration."

"You'll probably be fine," Edie mumbled. "When I left, he was really focused. He might not even notice you coming in."

The shieldmaiden left without another word, and silence fell. Edie had mostly managed to calm herself, though she couldn't deny the little twinge of irritation still left. It helped that Adam seemed to have forgiven her already; he smiled weakly at her as she sat down next to him.

There were so many questions she wanted to ask. She had been a fan since her childhood, and now they had something crazy in common—they were two of the last hellerunan left in the world. Chances were they shared a distant ancestral past. His powers seemed so much stronger than hers had; had he always known there was something different about him? Or had he been completely unaware, like she had? Was there something otherworldly about his music that had attracted her and her dad, or had it just been chance?

Were these even questions he could answer?

Her window of opportunity closed, however, as the back door opened and Marius entered with Basile in tow. The priest wore a hat and overcoat, which he quickly discarded to reveal the cassock he'd been wearing earlier.

He scanned the apartment, and when his gaze landed on Adam, he adjusted his tortoiseshell glasses. "Ahh, there you are, kiddo. I always wondered when you and I would finally meet face to face!"

Adam looked perplexed as he rose from the couch. "I'm sorry, what?"

Edie stood up after him. "He's part of the, um, group that we mentioned earlier. He's sort of the ... leader of this area."

"Don't lie to him," the priest scoffed. "We're less of a group and more like a scatter of stubborn, *slightly* unhinged people."

She sighed. "Anyway, he's been watching after you for..." She waited for Basile to fill the gaps in her knowledge, but he said nothing. "For a long time, hiding you from the Gloaming."

"The Gloaming. Right." Adam adjusted the strap across his chest.

"Satara gave me a little bit of a rundown on the ... nomenclature. Those are the bad guys, right?"

Basile chuckled. "That's right. And let me tell ya, keeping your power hidden to throw them off your trail was a hell of a job. You *really* pack a punch, you know that? Anyway, you're welcome."

"Keeping my power—"

The priest cut him off with a loud clap that made him flinch. "All right, where's the stiff?"

The surge of magic around Adam was palpable. "*Elle* is in her room. First door on the left." He was already stalking forward as Basile started down the hall, and came abreast of him before he reached the bedroom door. "What do you mean, you were keeping my power *hidden*?"

Shadowy energy clouded around him like a swarm of flies, knocking out the hall lights. Holy moly. Well, there could be no doubt as to what his preferred type of magic was. All that time spent with it bottled up seemed to make it even more volatile than it already was.

Indriði had been right about some things—the pressure of built-up magic was immense. But at least Adam wasn't exploding. Yet. Unlike Edie, he must have had some sort of outlet, even if he hadn't realized it.

Basile turned and frowned at Adam like the question he'd asked was out of line. "We'll get to that later. Did you want me to handle this situation or not, Adam?"

The hellerune seethed but gestured stiffly for Basile to enter the room.

He opened the door, and Edie peered in to see Cal sitting right where she'd left him, almost in a state of meditation. He was holding Elle's hand in one of his, the other on her paper-white shoulder. A thin sheen of pale orange light enveloped the young woman's body, which was still mostly covered by the sheet they'd found her in.

Satara leaned against the wall near the foot of the bed and looked up when the door opened. When she spoke the revenant's name softly, he came out of his trance at once, dazed.

With a quick glance over his shoulder, he stood. "Took ya long enough. Whew. It's been a while since I had to do anythin' other than maintenance on my own decomp wards."

He looked like he needed some air. Sure enough, without another word, he slipped past the people in the cramped hallway and made a beeline for the back door.

"Probably just taking a smoke break," Edie mumbled when she noticed everyone looking at her for an explanation.

Well, everyone except Adam. He had drifted into the room like a spirit himself, eyes glued to Elle's body. Except for a little crusted blood around her nostrils and the awful color of her skin, she was pristine. From Adam's back, the guitar cooed softly; a misty light emerged from the pickups and crawled down the neck to touch Adam's arm. After a tiny jolt, he relaxed a little.

Basile scooted past him, rolling up his sleeves. "All right, if you're gonna insist on being in the room while I do this, I'm going to need space. And absolute silence." He glanced at everyone but Adam. "And any energy you can spare would help."

Edie leaned against the door frame, arms crossed. "If you can figure out how to take it from me, go ahead, I guess."

"Try not to kill anyone," Marius mumbled from just behind her.

Satara traded places with Adam and cleared the computer chair from Basile's path. Once she had joined the others near the doorway, the priest began to prepare himself with long, deep breaths.

Eventually, he held a hand out toward Adam. "Give me the guitar."

The Genesis responded with a grinding screech, then several plucks that somehow got across the bitchy tone of whatever Elle was trying to say.

Adam pulled the guitar to his front and awkwardly patted the body. A minute ago, he had been ready to wreck Basile's shit; now, he was nervous again. "She's not sure about it. Do you actually know what you're doing?"

The priest sighed. "Do you know how many exorcisms I've performed?"

"No," Adam snapped, "I don't. I clearly don't know you as well as you seem to know me, man. I don't even know your name."

"It's Basile. Basile Bolet." He sighed. "I assume you'll thank me for keeping you alive for years once all this is smoothed over, so we'll just move on for now, shall we?"

Adam said nothing, simply looked down at the guitar. It trilled once more, and he nodded, seemingly in response. With a sigh, he lifted the strap over his head and handed the instrument to Basile.

CHAPTER TEN

WITH THE GUITAR IN HAND, Basile stepped closer to Elle's curled-up body. "Well, at least she's in pretty good shape. That'll be a plus."

"What will happen exactly?" Adam asked, sitting on the end of the bed, close to Elle's feet but not touching her. "If you can put her back in there, will she be ... alive again? Normal...?"

The priest hummed. "I can't say. A little resurrection before the soul leaves the body is possible, but that's not the case here. Still, we've got her soul with us ... so ... well, I guess we'll see."

"So she'll be a ... revenant?" Edie tried.

"I can't be sure. I don't think so. Revenants are made to be controlled by the ones who raise them. You leech the life from someone else, and they spring up, ready to obey your whims or whatever." Basile waved a hand. "Whether she's technically *undead* or not, does it matter?"

The guitar screeched.

"No," Adam translated quickly. "This is what she wants."

"Then let's get to it." The priest lifted the guitar strap over his head, letting the instrument hang against his chest as he stretched and flexed his hands. "So, here's what's gonna happen. First of all, I'm going to carefully, er, *separate* her soul from the guitar. It's not as easy as just tearing her out of there, which is usually my preferred method—it's more surgical. Then, I'm going to lead her back into her body. While trying my best not to absorb her completely," he added quickly.

Adam looked horrified, and the guitar protested, vibrating slightly against Basile's chest. "*Absorb* her? What are you talking about?!"

"Well ... my kind are sort of in the business of eating souls, you know, since we haven't got any ourselves." Before Adam could go off on him again, he continued, "But I've been doing this for a long time! I've exorcised plenty of souls without consuming them. I just need to concentrate. And like I said, a little extra energy wouldn't go amiss."

"Take whatever you need. Just fix her."

Wordlessly, Basile looked down at Elle's body. Silence stretched on as he stared. Then, with both hands cradling the guitar, he began to mutter something.

Edie winced as a familiar flash of pale light flooded the room. When it faded, Basile had changed: instead of an older man, a skeleton now stood in his place, bones a bleached white, eye sockets empty and dark. Adam balked but didn't move from his place by Elle's side, simply looking on in awe.

The skeleton priest almost seemed to emit a sigh—a low, tired sound that wove through the room, making Edie shiver. It was the sigh of someone who'd been alive far too long, had seen far too much, and had done this far too many times. His fleshless fingers stroked the surface of the guitar in an odd repeating pattern, and she wondered if he was tracing some sort of sigil to help him focus the spell.

After a moment, a few whispered words left his unmoving mouth. His posture changed. He clenched the fist that had been stroking the guitar and planted his feet, like he was trying to pull something particularly heavy. The faint sound of grinding teeth caught Edie's ear. Was he in pain or was he really concentrating that hard?

Finally, subtly, she began to see it—a faint periwinkle shimmer around the guitar, the same shimmer she'd seen around the Watchers' bodies as he'd flayed their souls. The luminous energy trembled and jerked as it was pried away from the guitar. And as it emerged more fully, Edie could see that Elle's soul had not taken the shape of the Genesis—it still looked like her, the faint outline of her face contorted in horror and agony.

It was taking an achingly long time to drag her soul out, and if Elle's hazy expression and the distant wails filling the room were any indication, it was a painful process.

Adam jumped to his feet, eyes wide and shiny. "Wait, no. You're hurting her!"

"Shh!" Basile hissed, teeth grinding louder. His shoulders were trembling, chest heaving with the effort it took not to tear her soul out and swallow it whole.

A ghostly shriek of panic filled the room, and Edie could see Adam struggling to hold himself back. He crossed his arms tightly against his chest, worrying the ridges of his tattoos.

"Dammit," the priest breathed. "She's losing focus. She's fighting me."

Satara took a step forward. "Why?"

"She's upset that it hurts. But there's ... not ... a lot I can ... do!"

The shieldmaiden turned her head and motioned for Edie and Marius to enter the room. Once Edie was by her side, she took her hand. "He's going to need some of our energy to carry on, I think. Just take deep breaths, relax, and open yourself up."

Edie was still uncertain of how exactly to *give* someone her energy, but she tried to do as Satara said. She let her shoulders slump, closing her eyes and relaxing her whole body.

At first, she wasn't sure anything was actually happening—then she began to notice the weakness in her knees. Her biceps began to burn slightly, like she'd just finished an exhausting workout. Eventually, she wasn't sure she could lift her shoulders even if she wanted to. It was like a weight held her down.

She opened her eyes. Adam seemed to be in a similar state, sitting on the end of the bed once more, head in his shaking hands. Satara's grip was weak in Edie's, and beside her, Marius looked deflated.

Try not to kill anyone, he'd said before Basile had started the ritual. Was that possible?

"Basile," she croaked, "we're, uh, running kind of low."

"Dammit," he cursed again, inhaling sharply. "I'm trying not to— take her, but she's— I can't hold—"

Basile's knees buckled, and he cried out. He tried to steady himself, but faltered, his arm jerking. In an instant, bright periwinkle light exploded out of him—and by the time it faded, he was humanlike again, on his knees with the Genesis hanging from his neck like an albatross.

"*Dammit!*"

His usually neatly combed hair hung in his face as he pulled himself up to his feet, panting. Adam stood, too, eyes locked on Elle.

"Did it work? She's not movi—"

"No! No, dammit, it didn't work." The priest's voice was gruff. "I was just a second away. If I'd had a little more time—"

"What happened?" Edie asked, coming closer. "What was that explosion?"

"I was *going slow*, but she put up a fight. It made it tremendously hard not to consume her." He straightened out his clothes and hair as he spoke. "At ... at the end there, I nearly tore her soul out, and my body would have absorbed it. I *had* to stop. But then I couldn't hold on to her. *Dammit...*"

Adam's breath was uneven. "Couldn't— Where is she? Back in the guitar?"

The priest shook his head. "I managed to pull her out, but I stopped the ritual at the last second." He gestured to the bed. "And she's not in her body, so ... her soul must have crossed the veil."

Edie's heart sank. Behind her, she heard the back door close and shuffling as Cal entered. When she looked over her shoulder, she saw him lingering in the doorway, a dour expression on his face. "Uh ... how'd it go?"

"You let my kid's *soul* just fly off into the ether?" Adam managed, squaring up to Basile and yanking the Genesis away from him. One by one, the fairy lights on the wall flickered out. When the priest didn't answer right away, he became frantic: "Are you telling me she's *gone*? She's fucking gone, passed on into the afterlife or something—is that what you're saying?"

"Calm down!" Basile snapped. "Odin's ravens, you lunatic, pull yourself together."

"Hey, hey, hey!" Cal entered the room, coming to stand just behind Edie and Marius. "You *both* need to cool your jets for a hot sec so we can figure out what the fuck is going on. Got it?"

They seemed to, at least a little. Adam continued to fume silently, and Basile turned to the others, arms crossed.

"Tell us what this means, Basile," Marius said grimly. "Has she passed into one of the gods' halls?"

"No. Considering the circumstances, she's more than likely a lost soul. So she's crossed the veil, but we won't find her on the way to Hel or anywhere else." The priest sighed. "She's probably in the Wending."

Cal wrinkled his nose. "She died and went to Wendy's?"

"I've heard that name," Satara said softly, face drawn from having her energy siphoned. "I can't remember where, though."

"It's the plane of lost souls. The people there are sometimes like Elle. Sometimes they're those who weren't buried or honored properly when they died—if they don't turn into a ghost or a draugr, they're stuck in the Wending. But most of them are people who got lost trying to travel to their afterlife. I understand the plane is a never-ending journey; the spirits can never rest, never linger. Always moving forward but never going anywhere. Never getting home."

Adam's distress only grew. He shuddered all over. "Oh my fuckin' god. No ... Elle..."

"Hey," Basile said, fixing the hellerune with his intense gaze, "it's better than the alternative. If I'd eaten her, she *would* be gone. Forever. As in, no existing energy in *any* universe. Oblivion."

Adam sat on the bed again, his skin almost as white as the corpse lying nearby. He looked like he might pass out. If Edie was honest, after giving up all her energy, she wasn't that far off herself. Wordlessly, she released Satara's clammy hand and sat on the floor, taking deep breaths to try and keep conscious.

"Please," Adam whispered, looking up at Basile. "Please ... I need to help her. She's— she's all I have, I can't lose her. I ... if she's not gone forever, we can get her back, right? We can still bring her back?"

The priest took off his glasses, rubbing his forehead and the bridge of his nose. "I'm not really sure of any way to get living people into the Wending. Your kind aren't really supposed to be able to exist in the realms of the dead."

"But you said people have brought loved ones back before. There must be a way."

"That was a long time ago. But ... I suppose I can look into it." He replaced his glasses and glanced around the room at the others. "I won't be able to do it myself, though. I have a lot of material to research and only two eyes."

"I'll help," Satara said. "I'll need food and water and somewhere to sit, but I can do it."

Marius nodded. "I can, too."

"I'll park here and keep working on the decomp spells," Cal mumbled as he approached the bed. "I'm gonna need some space to concentrate."

Edie rose shakily. "If you end up needing more people to research, I guess I could try, but I might be more of a hindrance than anything."

"Eh, someone's gotta watch Frankenstein."

Adam shook his head. "No, I should do something. I need to do something. I ... I need to actually make myself useful for once in my life and help."

"What you need to do," Satara said, "is rest and keep sane."

"Yeah. Let Edie keep an eye on you, big cat." Cal reached over his head and examined the blown-out fairy lights. "And, uh ... if she can teach you a thing or two about controlling your magic, all the better."

CHAPTER ELEVEN

BASILE and his two volunteer researchers left in short order, and Cal pulled the computer chair up again to work on his decomposition spells. It was a bit easier than before to convince Adam to leave Elle's body, considering how drained he was. With the Genesis still at his back, he went to his room to decompress. Edie wasn't too far behind.

His bedroom was a continuation of the living room in many ways. His various collections had found home on a bookshelf near the door as well as the top of the dresser. Not as many posters hung here, but there was an impressive selection of guitars against one wall, some hung up and some sitting below on stands. She recognized a stippled JEM7D, a black-and-white Reverse Flying V, and an ultra violet Hellraiser Hybrid C-1 among them. In one corner, there was a custom gaming PC set up with a chair that looked like it should be at the helm of a spaceship. The keyboard had been moved aside to make room for a huge, shiny drawing monitor.

Adam went to the bed and sank down, slumping with his forearms resting on his knees. Edie took the room in for a moment before sitting down next to him. She instinctively reached out to pat his back.

"I don't know how I let this happen," he murmured miserably. "If I had been able to save her ... if I had forced her to go to the doctor sooner—"

Edie sighed. "It's not your fault. I get that you want someone to blame, but there isn't anyone. You wouldn't have done anything differently, 'cause how could you have known?"

He simply shivered in response.

He wanted to help, and that was understandable, but Satara was right —he'd had a rough twenty-four hours, and he needed to take a breather before he lost his mind completely and blanketed Brooklyn in darkness or something. "Why don't we get out of here? Get some fresh air. You could use it."

"I don't know. I really ... really should stay here. In case I need to do something."

"Yeah, but all the bases are covered for right now. The only thing you can do is wait for the, uh ... professionals to figure out our next step."

Adam worried his bottom lip. "I guess, but I just ... I don't know. No one else is here with..."

He trailed off, but Edie got the gist—he was still nervous about leaving Elle alone with Cal. She took a breath, determined not to get upset this time. This guy had had the shittiest couple days she could imagine, and she got the sense he was pretty neurotic even when things weren't going to hell.

"Adam." She managed to catch his gaze and hold it. "You have to believe me when I say that Cal would *literally* rather *die* than hurt her. She's in safe hands. Like, I can't think of any way she could be safer, actually. I swear on ... on—" She frowned. "I guess I don't have much to swear on."

"Beats me. I always said if I ever had to swear an oath, it would be over *Xanathar's Guide to Everything*." He scrubbed his face and finally conceded, "I probably should get out of here for a couple hours."

Minutes later, he was ready to go and following Edie out the back door, leaving the Genesis behind. The two of them could be siblings with their dark hair and leather jackets.

It had finally stopped raining, and a lot of the snow had melted away, but still, she was surprised when she turned and saw two helmets under his arms, one standard black and one glossy pink with cat ears.

Dread settled in her gut. "Please tell me that one's yours."

"Sorry." He tossed it to her. "Be careful on the stairs."

As she crept down, she turned the pink abomination over in her hands. It wasn't ... ugly, per se. It just really wasn't her style, to say the least. "Do you have anything else?"

"Sorry," he said again, wincing this time. "But it'll keep you from cracking your skull open, so that's a plus."

He led her to a small, double-padlocked shed in the corner of the yard. Once the truly excessive amount of locks and chains were removed, he rolled out a compact urban motorcycle.

"Cool," Edie said. "A Yamaha?"

"Yeah, an MT-07. You can't ride until you suit up, though."

With a sigh, she pulled on the horrific pink helmet, hissing. "It burns us."

Adam put his own on, flipping the visor down and glancing at the sky. "The rain's let up, and I'm a careful driver, so we should be okay." He sighed. "I got it all ready for summer, but it doesn't look like summer's coming."

Edie followed his gaze, gnawing on her lip. The weather had been weird for a while now—but a blizzard in July in New York City? It was starting to feel like whatever was going on was beyond climate change or anything easily explainable.

They walked the bike down the alley, and at the curb, she climbed behind Adam. Navigating the streets of Brooklyn was a silent affair. Edie assumed Adam was just as lost in thought as she was, and she couldn't blame him, considering the circumstances. It wasn't until they were parking on Flatbush Ave that he spoke.

"So, you're a fan of Death Benefits, huh?" he asked as he took off his helmet.

She followed suit. "My dad was a big fan. He got me into you guys. That was one of the reasons I started wanting to do music, actually."

He looked over at her earnestly. "Fuck, I'm sorry. You guys showed up to help me and I didn't even think to ask you anything about your lives."

"It's fine. I mean, you have some stuff going on."

"So you're a musician? What do you play? Are you in a band?"

Edie had to admit, she felt a surge of excitement when he started asking her questions. And he was listening attentively, like he was actually interested in the answers. "Yeah, I'm a bassist. Mostly. My friend Mercy and I have a band, DYSMANTLE. Or, well, we did ... before all this."

His expression sobered a little, but he didn't press that particular subject. He switched the alarm on his bike, and they continued along the sidewalk, bracing against the cold wind as they entered Prospect Park. "So are you a Schecter girl, or what?"

"Fender. It's a Jaguar. JAB-90EQ."

"A Jag, nice. My friend Brian"—she tried not to freak out when she realized he was talking about DB's own bassist—"usually plays a Hellraiser. He swears by it."

Edie couldn't help but snort. "Yeah, if I have an extra thousand bucks, maybe I'll look into it." It took a second for her to remember she *did* have an extra thousand bucks—many times over. But she wasn't looking to spend it on guitars. Besides... "My dad bought me the Jag, actually. Right before he died."

Adam was silent for a moment before nodding slowly. "That's rough. I can see why you're still playing it." After another pause, he added, "You talk about your dad a lot. He must have been an amazing guy."

She wasn't sure what to say. Frankly, she was used to people knowing her father's situation without her even having to say a word. A selfish part of her almost wanted to let Adam continue to think Richard Holloway had been a good person. It'd been a long time since she'd heard a nice word about her father.

But her rational brain overruled that urge a beat later. "Ah ... not really."

As they entered the park and slowed their walk to a stroll, Adam quirked a brow at her. "Oh?"

"Yeah, he ... I'm not sure if you were able to sense it or peek through his glamour or whatever, but Cal isn't ... human. He's not even alive."

Adam looked at his feet. "I thought something weird was up with him. You guys kept calling him a revenant."

"Yeah. It's like a zombie, except that's considered a rude word. It's a kind of undead necromancers can raise, one that's sort of ... connected to your brain and has human-level intelligence, unlike husks, which are basically mindless. Revenants can follow orders and carry out tasks and stuff, but they can also devise their own plans, do magic ... they're pretty much just like you and me."

"Okay." Adam tilted his head. "But what does this have to do with your dad?"

She heaved a long, deep sigh. "My dad was a hellerune like us, and he raised Cal as his revenant. But the thing about revenants is that, even though they're basically humans, they're bound to the person who raises them ... and to their bloodline. So, basically, my dad told him what to do and he had to do it. And when he died, that passed on to me."

Adam looked ahead of them, brow furrowed as he digested this. Eventually, he said, "So your dad kept him like ... an indentured servant?"

"More like a slave, to be honest."

"And you..."

"To force him to do something, I have to order him magically. I'm not clear on the specifics. I only ever did it once, on accident, and I never want to again." It was her turn to look at her feet. "But yeah. My dad was a horrible person ... for a bunch of different reasons."

Adam peered at her. "If Cal's staying with you willingly, then he doesn't need to be bound to you, right?"

"Well, being connected gives us access to each other's brains ... so that's useful in a pinch. But we don't use it for anything besides that. I don't think."

"Have you thought about trying to find a way to release him?" His tone was serious, like he thought he might have to argue with her about it. "Seems like there's more downsides than there are upsides. And even if you're not planning on controlling him ever, sometimes it's the principle of the thing, you know? I'm sure being trapped doesn't feel good."

Edie wasn't sure where his sudden empathy for Cal had come from, but she wasn't opposed to it. She considered his words for a moment. "We haven't really talked about it before. I don't think he likes to acknowledge it. But..." She shrugged. "If we could find a way to break the bonds without hurting him, I would. I'd just have to talk to him about it."

Silence fell between them again. After a minute or so, they came across a bench, and Adam veered off the path toward it. He took deep breaths as he sat.

"Feel a little better?" Edie asked, taking the spot next to him.

"A little." He crossed his legs at the ankle and stretched out, sighing. Slowly, though, his miserable expression returned. "I was having a nonstop panic attack, and now I'm having a nonstop panic attack but outside."

"At least we're away."

She hesitated, thinking of all the questions she'd wanted to ask him earlier. One in particular was at the forefront of her mind, but she wasn't exactly sure how to approach it. At length, she peered at him.

"Adam ... you were defending Cal just now, but you keep acting all suspicious of him. Why? Why are you so afraid of him?"

He blinked. "Afraid?"

"It's pretty obvious. Cal noticed, too. He told me."

Adam shifted uncomfortably and didn't speak for a close to half a minute. Finally, his shoulders sank, and he sighed. "Yeah, I guess it is pretty obvious. He just gives off a certain ... vibe. The way he moves, the way dresses, the way he talks. The way he smells. It's all— It reminds me of someone."

Edie took a shot in the dark based on some of the things he had said throughout the day. "Your father?"

"Yeah." Adam scrubbed his face. "I didn't mean to make him uncomfortable. That was shitty of me. I usually wouldn't be such a dick about it, but I ... I feel like I'm losing my mind."

"I know exactly how you feel." She paused for a moment before adding, "You can, um, talk to me about it if you want. You don't have to. But you can."

Adam scanned the park. There weren't many people around, but he seemed more at ease that way. "I'll tell you some other day, maybe. Just ... let's say he was abusive and leave it at that."

"Is he still alive?" she asked softly.

"I don't know. I haven't spoken to him since I left. My mom's tracked me down and called a few times in the last ... twenty-five years, but it never comes to much. It's just awkward." Adam shrugged limply. "I don't really care if he's alive or dead anymore. When I was younger, I'd have given anything to kill him, but..."

"Yeah," Edie said, "a lot of your songs kind of, uh, give that impression. Plus, I mean, the fact that you named yourself after the only movie monster famous for having daddy issues."

Thankfully, he was amused instead of offended, giving a tiny chuckle. "There are a lot of reasons I chose that name, not just that. Have you ever read the Mary Shelley book?"

"Eh ... I have a hard time paying attention to books. I didn't do great in school."

"That's fine. I was just a really weird teenager, I guess." He cracked a weary smile. "The monster that Frankenstein creates actually gives himself a name in the book, y'know."

Her eyebrows shot up. "Really? What is it?"

"His name is Adam." He gestured to himself. "When I was young, it seemed like a sign. I felt just like him. A mistake. Made out of parts that didn't fit together right. Then, when I came out wrong, I was rejected. Desperate to find a place to belong. Trying *so hard* to be a good person and sometimes seeing no point. Feeling like I was dead before I was even born."

It sounded to Edie like he needed some serious therapy, but she was hardly one to judge. "So, you always felt like an outsider," she said. "I guess I can relate. When I was a kid, everyone my age thought I was a weirdo ... although even as an adult, I'm not exactly popular."

Adam fingered the tattoos on his wrist in thought. "I wonder if that has anything to do with our ... powers. You know, the hellerune thing."

"Nah, I'm just kind of a freak. My powers didn't actually show up until a few months ago, when I touched my dead hamster." She looked down at the tattoo on her own wrist—*ingwaz*, the beginning. "Even after that, it was a real bitch to figure them out. It still is. But yours seem to be, um ... active."

"I've touched dead things before, but my powers—" He loosed an unhinged laugh. "That still feels so weird to say. My *powers* were definitely around before then. I just ... buried them as deep as I could, however I could."

"You've used them before, then?"

"A bit. I could do weird little things. I ... I knew I was different, but I always brushed it off." He sighed and rubbed his forehead. "It wasn't until a little over a decade ago, I think, that it started getting really hard to ignore. But I couldn't figure out how to use it, even when I really, *really* needed to. When—" He cut himself off with another sigh.

Edie raised a brow and waited for him to go on.

"It was Mikey," he said after a moment.

"Mikey Mausoleum? Your drummer?" It took her another moment to realize what he was talking about.

Around a year after Death Benefits had broken up, she remembered her dad telling her Mikey had overdosed and died. If she wasn't mistaken, there had been some speculation that it was a suicide. Dad had been pretty upset about it, so it had upset her, too, even though she hadn't understood the full context. That had been only a year before Dad had died, now that she thought about it.

"I was there that night," Adam said softly. "I got a weird voicemail and a text from him, so I went over to his place. And I found him, unconscious. I called 9-1-1, but I knew they wouldn't get there in time. His heart was barely beating." He closed his eyes. "But when I touched him ... when I touched him, I could *feel* that I could save him. Like if I tried, I could keep him alive for a little bit longer."

Edie nodded. She'd done the same thing for Mercy months ago, but she knew this story didn't have a happy ending.

"I had no idea what the hell was going on, but I had to try. But I couldn't get it. No matter what I did, I kept slipping, or my magic came on too strong, and..." He hung his head, and she could hear him starting to choke up for the first time since they'd left his apartment. Even talking about his father hadn't gotten such a reaction out of him. "I couldn't do it. Just like with Elle. It was the same fucking thing; I couldn't do it."

She reached over and took his hand, squeezing it gently. "Yeah, I know what you mean. I had to do that once, too, for my friend ... if Cal hadn't been there to guide me, I probably wouldn't have been able to save her. It's not your fault you didn't know what to do."

Adam looked up at her, tears sticking to his dark lashes. His hand shook in hers. "I would have done anything to keep him away from those pills. Anything I needed to do. He and I ... if it was because I married Karen, we could have talked. We could have worked it out."

At that, Edie tilted her head. This was starting to sound less like a good friend had died and more like ... something else. She searched his face for a moment as she considered this.

Every Death Benefits fan had heard the rumors that Adam and his drummer had been in a secret relationship in their early career, but she'd always brushed that theory off. It seemed disrespectful to speculate on other peoples' lives like that, especially when one of them was a dead guy. Now, she couldn't help but wonder.

Would it be rude to ask? She waffled before saying to hell with it and taking a leap of faith. "Were you two ... together?"

There was a brief silence, and Adam drew away, hands fidgeting in his lap. "We ... for a while, yeah. We were together. It wasn't really anything serious. We were both in awful places in our lives. We dated around, sometimes came back to each other, but we never really talked in depth about it. I mean ... you didn't. It was the nineties. HIV was still killing people. Mikey and I tried to be careful, but if you were bi and you ever wanted a girl to touch you, you *never* fucking talked about it. Eventually, I met Karen, and it ended for good."

"You weren't still...? I mean, you didn't..."

Adam frowned. "Are you asking if I still had feelings for him?"

She shrugged in response.

"Not romantically, but he was still my friend. Things were pretty much how they had always been. But the thought that he never moved on, that it might be *my* fault that he ... did what he did? I can't handle it."

Edie shifted on the bench, her mind buzzing with about a million more questions than when she'd started. Best not to acknowledge that she was comforting one of her musical idols on a park bench as he cried about his ex-boyfriend, or else her mind would explode. "Sorry, this is a little off-topic, but— You like men and women?"

"What, you don't?" he returned.

"I don't really like much of anyone."

"Fair enough."

"If I decided to be with someone, I guess I'd choose regardless of what gender they were." She considered him. "But why not come out now? No one cares anymore."

"It's still scary. I had a hard time even admitting it to myself. I've just been ... terrified of what people will say. What if I do it wrong? Like, what if I'm too old to get the culture and stuff? And what if—" He cut himself off and said no more on that subject. Instead, he mumbled, "Maybe don't tell Cal."

Edie squawked. "What, you think he's going to hassle you for being queer? If you ever heard the way he talks about Cillian Murphy, you wouldn't be so worried."

"Oh. Interesting." Adam was thoughtful for a moment before sighing miserably. "I just overthink everything. I'm worried about ... *everything*. I've always been terrified that I'll end up a monster like my father. That I'll hurt someone. I was told that meant I had OCD, but I don't know if that's even true. If I always sort of knew something was wrong with me— if I always knew I had these powers—then maybe that fear isn't as irrational as everyone says."

"If your powers make you a monster," she said, "then I'm a monster right along with you. Do you think I'm a monster?"

"I don't know."

She rolled her eyes. "The truth is that our parents were terrible. My father ruined lives; yours traumatized and abused you. Basile's mother created him so she could be a queen forever. But the people we come from don't have to be where we go. Genetics aren't destiny. Being a good person or not is a series of choices you make. Some of those choices are easy ... some suck, or are painful, or expensive. But no one else makes them for us, parent or not."

Adam looked down at his lap, fingering his wrist again. "That's not necessarily true. The hellerune thing ... if I don't learn how to control it, my powers *could* make that choice for me. I could fuck something up and hurt people."

"We'll work on that," Edie said, then huffed. "At least you have access to your powers, even if you can't wield them right. I was, like, magically constipated for months."

He simply smiled in reply.

"And," she added, "I hope you like free tattoos."

"I guess I couldn't complain, considering. Why?"

She glanced down at her wrists. "Uh ... you'll know when it happens."

CHAPTER TWELVE

SCARLET TAPPED her pen on the blank sheet of paper, head in one hand, trying desperately to concentrate. Penning letters by hand was loathsome, but she still kept a few old friends here and there who couldn't be reached by email. She was starting to think nothing would come of her effort, however; the light that poured through the windows of Indriði's home was cold and harsh and, for someone who preferred the dark, not exactly conducive to focus.

She'd have liked to claim that the apartment's lighting was the reason she spent most of her time in the Baccarat bar, but, though wights tended to prefer the night, there were no real drawbacks to being in daylight— just that it was annoying, and would probably give her a headache if she got too much of it. No, the real reason she haunted the bar was more humiliating than that.

For the first time in almost a century, her slow climb up the social ladder had ground to a sickening halt.

When she'd been assigned to command the Watchers, she'd had such hope. She'd worked her ass off to impress, and when she'd been asked to leave Anster, it had felt like her tenacity and ambition were finally being rewarded.

Now? It seemed Indriði didn't care how hard she was working, or what progress she was making. She was so focused on Daschla's little side project that it was like Scarlet didn't even exist. And Daschla herself had made it very clear that she thought Scarlet was insignificant.

It drove the vampire mad. She had traded Zaedicus's tiresome attitude for more of the same garbage. Being around other powerful women was *supposed* to have given her a place at the table. But it hadn't. She should be part of the conversation. Under her command, the Watchers had been the catalyst for a Gloaming-occupied Anster.

The only one who seemed to care about what she was doing was the Wounded. Whenever they spoke, he looked her in the eye; he listened, he considered her input, he trusted her to do what she needed to do.

That was what had given her the confidence to tattle to him about the Blood Eagles.

The Wounded had given Indriði a stern talking-to, according to Ilphas. He had let her continue with her pet project but demanded that she divert more time and attention to the New Gloaming and the Watchers. He had even waited for Scarlet to come home so they could go over her plan of action.

He saw the leader in her. The Gloaming Lord that should be. In return, Scarlet would bring this city to its knees.

And that was what it needed, wasn't it? She didn't have to wait for Indriði's permission. She was ready to execute her own plan. If it happened to interfere with Daschla's little human club? Oh well.

The vampire rose to her feet, abandoning her attempt at letter-writing. There were more important things to do—memos to send, orders to give, supplies to prepare. If she started carrying out her plan now, New York City could be occupied within a week.

As she reached for her laptop, however, she heard the apartment door open. Daschla's voice called out, "Hello?"

Scarlet quelled her disgust and reluctantly changed course, heading toward the lounge. As she entered, the blond bitch was peering around the room, two of her red cloaks stationed just outside the open door.

When she saw Scarlet, her expression flattened. "Oh. Hello."

"Hello." The vampire refrained from going for the throat, managing to keep her tone friendly, if a bit strained. Daschla's attitude sickened her, and she was a human, not to mention a century her junior—but a secret, shameful part of Scarlet still longed for her approval. "Can I help you with something?"

There was no attempt to reciprocate even the facade of civility. "No. I'm here for a meeting with Indriði. Where is she?"

"A meeting?" Scarlet frowned. "What for?"

"Assessing the state of the Gloaming in the city. Determining what's next. Important things like that."

Flames licked Scarlet's heart. "I wasn't informed of any meeting."

"I guess you weren't invited." Daschla shrugged. "I'm sure that elf will be taking notes. Maybe you can ask for a copy."

"Unless you two are going to be talking about your rallies," the wight returned, "I should be involved. I command the foot soldiers at our disposal, remember."

Daschla sighed wearily and passed her. "How could I forget, Scarlet? You tell us every two minutes." She sat on the end of the sectional, setting her purse aside and crossing her legs. "I know it's exciting to finally accomplish something in your life, but parading it around doesn't make it more impressive."

There were no words. It would be so easy to dart over to his *worthless*, weak child, grab a fistful of her hair, and yank her head right off her shoulders. The pop of her vertebrae separating, the wet, rubbery snap of her tendons and skin being pulled apart—

Remember the spire. Just imagine her hanging from the spire.

Scarlet turned away and fled to the washroom, locking the door behind her. She turned the tap and held her shaking hands under the cold water, then ran them up and down her bare arms. For someone to speak to her like that, and to know she could do nothing to punish them ... it transported her to another time and place.

The baron had taken everything from her. First, he had taken her life: when a brutal illness had swept through her village and killed most of the females, he had done nothing, *nothing*, to help the people who needed him most. Then, he had taken her death. Improper burials in shallow graves had caused unrest; women, gray-skinned and thin, tattered and starving, had risen en masse from the ground. He had been there to collect them and bring them to his castle.

Then, her freedom: he had groomed, fed, and dressed her and the others. He gave them a home, luxuries they never could have dreamed of in their human lives. But his price was undying loyalty, and the penalties for angering him were even more sickening than playing sycophant.

Some escaped the horror by needling him into killing them; others allowed him to cloud their brains with hypnotic magic. Some, like Scarlet, gave in to his fantasy. It was easier to pretend she was important and treasured than to face the horror going on around her.

Eventually, she was the only one left. It was only then that she saw the baron for what he truly was: a pathetic old man who was, as it turned out, easily ended. As she walked the world, she soon found there was an overabundance of male wights who were just as beastly and just as easy to kill.

She let them believe they were above her. She nestled herself in their courts and jumped through their hoops, found her way into their chambers and war rooms. In the end, they all made one final mistake. And they all died for it.

No one would ever dominate her again, man or woman. She had sworn to herself.

And yet.

Scarlet looked up as she heard someone else enter the apartment, heels clacking, happy greetings. The fire in her chest was gone, and her heart and lungs felt like stone. In the mirror, her face was devoid of emotion.

She turned off the tap and left. If Indriði didn't want her present, she would have to say it to her face.

But when she entered the living area, there was none of the stony silence she'd gotten from Daschla. Indriði smiled and waved her over. She even ordered Ilphas, who must have come in with her, to add a third glass to the cocktails he was making.

"Scarlet! I'm glad you're here," the Norn said. "I have some news."

If she was so glad Scarlet was here, why hadn't she asked her to come to the meeting? Regardless, Scarlet sat on Indriði's other side, refusing to acknowledge Daschla. "News?"

"Big news. But first—Daschla, anything to report?"

"Things are progressing like we wanted. I know you said you thought the snow might hold things up, but I think I've found a way to spin it in our favor. I guess we'll see. We should see results within the next month."

"Good. And, Scarlet, your Watchers?"

The vampire smiled. "My plan is ready to go. Everything could be settled within a matter of days if we start now."

"Hold off," Indriði said. "There are some things we should finish up first. Then we'll set you loose."

If Scarlet had blood pressure, it would be spiking, but she schooled her expression and smoothed out her skirt. "Very well."

"So, what's your news?" Daschla prompted, taking the drink Ilphas offered her.

Indriði did the same, apparently unable to keep from smirking as she sipped the pink cocktail. "You'll never be able to guess. It's just too good."

Scarlet didn't take her eyes off the Norn, even when handed her own glass. "What is it?"

"The Reach. They all followed me here, just as I thought they would." Her smirk grew wider. "It's too bloody good. I thought they might, but I never imagined how funny it would be. What are they planning on doing? Hunting me down and making me apologize or something? Good lord."

Daschla crossed her legs. "Is this good or bad for us?"

"Ah, well ... there's good news *and* bad news. Good news is, their fumbling led me right to the hellerune. Some guy living in Brooklyn."

She took a long sip. "Bad news is, they've already found him, and they're hanging around him like vultures. But," she added, "with Astrid dead, they're significantly weakened. They're probably having to rely on whatever pitiful Reach presence there is in the city to help them."

"And that's ... what?" Daschla deadpanned. "Two, three people?"

"Enough to cause an issue." Indriði stood. "But the powers that be are adamant we recruit all the hellerunan we can find. So we'll have to figure out something. Blackmail, perhaps."

Scarlet set her drink aside. "With all due respect, I doubt we'll even have to go that far. The Gloaming has infinitely more power than the Reach to begin with. If we appeal to the hellerune, we may still be able to bring him to our side willingly. We'd just need to know more about him. What's his name?"

"Adam Einan. He's some washed-up punk singer—"

"Of Death Benefits?" Scarlet squinted. She wasn't a fan, but Nocturnem's DJs had played their more popular songs with semi-regularity.

To her surprise, Daschla perked up with recognition. "Death Benefits. That's the name of the band he was in?"

Scarlet didn't answer, but when the blonde reached into her purse and took out her smartphone, curiosity got the best of her. "What are you doing?"

"I'm going to place a call. I think I know someone who can help."

CHAPTER THIRTEEN

ADAM WOKE SLOWLY, as if the deathlike sleep that had consumed him last night was reluctant to release him from its clutches. His first groggy thoughts as he turned over and buried his face in the pillow were standard—he had work to do today, Elle was home from school, he had to get up but he wished it wasn't so cold in here...

It wasn't until his mind cleared that all the memories came rushing back. Elle. The Genesis. The Reach. The priest. The Wending.

The force of it all pressed him into the mattress like a demon sitting on his back, making it hard for him to breathe. In an instant, despite having slept deeply, he felt tiredness seep back into his bones. He struggled to lift himself into a sitting position.

Why did he have to wake up?

He wanted to wonder if he had dreamed it all. But he couldn't, not even for a moment. Things *felt* different. His body, his brain, the apartment. There was no denying that he had woken in a new reality, one he was dangerously unequipped to handle.

At least banging in the kitchen—which startled him for a moment—reminded him that he wasn't completely alone. He couldn't help but feel embarrassed that one of his guests was up and moving around before he was, even if the situation was a little ... unorthodox.

As much as he wanted to lie in bed forever, he had to get up. There was shit to do.

With a groan, Adam dragged himself out of bed and started toward the door. But just before he left, he paused and looked over one shoulder, brows drawn. The Genesis was sitting in its stand a few feet from his bed, as still and silent as any normal guitar. He hadn't liked the idea of Elle's soul being trapped in there, but he liked the idea of her out there somewhere, wandering and lost, even less.

He had to keep going for now. He had to make things right. Maybe he could lie down and die soon, but not now.

As he stepped out into the hall, the smell of burning food invaded his nostrils. In the kitchen, Edie was juggling two plates, a frying pan, and a spatula. She wore the same clothes she'd had on yesterday and didn't look much better than he felt, pale and obviously tired.

"Hey," he said as he approached, peering at the frying pan. "Are you, uh, okay?"

"I'm fine!" she replied, shuffling things around on his small counter. "How are you? Did you sleep well?"

Adam shrugged in response. That pretty much summed it up without going into morbid detail.

"Satara texted me this morning," she continued, trying to plate their breakfast. It had to be eggs, but the color was a little concerning. "She and Marius just arrived back at Basile's to do some more research, but they haven't found anything yet. He apparently has an assload of books and scrolls to search through, though, so..."

Adam nodded and glanced around the apartment. "Is anyone here with us?"

Apparently, the question was not very subtle, since she answered straight up: "Cal's been up all night working on Elle."

"All night?"

"You know, in between smoke breaks. He doesn't really need to sleep."

"Oh. Right." Adam shuffled, crossing his arms as he looked her over again. "Where did ... *you* sleep?"

"Oh, uh, just on the couch. Is that okay?"

"Well ... yeah." He suddenly felt terrible for not offering her better clothes to sleep in. She'd been kind enough to stay here with him even though she had a luxury apartment waiting for her in Manhattan. It was the least he could do. "I'm, uh, sorry for keeping you away from your friends and everything. You're really not obligated to care for me. I'd get over being here alone with Cal. I get nervous, but I'm still an adult man."

Edie smiled tiredly and swept a loose hair back into her bun. "It's not a big deal. And like I said, I'd just get in their way, anyway."

That didn't seem likely. From what he'd seen, she was a bright enough person, and her friends clearly liked having her around. Even if she didn't research, he assumed having her near wouldn't be a problem. And there was no way she *preferred* to be here, babysitting a neurotic forty-two-year-old man she'd only met a day ago.

She seemed so ... insecure. Was this how *he* came off to other people?

Plates in hand, Edie motioned him toward the dining table. Once they both sat down, he picked up his fork and prodded her creation. Definitely eggs, but they looked dry as a desert and were a weird, burnt-orange color. Despite this, he could feel his mouth watering. It had been a couple days since he'd eaten.

"So," she said, also tentatively digging into her food, "I thought while we were waiting, we could talk about your powers a little bit. You know, try and teach you a few things. I'm not exactly a scholar in magical theory, but I can answer some questions, at least."

Adam was considering this when his phone vibrated in his sweatpants pocket, making him jump a little. He took it out to set it on the table. Normally, he'd put it aside and get to it later, but one glance at the screen stopped him in his tracks. Setting his fork down, he hastily unlocked it.

Edie must have noticed a change in his posture or something. She tilted her head. "What's up?"

Sitting in his unread messages was a contact he hadn't heard from in a while. He had to stare for a moment to make sure he was actually reading it correctly.

[Brian Morison]: hey frankie, long time no see bitch. why the fuck havent we hung out since like your divorce? we live in the same city man. I wanna see your stupid face again. get back at me mothafuckaaaaa

"Um, Brian just messaged me and asked if I wanted to hang out."

"Brian ... as in Brain Damage?" Edie was clearly trying to rein herself in. "Like, your bassist?"

"Well, he's not my bassist anymore," Adam said with a chuckle. "But yeah. Weird."

"Why's it weird?"

"We just..." He shrugged. "We haven't met up in a long time. Life just got in the way and stuff, and we've been busy with our own shit, I guess."

Brian had been one of the only reasons he'd gotten through Karen leaving him. But he'd also been one of the biggest critics when Adam had stepped up to support her through her breast cancer treatments and double mastectomy, after her second husband had filed for divorce. Brian had thrown a pretty stupid tantrum when it had all gone down, and Adam was sure they'd drifted for good, but this ... this was a really pleasant surprise. He couldn't fight the grin that spread across his face.

Edie was smiling slightly, too. "You should totally go hang out."

"I dunno. Now's not really the time, with everything going on..."

"Yeah, but there's nothing we can do for now, remember? Getting out of the house and seeing friends would take your mind off it." She gave an exaggerated shrug. "That's always what helps me."

"I don't know if it'll help," he mumbled, looking at his phone uncertainly, "but maybe..."

"And while you're gone, I guess I could go to Basile's. Maybe I can help with something that's not research. Getting them food and drinks and stuff. I dunno." As she chewed, she reached into her back pocket for her own phone. "I'll add you to our group chat. That way you'll know to come back if there's any change?"

He nodded wordlessly. He had to admit, he wanted to see Brian. Even if he couldn't tell him about all the weird shit happening, Adam could at least be around someone familiar, talk about familiar things. Normal things. Maybe, for just a few hours, he could forget everything was falling apart.

As he finished his sad breakfast, he texted back:

[Adam Einan]: That sounds great, man. Meet at Sophie's? :)

He was surprised when Brian replied almost immediately:

[Brian Morison]: nah bro Sophies is closed. the blizzard fucked up the power or something. just come over to my place, I got beers and a 65 inch
[Brian Morison]: TV

[Adam Einan]: Sure. I'm sure we'll find something to watch. lol
[Adam Einan]: When should I come over?

[Brian Morison]: asap. if thats good for ya
[Brian Morison]: if your busy just clear your schedule lol hahaha

The notification that he'd been added to Edie's group chat dropped down on his screen, and she stood up across from him a second later, taking her empty plate to the sink. "I'm gonna tell Cal what's going on, then head out." Turning to him, "Is that okay?"

He sighed. "Edie, I'm really fine. I'm not gonna jump off a building or anything. I just ... what if they *do* need me for something?"

"There's nothing you can do. Trust me. Just go hang out with Brian for a few hours, take your mind off things. Once they figure out how to get us into the Wending, you're gonna need to be ready, so ... rest."

"Marius and Satara aren't resting," he said quietly.

"That's true. But the thing is..." Edie turned and approached, standing before him with her arms crossed. "Your life is never going to go back to the way it was. You'll probably have to leave your apartment, maybe even the city depending on how this pans out. Who knows what's going to happen to your comic or your art? For Christ's sake, your *daughter* died." She shook her head. "Just rest. For one day."

"Okay ... okay." Reluctantly, he rose from his seat, trying not to think too hard about what she'd just said. He'd been taking everything one step at a time, trying to focus on the crisis at hand. He hadn't considered what would happen *after* all this. If he started now, he'd crumble. Blocking it out of his mind as best he could, he texted Brian back:

[Adam Einan]: Alright sure. I'll head over in a couple minutes?

[Brian Morison]: do itttttttt broooooooo

With a sigh, Adam dumped his plate in the sink before heading to his room.

The moment he entered, his gaze touched the Genesis again. He couldn't bring it with him—Brian would think it was weird if he brought it over, and strapped to his back no less—but he wished he could. The past day and a half had felt more like a week, and having it near had started to give him a sense of security. Or maybe that had just been the feeling of having Elle's soul close. Maybe the guitar wouldn't feel the same now that it was empty.

Trying to keep his head clear, monitoring his breathing, he got dressed, pocketing the wallet and keys resting on his bookshelf. When he exited his room, Edie seemed to already be gone, and he could hear Cal mumbling to himself in Elle's room.

He hesitated outside the door for a moment, wondering if he should go in and see how everything was going. According to Edie, Cal had noticed Adam's odd behavior. The least he owed him was an explanation. But the thought of explaining himself twice in such a short period of time made his stomach turn. He left by the back door, locking it behind him.

It had snowed again last night, and the roads were slushier than yesterday, so he skipped his bike and headed to the subway instead, going through the motions robotically. Navigating the city was in his nature, as integral as breathing or blinking.

Aside from the odd roadie or sound tech who still kept in touch, he, Brian, and Mikey had been the only members of DB to stick around New York. Dead Thing and Clottia had gotten married and moved to LA pretty much straight away. With Mikey gone, Brian was the only band friend nearby, and it had hurt to grow apart from him. Hopefully, this was a sign that he wanted to patch things up. Despite all the awful shit going on around him, Adam couldn't help but feel relieved, even excited. He'd made new friends, but only a few people knew his whole story. That meant something.

His mind drifted, lost in anxieties and memories even as he arrived at his stop and hopped off. The next thing he knew, he'd entered Brian's apartment building and was quickly approaching his door.

Adam stopped in front of it, hands squeezed tightly in his pockets. He took a deep breath before knocking.

It's fine. It's just Brian. Just keep it cool and don't tell him anything. You don't need to be sent to a psych ward right now.

There was no answer for a few long moments, though he swore he could hear something on the other side of the door. He texted that he had arrived, and was about to try knocking again when it finally opened.

Back in the day, Brian had always worn platform boots that made him taller than Adam, but the Brian standing before him now was a couple inches shorter. His complexion was pale and lightly freckled, his face square with round cheekbones, and he wore his sandy hair in a high-and-tight style. The hair always threw Adam off. In the DB times, he'd shaved it pretty closely. Instead of the black tank top and dark jeans that had once been his signature look, he wore a T-shirt and cargo pants.

A "Hey, bitch!" and a big grin was his greeting. Typical.

Nevertheless, it was familiar, and it made Adam crack a smile. "Hey, man."

Brian stepped aside to let him in, and once he entered, Adam went for a standard handshake and bro hug. As he did, though, he couldn't help but notice how Brian tensed up, how he pulled out of the embrace hastily.

Adam shoved his hands back into his jacket pockets, biting back a grimace. Maybe the hug had been too much after so long. "How you been?" he tried instead, glancing around the apartment.

He was barely able to take anything in, however, before he noticed that they weren't alone. A woman sat on the couch, watching them with a smile. She was porcelain-pale, with precise but dramatic makeup and black hair so glossy and straight it almost looked like a wig. She wore a pentagram strap mini dress and velvet wedges, and he couldn't help but stare.

Was this a new girlfriend, maybe? Whoever she was, she was way out of Brian's league. It was fine that she was here, but he'd been under the impression that this hangout would just be the two of them. It seemed weird that he'd been given no heads up.

His moment of staring only lasted a second before Brian caught on:

"Oh, by the way, Adam—" He led him over to the couch. "This is my friend."

Before Adam could respond, she rose from the couch, tugging at the hem of her mini dress and leaning to extend her hand. "Nice to meet you, Adam. I'm Scarlet."

CHAPTER FOURTEEN

"Scarlet. Hi." Adam smiled and extended his hand, too. "I'm Adam."

Her skin was cold to the touch, and she didn't shake his hand so much as hold and squeeze it for a moment. "I've heard a lot about you."

Scarlet's tone was ... weird. Almost a purr. Her red-painted lips were curled into a sweet smile, her black eyes glinting. If he didn't know any better, he'd think she was flirting with him. But that couldn't be the case —they'd just met, and he looked half-dead.

Apparently, that fact hadn't escaped Brian's notice. As he sat on one end of the couch, he said, "You look like absolute shit, Frankenstein. Is this what being an artist does to you? All that time inside doodling?"

"Heh. Yeah, I guess so."

"It pays the bills, I guess. Or does it?" he added with a chuckle.

Adam wondered if it would be rude to say that, yes, these days, it paid the bills and then some. He settled for simply sighing and sitting in the empty space between Scarlet and Brian. "I was promised beer."

"Oh, yeah." Brian rose and started toward the kitchen, then came back shortly with a six-pack. "You sure you'll be able to handle it, Frankie? I know you're terrified of this stuff."

Adam looked up skeptically as he was handed a bottle. "Bri, it's a Heineken Light."

"All right, big guy, if you think you've got it under control." He glanced at Scarlet, laughing. "He used to get so fucking mad when I came to rehearsal drunk. Threatening to beat the shit out of me. 'I play way better when I'm fucking wrecked!' I'd tell him. Yeah, right, like he could take me anyway."

Adam suppressed a sigh as he opened his beer. Good to see Brian hadn't changed a bit. Granted, he didn't remember *quite* this much needling, but then again, rose-colored glasses and all that.

Brian handed Scarlet a beer before relaxing back on the couch and smirking at Adam. "So, what you been up to, besides drawing big titty anime girls? Making any music?"

"Eh, here and there. I've helped write a few things for Dead Thing and Clo, but my own stuff has kind of slowed down. What about you?"

"Oh, yeah, DT's new band. What's it called again?"

"Powerburial. Clottia has—"

"I don't know, man, DT's always relied so heavily on drum kits and stuff, I feel like he wouldn't need you to help him."

Dead Thing had actually been using gender-neutral pronouns for a few years, now ... but maybe Brian didn't remember, or hadn't seen them posting about it. Or maybe he just wasn't used to it. After a pause, Adam decided to proceed as normal. "I'm sure they and Clottia have a ton of people to bounce stuff off of in LA. It feels kinda good that they still ask me for advice and stuff. I haven't seen them in person since Mikey's—"

"Can't relate, bro." Brian took a deep sip of his beer. "Clottia blocked me on Twitter like a year ago 'cause of some Harambe meme I retweeted."

Adam wasn't even sure what to say to that, so he just shrugged and asked again, "What have you been up to, though?"

"Y'know, whatever. I got laid off last year, so I basically had to start over at a new company. *That* was fun." Brian rolled his eyes. "I guess you kinda had to do that when you got kicked out of your cubicle, huh?"

"Yeah, I mean, I quit, but pretty much. I'm sorry that happened to you, dude. That means more time with your own band, though, right?"

"Nah." He took another long sip and pulled a face. "We broke up like six months ago. Our other guitarist left and they wanted to hire some chick who had no idea what the fuck she was doing."

"Hm?"

"It was a thirst thing. She was a major slut. And a crazy-ass bitch, so, yeah ... there was basically this whole big fight and they— and we broke up."

Adam still hadn't taken a sip of his beer, and the more he listened to Brian, the less he wanted to. The discomfort level had been rising steadily since he'd stepped into the apartment. Either Brian didn't notice or didn't care—or maybe he was trying to save face by acting like a tough guy. Whatever the issue, he was being a total dick.

Adam glanced at his phone. Had it really only been eight minutes? "What else has been goin' on?"

"Eh." Brian shrugged. "By the time I get home from work, I'm so fucking tired I don't have energy to do anything. Except bitch on the internet, I guess."

At least Adam could partially relate to that. He nodded a little. "Yeah, I don't miss that. The tiredness. I'd kind of just get home and play *World of Warcraft* until it was time for bed." He smiled. "I guess I sometimes still do that on my days off."

"I remember, dude. Oh my fuckin' god, you were a mess." Brian laughed, then turned sour a second later. "At least you got to sit at a desk and jerk off all day. Most of my time is just moving shit around and cleaning up other peoples' fucking messes. And management's got cameras fucking everywhere, so I can't even take two seconds to check my phone or smoke or whatever. The higher-ups are garbage."

Okay, now he was talking. Adam tried to forget the comments he'd made a moment ago and focused instead on the topic at hand—one he was intimately familiar with. "Yeah, my company used to have this software where they monitored everything you did on the computer. I mean, I was usually working, it was just ... annoying to know they didn't trust us."

"Right? I work my fucking ass off." Brian sank into the couch a bit more. When he spoke again, frustration shone through his tone. "I swear, it's like a ... like an epidemic or something. It's not s'posed to be like this, man. Nothing is ever for us anymore."

Adam tilted his head. "For us?"

"You know, people like you and me. We get treated like shit and we're expected to just take it."

Adam still wasn't following him. Was he talking about class, or what? "Well, you know, punk is making a comeback."

"Not punk, dildo," Brian said with a snort. "Just ... you know."

"I ... don't think I do, man."

"You know! Us." He sighed. "You know, like, all these things they're forcing into the media now."

Still perplexed, Adam struggled to find the words. "Uh ... can you give me some examples?"

"Just, like ... all those soy boys triggered about how you can't have a fifth gender or whatever in video games. Having to get women in on everything now, even if they're dumb as rocks. Affirmative action and that diversity quota shit." The words were spilling from him now. "Did you know I applied to a job that was the exact same as the one I had before, different company? But two Jews and some Black chick were in the running, too, so I obviously didn't get it."

Oh. *What. The. Fuck.*

Adam's voice caught in his throat, gaze searching his friend's angry, sour expression. Had he actually heard that? He'd never considered Brian the most rational man in existence, but....

"I ... um." Adrift, Adam glanced at Scarlet, hoping she'd throw him a life preserver. But she was simply observing them, her expression impassive. He looked back at Brian. "That's, uh ... Bri, I get you're frustrated, but that's not cool, man."

Brian shrugged, trying to look nonchalant. "Maybe I'm tired of being cool, Adam. I'm tired of pretending everything's fine when it's not. It just keeps getting harder and harder to get by."

"Yeah, it does. But I don't think those things are why." Adam frowned, voice soft. "Don't talk like that, man, that's fucked up."

"You only think that because you're scared of being canceled or whatever. The media is brainwashing people to believe all that crap so it's socially acceptable for the minority to take over. They literally wanna wipe us out."

Adam couldn't do anything but stare at him in horror. He'd tried to empathize, but this was more than off-color remarks. This was something ... else.

"Where are you getting all this?" he asked carefully. "You've never said any of this stuff to me before. We would've beat your ass in the nineties."

"Yeah, Adam. We would have. But I've grown up." Brian clamped his jaw tight and crossed his arms awkwardly, drink still in one hand. "I've been tired of all this garbage for a long time, but I couldn't say anything, because I was afraid. Not anymore, though."

"Not afraid to do what, be a total dick?"

"And now I have people who actually understand what I'm going through." Brian sat up a little straighter, setting his beer on the coffee table. His eyes were alight as he turned to Adam. "You should talk to some of my guys, or listen to this podcast some of our admins have. They make a lot of sense, man, you'd be surprised."

"Who exactly are your 'guys'?"

"It's this forum I joined a while back. They're called the Blood Eagles. They meet up in NYC, so we could even go to a rally or something together. Remember when we used to do that?" he added with a laugh. A *laugh*. Like everything about this situation was completely normal.

"Those were *protests*, Brian. To keep us in our *homes*."

"We're being driven out of our homes, aren't we? All the Muslims and Mexicans they're bringing in and shit." Brian turned his hands palms up, looking like *Adam* was the one being irrational. "Bro, you know you're struggling with the exact same shit. Even if you don't know it, we're all going down together. The degenerates don't give a damn about you, so why are you so obsessed with pandering to them?"

"*Degenerates?*"

"Yeah."

"Okay, explain to me exactly what is degenerate to you."

"Someone who's weighing on society." That casual tone again. "Retards. Fats. Pronouns. Thots. Illegals. We've got welfare queens and pedophiles looking after kids—"

Adam stood, staring down at Brian's smug face. He could barely form a coherent sentence through the heartbreak: "Stop. Talking."

Brian glared. "What, too close to home? Since when did you turn into such a—"

"I don't want to meet your friends, I don't want to go to your rallies. You and I have nothing in common. Okay? So shut the fuck up."

Scarlet hadn't said anything this whole time, simply sipping her beer and listening. The few times Adam had tried to catch her eye and pull her into the conversation, she'd only smiled politely and gone back to her drink. Now, however, she cleared her throat. As Adam turned to look at her, she touched his elbow.

"Ignore him," she purred, gently pulling him back down to a sitting position and scooting a little closer. "We both know this isn't about any of that, right?"

"Excuse me?"

Scarlet tilted her head thoughtfully, pursing her lips. "The people who set this all up thought maybe you'd respond better to the plight of an old friend. Relate to the things he said. But you're different, it seems." She smiled. "You don't play games. I can respect that. I don't either. So why don't we get to the heart of the matter?"

Adam shook his head. "What do you mean someone set this up? What are you *talking* about?" He glanced at Brian. The man was sitting with his arms crossed, clearly pissed she'd cut him off.

"Let me frame this another way." Scarlet rose and sat instead on the coffee table, right in front of him. "I assume your new friends have told you about the Gloaming?"

This woman certainly commanded his attention. But when she mentioned the Gloaming, Adam swore he saw something flicker behind her—in the doorway of the kitchen, perhaps. A dark shape. He searched for it for a moment before looking back at her.

"I'll take that as a yes." She crossed her legs, drumming her fingers on her knees. "I'm not sure what they told you, but let me assure you, the truth is much more complex."

"You kill people," Adam murmured nervously. "You're the reason Anster is going nuts."

"I know it sounds scary, Adam. But certain sacrifices have to be made to establish ourselves as the ruling faction. We must rule if *anyone* is going to survive what's coming our way." She shrugged. "It's as simple as that. Perhaps it seems bad now, but if we win, things will get better for *everyone*. Even normal humans. But..."

"But ... what?"

"We have to act fast. Fate isn't going to sit and wait for us. Our leader, the Wounded, rubbed out the old Gloaming well enough, but all this opposition from the Aurora and now the Reach ... it's slowing us down."

Adam gritted his teeth. "What— what exactly is coming that you think you need to prepare for?"

"I can't say. There are rumors, but I couldn't tell you, truthfully." She leaned back. "But regardless, you're special. A hellerune. The Wounded has been looking for a hellerune to help him lead. Do you understand? You could help us bring order. You could save people."

He said nothing.

"Adam," she said, tone slightly harsher, "you've been nothing but powerless your whole life. Your father ... your career ... that desk job? Karen? *Mikey*? Don't you want to control your own fate for once?"

...Didn't he?

"I—" That shadow again, flickering across the wall behind her. What the hell *was* that?

"Once we saved the world, you'd be a hero. You'd be loved. The Wounded would protect you, make it easy for you." Scarlet threw a disdainful look in Brian's direction. "You would never even have to interact with Daschla's Blood Eagles."

"I..." Adam rose, and was silent for a moment before shaking his head, setting his beer aside. "I don't care if you think you're gonna save the world. After the things you've done, I'm not interested. Sorry."

He made a move to scoot past her, but she grabbed the sleeve of his jacket. Her expression had turned cold. "If you go now, you'll be making the biggest mistake of your life. If you stay with the Reach, you and all your friends will die."

Adam wrenched his arm away, and as he did, he noticed another shadow whisk across the wall—not attached to anything, it seemed. It distracted him for a half second before he returned his gaze to Scarlet, backing away toward the door.

"I'll ask you one more time," she said, rising after him. "Will you join us, or will you lose your life?"

Brian interjected: "Just do what she says, man!"

"No!" Adam snapped. "The answer is no!"

The woman's expression cleared. She didn't look angry so much as focused, her eyes boring frigid holes into him. "Fine. If that's your final answer, then I'm afraid I can't let you leave."

Before Adam even registered the words, she was on him. A millisecond later, he was on his back on the floor. Her cold fingers wrapped around his throat, squeezing.

He tried to buck her off him, but her body was like a lead weight—the strength with which she was strangling him seemed almost impossible. Too late, he realized that she must not be human.

Desperately, he jerked his head to look at Brian, in a vain attempt to yell for help. The man had risen from the couch but was frozen, simply watching the scene in front of him. A couple seconds later, he snapped out of his trance, but he ran from the room instead of pulling Scarlet off.

Adam's well-honed fight-or-flight instinct was the only thing spurring him on as adrenaline pumped through his body, giving strength to muscles that admittedly didn't get much use. With a croak, he managed to throw Scarlet off-balance, and they tumbled across the carpet together until he found himself on top of her. He scurried backward and tried to pick himself up, but she recovered with preternatural quickness, grabbing a fistful of his hair.

Planting her feet, she stood above him, yanking his head back and forcing him to look at her face. She opened her mouth, and he had no choice but to watch as all her teeth elongated till she had a jaw full of railroad spikes.

Panic screamed through his body. Even before Scarlet secured her other hand around his throat again, his world began to blacken, limbs numbed; he couldn't feel his face, and no matter how wide he opened his eyes, he could barely see. Darkness enveloped him.

And then, just behind her head ... that shadow again. That flick of solid shadow that had been dancing at the edges of his vision for a while now—

She faltered. Something caused her to cry out, and when she did, her grip loosened. He couldn't stop to wonder why; there was no time. He reacted instantaneously. The darkness clouding his head drained from him all at once, flowing down his arm and coalescing in his hand.

With a blast of deep purple energy, Scarlet was thrown away from him.

The lights in the room went out like snuffed candles as Scarlet hit the wall to the left of the bedroom door, shaking the whole apartment. Black and purple shadows curled off her skin like flames. She slumped, struggling to move for a few seconds, and by the time she scrabbled to her hands and knees, the shadows had spread to her face, clinging to her eyes.

Adam watched in awe as she rubbed at them, screeching, frantically trying to get her sight back. But there was little time to marvel at what he'd done—next to her, the bedroom door flew open, and Brian emerged, leading with the muzzle of a semi-automatic rifle.

The moment they locked eyes, that shadow flickered again. Now that he was more aware of his surroundings, Adam could perceive it properly: a solid black shape, angular, with a tail like a comet. It swirled around his body, and suddenly, he somehow knew that he had created it.

It was his to command.

With a flick of his wrist, the shadow hit the floor and slid across it, slipping under Brian's feet.

The man yelped and staggered. Gunfire ran out. Bullets sprayed the floor and wall, shattering a window. But the shadow was undeterred. Adam gaped as the silhouette of a human form sprang from the shadow's depths and jerked Brian into a choke hold.

With another sharp yank, the silhouette forced him to drop his rifle and then quickly had him on the floor, either dead or unconscious. When the shadow straightened to look at Adam, he recognized the shape of it. Leather jacket, chin-length hair...

Himself.

In the back of his mind, a voice echoed. Not his own voice—or ... not a *him* he recognized: **Get 'em, killer.**

The shape was gone as quickly as it had appeared, melting back into the shadowy spot on the floor. Then the shadow was gone altogether, and Adam was left alone with his two attackers.

Scarlet clawed at the wall, dragging herself to her feet. As she did, she scented the air. Her voice ground like a demon's: "I may not be able to see you, but I can still *smell* you..."

Sure enough, she turned toward him and broke into a sprint, teeth bared.

He dodged, but she caught him by the elbow, throwing him into a spin that sent him careening into the nearest wall. The force of the impact made him see stars.

That was it. Something about the sudden pain, the sting of his face and shoulder hitting the wall, stirred a hatred in his chest that was too sharp too quickly for him to contain it. The violent heat of it was frightening, and yet as he turned—as he thrust his arms toward her and let wave after wave of lethal shadow magic batter her—the feeling fed him.

Kill the bitch. **Kill the bitch. Break her apart, feed 'er to the ground.** He lashed his arms like whips, anger unrelenting, feverish to throw more magic at her. But the shadows only escaped him in bursts, imprecise explosions that marred the walls and furniture.

This wild magic only lasted a few seconds before he felt so weak he could hardly stand up. The loud crashing and sizzling of the shadows disappeared. The horrible voice ricocheting around his skull disappeared. The world was silent save for distant shouts and police sirens.

Adam panted and staggered to the side, barely registering Scarlet sprawled across the floor or the writhing shadows coating her body.

Barely lucid with exhaustion, he somehow managed to find the door. He flailed for the doorknob. Finally, with wisps of shadow clinging to his heels, he fled the scene.

CHAPTER FIFTEEN

THERE WEREN'T many things in this world that disturbed Cal. Heights? He wasn't raring to go jumping off no buildings, but it was hard to destroy a revenant. The dark? He could see just fine whatever the lighting. Dead bodies? Well. That'd be kind of hypocritical, wouldn't it?

But something about this goatfuck they'd been dragged into was getting to him. And he couldn't seem to pin down *why*.

Sure, a young dead girl was a terrible thing. Especially when you were the guy who had to pry her cold corpse out of her dad's refrigerator. Being the only one keeping her body from decaying wasn't exactly Cal's idea of a fun vacation either, but still, he couldn't put his finger on why the whole thing was bothering him so much.

The pale orange light surrounding Elle's body thinned a bit as he sat back, scrubbing his tired eyes. He might not need to sleep, but fucked if using magic nonstop didn't drain him—and this tiny pink computer chair was hurting his ass.

But no matter how much his ass hurt or how much he wanted to lie down and close his eyes, he couldn't. Besides quick breaks, he found himself drawn to Elle's bedside like he was tethered there. Whether it was out of pity or some sense of duty, he couldn't tell. He didn't even *know*.

He crossed his arms, keeping his eyes closed and trying not to wince at how the chair squealed as he leaned back. It was moments like this that made him wonder about his past. Or, more accurately, the past of whoever this body had been before it had been *Cal*. Was there an explanation there? Some feeling or experience that had been so intense that he still remembered it even if he couldn't recall it?

If that was the case, did the memory even really belong to him? He was just a bundle of energy zipped into someone else's meatsuit. Technically, none of those experiences had ever really been *his*.

He cracked an eye open to look at Elle, who was still serene as a sleeping baby. If there was something as awful as *this* in his memories somewhere, maybe he didn't want to know.

It didn't help that her traumatized father was treating him like some kind of criminal. He hadn't done anything to deserve it. Hell, he was the only bastard around here who'd done anything practical so far. Satara and the others were researching stuff, sure, but he was actually getting results, and without hardly any breaks, too.

Besides it being annoying as hell, it made him feel … well, like a monster. He already knew he was big and scary looking; he didn't need to be treated like he was some big, dumb animal, too. You'd think a guy who called himself Frankenstein would understand that.

If he only knew *why* he made Adam so nervous, he'd feel better. Might even be able to fix the problem, given the right context. But no, on top of everything else going to shit around him … this.

Adam didn't know the half of what it was like to be a Frankenstein, the douchebag. Typical fuckin' humans.

With a sigh, Cal scrubbed his face again and rose from the chair, rolling it off to the side. It was time for a well-deserved break.

Edie had insisted on leaving a glass of water with him, and though he'd waved her off earlier, he was happy to take a big sip now. He didn't need water to live, but it felt nice to have a little in his system. If he ignored the taste, he could even pretend it was a nice silver rum.

Water wasn't going to cut it, though. He looked at Elle one last time before slipping from the room, gently closing the door behind him. By the time he stepped into the kitchen, he already had his pack of Newports in one hand and a cigarette tucked between his lips—such as they were.

The knob of the back door was under his hand when it turned violently, and he staggered back just in time to avoid getting hit as the door swung open.

Adam.

On recognizing him, Cal was hit with a wave of dread, but it was soon replaced with concern. The guy looked like a corpse himself, *worse* than when they'd first found him. The dark circles around his eyes were deeper, his complexion like a melted candle, his face and neck bruised.

When their eyes met, the hellerune loosed a yelp and practically leapt across the kitchen. It was then that Cal remembered he'd dropped his glamour to conserve energy.

"Whoa, whoa, chill out! It's me. What the—"

"Where's Edie?" Adam managed, looking around the kitchen frantically.

Something really must be wrong if he was asking a question he already knew the answer to. Or maybe he was just being a dickhead. But something told Cal that wasn't the case. "Uh ... she's out. At the priest's place, 'member? You guys made a whole plan about it."

"Fuck!" Adam's voice was strangled. Before Cal's eyes, he almost seemed to ... crumble. His whole body shook, gaze somehow frantic and unfocused at the same time; his shuddering breath quickened until he was almost hyperventilating.

Deep discomfort, paired with a good measure of irritation, tore at Cal's chest. There was always some sort of issue with his guy. "Calm down," he said, a little tersely. "What the hell happened?"

It almost seemed like Adam didn't hear him. His gaze was distant, and if Cal didn't know any better, he'd think he was about to sink to the floor.

Before he could, Cal huffed and reached out. That was about enough of this. If he couldn't pull himself together, Cal would *make* him pull himself together. He grabbed Adam's forearms and practically lifted him, turning and planting him in the nearest dining room chair.

He tried to keep his hands steady, but Adam—who had frozen up for the second it took to move him—shook him off, teeth chattering. "Do- Don't touch me."

Cal pulled his hands away. "Just sit down and chill the fuck out, hombre. And for god's sake, tell me what the hell is wrong so I can help you." When Adam continued to shake, the revenant gestured to his neck and face. "Who did this?"

"It— Scarlet. Her name was Scarlet."

That gave Cal pause. "Scarlet? The vampire?"

"I don't know what she was."

The revenant took a deep breath, willing himself with what little energy he had left not to yell. "Tell me what happened."

At last, the haze over his mind seemed to clear a little, and he shook his head. "My ... one of my old friends asked me to go hang out with him, at his house. Edie thought it'd be good for me to take my mind off of ... everything. I wasn't sure, but ... anyway, when I got there, there was some woman I've never seen—"

"What'd she look like?"

Adam scrubbed his wrists hard. "Um ... really pale. Long, shiny black hair. Kind of goth, I guess."

Definitely his Scarlet, then. Cal gritted his teeth and motioned for Adam to continue with his story.

"Everything was normal at first. Awkward, but normal. I thought maybe she was just his new girlfriend or something. Then he started ... saying weird stuff. He tried to get me to join that Blood Eagles thing." Adam avoided looking up at Cal, instead focused on his boots. "When I said no, Scarlet started asking if I wanted to join the Gloaming instead."

"And I guess you told her to take a flying fuck at a rolling donut."

"She got mad and told me if I said no, she'd kill me. And then she tried to."

Cal's brow shot up. He'd taken on a vampire and her pet human, both at once? Maybe he wasn't as wimpy as he looked. Still, the magic had clearly taken a lot out of him. He still didn't know how to use it proper.

Adam glanced up at him. "I was able to fight her and Brian off. I ... fuck, I don't know if I killed him."

"Well, did he try to kill *you*?"

"He had a gun. He tried to use it. I..."

There was something eating at him. Beyond his friend's betrayal, beyond getting the shit beat out of him, something else had happened. And Cal had a good feeling he knew what it was. "Using your powers didn't feel good, am I right?"

"No," Adam mumbled, "that's the thing. It felt too good. I ... *liked* hurting them. And I heard this ... this *voice*." The more he said, the more agitated he seemed to get, until he was nearly squirming in his seat. "All my life, I've been obsessed with this idea that I was going to hurt people. That I would like doing it. That deep inside, I was this ... awful monster, and it was only a matter of time before I showed my true colors, and I— I can't let that be true. I don't want to hurt anyone!"

"Hey, hey, hey!"

Cal reached for his shoulders as if to steady him but stopped short when Adam flinched away. Confusion and anger mingled, and the pressure of their combination was too much for Cal to handle this time.

"What the hell is wrong with you?" he snapped. It came out louder than he meant it to, and Adam grimaced. "Stop acting so fucking scared of me, all right? Jesus! I know what I look like. I know I'm a *zombie*, okay, I get it. How could I fuckin' forget? Just stop wincing like I'm gonna go crazy and tear your throat out or somethin'." The last bit came out as more of a plea than Cal had meant it to, but at this point, he was desperate to get this guy to understand.

Adam curled inward on himself slightly, but it must have been an involuntary reaction, because he responded with just as much volume and enthusiasm as Cal: "I'm not scared of you because you're dead. This has nothing to do with you!"

"And yet I'm the one getting treated like a convict when you don't know the first thing about me!"

"How am I supposed to act around someone who drinks and smokes and— and walks and talks just like my piece-of-shit rapist father?" It all came out like a bullwhip, and the second it struck, Adam was out of his seat, pacing toward the living room with his fingers tangled in his hair.

Piece of shit. Rapist.

Even after a few long moments of silence, Cal felt the sting of those words keenly. A rift opened in his chest, pulsing deeply and slowly like a bleeding wound. He was suddenly consumed by and ashamed of the feeling. That ... that *hurt*.

It hurt so bad that he didn't have anything smart to say. Memories of when that breathstealer had attacked Mercy came flooding back to him. The damn thing had shifted into his form, and when the real him had arrived to help, Mercy had been terrified. She'd accused him. This was like that.

What made people think he was one move away from hurting them?

Cal was so focused on regulating his emotions that he didn't notice Adam until he reentered the kitchen.

The hellerune watched him for a moment before raising a hand to rub the scar on his forehead. "I'm sorry. I ... I didn't mean to come right out the gate with that."

Cal shrugged a shoulder, trying to pretend a little too late that the comment hadn't affected him. "Whatever."

"No, I'm..." He sank down into the dining room chair again with a sigh. "That was a shitty thing to say. You haven't done anything but help me, it's just, I'm kind of—"

"It's fine."

"No, let me finish. Ellie is *dead*, and everything I worked *so hard for* is gone, and it ... it's just killing me. I can barely sleep, I can't eat; forty years of demons have come back to bite me in the ass within the last two days." He squeezed his eyes shut and sighed again. "And every time you talk or move, it's like bolts shake loose in my brain, and I wish I could control it, but I *can't*. If my life wasn't falling apart, I'd be able to handle it, but on top of everything else..."

"I can't change everything about the way I am," Cal mumbled. "If I could, my life would probably be a hell of a lot easier."

"I know. And I'm sorry. You've already beyond proven that you're nothing like him. It's just ... something I have to get over, I guess." Adam sighed and looked up at him. "It would help if you refrained from, you know, shouting and grabbing me."

Embarrassed, the revenant crossed his arms and shuffled from foot to foot. "Oh. Yeah. I guess that would be a good start, huh."

"I'd be a lot less likely to blow up at you." He sank further into the chair. "What are we going to do about Scarlet and Brian? What if I killed him?"

Relieved to have the previous topic dropped, Cal uncrossed his arms. "Don't worry about that right now. Now we know that vampire bitch is here, so all the better."

"You know her?"

"She knows me more than I know her." With a huff, Cal pulled a chair up and sat across from Adam. "She's a psychic vampire and a memory leech, emphasis on the *leech*. Back in Anster, she fucking roofied me and hauled me off to the Gloaming. I don't remember any of it, but I guess they had her digging around in my brain to figure out what we were up to. While she was in there, she *took* something from me. Memories. I know she did. I can feel it."

Adam stared at him. After a moment, he said, "Oh. That's ... wow. I'm so sorry."

"Yeah, well. Next time I see her, I'm getting whatever she stole back from her, one way or the other. If she's close, then there's a higher chance of us running into each other. And this time she won't be able to drug me."

He let the words fall there, and they sat for a few long seconds. Across from him, Adam seemed to be deep in thought. What he was thinking about, Cal could only guess. As long as he was done accusing him of being some monster, he wasn't sure he cared.

At length, Adam looked back up. "So," he said quietly, awkwardly. "I, uh ... heard you like Cillian Murphy."

CHAPTER SIXTEEN

SATARA LOOKED UP, past the planes and valleys of the mountain of tomes before her, out the window. From where she sat on the floor, legs crossed and book in her lap, she could only see the sky. The sun hid behind a grim cloud cover, rays so weak they barely pierced the rolling gray. But at least Sól was up there, riding her chariot ever onward—and for the time being, it had stopped snowing. Both good signs.

The fledgling valkyrie simply prayed that the things she feared would never come to pass ... that her suspicions were wrong.

Aside from the ticking of the clock and the occasional sigh from Basile, the room was entirely quiet. Edie had left a quarter of an hour ago to get lunch for everyone—those of them that could eat, anyway—and Marius had followed to assist her. But even with complete silence, Satara could hardly focus.

The ache in her wings had built more than she'd anticipated in the past couple days. The first two weeks had been concerning but not unbearable, and she'd expected the next two weeks to carry on more or less the same, but no such luck. The rot seemed to have gained momentum, a slow poison building up and threatening to spill into her bloodstream. The thought of it alone made her breath irregular.

All of this, paired with lack of sleep and the memories of Astrid's death, and she could barely focus on the task at hand.

It didn't help that the task at hand was tedious: poring through archaic texts, trying to piece together a solution to save another woman's life. She felt awful for Adam. He was a good man, and of course he wanted to see his daughter alive again. But Satara was dying, too. And though investiture frightened her, it was hard to fulfill these obligations with that thought in mind. It was difficult to help others when she was acutely aware that every passing moment brought her closer to an eternity in Náströnd.

She rubbed her tired eyes and glanced up at Basile, who sat on the couch, working diligently. He was a fascinating man, but he could be very irritating. Did he even care about her problem? Did he know something she didn't—was her condition not as urgent as the pain made it feel? Or had his immortality wearied him to the point that he cared little for humans?

Whatever the case, she was starting to regret their deal. When she had thought it would be a matter of a couple hours, maybe a day, that had been one thing, but it was shaping up to be much longer—*if* they ever *could* find a solution to this problem. It was a vicious cycle: the longer she waited to transition to a valkyrie, the more pain she was in; the more pain she was in, the less she could focus; the less she focused, the slower they found a solution to the Elle problem.

Satara took a sip from her mug of tea and gazed down at the "coffee table." She had been around dead bodies her whole life, but the thought that there was a *lich* just inches from her, and possibly still conscious, made her shudder.

She had read a bit about liches. Commander Coldheart, the hero of her favorite book series, was in fact a servant to a lich king. But she'd never actually met one in person, nor would she want to, in most cases. Some were harmless, but the majority tended to be egotistical and power-hungry.

If Basile's mother had been a lich queen, was he a lich prince? The imagination ran wild. Her favorite author would have a field day if they knew that such a thing existed. Think of all the drama...

Her shoulder blades spasmed suddenly, and a jolt of pain flew up the arms of her unseen wings. She grimaced, inhaling sharply through her teeth. *Dammit.*

When she opened her eyes again, Basile had looked up from his book to peer at her. "You all right?"

A twinge of heat pricked her heart. "I ... could be better," she replied stiffly. "Let's just put it that way."

"Ah. Right. The wings."

"Yes, the wings."

To his credit, Basile's expression was grim as he adjusted his glasses. "Hopefully we're close to a breakthrough on this. Then we can ... you know, proceed."

"Exactly how close to a breakthrough do you think we are?" she asked, relaxing slightly as the pain evened out. "And how long do I have?"

"I promise you, you'll know when you're close to the end. We have time."

Satara sighed. "I figured. But I'd rather not wait until I can't walk from pain. How long?"

She asked the question not only because she was afraid of turning into a twisted fledgling, but also because she was frankly afraid of the alternative. The thought of becoming a valkyrie terrified her.

"I'm not going to let you die, young lady." He spread his arms in a grand gesture. "Even if, for some crazy reason, we had to stop what we were doing right now and save you, I'd buck up and do it. No one's going to Náströnd, all right?" He waved a hand toward the mountains of books. "I give this whole business a day and a half at most. Maybe two days including your trip to the Wending. That's plenty of time left."

"You think we're close to resolving this, then?"

"Pretty sure. I just don't want us to lose momentum, you know?" The priest adjusted his glasses again.

Two days. Satara took a deep breath. She could do that. It was two more days to collect herself and prepare for what happened next. And if it turned out she couldn't wait, one word to any of her friends and they would put the heat on Basile.

Silence fell again, and her gaze drifted down to the book. It wasn't more than a few minutes before she realized she'd read the same paragraph about eleven times, however, and lowered her head to rub her brow.

As she did, she peered at the sarcophagus. He'd given them some brief backstory, but she had so many questions. Maybe her focus would improve if she took a break? At this point, the least he owed her was some further explanation, if only to relieve her curiosity.

"Basile," she said, drawing his attention, "I understand why you put your mother in this coffin. But why do you keep it here with you?"

The priest seemed surprised she was asking. "Well ... I decided to keep it with me so that people wouldn't find it and open it in ignorance."

"But so close? Right here in your living room? Why not just keep it in storage, or somewhere else that only you can get into?"

"Yeah," he sighed. "I was afraid you might ask me that. I really *don't* want people to screw around with it, but..." A pause. "I also keep it as a reminder."

She tilted her head. "A reminder of what?"

A somber expression crossed his usually so pleasant face before he was impassive again. He looked away from her and, after a moment, sighed heavily and closed the tome he'd been thumbing through. His air was suddenly so gloomy that she wondered if he would actually answer.

"Well, Satara ... it's a reminder of what I am, what I could become ... and what I've already done." He stood, fixing the sleeves of his cassock. "Sometimes I need to remember that, even if I died tomorrow, I've already done a little good in this world."

He left her, then, and went to the window, arms crossed behind his back. What he saw out there, she didn't know. She got the feeling that if she joined him, she still wouldn't.

At length, he spoke again. "I didn't always dress like this, you know.

There was a time in my life where I wore pants, can you believe it?" After a brief glance over his shoulder, he went back to his hawklike vigil. "But it wasn't the same. When I started putting on the cassock, everything ... changed. People—everyone—started to notice I was there. Even here in New York. They'd look me in the eye. They'd stop me. They'd touch me. People won't touch a police officer or a doctor, but a holy man ... any holy man, they'll touch."

"Is that a good thing?"

Basile shrugged a shoulder. "It's good for them. For me, it's ... I don't know. Draining? On top of being a priest, I'm a soul guy. You all fight about who's more important, who's too different, who's better and stronger and why." He planted his hands on the windowsill and leaned forward heavily. "But no matter how hard I look, all I can see is how you're *alike*. *All I can see* is your souls. And the souls of the people you forget about are just the same, you know? Homeless families reach out and stop me—they touch me—and all they want is to know that I can see them." He huffed and shook his head, gesturing upward. "If *He* can see them."

Satara hugged her knees to her chest. He sounded perturbed, almost. But not as though he was annoyed. More like ... bitter. "Does that bother you?"

"I—" He was quiet for a second. "I don't know, Satara. Should it bother me that I've been lying to these people? Should it bother me that I wish I wasn't?"

"What do you mean?"

Basile threw up a hand, apparently at a loss briefly. "Catholic, Jewish, Muslim—it doesn't matter what it is. I just figure it's nice to believe in unconditional love. If *I* screw up, it's all over for me; Odin doesn't have the patience or frankly the capacity to forgive me. He can be a real selfish bastard."

Satara tilted her head. "You could believe if you wanted. There's nothing saying you can't. The Pantheons were born; something needed to create them, create the universe. You could decide what you wanted to believe in."

"I don't know how to believe in anything anymore. Maybe I never did." One of the hands on the windowsill turned into a fist. "I can't be sure of even one thing I'm doing. I can't be sure if this is all for nothing. I can't even be sure..."

He trailed off, and Satara waited for him, watching his back with a dour look of her own. This was not the same man she had met two days ago. This was not the man who spoke carelessly of human lives and dismissed peoples' suffering. Something inside of him was festering—poisoning him as surely as her wings poisoned her.

"If I keep doing this," he began, voice quieter than before, "if I keep trying to help people, taking spirits into me ... is it true that I'll get emptier? If I don't stop, one of these days, am I just going to wake up so *hungry* that I ... I'll be evil? All because of the damn soul?"

She watched him closely. "If you did, what would you do?"

"Well, now that you're here, you can kill me." Basile looked over his shoulder. "Eternal life isn't worth much; take it from me. I'd rather die well and have people say I was a good man. Or whatever I am."

"You are a good man," Satara murmured. She patted the stone coffin. "And you always have been. Remember?"

Basile watched her for a long moment. Then, as if they'd never had the conversation, he turned and switched gears immediately. "That's enough of a break. We don't want Edie and Marius to catch us shooting the breeze when we're supposed to be plugging away. Plus, I've only cleared my schedule for the next week."

He sat down again, opening his book. Satara returned to hers as well, but the thoughts racing through her brain did little to help her already struggling focus.

After a few minutes, Basile relieved her. With a hum, he pointed to something on the page he was reading. "You know, I've only visited the Wending a few times, but I always forget that for you living people, it doesn't really feel like a physical place."

"The other Worlds are physical, though, aren't they?" Satara asked. "If I knew the way, I could walk to the gates of Asgard right now."

"That's right. But the Wending isn't like Hel or Midgard or Alfheim. It's not a World, it's a plane. A ... layer. A space in between." He waved a hand. "They're easier to get to from other in-between places. Something to think about."

She nodded.

"There's also the issue of figuring out how to get you inside while you're still alive." And as suddenly as he'd switched gears a moment ago, the priest switched them yet again. He pinned her with a stare. "Why don't you want to be a valkyrie?"

Satara was taken off guard by the question, and she hesitated for a moment. He was an agent of Odin, Lord of the Valkyir. Was this some kind of test? "I don't know what you're talking about."

He squinted. "Now, that's just not fair. Anyone with eyes could see it. You're a melancholy one, you know that?"

"I really don't—"

"Whenever we talk about your investiture, or valkyir, or anything having to do with any of it ... you freeze up. Go cold." He huffed. "I mean, good lord, you're more scared of dying than you are excited to become one of the most important beings in the universe. Do you know how crazy that is?"

"It's not crazy," she returned firmly. Her patience for his attitude was wearing thin. She much preferred the thoughtful, frightened man she'd conversed with a few minutes ago. "If you knew the life I have ahead of me, you wouldn't have to ask."

"I know a thing or two about valkyir."

"And I lived with one. I *saw*."

Basile searched her face thoughtfully. "All right ... then tell me."

Satara took a deep breath, setting aside the book in her lap and pressing her temples. Perhaps it was best to start at the very beginning.

"In the forest surrounding the village I grew up in, there was this oak.

It was huge, and ancient, and there was a hollow in the trunk so wide that my brother, Darras, and I would climb in and hide for hours. As he grew older, he couldn't fit into it anymore, and it wasn't any fun without him, so I abandoned it, too.

"But we still went to the forest together. He was training to be a defender. Not a warrior; he was adamant about that. A *defender*. He was always armed with this enormous shield, and no matter how hard I pushed on it, as a child, I could never make him waver. We'd play games where we faced a challenger, and he'd guard me as I pretended to cast magic and heal him.

"One day, while we were playing, he ... he suddenly went still. Looking into the forest, like a deer. Listening. I yelled to ask him what was wrong, but he never answered. He just picked me up, shushed me, and shoved me into the hollow of the oak. I was barely small enough to fit."

Her hands shook. She almost paused to collect herself, but no—she had to be out with this story in one stroke, or it would never come out at all.

"Before I could even guess at what was happening, a troop of men tore out of ... nothing. Darkness. There were so many of them, and they all jumped on Darras. I shut my eyes and hid my face, but I could hear them fighting: the cries, the swords, his shield digging into the dirt. Then I heard ... it sounded like water—"

Satara closed her eyes. No. She couldn't touch that memory.

"My brother died defending me, and when his attackers stopped to search his corpse, I slid out of my hiding place and I ran. I warned the village that there was a hostile party coming, but ... the men never came. Our scouts only ever found Darras's body. And a few months later, my training began. Training to become a warrior." She could feel her face crumple but could hardly stop it. "They trained me to fight, like what I had done wasn't good enough. But I was only a *child*."

Basile slid off the couch, sitting on the floor across from her. "And what does all that have to do with being a valkyrie? You don't strike me as the type to be contrary for no reason."

"I've seen Astrid," Satara whispered. "I saw what her life was like. She was sad and lonely and angry all the time, Basile. *I don't want* to forget what it's like to be human. I want to love and be loved, without weapons and armor strapped to me. I don't want to be waging war my entire life." Tears spilled down her cheeks before she could stop them. "I can't spend every day on the warpath like Astrid did."

"Right. Astrid." The priest was thoughtful for a moment. "Tell me ... if you weren't forced to be a shieldmaiden, if you weren't destined to become a valkyrie, what would you do with your life?"

She blinked, wiping her eyes. No one had ever asked. Not even Edie, who had a penchant for absentmindedly asking deeply personal questions. "I always wanted to tend the dead ... to help them and their families move on. Like my mother and father. They're a death priestess and an undertaker, respectively. Or to maybe be a battle healer, like my great-grandmother."

"My gods." A bemused grin split Basile's face, and he laughed, gesturing to her. "You know you can do exactly that as a valkyrie, don't you?"

"But—"

"Valkyir choose who lives and dies in battle—and yeah, that's hard. But listen ... a battle healer cuts throats just as much as they patch up wounds. A death priest helps the dead pass on and leave their bodies behind. Both of those things are exactly what valkyir do."

Satara simply stared. "Valkyir go to war all the time. That's how *Astrid's* battlemother died."

"Yeah, valkyir sometimes do battle." Basile held his hands up. "Sure. But everyone does once in a while. Most of the time, they're either reaping souls or just sitting around doing whatever the hell they want. Whatever they're good at, ideally." He quirked a brow at her. "Apparently Astrid was good at sitting around being angry."

"But she always said..." Satara trailed off and frowned.

"Well, she *would*, wouldn't she? What immortal being isn't convinced they're right about everything? But her box isn't yours." He laughed again. "You know, I once saw two men after a battle, both soaked up to their elbows in blood. One was a warrior, bathed in the stuff after mowing his way through the battlefield. The other was a medic, covered because he'd been amputating limbs and suturing gut wounds." He clapped his hands together, apparently proud of his anecdote. "They looked the same, but those are two different vocations. See?"

"You say I can just do whatever I want"—Satara sighed—"but valkyir are aspects of Odin. We have duties we have to see to."

"Yes, but like I said, they're duties you seem to already like. And besides those? It's all up to you. Hell, I've met valkyir who are *poets*." Basile shrugged and sat back on the couch. "Odin is the god of poetry, after all. War, too. And death. He's got lots of facets, and so do valkyir. No two of you are exactly alike."

Satara went quiet, idly flipping through one of the books in front of her. She wasn't sure what to make of what Basile was saying. Even beyond her apprehension, there was still so much to think about—going from human to valkyrie was a transition she could barely comprehend. Her life, her very being, would change in every aspect. And not to even know what to expect ... even if she decided she didn't mind the idea so much, it was a lot to think about.

After a period of silence, the priest stood, grabbing his empty mug in one hand and a book in the other and meandering into the kitchen.

Left with her thoughts, Satara spared a glance over her shoulder. As if in answer, her fledgling wings sprouted from her back, stretching out with a gentle shimmer and a puff of down. They were more opaque than they had been when they'd first appeared. But the past couple days, she'd noticed how easily the shadowy feathers came loose in her hands.

These wings were heavy, so much heavier than she ever could have imagined. They truly had no substance, were barely corporeal at times, and yet her body strained to hold them up.

Why had Astrid left her with these, and no guidance on how to be rid of them?

Satara folded them up again, and they disappeared. With Astrid gone, she would never get a definitive answer. It was time to stop asking the question.

She could either forge ahead into the unknown, or let this kill her.

CHAPTER SEVENTEEN

"YOU SAID *SCARLET* WAS THERE?" Edie said into her phone, already passing the bag she was holding to Marius so she could block out the sounds of traffic with her other hand. Whatever Cal had just said, she must have heard him wrong.

"You got bugs in your ears, Holloway? Yeah, Scarlet. The bitch herself. She was at this asshole's house tryin' ta ice Frankenstein."

Edie exchanged a glance with Marius, mumbling, "One sec, Cal," before lowering the phone. "Adam's friend asking him to hang out was an ambush."

"Wonderful," the vivid replied with a sigh, watching the traffic from the sidewalk where they had stalled. "I suppose that means lunch is canceled?"

"For me, anyway. He got out alive and he's home, but I should probably go over there." She turned, looking at the nearest subway station, then back at Marius. "Can you tell them what happened?"

He seemed apprehensive but nodded anyway. "Fine. Just take care. Wait, your food—"

Edie had already started trotting away. She called over her shoulder,

"I'll be fine! Just keep it!" When she reached the subway entrance, she lingered, lifting her phone again. "I'm on my way."

"Make it snappy," Cal replied, and hung up.

She made the trip in record time, and when she entered Adam's apartment, she found him and Cal sitting at the dining room table, a large book open between them.

"So ... the dice tell you how strong you are?" Cal was saying.

"Yeah, you roll the dice to get your stats, and your stats determine what kind of armor you can use, your weapons, what skills you're good at, things like that. There's lots of different ways you can roll them—"

"Wait, but what if the dice give me a real shitty number?"

"Then ideally you want to put that number into your dump stat. Your least important stat, basically. So if you're a Wizard or Warlock, you could dump strength, or a Barbarian might want to dump intelligence—"

"What, my guy can't get his GED? I can't roll to watch some PBS or somethin'?"

"Uhhh, well, I guess you could use your Ability Score Improvements if you really wanted to."

Edie crept a little farther into the room, closing the back door behind her. "Whaaat is going on here?"

Adam almost jumped, looking over his shoulder sheepishly. "Oh, Edie. Hi."

She approached the table, lifting the cover of the book. "*Player's Handbook*." She glanced at Cal. "For what?"

"*Doorknobs and Dickholes!*"

"*Dungeons and Dragons*," Adam corrected.

"*Dragons, Drive-Ins, and Dives.*"

Adam looked at Edie. "I give up."

"Thought it might make him feel better to talk about somethin' ... ya know, familiar." Cal leaned back in his chair, crossing his arms. "Imagine my surprise when he starts talkin' to me about elves and dwarves and shit."

"It was a little less overwhelming when I thought those things weren't real," Adam mumbled. He closed the player handbook, addressing Edie. "You didn't have to come over here if you were in the middle of something. I'm okay."

It was nice to see him doing all right emotionally, but he looked like he had one foot in the grave. She was used to a similar sight in the mirror after using a ton of magic. "Judging by your face, I'm guessing you were able to fight her off?"

He nodded. "I mean, as best as I could. It was more of an ... expulsion than anything."

Cal pulled a face. "*Expulsion?*"

"It could be worse," Edie said with a shrug. "You could be magically constipated."

"*Consti*— You motherfuckers are gross."

"I'm not sure if my situation is any better, Edie. I don't wanna hurt anyone."

She sighed. "When you see more from the Gloaming, you *will* want to."

"That's what I'm afraid of."

"Well," Cal said casually, "if you wanna make sure you don't hurt anyone on *accident*, you'll need to manage your magic better. Make it less like explosions and more like lasers. You thought about getting a focus? Like a wand or somethin'?"

"If you're about to send me to Diagon Alley, you can shove it up your ass, Cal."

The revenant raised his hands in defense. "Well, excuuuuuse me for trying to fix your problem!"

"Are there any focuses that won't make me look like a complete tool?" Adam asked with a smirk.

Edie put her hand on the back of Cal's chair and leaned against it slightly, the wheels in her head turning. "How does a focus work exactly? Some of the stuff I researched a couple months back mentioned them, but I never looked into it."

"It's just a thing you channel magic through," Cal replied. "It could be anything."

"Can you be more specific? Are there any rules?"

"Uh ... I guess it's better if it's something important to ya. Like a special ring or family heirloom or whatever. I knew a girl in Vegas who used her cell phone. But I think earthy crap like wood or metal works best. And there's some rule about it being given to you as a gift. I dunno, I'm no fuckin' wizard."

Edie couldn't hold back her grin. Perfect. She left before anyone could say another word, trotting to Adam's room.

When she came back, she held the Genesis in her hands.

"Adam? You ready to tear shit up?"

It was only a few hours before they got the news they had been waiting a day and a half for.

Cal had quickly resumed his work on Elle's body, so Edie and Adam had been left to figure out how exactly he'd use his Genesis as a magic focus. That was an exercise in the helpless leading the clueless, as far as Edie was concerned, but it was better than sitting around doing nothing.

Adam was testing out a few riffs, trying to see what might spark a reaction, when Edie's phone buzzed in her pocket. A new message in the group chat.

[Satara]: We found something. On our way.

"Adam." Edie stood from where she'd been sitting next to him on the couch and flashed him the message. "It's time."

His drawn face lightened a bit. He glanced down at the Genesis. "I guess there'll be time for this later. Hopefully we don't run into anything we have to ... y'know ... kill."

Logically, Edie thought, the chances of running into something that wanted to kill them in a plane of lost souls was kind of low. Realistically, however, it was a rare thing if she and her friends went somewhere things *didn't* want to kill them.

But they had to go. There was nothing she could do but hope.

When Basile and the others arrived, they were decked out for battle. Or, rather, Marius and Satara were; Basile was dressed in his cassock as always, a messenger bag over his shoulder.

As they entered, he whistled. "Do you know how hard it is to sneak swords and crap through Brooklyn?"

A second later, Cal emerged from Elle's room, frowning when he saw the others. "All done?"

"Hopefully," Satara replied. "If everything goes according to plan."

"Which it will, of course." Basile stepped into the center of the room, looking around before noticing Adam, who was just rising from the couch. "Ah, there you are. I heard about your little misadventure."

Adam didn't seem interested in small talk. "You found a way in?"

"Yes. Well. Sort of."

Cal leaned against the wall and crossed his arms. "So, what's the plan, Father? How're we doing this?"

"Well, since we can't get to the Wending from Adam's living room, the first step is to go somewhere we *can* get to it."

"Right. So, traveling." The revenant sighed and jerked his head over his shoulder. "Guess that means I'm staying behind."

He didn't look happy about it, and Edie had to say she shared his apprehension. Every time she and Cal separated, something awful seemed to happen. They had long since agreed never to do it if they could help it, but the magic he was doing required near-constant vigil—he couldn't come with them if they wanted to keep Elle's body from rotting.

"I'll be okay," Edie said under her breath, glancing at him.

He grumbled in response.

"All right." Adam adjusted the guitar strap across his chest. "We need to go somewhere else to get to it. Do you mean like a ... I dunno, a portal or something?"

"Sort of. Satara was saying to me earlier, you could *walk* to the entrances of the other Worlds if you wanted. As long as you knew the way, you wouldn't have to do anything special. But the Wending doesn't have a heimdyrr—it's a plane, woven into the fabric of the universe. No doors, not for living people, anyway. And, well," the priest scoffed, "I don't really have enough power to open a hole in the fabric of the universe from the physical realm. Not *here*."

Marius glanced at the others with a smirk. "The draugborn admitting he doesn't know something? Impossible."

Basile sighed. "Anyway, I can't get you there from your kitchen ... but there are in-between places. Even in the physical world. Even in a city like this. Lost souls are drawn to them, too—that's usually where they pass through and eventually get to the Wending. Have any of you ever heard of liminal space?"

Edie was pleased to actually be able to raise her hand for once. "Mercy's talked about that. It's like ... a period of transition from one phase of your life to the next. 'The past is left behind us and the future doesn't exist'—she says that a lot."

"God, that girl is weird," Cal mumbled, rubbing between his brows.

"You're right in a way, E. But liminal space can be an actual, physical space, too." Basile went to the apartment's front door and opened it, pointing at the threshold between the hallway and the kitchen. "What room is this?"

"It's ... not," Adam replied.

"But it exists in this house, doesn't it? Everything in this house is a room, isn't it? So this must be a room."

Cal sighed. "Am I the only one here who doesn't smoke crack?"

"It's not a room," Marius said, tilting his head. "It's not really ... anything."

Basile nodded and slammed the door. "And that's what liminal spaces are. Cosmic thresholds. A place always in transition between what was and what's about to be. A place where something is always *happening* but nothing ever *is*. And you know where one of the biggest ones in the world is, right now?" He looked at each of them, grinning. "Under our feet."

Adam's face cleared in realization. "The subway."

"That's right." The priest laughed and clapped his hands. "Any subway station'll do, but for our specific needs, I'd prefer an empty one, you know? I don't think the turnstile guards are cut out to deal with weirdos doing Norse soul rituals."

"What about Hoyt St?" Adam suggested. "It's under maintenance because of the blizzard, and it's not far from here."

Basile nodded. "I know the place. Probably our best bet at this point." He looked around at those gathered. "All right, if you're in, come stand around me. Close as you can get."

Edie couldn't shake her anxiety, but there was no time to wait. She went to the door to pull on her jacket and boots. Just as she was wishing she had a weapon other than her magic, Marius approached her.

"You can use this," he said from above her as she tied her laces. "I don't need it."

When she looked up, a familiar dagger glowed in his hand. Radiant Hærfríðr's blade of truth. After the battle in the Temple of the Rising Divine, she had stolen it, sort of as a last fuck-you to the Aurora. Marius had been carrying it since she'd given it to him, but she hadn't seen him use it yet.

Edie hesitated for a moment before straightening up. "You sure? I'll probably be fine."

"Go ahead. We won't have time to go back to Yuval's apartment to get anything else, so you may as well."

"Thanks." She accepted the dagger and sheath and secured them to her studded belt. "Maybe after this I can get my own weapon instead of having to borrow everyone else's."

Marius replied with a surprisingly warm smile.

Across the room, Basile had turned to Adam, who'd also suited up in his jacket and boots. "I assume you're staying behind. You look like hell."

"What? No." The hellerune frowned. "Elle is my daughter. I'm going."

"Suit yourself," the priest replied uncertainly before motioning to corral them all in close to him.

Cal still leaned against the wall, brow quirked, rubbing his chin. "So explain to me why all the kids have to hug you for this to work? Or is that just a typical Catholic priest thing?"

"Hilarious, Cal, I'll laugh as soon as I can." Basile rolled his eyes and stooped down, taking something out of his bag. Whatever it was, it glowed slightly, and he began using it to draw runes on the floor around them. "I'd normally teach you how to create a teleportation circle yourself, but let's not deplete what little energy you have, shall we? At this point I got no idea what you might face in the Wending."

By the time he stood, they were surrounded by a circle of runes, with one large sigil in the middle. He mumbled a few words, and the writing lit up, wreathed in silver fire. The world around them wavered like heat over asphalt. Edie could barely hear Cal wish them luck as the world began to blur and shift around them.

The next thing she knew, she was standing at the bottom of a subway staircase.

Edie hugged her coat closer as she stepped out of the circle. The ring of glowing runes had translocated with them but was now fading away with a final flash of light.

As she looked around, she couldn't help but notice how the hairs at the back of her neck stood on end. Where they were standing, the lights were on, illuminating ugly red-and-yellow tiles, but it was dark beyond the turnstiles. Nearby, she could hear wind rushing through the tunnels, and distant noises of trains going to and from other stations.

As the others joined her beyond the circle, Basile took point. His head was lifted almost as though he was scenting the air, and she could have sworn his irises were shifting between a light and slightly darker blue.

"Hm..." After a moment of silence, he drummed his fingers against his chin, then pointed ahead. "That way. Adam, get the cameras?"

Basile started off without waiting for them, his pace brisk. Without breaking stride, he hopped the turnstile, leaving Adam to interpret his words. The hellerune craned his neck to look at the security cameras, and a moment later, they were shrouded in shadow. With that done, the others followed him over the turnstile to the platform.

To their left, Edie could hear the distant sounds of equipment and men shouting back and forth, and she became even more tense. One wrong move or too-loud noise and they'd be found out—and they were a weird-looking bunch, decked out in armor and carrying strange artifacts and weapons.

She didn't want to know what would happen if they were found.

What was *really* bothering her, though, was how ... strange this felt. She'd used subways her whole life, but the absence of people seemed so wrong. It robbed the metro system of its sole purpose.

Thinking about it, she understood what Basile had been talking about. People didn't stay in the subway very long. Most people didn't even think that hard about using it. And yet without them, it was nothing. Without them, the future didn't happen here.

Edie braced herself—and she could hear Adam take a deep breath beside her, too—as they went further down the platform, away from the entrance and deeper into the darkness. She slowed her pace and whispered, "Basile, shouldn't we stick closer to the light?"

"Not if you want this to work. I'm trying to find where the weave is thinnest." Basile stopped at the very edge of the platform, looking both ways down the tunnel.

"I think this is as far as we can go," Adam whispered, an edge of urgency to his voice.

"No." Basile's voice was stark in the darkness; he didn't seem to be trying to regulate his volume at all. "We need to go deeper."

Edie shivered. "I'm pretty sure that isn't possible. We're on the deepest level."

"Not deeper *under*. Deeper..." He waved a hand vaguely. "It's hard to explain. This station isn't good enough. Just follow me, my little lemmings."

And without further ado, he jumped down onto the track.

He landed just short of the rails in a surprisingly effortless motion, then turned and looked up at them expectantly. "Well? Come on, we don't have all night."

Marius in particular balked—when Edie had been teaching them how to navigate the subway, she had impressed upon them that they should stay away from the gap, and he had clearly taken it very seriously. "You're going to get yourself killed, priest."

"I'm not worried about it." He motioned for them. "Come on!"

Adam was the first one to take the plunge; he stepped up to the edge of the tunnel, took a deep breath, and jumped in with a resolve Edie hadn't come to expect from him. Either she'd misjudged him or he was really that desperate to get Elle back. Or maybe he'd explored abandoned subway stations before. Probably a mix of all three, now that she thought about it.

Satara went next, with Edie following close behind. Finally, with a fair amount of grumbling, Marius jumped down, too.

Basile was off again, completely unconcerned with the darkness engulfing him. The airflow told them no trains were coming, so for now, they simply walked along the floor of the tunnel, dodging rats and litter. Wires and pipes snaked along the walls on either side of them, and to their left, a concrete ledge for workmen waited should they need to get off the rails quickly.

"When I said 'deeper,' " Basile said, breaking the silence, "I didn't mean deeper underground. I meant more like ... deeper into this feeling. Right into the center of the in-between."

Edie noticed Marius's bulbs of light getting weaker but didn't think much of it. It was so dark, anyway, that even the barest light seemed bright. "And what happens when we get to the center?"

"Then we're the closest you've probably ever been to oblivion."

"Uh…" Adam cleared his throat and looked around. "Anyone ever read *Midnight Meat Train?*"

As soon as he spoke, Marius's orbs were extinguished completely.

CHAPTER EIGHTEEN

WHEN IT CAME TO PHOBIAS, Edie didn't consider herself afraid of the dark. Deep water, maybe. The stench of blood. But darkness was fine by her; she even found it calming in the right circumstances.

This darkness, however, was different.

In the complete absence of light, her eyes strained, trying to work for a scrap of illumination so they could adjust to the darkness. But they were gods only knew how many feet underground, inside the earth. They'd long since left light behind. There was nothing. Just an endless black void.

Her brain sent panic signals to her body: *No one will ever find you. The walls will close around you, pressing down on your bones until they warp. Your eyes will never see again. Your ears will never hear anything except the rusty razor sound of your parched-throat screaming—screaming for help that will never, never come.*

It took her a moment to realize that those thoughts were more than a primitive panic response. Her entire body seized as she felt something lukewarm slither under her jacket, up her arm, smooth and muscular like a snake.

You have to stay. We've been waiting for you for so, so long. We made this darkness for you, Edith ... all for you. Stay just like this, still, in your new home forever.

A fear she had never experienced before, even in the heat of battle, crawled up her spine. She could already feel her mind begin to slip, a shivering, maddening dismay gripping her just as surely as whatever had attached itself to her arm.

It was right. Just like an empty subway, if she wasn't perceived, she might as well not exist—and no one would ever perceive her again. She was trapped. The walls were pressing in...

From somewhere in the endless void before her, a scream echoed.

It brought her to her senses long enough that she was able to reach for the Puretongue's blade. With a cry of her own, she lashed out, slicing at the thing around her arm with a fury only terror could muster.

The thing retracted as her blade made contact, and a grating squeal rose somewhere faraway in the tunnel.

That was a terrible mistake, Edith. Now we are coming to you.

Edie staggered forward, arms out before her, trying to find Satara or Marius or anyone—but none of the people who had been right next to her seemed to be in arm's reach anymore. Her protective streak flared up.

"Coming to me?" she whispered, her voice nothing more than a trembling breath. "Where are you? Hurt my friends and I'll come to *you*."

She nearly jumped when, in her hand, the Puretongue's blade began to glow softly. It wasn't enough to illuminate the tunnel—it was barely enough for her to see a foot in front of her—but the sight of it was comforting. She felt a little confidence return to her as she reeled, trying to find a familiar face in the darkness.

From her left, she heard shuffling, and when she swung around, the blade's light just touched something black and glossy. It took her a second to realize it was a leather jacket.

Trotting forward, she found Adam lying on his side, eyes wide. His wrists and mouth had been bound with what looked like thick white rope. As she knelt and grabbed hold of the tentacle covering Adam's mouth, it pulsed; in her hand, its texture was more fleshlike than rubbery.

Screw this thing.

She pulled it taut and sliced it in half in one stroke, freeing Adam. The tentacle zipped from around his wrists as well and disappeared into the darkness. Another squeal drove into her mind like a railroad spike.

Stop hurting us...

"Not a fucking chance, asshole," Adam panted.

Edie helped him up. Thankfully, he and his guitar were still in one piece. "You can hear it, too?"

"I can hear it all right." His voice was strangled. "What the hell is that thing?"

"I don't know. But it knew my name."

"Mine, too." He shivered and squinted into the oppressive darkness. "Everyone else has to be around here somewhere. Right? They've gotta be."

She wished she could produce more light, but they'd have to make do with the blade. "Stay close to me," she whispered as she began to creep forward. "Try calling for them."

"Satara? Marius? Basile? If you can't talk, make a noise!"

A clanging somewhere to their right made them both jump, but they sped in its direction just as quickly. It wasn't long before Satara's kicking feet came into view, her steel-plated boots banging against the rails.

Before their eyes, a white appendage glided through the darkness and wrapped itself tightly around her ankles, stopping the noise. Hissing echoed through the tunnel.

Edie handed Adam the knife and murmured, "Start cutting." She rushed forward, braving a few feet of darkness so she could find Satara's upper half—almost completely wrapped in the fleshy ropes. With a deep breath, Edie summoned her magic. Blue fire ignited and skimmed across her palms in a thin layer as she seized the tentacles.

They pulsed and jerked under her hands. Screaming echoed in her mind, but she held fast. By the time the twitching limbs had rotted into dust, Adam had freed Satara's mouth and helped her up.

"Marius!" the shieldmaiden gasped, and gestured wildly ahead and to the left.

With Edie's help, she collected her fallen spear, and they crept forward in the darkness as a cluster.

It was only a few feet before they came across Marius. Edie was surprised to see Basile next to him, completely freed of his bindings. Marius, too, was unbound—and yet he faced the wall, perfectly still and silent.

The priest waved a hand in front of his face. "Hello? Earth to Auroran?" He glanced at the rest of the group as they crept closer, guided by the glowing dagger. "Hey. Is he broken?"

Edie frowned and took a couple steps forward, lingering behind Marius. After a moment of hesitation, she reached out to grab his shoulder. "Marius?"

A whimper escaped him—not a sound she had ever heard from him.

"It's just a trick," she said, daring to speak above a whisper. "Marius? You're okay. We're right here."

She pulled a little harder on his shoulder, trying to get him to turn around, and finally, he seemed to snap out of whatever was holding him. His eyes glowed a vibrant gold for a moment, darting around in the darkness before his gaze settled on Edie.

"What in the Wolfbinder's name is this?" His voice was scratchy. "How could you bring us here..."

Basile shrugged. "I didn't know they came up this far!"

"*What?*"

"Don't know exactly. I call them afterthoughts. They seem to be little manifestations of sorrow or abandonment or something. They love places like this ... and, uh, apparently this one is pretty powerful." He sighed. "We just need to get out of the tunnel. If we're on one of the platforms, it'll leave us alone."

"Why the *fuck* would that stop it?" Edie snapped. "Why'd you bring us into the subway at all if you knew something terrible was in it?"

Without warning, a fierce wind hit her left side. Her hair whipped her face, and a second later, a foul smell filled the tunnel. The smell of something that had been sitting and decaying for a long time. The word *forgotten* filled her head, and the feeling that came along with it was so intense that her heart seized, eyes beginning to water. She knew the wind wasn't an incoming train.

All we wanted was for you to stay still. You've been down here for too long. No one remembers you. No one needs you. Become nothing. Become us.

"We can talk about this later," Basile said tensely. "Everyone turn to your left and just start walking."

Adam stared at him. "Left? But that's where the wind is *coming* from."

"As long as we make it to the next platform, we'll be okay. But we won't be if we just stand here arguing about it!"

With no other options, they followed his orders, falling into line behind him.

It went against every instinct to walk *toward* the thing that was no doubt racing in their direction, and Edie's body wasn't letting it go without complaint. Chills racked her torso, and if her heart beat any faster, she thought she might pass out.

Almost there. You will see us soon.

With the dagger's glow beginning to fade, she couldn't *see* much of anything, but she could feel the track turning slightly to the left under her feet. They must be approaching a bend. She focused on keeping her steps in line with it.

Sure enough, within thirty paces or so, she started to make out shapes: the curve of the wall, blacker than the rest of the tunnel beyond; the ledge, which had become smaller, and its railing; distantly, a small light flickering against unpainted concrete and corrugated metal. A new platform?

Beside her, Adam looked behind them, then forward, seemingly calculating something. "If we're southbound from Hoyt ... this must be the Bergen St station. The lower platform has been abandoned for forty years, but they reroute the F train through it sometimes. Holy shit."

The wind picked up its pace, and the stench of it had become almost unbearable. Their group broke into a run to reach the platform before whatever was coming for them did.

We can see you. Running toward us. Into our embrace.

Beside Edie, Marius loosed a noise of frustration. "I keep trying to summon more light, but I ... can't. I can't even get my weapons. What *is* this thing?"

"Stop talking!" With a burst of inhuman speed, Basile reached the platform before any of them and hoisted himself up with a grunt. In the thin flicker of the maintenance light, Edie could just barely see him adjust his glasses before reaching both hands out for the next person.

Adam made it there first and in his frenzy barely needed the boost from Basile. Next was Satara, who was pulled up in less than a second by the other two. They hoisted Marius up next and—

And Edie found herself the last person standing in the tunnel.

The subway trembled all around them. Her breath came heavier, and she threw the dagger onto the platform first, not wanting to cut herself when she climbed up. She made to move forward, to grab the hands reaching for her, but...

Just one look.

She turned her head toward the wind and strained, trying to discern shapes within the solid black darkness of the subway tunnel. For a second, it was to no avail, and then—

"*Oh my god!*" When she glimpsed it, the words spilled from her lips.

She couldn't quite comprehend what she was looking at, only that it was a mess of flushed, moist white limbs twisted together in the shape of a huge humanoid. It lurched toward her, its form frenzied, untwisting and wriggling in places. If it had a face, it was completely obscured, bound by barbed wire and melted metal wreckage.

"Edie!" Before she could discern much more, arms encircled her chest and shoulders, hauling her onto the platform. As her feet went up over the ledge, the afterthought gave a grinding croak, and a tentacle shot toward her.

Darkness bathed the subway again.

The next thing Edie knew, she was sitting on cold concrete, her knees curled up to her chest. She could sense light behind her squeezed eyelids, and as she gasped for breath, she could no longer taste the rancid smell of the wind. It was another moment before she dared open her eyes.

She was on the platform, surrounded by the others. Basile, Satara, and Adam stood above her, trying to catch their breaths; Marius knelt next to her, holding her tightly in his arms as he searched her face.

The vivid lingered a beat before releasing her. "I thought you were gone for certain."

Edie shivered. After what they'd just witnessed, the last thing she wanted to be was *gone*.

"What did you see?" Adam asked as she stood.

What *had* she seen? How could she even begin to describe it? She shook her head. "I ... don't want to talk about it."

He nodded, brows drawing together.

"Sorry about that," Basile said absently, already roving around the platform and feeling the air. "Afterthoughts usually stick to the rail yards and abandoned bits. I suppose I should have known. But, we could've killed it if we had to."

Edie simply sighed, scrubbing her face with both hands. "I— let's not talk about it. I just ... let's move on."

"I'm afraid the place you're off to isn't much more pleasant." The priest clicked his tongue, adjusting his glasses with a smile. "Oh, this is a good spot. This will do very, very nicely."

Marius followed him with a suspicious gaze. "Nicely for what, exactly? You still haven't told us how you're planning on getting us into the Wending."

"Oh, I can open a portal fine *here*. That won't be a problem. A little reach-through, a little finagling ... yeah, that's not the problem at all."

"Then what is?"

"Ah ... well." Basile turned to them, and it was clear from his expression that his news wasn't good. "Here's the thing..."

Edie could already feel her blood pressure rising.

"The Wending isn't *for* the living. You wouldn't be able to process it, and it certainly wouldn't be able to process *you*. So ... you won't be able to enter it as living people. Per se."

Edie blinked. "And the alternative is...?"

"I don't think you'd like the alternative. But don't worry, I have a solution."

"Brilliant," Marius deadpanned.

The priest cut him a look. "What we need to do is trick the plane into thinking you're *not* living. Now, I did some research, and there's only one surefire way of doing this without potentially actually killing you. I'll need to take a part of each of your souls. Just a small part should do the trick."

"Take a part of our souls?" Edie repeated. "You *just lost* one!"

Satara frowned. "How are you planning on flaying a part of our souls without consuming them? Edie's right; struggling with that is how you lost Elle."

"Ah. I'll use this." Basile pulled his messenger bag to his front and produced something from it—a diamond prism of what seemed to be clear, if slightly frosty, glass.

Edie recognized the object at once, despite the fact that it wasn't fashioned into a necklace. "You ... have a keeper paragon? An actual keeper paragon?"

He lifted his brows, apparently surprised that she knew what it was. "I have others."

"Others?" She gaped in exasperation. "Do you know what I had to go through to get one of those things?"

Basile shrugged. "Being a priest of the god of magic and secrets has its perks, I guess."

Though they were all clearly on edge, Satara looked most disturbed. That made sense, given the last time she'd seen one of these things, Indriði had used it to obliterate Astrid. "Are you going to use it to trap our fylgjur, or some other part of our souls?"

"I'm not that well versed in time magic, so I'm not sure I could even *find* your fylgjur. I'll just see what I can trim off here and there, from various parts." He held the paragon up to the light. "I should be able to fit you all in just this one. I don't need to take that much."

Adam stared at him. "This whole operation is just jerry-rigged from start to finish, isn't it?"

"We're not supposed to be able to do this at all, so be grateful for what you have." The priest nodded around at the group. "Ready?"

There was a heavy silence for a moment. Finally, Marius broke it, shaking his head. "I'm ... sorry, but I can't. I can't do this."

Basile raised a brow.

"I can't allow you to take my soul," Marius continued more firmly, brow twitching. "And I shouldn't allow you to take theirs, either, not after what we saw happen with Elle."

The priest sighed. "I *know* I screwed up; you don't have to keep reminding me. But this is different. Souls don't wanna go back in their bodies, but they like keeper paragons."

"How do we even know we can trust you?" The vivid jerked his head in Edie and Satara's direction. "They've been tricked before."

"Marius—"

Adam rubbed his brow, shaking again. "I'm still going, even if I have to go alone. I have to get Elle. It's the only way."

"Sometimes people die, Adam." Marius fixed him with an intense stare. "It's not worth getting yourself killed over, too."

Satara sighed. "We can't let him go alone. I trust the priest."

Edie considered her for a moment before nodding in agreement.

Their answers didn't seem to satisfy the vivid, who crossed his arms, pursing his lips grimly. "I'm sorry. Even if I was certain you were trustworthy, splitting my soul goes against my oaths. I'm no lich. There are limits to what I'll do."

Adam exhaled hard and looked to Edie pleadingly.

She shook her head. Marius had made up his mind, and he was certainly being less reckless than the rest of them—which was a first for him. He must be very wary of Basile. "Okay. I can't make you help."

"I said I won't let him split my soul. I never said I wouldn't help." Marius glanced at the priest. "I will stay behind and make sure Father Bolet doesn't ... taste of your souls."

That was a good idea, actually. But one less fighter on their team didn't bode well. Hopefully she was right and they wouldn't run into anything too horrible.

"Have it your way." Basile turned to the others. "What about the rest of you ungrateful chumps?"

One by one, sharing reluctant looks, those remaining accepted. What else could they do?

With a nod, the priest shouldered his messenger bag aside, holding the keeper paragon in both hands. He closed his eyes and began a ritual Edie and Satara were unfortunately familiar with. As he whispered, an eerie blueish light misted around each of them, slowly flowing from their veins out into the open. The paragon filled with the glow, casting strange shadows around the abandoned station, and a peculiar feeling shuddered through Edie—one she recognized.

It hadn't been that long since Indriði had convinced her that the only way she could unlock her powers was through empowering her fylgja, the guardian spirit connected to her soul. She'd gone so far as to let Indriði capture her fylgja briefly, and having it outside her body had felt much like this. She felt naked. Disturbed. Anxious, like something terrible was coming for her.

She noted, too, how much weaker she felt, like she'd had a bad night's sleep and little to eat. Across from her, Adam became even more wan before. She couldn't help but wonder if he'd even make it through this journey.

With the paragon now full and glowing like a tiny star, the priest wrapped it in a bit of cloth before depositing it gingerly in his bag. Then, he pulled something else out. He held it tightly in his hands, such that Edie couldn't quite see what it was.

"I have to stay on this side and keep the portal open, but since you'll have even less an idea of what you're doing than usual, I figured we needed something to communicate." He held the object up in one hand so they could see it clearly.

"Oh, good," Adam croaked. "A pretty princess tiara."

"It's a *circlet*, and if you don't stop dissing my magical artifacts, I'll make you wear it." Basile turned to Edie and placed it in her hand. "Put it on and I'll be able to see what you see, and talk to you."

With a little reluctance, Edie placed the circlet on her head. The silver was cold against her forehead. A moment later, a thin sheen of glittering magic surrounded her. It didn't seem to mute any of her senses, though, and within a few seconds, she barely even noticed it was there.

The priest assessed her before nodding in approval, then turned and said grimly, "Okay. It's time."

He felt the air again, and when he seemed satisfied, drew a small, curved knife from his bag, its blade etched with tiny runes. They glowed as he empowered them with his own magic, and Edie watched in fascination—and a little horror—as he grabbed ... reality.

She wasn't sure what to make of what she was seeing. He had grabbed within the air, something she couldn't see—and yet he'd caused a distortion around the area, incomprehensible to her brain.

"I'll have to reach through and trigger the proper response from the plane. Us being here isn't enough if we're not spirits." Under his breath, he added, "This whole damn operation is jerry-rigged, why not another thing?"

With one quick stroke, he sliced a hole through existence. It opened much like torn fabric would, and beyond, Edie could see what she thought was the starry midnight sky. But it shifted and morphed and changed, sometimes streaked with colors like an aurora borealis, sometimes dark like the night.

A terrible sound came from the fissure. Or, rather, a terrible lack of sound. The vastness of the silence pouring out reminded her of the vast silence of the Atlantic Ocean, when she had been trapped so deep under its waves ... no sound but the pressure of her own blood in her ears...

She shivered and hugged herself, watching uneasily as Basile reached into the void without a bit of hesitation. He groped around like he was trying to get at something that was just out of his reach.

After a few moments, his frustrated expression turned to one of relief, and he seemed to tug down on something before withdrawing his hand. "There we are."

Before Edie could ask what exactly he'd just done, a horrible wind filled the tunnel, coming from the same direction as the wind from before. For a second, her whole body seized, wondering if the afterthought had decided to come back for more. But no, she could hear other sounds besides the wind, now. Clattering. Squealing.

A train?

She looked toward the edge of the platform. They'd been slinking through the tunnels for a while now, and no trains had come this way, so she'd assumed the route had been diverted. "Where ... is that coming from?"

Her question was answered soon enough. A weak yellow light filled the tunnel, and when she peered down it, she could see two dingy headlamps approaching them. Debris seemed to be falling off the train even as it sped toward the station, its body slightly lopsided on the tracks and shuddering like it might fall apart.

When it finally pulled into the station and ground to a stop, Edie could hardly believe what she was looking at. The sight of it, the smell...

It was an old train, probably mid-century, but was barely recognizable as such. It was filthy, caked with dirt and smoky grime. Its rivets and siding wept rust, and it seemed to be decaying, the metal corroded to the point of having large holes eaten here and there. The stench was a mixture of rot and mildew, and Edie found herself wishing she'd brought a scarf or something to cover her face.

With a hiss, the discolored doors of the train parted.

Basile turned to them solemnly. "Choo choo. All aboard."

CHAPTER NINETEEN

As Edie boarded the ghostly train, the hair on the back of her neck stood up, chills racing down her arms. The smell of the car was even fouler on the inside.

Am I really doing this right now?

"Hold on tight!" Basile called behind them, and she looked back to see him and Marius standing almost shoulder to shoulder.

She met the vivid's eyes—gilded, lit with concern and something she couldn't quite place. Her heart twinged, and she waved as Adam and Satara passed her.

Then, the doors slid shut. Grime caked the windows, but through a rusty hole in the side of the subway car, Edie could see Marius turn away with a muttered curse.

The train shuddered and started, jerking down the rails for a few moments before finding its clumsy, off-kilter footing. She tore her eyes away from the hole and examined her surroundings.

The interior of the car was just as disgusting as the outside had been, coated with rust, mud, and a strange, organic sort of filth. Almost *bloody*. She had been in gross places before, seen and smelled dirt and gore, even been covered in it—but there was something unsettling about this filth.

Without knowing where it had come from, she could sense it was like a disease, a corruption. This filth spread on its own. If she listened closely, under the clapping of the train against the track, she could almost ... *hear* it. Crawling. Breeding.

Loath to touch anything, she planted her feet as best she could and shifted her weight against the train. Near her, Satara was in the same predicament; she stood near one of the poles and wedged it between her arm and her shield to keep her hands clean.

Adam, on the other hand ... though he seemed to acknowledge the filth, it didn't stop him. He sat heavily on one of the benches and put his head in his hands, shoulders rising and falling evenly as he took deep breaths.

Edie tried to exchange a look with Satara, but the shieldmaiden had already fixed him with a concerned gaze. "Are you all right?" she asked.

"I'm..." Adam raised his head, tugging on his guitar strap. "I don't like the idea that Elle had to ride this thing to get ... where she is now." Under his breath, he added, "Makes me wonder what the Wending is like."

They fell quiet again, and Edie broke her stance a moment later to walk to the other end of the car. They were the only passengers on this car, but when she looked out the window at the end, she could see into the one behind them. And there were people there.

Or what she thought were people. From where she stood, they were only faceless white-gray forms. They sat, mostly, but some stood, all with their heads bowed. The sight of them made her spine crawl, but she couldn't seem to look away.

"Edie!"

The voice made her jump. Basile. She glanced around, then realized the aura that had fallen around her previously was shimmering. He was speaking to her through the circlet.

"Don't look at those," he continued. "Just go back to where you were and keep your eyes ahead."

The tone of his voice sent a spike of panic through her, and she averted her eyes at once, turning back around.

Around them, the dingy train windows were completely black, but not with the close darkness of a tunnel. This darkness seemed ... more vast, somehow, and she could *hear* things in the beyond. A strange bubbling or murmuring, and a distant keening sound. Between those, a deep, cold, resounding silence, like what had poured from Basile's tear in reality.

Once again, she was reminded of the ocean off the coast of Maine. If something happened and they were lost in this void, would she be able to find which way was up? Or was there a riptide to pull her down here, too?

Without warning, the thundering of the train on the rails disappeared. Their ride felt smoother, suddenly skating noiselessly as if through open air. Edie gasped as the car around them began to shake, and instinctively, she reached out to grab one of the hanging straps.

Her gaze shot to her companions, but the lights flickered. She could barely make out Adam and Satara holding on for dear life before the car was plunged into complete and utter darkness.

The shaking continued, and Edie cried out into the dark. Her mind whirled with pleas and prayers and panicked questions. Was it happening sooner than she thought—the void taking them?

But a few long, terrifying seconds later, the lights flickered on again. Her feet felt steadier under her, and as she looked around at the others and their surroundings—all in one piece, thank whatever gods were listening—she realized the train had stopped.

The doors groaned open, revealing a new station, and stayed that way. Slowly, like newborn fawns, the group staggered out onto the platform.

The station around them was eerily familiar, almost a mirror image of the one they had left behind. Just like the train, it was dirty and decaying, even by NYC standards. As she walked forward, Edie spared a glance at the open doors of the car next to theirs, expecting to see the creepy figures she'd seen through the window. There were none.

Wordlessly, the group left the platform, starting up the stained stairs.

The lights were dim, yellowed and dirt-caked, and the bloody corruption climbing the walls and carpeting the floor pulsed and writhed as they passed it. Here and there, Edie noticed gray lumps breaking up the filth. It wasn't until she saw an ashen-skinned figure shuffling on one of the upper-floor platforms that she realized they were people. Lost souls who hadn't even made it out of the subway, swallowed up.

The smell was vile, smoky and tangy. She tamped down the horror welling inside of her and climbed, climbed, climbed, desperate for a breath of fresh air.

But even as they crept up the last set of stairs and breached the pavement, there was no fresh air to be had. They found themselves in a small paved court, boxed in by tall buildings. The world around them was dark and shining; above, there was no night sky, only dark gray clouds.

It was impossible to tell anything distinct about this place. There was hardly any light but a faint, muted blue glow from an alley to the street, beckoning them forward.

Edie looked to the others as they walked toward it, wanting to ask if anyone had a plan, but it felt too strange to talk here. Like in her reoccurring dream. She couldn't shake the fear that if the silence was broken, something would be alerted.

When they came to the end of the alley and turned the corner, though, she couldn't help but gasp at what she saw.

The city laid out before them was a decomposing nightmarescape. The dark buildings, huddled together, defied reality as Edie knew it: broken apart, the pieces still drifting near where they had crumbled off; stairs and fire escapes upside down and backwards, with ashen figures still sitting on them as though they were rightside up. Blue mist shimmered within the ruin, snaking around the debris like settling dust.

All around them, chunks of the road had been lifted, hovering lopsidedly over the craters they had left behind—some quite high in the sky and some just a few inches out of place, making the road pitted and uneven. Fissures in the asphalt glowed, leaking a bluish-purple energy. A constant low fog curled around Edie's ankles, and the sky above was dark and stormy, the roiling gray streaked with the same color as the magic seeping from the ground.

Ghostly wind whistled through broken stone, the only sound nearby; in the distance, what sounded like rolling thunder and the groan of distressed metal echoed through the entire city. From where they stood, this place seemed to stretch on forever.

Beside Edie, Adam was the first to break the silence, his voice soft with awe. "What is this place?"

The aura around her shimmered, and Basile's voice answered: "This ... this is nowhere."

At those words, Edie's heart clenched.

Uncertainly, they walked forward, glass and gravel crunching under their feet. The vulnerable, naked feeling of being without part of her soul intensified in Edie, almost bringing tears to her eyes. This place was not right. If they got lost here, they would never get home. Time would end before they found their way.

"This isn't really what I expected," Adam murmured, eyes lingering on the floating cement and debris. "With all the Norse stuff and fantasy creatures, I thought it'd be ... I don't know. Not a city."

Basile's voice rose around Edie again. "It didn't always look like this. And it doesn't look exactly like this everywhere, for everyone. It's complicated."

Satara raised her head and nodded. "I read about something like that recently. It said the universe is adapting to modern humans' presence, with the way we've separated ourselves from everything else. We are ... permanently changing the tapestry of existence." She looked above, brows drawing together. "If the Wending is all about eternal travel and being lost, then it must reflect modern ideas of what that means—never resting, never going home..."

Edie shivered. She tried to remind herself that they would be okay—they were living, not dead, and they had Basile to guide them—but she couldn't shake a niggling feeling of foreboding. Adam was right: this entire thing was jerry-rigged. Anything could go wrong at this point.

If Basile made a mistake, they'd pay the price.

They continued along the street for a while, mostly silent. This place was much bigger than Basile had made it sound, and the realization that they had no idea how to *find* Elle was beginning to set in. Where did you even start looking in a place like this?

Edie was about to ask but was cut off by a sudden tremor in the ground below them, one that threw them all off-balance. A metallic groan accompanied it, like a piece of old heavy machinery—too close for comfort. The noise thundered through the broken cityscape, pinging off buildings and narrow passages and creating a fierce echo.

Edie spun, trying to find the source of the noise, but it seemed to vibrate from every inch of concrete and steel around them. The tremors continued, and it wasn't until she looked up at the sky that she realized what was causing them.

Her breath caught in her throat. Without thinking, she grabbed Adam, pushing him and Satara into the darkened doorway of a nearby apartment building.

"What are—"

Edie cut him off, clamping a hand across his mouth. He shot her an indignant look. Then, his eyes caught on the *thing* behind her, and his gaze filled with terror as it drifted up toward the sky.

To say the thing was looming above them was not entirely accurate. In fact, it seemed to be standing several hundred feet away. But its sheer size gave the impression that it was gazing down from much closer and made Edie think it could probably still see them.

In form, it was similar to a human skeleton—a skull, ribs, limbs, a spine—but the proportions were all wrong. For starters, it had to be three hundred feet tall at least. The skull was slightly too small, the shoulders too broad, the arms and spine too long; there were too many ribs, and the points of each vertebra extended in bony spikes. It had stopped walking, and white light glowed from within its head as it observed the city streets below it, uncomfortably long neck craning down, then scanning left to right.

Edie flattened herself against the splintered door of the apartment building, holding her breath. That low metallic whine echoed again as the thing's head moved and it began to walk. It came closer but moved left, and was out of their sight within fifteen seconds.

Still, Edie didn't move an inch. Whatever that thing was, she didn't want to run into it. Fine dust fell from the buildings around them with every earthshaking footstep. It wasn't until the dust stopped falling and the tremors faded that she finally allowed herself to breathe.

Beside her, Satara exhaled slowly, still watching the corner of the sky where the skeleton had disappeared. After a moment, she asked, "And what was *that*?"

The air around Edie shimmered, and Basile spoke: "*That* is what's known as a Coveter. I'd hoped you'd get lucky and not run into one."

"Where did it come from?" Edie asked, daring to take a step past the doorway. In the distance, she could see its retreating form, its head bowed watchfully.

"No one's sure how they got here, not even the gods. Maybe they've always been part of the Wending. In any case, they serve as sort of ... the jailers of this plane. When they're not feeding off the lost souls, they roam around looking for people who shouldn't be here."

"Great," Adam said under his breath. "Giant skeletons. Why not?"

Edie had to agree. They'd just arrived and she was already done with this place.

She looked to the others. "There's no way we'd be able to take one of those things on. They're the size of the Statue of Liberty, for Christ's sake. We need to find Elle's soul and get the hell out of Dodge."

"Agreed." Satara sighed and glanced at Edie's circlet. "How are we supposed to track her?"

Basile's voice came through. "I figured we'd use whatever residual soul energy is left in that guitar. Do you sense any vibrations, Adam?"

The hellerune pulled the guitar across his chest, glancing up and down its length. "I ... guess maybe a little."

"What direction is it coming from?"

He seemed to concentrate for a moment, then shook his head, frustration creeping into his voice. "I don't know, I can't tell. It's faint."

There was a pause from the circlet, then another shimmer. "We're gonna have to get closer to her."

"*How*? We don't have time to play Hot and Cold with my dead kid's soul."

Another pause. "Well, souls are trapped here, but they still have a measure of sentience. They still act like people, and they can still be guided. If you could draw her to you somehow..."

Edie looked between Adam and Satara. "We could go around yelling her name?"

"Maybe," Satara said, "but look at how much ground we'd have to cover."

"It's not like we have a better option to get her attention. And I don't think we should split up."

Adam looked deep in thought for a few moments, fiddling with his guitar strings. Then, suddenly, his head snapped up. "I have an idea." His hazel eyes were bright with determination. "But ... it's kind of crazy."

"My favorite kind of idea," said Basile's voice.

Satara rolled her eyes. "Clearly."

Adam did a three-sixty, craning his neck to look up at the buildings around them. He seemed to consider his options before pointing up, past Edie and Satara, at one of the crumbling apartments—one of the only ones to have maintained its upper floors, taller than the others.

"If I go up there and play something she recognizes..." He lowered his hand and returned it to the neck of the Genesis. "The guitar worked without an amp when her soul was inside it, so ... maybe it won't matter here, either." He glanced between them uncertainly. "If the sound carries and she hears it, maybe she'll come?"

Edie frowned. "Yeah, but maybe something *else* will hear it and come." She gestured toward where the Coveter was still retreating. "What then?"

"I don't know, there are a lot of weird sounds in this place." Adam looked at Satara pleadingly. "Shouting would be just as likely to get their attention, right? And this might travel farther."

The shieldmaiden was quiet for a moment, turning to assess the building before glancing at Edie. "We could stand watch. If one of those things starts toward us on the horizon, we'd have plenty of warning, Lady knows."

Edie couldn't help the dread simmering in her heart. There were a million things that could go wrong here, and the plan might not even work. But they'd already taken great pains to get here; at this point, she was determined not to leave empty-handed.

She sighed at Adam. "Please don't get us killed."

With nothing more than a nod, he sprang into action at once, jogging past her with the Genesis now slung across his back like a rifle. She followed close behind, the splash of their combat boots in oily puddles and the jingling of Satara's armor the only sounds between them.

In a hundred yards, they came to the door of the building, covered by thick, dark boards. They seemed secure, but as Adam grabbed them to tear them off, they crumbled like charred firewood in his hands and fell to dust at his feet. After a pause, he disappeared into the void beyond. By the time Edie did the same, he was already climbing a cement staircase.

Gravel crunched under their feet as they made their way up. The staircase hugged the wall on one side, climbing up steeply, but the other side was open, with no handrail or guard. Edie stuck close to the wall, trying to match Adam's haste.

As they reached the door to the roof and burst through, she found herself gasping for breath. The air here was wrong. It didn't feel like she could ever get enough of it in her lungs, even when they wouldn't expand any more.

The view from up here was just as disconcerting, but it at least gave them a bigger picture. The city was broken and huddled, buildings leaning on each other, most streets no more than labyrinthine warrens. Ashen figures dotted the landscape here and there, scurrying between buildings or sitting on roofs, fire escapes, debris. She watched as a spirit trotted along the broken concrete and walked up a wall, never breaking stride or slowing down. After a moment, it disappeared into the ether.

She looked away, unable to suppress a shiver. The gray sky stretched on for an eternity, heavy and rolling without reprieve. In the distance, she could count the forms of several Coveters, and her heart dropped. She drifted to the edge of the roof to look to the west; when she glanced over her shoulder, she saw Satara had done the same on the opposite side.

Adam stood between them, staring out at the city with the Genesis in hand. Then, after another glance back and a deep breath, he began to play.

A long, keening note tore through the silence suddenly, the vibrations of it shaking the pebbles at Edie's feet. She could feel the noise carry far, snaking through the wreckage as Adam carved his melody—rugged and dark, but sad, longing. The opening riff of one of DB's first albums, if she wasn't mistaken. Nervously, she scanned the skyline, her ears ringing with the force of the tune.

It was so loud from where she stood that she almost didn't notice Satara say her name. She turned her head and froze.

Adam's head was bent while he focused on his melody, but his guitar was ... at first, she thought it was *smoking*. As he played, wisps of white energy coiled around his hands, slowly spreading to wrap around his body as well. Dark purple energy soon joined it. She didn't have to be holding the guitar to feel the vibrations coming from it; she could sense the power from where she stood.

And as she looked all around them, she noticed that the ashen figures had stopped to stare up at them. Just like her dream in the woods, when she could feel the eyes of the trees on her ... she had broken the silence, and something primordial and ancient had acknowledged her presence.

The spirits seemed confused and shy. The bolder ones flickered onto the roof with them, but only for brief seconds before flitting away again. She caught glimpses of one or two drifting by or above to see what was happening. Scraps of voices, mostly gibberish, caught in her brain. But by and large, the spirits avoided them, simply watching. A few even fled, disappearing from sight altogether.

Edie turned her gaze back to the skyline. Far in the distance, a few Coveters lingered; one had tipped its head as if to listen. Her heart jumped into her throat, and from between clenched teeth, a prayer leaked: "Come on, Elle, please..."

The sound of energy ratcheting up caught her attention, and she glanced toward the sky. A streak of bright blue mist had appeared above their heads and was darting between them intelligently, checking each one of them out. Another spirit, but ... brighter than the others.

"Elle?" she called, turning.

The blue mist paused before dropping to the ground and quickly coalescing into a figure. The figure was blurry at first; she was only able to make out their big boots, their T-shirt, and a mohawk. Finally, the image sharpened.

Edie's jaw dropped. She tried to say something to Adam, but there were no words.

The other hellerune must have sensed a change, though. Abruptly, his melody died in the air, and he turned to face the ghost.

It wasn't Elle, but they—both of them—recognized his face. Standing before them, completely lifelike save for desaturated coloring, was Mikey Mausoleum.

CHAPTER TWENTY

EDIE LOOKED between the two men standing in front of her. Adam's face had turned almost as gray as the specter's.

It was probably safe to say none of them had seen this coming. For a moment, Edie wondered if it was some sort of mistake.

But no, this ghost looked exactly like Death Benefits' late drummer. Same mohawk—usually candy-apple red but only a tinted gray here— same disheveled appearance, unlaced boots. His youthful, almost feminine face was worn and tired, framed with stubble. But his large brown eyes were alert, much more so than the other spirits here, and when he looked at Adam, they lit up with recognition.

Adam was the first to blurt out, his voice cracking, "*Mikey?*"

The spirit responded with an easy smile and a laid-back "Oh, hey, man," like they had just bumped into each other casually, not after a decade and in a plane of lost souls.

If nothing else, Mikey's reaction was disarming. Even Adam, who seemed constantly on the edge of a meltdown, relaxed when his old friend spoke, straightening up. He slung the Genesis over his shoulder again, awed and numb. "Mikey ... is that seriously you?"

"Yeah, it's me!" The spirit looked down at himself, fingering his oversized T-shirt. "I *think* it's me. Everything looks like it's in the right place..."

Even dead, he sounded stoned out of his mind. Edie took a step forward, glancing over at Satara. She had turned toward the others, too, watching cautiously.

"Mikey." Adam couldn't seem to find any other words. In one swift motion, he stepped forward and drew the shorter man into a tight hug.

To Edie's surprise, he was perfectly capable. Despite Mikey's ghostly appearance, he was corporeal, standing still in Adam's arms for a moment. Then he returned the hug, squeezing him and patting him on the back. "Wow, you look different." The drummer's voice was muffled by Adam's shoulder. "Like, all old 'n' shit."

Adam pulled back, looking down at him with a huffed laugh. But his calmness couldn't last forever, and soon, his brow furrowed, eyes shining. The implications of Mikey's presence here were starting to overtake the shock of seeing him. "What the hell are you doing here, man?"

"I dunno," Mikey replied pleasantly, gazing around the Wending like one might gaze around a Target. "I heard you playing our song, so I came to see. Where am I again?"

"You're in the Wending," Satara said as she approached. "It's where the souls of the dead go when they get lost."

His big eyes got bigger. "Whoa. That's *fucked up.*"

She hesitated before asking carefully, "You ... you know what happened to you, don't you?"

"Yeah!"

When he said nothing else, Adam prompted, "What happened? How did you get here?"

"Oh." Mikey nodded along, looking between him and Satara. "Well, the last time I went to sleep, I think I took too many pills. Usually it's okay if I make a mistake and take too many ... I just sleep a long time." He shrugged helplessly. "Then I woke up and wanted to go to the bodega to get some candy and booze? But I couldn't find the right way."

"Did you ride a train?" Edie asked.

"Yeah ... I tried to go somewhere else, but I couldn't find my stop." He pulled a face at Adam. "Man, the MTA really needs to put more money into cleaning the subway or something. It was totally grody."

The air around Edie shimmered, and Basile mumbled, "I want whatever this guy's having."

The heartbreak in Adam's face was obvious. "Mikey ... do you know you're...?"

"Dead?" the spirit finished forlornly. "Yeah, I kinda guessed after seeing all the spooky shit around here..." He perked up, tilting his head. "How'd you know?"

Adam's brows raised, drawn tightly together. "Mikey, I was there. I ... watched you die. Do you— do you even know how long it's been?"

Mikey shook his head. "Nope! Time feels all weird here. And no one has a watch or a cell phone or anything."

"It's been a while," Adam said, voice thick. "A little over ten years."

"Oh." The spirit considered that before smiling widely. "I guess that explains why you look like my dad." Then, for the first time, he seemed to fully register Edie, looking between her and Satara. "Who are the cute chicks?"

"Um, this is Edie, and this is Satara." Adam gestured to them in turn. "Satara, this is my ... former drummer. You're not, you know, *concerned* about having been in a plane of lost souls for over a decade?"

Mikey shrugged. "Can't go back and fix it now. Plus, I was all dead and stuff, so it's not like I missed anything. Except the fact that you're dead now, too, I guess." To his credit, pain crossed his face at that thought. "How'd it happen?"

"I'm not dead." Adam sighed heavily. "It's a long story. Basically, Ellie got stuck here on accident. We need to find her so we can bring her back."

"You can do that?" Mikey blinked, grinning crookedly. "Gnarly."

"Hopefully."

Edie nodded toward Adam. "He was playing that song hoping she'd recognize it and come."

"Yeah! But I came instead!" After a second, his grin died. "Uh, sorry. Do we need to play it again?"

"We might not need to," Satara said. "Have you seen Elle here? Could you take us to her?"

"Elle's here?"

Adam ran a hand down his face and sighed. "I just told you that, dude."

"Oh, right." Mikey smiled again, looking around lackadaisically, like he might spot Elle nearby. When he didn't, his smile turned to frustration instead. "I dunno where she is … I haven't seen her. Buuuut you were playing that thing pretty loud, so she probably heard it. Maybe she's busy?"

"Or trapped somewhere," Edie suggested, rubbing her upper arms.

"Ohhh, yeah!" The spectral drummer nodded, jerking a thumb over his shoulder. "I've seen those big skeleton dudes take people away. They put 'em in these big cages, I think. I followed one and saw it one time, but then … I can't remember what happened."

"Soul cages," came Basile's voice, along with the telltale shimmer from Edie's circlet. "I've seen them, too. No idea why they cage some souls and eat others, but … if you find Elle in one and get her, we can figure things out from there."

Mikey boggled at Edie. "Your hat is talking!"

"Where are they, Basile?" she asked.

"Beats me. This place looks nothing like I remember it. They used to be at the— Well, who knows what else has changed? Ask Space Case."

Edie turned to the space case in question, eyeing him up and down apprehensively. "Do you remember where you saw the cages?"

He frowned thoughtfully, swaying until he had considered the skyline in each direction. Finally, he shrugged, pointing behind Adam and Satara. "I guess we could follow that guy."

Edie spun, barely choking back a scream. Much closer than any of them had realized, a Coveter peered around a decaying skyscraper, neck craning searchingly. *How the hell did it get so close so quietly?* Edie's brain screamed, sending jolts of panic through her limbs.

The white light in the Coveter's skull pulsed, and a mournful whine rent the air.

"Hide," Adam hissed, and darted to slide behind the brick around the roof access door. Edie followed suit, and Satara split from them, concealing herself behind the central pipe of a rusted water tower. Mikey watched them go before turning into the same ball of light he'd arrived as, zooming over the edge of the roof and out of sight.

Edie pressed herself to the brick, trying to regulate her breathing. She could hear the creak of the Coveter's bones moving, the faint hum of the energy working inside of it. She had never been hunted like this—even in her dream, when the wolf chased her, she knew she could fight back. But against this thing, as tall as a building? Never.

The ground shook, the gravel at her feet jumping and trembling as the Coveter finally moved. Its shadow fell over them, and her body burned, a primal numbness overtaking her. She had to stay still. For all she was worth, she had to stay still. She had to get back home to Mercy. To Cal.

The shadow grew deeper. The tenements shook, raining fine dust, their steel beams protesting dully. The Coveter's form emerged from around the corner, and Edie cast her eyes down. It was *so close*. Its malformed hip bone alone, which was just level with the roof, was so massive it made her head spin.

And so she didn't look at it. She looked at the gravel, and watched it jump, and prayed.

It was hard to say how long it was before the gravel stopped jumping. The adrenaline and the Wending's strange air made it impossible to tell if it had been a few minutes or an hour. But when Edie finally looked up, the Coveter was gone, disappeared between the skyscrapers.

"How the hell did it sneak up on us?" Adam asked breathlessly beside her.

Mikey's ball of light rolled onto the roof and formed into a person again. He looked them over, then saw Satara round the corner and grinned. "Hey, he didn't see any of you!"

"Well, good," came Basile's voice. "Great exercise, team."

Edie finally allowed herself to relax, exhaling slowly.

"Captain Burnout could've made more of an effort not to get you all killed," the priest continued, "but his idea isn't bad. Try to follow that thing at a distance and see where it goes. Let's just ... not linger."

"Are we even fast enough to follow it?" Satara wondered aloud. "We aren't spirits like you, Mikey."

Edie's circlet glittered again, and Basile chuckled. "But you've got wings, remember? And, hell, the hellerunan can shadow jump. Easy peasy. Get moving!"

Edie balked. "What the hell is shadow jumping?"

The shieldmaiden glanced over critically, but Adam apparently knew what he had to do, his toes already at the edge of the roof. In a second, he had leapt off, Mikey trailing after him with a whoop.

Edie's chest clenched as she watched him fall, and she rushed forward like she thought she might be able to catch him. But in the blink of an eye, he was gone. It took her a moment to spot him at the base of the building across the narrow street, a form of solid black with shadows coiling around it.

He had hit the ground running, the shadow magic melting away from his body as he turned to look back up at them. He couldn't seem to find words, but his eyes were wide.

"It's like he's eager to get himself killed," Satara mumbled.

Edie wasn't sure that was entirely inaccurate. She simply shook her head and peered over the edge again. Every instinct screamed for her to turn around and take the stairs instead ... but by now, she was starting to get used to ignoring her body when it told her to stop. She took a breath and called, "Okay, how do I do this thing?"

"I can feel the shadows," he called back. "Just ... look for the right one and send yourself to it, meld with it."

Ugh. Usually, she would have bristled at such vague instructions, but somehow, almost begrudgingly, she knew what he meant. It had taken her months to learn how to harness death magic, let alone shadow, which she had barely touched, but perhaps the energy of this plane unlocked something in her. In any case, she *could* feel the shadows. She could reach out and touch them with her mind.

With a sigh, she sat on the edge of the roof, took another deep breath, and slipped off.

Her heart and stomach rebelled at the feeling of dropping. Even though she had seen Adam jump and knew very well that she could, too, she couldn't help the thought that ran through her mind once she was free-falling: *Well, that was a mistake.*

In fact, she was almost surprised when, as she fumbled for the shadows across the street, the world shifted abruptly, darkness curling in her vision. Her momentum disappeared completely, and the shadow magic washed over her skin like cool, soothing water. The next thing she knew, she stood on the pavement under a broken awning, both femurs still in one piece.

She shivered, adjusting her jacket as she went to stand next to Adam. Satara wasn't far behind, using her outstretched wings to glide to the ground. She landed with a wince and a light rain of feathers, and horror spiked in Edie's chest.

If nothing else, they had to expedite this so Satara could get the help she needed. Edie closed her eyes and turned, beckoning the others behind her.

When she opened her eyes again, it was as though a switch had flipped. The shadows crawling up the walls and across the broken asphalt had changed, no longer ghostly, transparent shapes. They were a deep black edged with purple flames, pulsing with life and exuding a deep, clean, soothing cold. Edie exhaled slowly from her mouth and eyed the closest one. She began to lift her hand, as if to reach for it—

—and she was there. Magic washed over her skin again, darkness closing in briefly before coiling away. Though to her eyes she stood in a void, she didn't fall. She glanced back at the others, thirty feet behind her now, then focused forward.

She felt rather than heard Adam materialize behind her, his magic colliding with hers with a hiss, and she reached for the next shadow. With a bit of effort, she was able to pull herself into the dark, living mass.

Soon, they were jumping ahead every few seconds, the sound of wings beating the air close behind. The streets twisted and turned, never consistent, never leading where they seemed like they should. It was Mikey's brightly glowing spirit alone that seemed able to parse direction —maybe because he was attuned to this place. Or maybe his perpetually stoned nature gave him some backwards insight.

As they wove through the warrens of the Wending's sagging tenements, slowly, the ground beneath them began to tremble, and Edie knew they must be gaining on the Coveter.

As the shadows cleared from her vision, she looked up and spotted it striding between two skyscrapers. That metallic whine rent the air again, fainter due to its distance, and the Coveter craned its neck to peer into one of the windows.

"These creepy fucking things are ... unnatural," Edie breathed as Satara touched down beside her, following her gaze. "Look at how it moves."

"No," the shieldmaiden murmured. "They are natural, in the purest sense of the word. Innate to this plane, as old as the universe itself."

Edie shivered. Satara was right, but she didn't want to think about it. She jumped again, following Adam, and caught his arm, pointing to a shorter building the Coveter had just passed. It was in the shadow of a skyscraper, and a purple-ringed void climbed the side and spread onto the roof. "Let's get a better vantage point."

He nodded and was gone in the next blink. Edie signaled to Mikey and Satara, and within a few seconds, they had all flown to the top of the building.

Adam was already standing at the edge, still with awe. As they approached, he half-turned and pointed at the horizon. "What the hell is that?"

Mikey coalesced beside him, expression brightening. "Oh, yeah, now I remember!"

Before them, the Wending rambled on, a flat land of the same dark, rotting buildings they had been blazing past. Skyscrapers rose up here and there, though most of them had lost their full heights to decay, but one far in the distance—a structure Edie wasn't even sure could be called a building—dominated them all.

Instinctively, she knew that was the center of the labyrinth, the place Mikey had seen. The end of their journey.

It was a huge black tower, so large and stark against the gray sky that she wondered how she hadn't noticed it in the distance before. It was so tall that it seemed to have shattered the "ceiling" of the Wending itself, and shattered its upper floors, too, in the process. Chunks of debris floated within whorling streams of blue and purple power that circled this catastrophic union, and what looked like lightning lit up the clouds around it, bright but completely soundless. Flat black figures, stretched and malformed, floated stilly against the sky.

"That's where they go," Mikey said, and even he had sobered. "I remember now."

"What the hell is it?" Adam repeated.

"Ah. That," Basile said with a shimmer, "is called the Seat of the Master. I guess some things never change."

"Do I even want to know what 'the Master' is?"

"Probably not," the priest said. "But if you figure it out, tell me."

Satara stared at the circlet. "You realize how concerning it is that a god of secrets and magic doesn't know the answer to that question, right?"

"Maybe he knows and he's not telling me, I don't know. In any case, you all should spend less time asking questions that make me look like an idiot and more time saving the girl." There was a pause. "Souls don't last forever in those cages."

When Edie looked back at the edge of the roof, Adam was already gone.

The Coveter diverged from its path, searching far to the left, but they made a beeline for the tower ahead. They crossed the distance as quickly as they could, but as the minutes turned into what felt like hours, the Seat of the Master only seemed a little closer. Edie realized just how massive the structure must be. Big enough that the Coveters pacing near it looked like normal-sized people next to a normal-sized tower.

The thought made her head spin. She tried to focus on the shadows instead.

By the time they were close enough to see the base of the Seat, it was filling their vision, stretching on forever either way, more like a wall than a building. Edie's eyes adjusted, tuning out the pulsing shadows, and she noticed that the wall wasn't black as she'd assumed but a very dark, very deep, shimmering blue.

Around the tower's perimeter was a low wall made of white stone, though as the group cautiously approached, Edie realized it wasn't stone but bones—not any identifiable as human, warped and sharp and locked around each other, but bones nonetheless.

She glanced from side to side. The only Coveters she could see were far in the distance. No one guarded the enormous open archway leading into the tower, so she signaled the others before shadow jumping to the other side of the bone wall.

They joined her moments later, peering through the archway. A long hall of the same dark material as the outside of the building greeted them, looming and completely unornamented.

At first, it seemed as though they would be able to enter without any problems. Then, as Edie stepped over the threshold, a peculiar energy hummed through the structure. A deep, echoing sound like a whale's call reverberated around them, and the wall rippled.

A ghostly feeling, rather than an actual voice, skimmed over her soul: *Intruders.*

CHAPTER TWENTY-ONE

Intruders.

Adam shook as the voice whispered through his body, his ears clutching though it wasn't a sound he could hear. Two words came to mind: *Fuck. That.*

With a faint wet sound, a figure emerged from the tower wall, clawing its way into the open air. It was vaguely humanoid, though its bottom half was engulfed in smoke, and its body was the same shimmering dark blue as the building. It wheeled around in a daze for a moment, getting its bearings.

Then it threw its head back and shrieked, its featureless face tearing open to form a sharp-toothed, dripping mouth.

A few feet in front of him, Edie had already summoned blue magic in her hands, and she fired a blast at the creature. It didn't have much effect beyond partially dissolving the creature's right arm, and before their eyes, five more of those things spilled out of the wall after the first one.

That almost-voice whispered across Adam's soul again: *Bring them to me.*

Nope. Whatever was waiting for them, he didn't want to meet it. Another azure spell roared up Edie's arm, her dark gray eyes tinting the same color; beside her, Satara raised her shield just in time for one of the creatures to glance off it and run into her spear.

Adam looked down at himself, armed only with the Genesis. This was bound to go well.

Without warning, Mikey winked into existence behind him, scared for the first time since they'd found him. "Don't let those things get near me!"

There was no time for Adam to react before one was rushing their way. He was paralyzed as it charged. No time to summon a shadow copy to pull it back, Edie and Satara too occupied to help, hands full—

It was upon them the next second, shrieking, its long, dark claws raised to maul him. No time—

Reflexively, Adam gripped the Genesis by the neck, flipping it. Then, with a shout, he swung like a batter going for a homerun, cracking the creature across the face with the body of the guitar.

As the thing crumpled to the ground, relief surged through him, followed quickly by panic when he realized he'd just full-force beamed something with his thousand-dollar Ibanez.

Quickly, he gathered the Genesis to his chest again, expecting it to fall apart in his hands. But when he looked, it was perfectly intact—not even a scuff where it had made contact. A quick strum confirmed that it was working as intended, too.

How could that even be possible?

Before he could think too deeply about it, Edie's voice came: "Adam!" Blue magic coiled around her as she summoned more death to fight the multiplying creatures.

His body tensed, and he secured the guitar's strap over his shoulder again. With a glance to the side and the briefest of thoughts—*Could use some help, now*—a shadow fluttered from him, dashing to take shape behind one of the creatures just as it had behind Brian. With a quick movement, the silhouette caught it in a headlock, but the creature was flexible, almost liquid, and slid from its grasp.

With a curse, Adam held out a hand, trying to summon the blue magic that burst from Edie, but he stopped short. The explosion he'd inflicted on Scarlet had been brutal. If he let loose now, he might kill everyone in a ten-foot radius, not just his enemies.

"Adam!" came Edie's exasperated voice again. She and Satara were cutting through the creatures quickly, but more kept coming, pouring from the wall. Fifteen, now, instead of six.

"I'm— I can't!" he snapped.

"Use the Genesis!" she snapped back as she dodged swinging blue claws. With a grunt, she overtook the creature, dissolving its head with a blast of magic. "I don't particularly feel like dying today!"

The Genesis. What had Cal called it? A focus. Adam had wielded magical foci in more video games than he could count; he might have been able to fumble his way through on instinct alone. But a guitar was no wizard's staff.

Unless...

He'd always thought the feeling he got when he played was universal. That deep rhythm, like a dark river, flowing just beneath his fingertips. That electricity that built up and needed release, *needed* a driving melody, aggressive lyrics. He had thought that was just the feeling of music.

But it was something more, wasn't it? Somewhere deep down, he already knew. When he'd played on the roof, looking for Elle, it had become obvious.

And anyway, what was an adventuring party without a Bard?

He slid his pick across the strings, drawing a metallic growl from them just as though the guitar was plugged into an amp. A few of the Seat's creatures had become interested in him and Mikey and were beginning to breach Satara and Edie's defenses. As they snarled and slipped through, lurching forward, Adam positioned his fingers and began to play.

The riff was quick and complicated, something from one of DB's earlier albums. He wasn't sure why it had come to mind first, but as he hit each note, he could feel the buzzing power leaving him and flowing into the Genesis. He could almost *see* it pooling in the center of the body, racing up and down his strings, a seething purple against the black of the guitar.

A few shadows fluttered from him, slipping into the center of the fight before springing into full-sized silhouettes. The Seat's creatures glided toward him, teeth and claws ready, and the power peaked in his hands. With a solid stroke down the middle, that power finally took form, arcing in a sideways slash of glittering black and violet magic.

The magic hit the creatures like a blade, slicing them cleanly in half. They dropped to the ground, but there was no time for Adam to stop and celebrate—he found he could only carry the melody, almost entranced, unable to keep his fingers from dancing along the neck of the Genesis.

Before him, his silhouettes had grown more solid, and they lashed out with fists and whips of darkness, assailing the creatures without Adam even having to think about it. The damage they did was trivial, but they provided a good distraction, and Satara and Edie began plowing through the opposition.

To his side, Adam heard a ghostly shriek and turned to see that more creatures had formed from the wall behind him. A second later, one lashed out, and he was knocked on his ass with a grunt.

He pushed through the daze to drag himself to his feet, staggering as he caught hold of the Genesis again. With a keening note, a wave of smoke knocked his assailant back, putting distance between them again.

He had to keep playing. As long as he had his flow, he could call on the magic without losing control and hurting his friends.

So the melody continued, slower now but no less intense; shadows wavered from the pickups, the guitar barely able to hold the chaotic ocean of magic raging inside. The power buzzed like amp feedback. With a few hard, decisive chords, he released it, and blasts of darkness hit the creatures, stopping them mid-charge.

And then his fingers stilled. The creatures were all dead, but Mikey was nowhere to be seen. As Adam turned to look for him, he spotted something in the distance.

A tinny whine resounded, ringing in his ears. The same second he registered what he was seeing, the earth beneath them began to shake, and he cried out.

A Coveter was sprinting toward them, the white light in its skull blazing. Another almost-voice, this time more of a punch than a whisper: *Intruders!*

The massive skeleton was still a ways away, but with such a large stride, it'd be on them in seconds, and if they ran through the open archway yawning before them, it would only follow them in. Adam slung the Genesis over his shoulder and searched frantically for somewhere to run.

"Hey, over here!"

He turned toward Mikey's voice and saw that the specter was hovering just over the ground, beginning to crawl *into* the Seat of the Master. For a moment, he thought he was melding with it—but Edie and Satara soon followed his lead, and Adam realized they had found a passage.

He booked it over, the ground shaking so hard he almost lost his footing. A roar split his ears as he dove into the passage and clawed deeper into the darkness.

When he looked back, his eyes were blasted with what felt like a searchlight. It took him a moment to realize the Coveter had reached them and was peeking through the small hole, watching their retreat.

His stomach leapt. After a few moments, the thing gave up with a mournful roar, and the earth began to tremble again, quickly. He could only hope it wasn't running to find backup. But with their luck...

As Adam reached forward to pull himself deeper, he caught something—an ankle—and he heard Satara yelp a few feet in front of him. Relief filled his chest. Even though it was dark as the void in here, they were still physical. They all still existed.

It was a cramped shaft, though. And it felt like an hour passed before they finally saw a hazy, cold light at the end of it. Ahead, Adam could finally make out the shuffling forms his friends.

"A light might've been nice, Mike," he called ahead.

"Sorry, I quit smoking!" the ghost called back.

"I meant from your body, you..." Adam trailed off, wincing from the ache in his knees. How long had they been crawling like this? He was getting a little too old for it.

The light got brighter and brighter until they finally reached the end of the shaft, and he watched as the backlit forms of Edie and Satara straightened into a larger room. With some effort, he straightened, too, thankful to be on his feet again.

When he took in the chamber before him, however, he almost wanted to dive back in.

The room was large, cavernous, packed with what looked like gibbets made of rough-hewn, sharp stone. Ashen figures filled most of them. In the center, an impossibly large spiral ramp extended for miles upward. It was wide enough that the Coveters would have been able to ascend it comfortably, and it looped around what looked like a ... he wasn't sure what the hell to call it. A cylindrical tower of glass, filled with blazing blue-purple light, a dense white glow in the center.

It hummed evenly, loudly, like an engine. Some kind of power source?

Adam realized his jaw had dropped, and he quickly closed his mouth, looking to the others. There must be millions of cages. If Elle wasn't in one of them, where else could she be? "What now?"

The air around Edie shimmered, and that asshole priest's voice came from her circlet: "Elle's spirit probably left residual energy in your guitar, like I said, when she passed through it. Try tuning into the signal now."

It wouldn't be a problem if you had been more careful in the first fucking place, Adam thought, though he said nothing, simply sliding the Genesis across his chest.

When Elle had been inside of it, holding it had felt different than usual. It had honestly felt like holding her, like he had done when she was a kid, like he sometimes still did when she needed her dad. The thought made his eyes heat with sorrow, but he suppressed the feeling, concentrating on the Genesis. Elle's energy *was* still there, vaguely: a breath of a memory, a faint mark left by her transition.

If he let it, it seemed to tug him: a stronger vibration high to his left. He glanced upward, then back at the others. "She's here."

As they took to the ramp, shadow jumping or flying where they could, Adam didn't take his eyes off where the energy was tugging him. The sound of the engine in the center of the room, the feeling of his hairs standing on end, the adrenaline screaming at him that the Coveters were coming—he tuned it all out, focusing only on Elle. He was convinced he could almost *hear* her now.

The light in the engine flared slightly brighter, enough that he noticed and almost looked. *Intruders.* It was the same almost-voice from earlier.

"How far is it?" Edie called from behind him. "I don't think we're gonna be alone for long."

He grumbled an affirmative, heart lifting as they reached a bridge connecting the ramp to a block of cages. The bridge wasn't any different from the dozens they had already passed, but somehow, he knew this was the one. He broke into a sprint across it, jumping over the massive chains that crisscrossed the floor.

His feet led him onward, eyes scanning the ashen figures in the cages until they finally fell on a familiar one.

Practically throwing himself against the bars of the cage, he shouted, "Ellie!"

Her form—sitting, curled up—was desaturated much like Mikey's, the vibrant pink of her sweater barely tinted, but when she looked up, there was no mistaking that sweet face. His girl. His baby.

"Dad?" She almost never called him that. Her voice broke his heart. Parched, hopeless, dead.

"It's me. I'm here." He went to close his fists around the bars but drew back quickly with a hiss. When he looked down, blood dripped from his palms. Apparently, they were as sharp as they looked.

Elle's spirit stood and glided to the cage door, dark eyes touching each of the forms beside him. "You came!"

"Of course I did."

"But ... how? How did you get here? How did you know where I was?" She shook her head. "Never mind, just get me out!"

She didn't have to ask twice. But how they would get her out was another problem altogether. As he searched the cage, careful not to cut himself this time, he couldn't seem to find a lock.

"Here, try this." Satara stepped forward with her spear and slid the silver shaft behind one of the rough stone bars, motioning for Adam to hold the other end.

Together, they pried it forward, trying to crack the stone open, but after a few seconds, it became clear that the spear would give before the cage did. Despite its sharpness, the stone wasn't thin or brittle.

With a huff, Satara pulled it out and instead wedged the head between the door and the frame, trying to pry it open.

As she worked, Elle kept close to the door, her face filled with worry. "Where am I, anyway? I thought I was in the city, but everything looked weird, and then there was this huge skeleton guy..."

"You're in the Wending," Edie said over Adam's shoulder.

Elle's eyes opened wider. "I died and went to Wendy's?"

Mikey gaped, his face lighting up. "Oh, man, I've been here for ten years and I didn't know there was a Wendy's!"

Adam loosed a half-mad laugh. Maybe Elle and Cal would get along.

Satara only pried for a few moments before it became obvious there was no way to break the door. She lowered her spear, brows drawn together, and looked at Elle. "Is there any key to open this? Have you seen them open?"

"Sometimes the skeletons come and take people or whatever, but I've never seen what they do. I—"

Without warning, a surge of energy cut her off. The engine behind them hummed, and blue power skated across the floor in a grid, slithering into each of the cells with lightning quickness. It curled around her, shocking her with something like electricity. Her body shook, and a million cries rose with hers as she fell to her knees.

"Elle!" Adam bent down, reaching for her only to cut his hands again. He pulled back with a growl—a noise he could hardly believe had come from him—and glared over his shoulder at the others.

Satara and Mikey were watching Elle with concern, but Edie had turned. Her hair blew around her head in a light breeze as she stared at the power source in the center of the room.

Whatever that thing was, it had shocked not just Elle but every spirit trapped in this place. It had had access to every cell.

Given everything they had learned so far, Adam suspected that connection went both ways. It could administer a shock, and it could take their energy to keep itself running. It wasn't a huge leap to assume it could lock and unlock cells, too.

Somewhere far away but not nearly far enough, he could hear the whines of several Coveters echoing. They were inside the building, coming closer. Adam rose and took the Genesis into his hands, gliding forward almost without realizing what he was doing.

Basile's voice shimmered into existence: "You better not be doing what I think you are, Frankenstein! You have no idea what that thing is or what it controls. You could bring the whole damn place down around you."

The priest was right. But it was draining these souls. Millions of people. It had hurt Elle.

If the only way to end this and get her home was to destroy it, he'd take the risk. Would they?

He looked back at Edie and Satara. Their eyes practically glowed with apprehension. He could see Edie's jaw working as she ground her teeth. But neither of them reached out to stop him.

An unfamiliar feeling washed over him. He was so used to being racked with anxiety and uncertainty ... but now, a calm stilled him. He knew what he had to do. All that was left was to do it.

The room began to shake, and Adam rocketed forward, sprinting back over the bridge toward the engine. Two Coveters filed into the room with fast strides, then two more, then three. They looked up and roared as they spotted him, hurrying to climb the ramp.

But he was already in the last stretch, the engine's buzz deafening as it licked his skin, trying in vain to force him back with its power. The overwhelming feeling of the primordial magic drew a long, strangled cry from him, but he didn't stop until he reached the glass.

Bracing himself, he raised the Genesis over his head, then swung it down with all his might.

CHAPTER TWENTY-TWO

THE SOUND of cracking glass and a horrible, ghostly shriek filled the room. Edie shielded her eyes as the bright light of the engine flared, drowning the cavern in a sea of blinding nothingness. A gale threw her against something hard nearby and knocked the breath from her lungs, and for a few long moments, the whistling screech blocked out any other noise.

Then, slowly, the light faded, the pressure that had washed over her body easing enough that she could sit up. Satara sat nearby, against Elle's cage, looking as windblown and bruised as Edie felt. Beyond her, the blue-purple magic that had been contained within the glass tower was writhing freely now, slowly billowing from the center of the room.

As wisps of it reached the stacked cages, the oppressive shrieking was replaced by the sound of stone grinding on stone. Edie blinked, dazed, as she watched the cages around her swing open and the ashen figures within bolt toward the exit.

She struggled to her knees and crawled toward the edge of the platform, watching as the Coveters below swung their arms, grabbing for the runaway souls—but there were so many that they only caught a few each.

Edie's heart sank, looking toward the engine. She could see a lot of light and magic, but no sign of Adam.

Almost as if in answer to her thought, a faint groan reached her ears. She shuffled a few feet in its direction and watched with wide eyes as a pale hand emerged from the torrent of power, gripping one of the chains crisscrossing the floor. With what looked like a monumental effort, it pulled forward, revealing a tattooed arm.

The other hand came next, dragging a guitar; then, his head. His face was screwed up with effort, and it was only then that Edie realized he was fighting against the whirlwind. It was trying to pull him into it, consume him.

With a cry, she leapt up and staggered to him, falling to her knees just in time to grab his wrist. With both hands, she tugged, muscles burning as she helped him fight against the undertow. After a moment, she felt arms around her waist, and she knew from the jangle of armor that it was Satara. Together, they pulled, planting their feet, straining—

Finally, she felt the power give way. She and Satara practically fell backward as they gave the final pull and hauled Adam back onto the platform.

"Adam!" Elle, now free, dropped beside them, gathering her father into her arms. Mikey wasn't far behind, kneeling beside them.

"I don't want to interrupt your reunion," Edie croaked, brushing hair out of her eyes and mouth, "but we have to get the fuck out of here." She nodded to the Coveters, as well as the sea of dark blue creatures that were now surging up the ramp toward them.

Elle squawked and stood, helping Adam to his feet. He sagged against her and almost dropped the Genesis, but Mikey caught it, sticking close beside.

"Over here." Satara's voice came from behind them, and Edie turned to see that she'd found another shaft.

Thank the gods. Hopefully it would lead them out, though anywhere was better than here. She let Adam and the two spirits struggle in front of her, glancing from them to the tide of creatures surging ever closer.

Once the others had crawled in, she gestured Satara forward, then climbed in herself.

This shaft was just as void-black as the other one had been, but up ahead, Elle glowed softly, at least assuring them there were no sudden drops. Eventually, after a while of twisting and turning, a pale grayish light filtered in from the other end. Freedom.

And just in time, too, because Edie could hear screams echoing down the shaft toward them.

"Basile," she whispered, "the streets out there are like a maze. When we get out, can you tell us where to go?"

"Uhhh ... one sec." There was a pause, and Edie continued to crawl forward, dread heating her neck. Finally, his voice came back: "I can pull a few strings and send up a beacon outside the subway station. Can you take it from there?"

A beacon. Hopefully it'd be bright enough for them to see it. "Thank you!" she said, the relief of seeing her friends climb from the end of the shaft making her almost giddy. Screw this place.

Her soaring heart shriveled, though, when she crawled from the shaft herself.

Where before the Wending had been stagnant and eerily calm, now, all around her, chaos reigned. The perimeter of bone around them had broken and was flying in a whirlwind around the Seat of the Master; the bluish energy roared through the sky, creating violent tornadoes; spirits whipped like flags in the wind, howling, torn from their resting places and drawn closer and closer to the tower; buildings had been upended, revealing crumbling dirt and networks of roots, as though they were trees.

The ghostly screech of the engine was present out here, too, as well as the unhearable voice. For a moment, Edie thought it was coming from the Seat itself, behind them. But no, it was leaking from the eddies of energy, from the glowing cracks in the ground, from every building: *You have defiled the Seat of the Master. You will be punished.*

"Basile?" Edie whispered, but there was no response.

A now-familiar whine reverberated, signaling another Coveter nearby. But other than that, she saw none on the horizon—their trespassing must have caught the attention of all the others.

Edie squinted into the distance, looking for the beacon. For a few seconds, she couldn't see it, frantic. Then, she spotted a pillar of light far away: the only constant, unwavering thing in this new chaos.

She ducked a chunk of flying debris and pointed ahead, shouting over the vicious winds: "There!"

Without checking to see if the others were behind her, she shadow jumped forward, then again, keeping her eyes on the pillar of light. Even when the earth began to shake under her feet, she didn't stop moving. Even when her breath became ragged, her shoes slipping on the gravel of the slanting roofs, her body pelted with stray magic and rubble, she didn't stop.

"Basile," she gasped out again as the beacon came closer, "we're almost there!"

No answer.

Above her head, two wisps of bluish light streaked toward the beacon. Wings beat a quick rhythm on the air, and someone else's shadow magic twined through hers with each jump. She had all her companions and the beacon, but why wasn't the fucking priest answering?

Finally, the streets became slightly more familiar, the beacon much larger and brighter. She recognized the apartment building where they had first met Mikey—and not too far away, the mouth of the alley through which they'd first come. The court it led to was completely shadowed, so she jumped into the middle of it and ran the rest of the way to the subway entrance.

The ground shook, but these tremors were different than the massive footsteps of the Coveters. They were faster, more like something was shaking rather than stomping. Fine dust and debris began to rain down as if the place was destroying itself in defiance of their presence.

Inside, the subway was just as filthy as it had been before, but Edie almost welcomed it. At least it was a sign that the end of their adventure was near.

"Basile!" She was shouting now. "We need the train! Call the train!"

Again, he gave no answer, but there wasn't time to stop and try to figure out why. Footsteps filled the abandoned terminal as the group descended to the bottom floor once more, and finally, the decomposing train came into view.

The doors shuddered open, and Edie stood by them, waving people in—first Satara, then Elle stepped nervously over the threshold. She waved more frantically for Adam, who looked like a dead man walking at the moment. They had to get him home.

But just before he crossed over, he stopped short and looked back. Mikey still stood on the platform, shoulders slumped, the Genesis in his hands. His brown eyes were wide and achingly sad.

There's nothing you can do, Edie told herself, gritting her teeth. *He has to stay here. There's nothing you can do.* But even as she thought it, she couldn't bring herself to rush Adam. Despite the quaking of the station around them, despite the unholy, screaming wind, she couldn't.

All she could do was watch.

"Mikey..." Adam approached the spirit, and the spirit raised his guitar.

"Here ... you're gonna need this."

Adam hesitated, looking into his eyes. There had been such a rush to find Elle, he'd barely had time to register that this was really Mikey. Now, it was hitting him. Hard. "Mikey," he said again, barely audible, as he took the Genesis.

The middle of a gore-crusted subway in the land of lost souls wasn't the best place to have an intimate conversation, granted, but Adam found he didn't care. This moment echoed a hundred others. A hundred mornings Mikey and Adam had parted ways, knowing their secret flings could never be anything more than that. A hundred mornings Adam had seen the same sadness in Mikey's eyes.

"You should go, man." Mikey's voice tilted with sorrow. "It's bad here. You don't want to stay here."

"Mikey..." he said again, then abruptly switched gears as a burning question entered his mind: "Mikey, I need to know why you did it. Was it an accident?"

A pause. "I dunno. It was just ... with the band gone, and I lost people I thought were my friends ... you were busy, all married with a family."

"If it was because of me and Karen, I'm—"

"No, it wasn't." Mikey paused again, then cringed. "I love you. I wanted you to be happy."

Adam gripped the Genesis tighter. They'd never stated it so plainly. Ever. "I love you, too, Mike."

"Things were changing, but I..." Mikey looked down at himself. "I was the same. I was the same stupid fifteen-year-old that ran away from home. And now I'm the same forever."

Every one of those hundred mornings, Adam had turned his back on that sadness. It had hurt to see. Every one of those mornings, he'd said goodbye and walked away.

He couldn't do that again. "You could leave. You don't deserve to be here."

"Maybe ... but I dunno how."

Adam looked down at the guitar, then at Mikey. Was it possible?

After a moment, he peered over his shoulder and met Edie's tentative gaze, trying to ask her the question silently. Above them, there was a horrific crack, and the subway station shook harder, fine dust falling around them.

Edie spared a glance at the ceiling. "Whatever you do, do it fast."

He looked back at Mikey and held out the guitar. "Come with me."

For a moment, the spirit's eyes lit hopefully, but uncertainty still marred his expression. "But I've been dead awhile, Frank, and you've— you've got shit going on!" He gestured to Edie and the others, teeth chattering. "I'd just— You have to get out of here!"

"Mikey," Adam said one more time, raising his voice over the shaking. "Come with me. I *want* you to come with me."

Something gave way in Mikey's face, and he took a step closer to Adam, only the Genesis separating them. He put his hands on the guitar, too, stroking it reverently. Weakly, voice choked, he said, "I always wanted a body with sexy curves."

That drew an equally weak chuckle from Adam. "She's all yours."

Mikey looked at him again, searching his face affectionately. Then, with a deep breath, his body faded, glowing faintly white. After a few moments, he was no more than a mist, and slowly, he seeped into the body of the guitar, climbing up and down its strings and coalescing around the pickups.

Another bang, loud enough that it took Adam's breath away for a moment. Edie shouted something that sounded like gibberish to his ears, and he turned quickly and sprinted into the car, huddling close to Elle with the Genesis pressed to his chest. He could almost feel Mikey's heartbeat against his own.

Edie jumped in after and hauled the train's doors shut, banging on the walls and shouting: "Basile! Come on, get us the fuck out of here! *Basile!*"

With a lurch, the train started forward, jerking along the track fast enough that she nearly fell over.

It wasn't long before darkness swallowed them up, the world beyond the train's windows more of a void than a tunnel. The oceanlike silence was now like the sound of blood rushing through one's ears, somehow oppressively loud despite not really being a sound at all. Their last trip through this void had been smooth, but now the train shook like it was going to fall apart.

A particularly loud thud from the far end of the train made Adam start, and he looked up to see faces pressed to the end window of the next car. The white figures that had been in the next car over when they'd entered this place—the ones that Basile had told Edie not to look at. They were staring inward now, their bodies and faces indistinct, their eyes nothing but scribbles. One of them jerked its arm down, pulling at the car door's handle.

Adam gasped and averted his eyes as quickly as he could, remembering Basile's warning. The priest was a total douchebag, but he knew what he was talking about. Adam didn't want to know what would happen if he acknowledged those figures for too long.

The train banged and screeched, his friends cried out, sparks flew somewhere nearby. The acrid scent of something burning reached Adam's nose, and he shut his eyes tight, not wanting to see which of the train's parts were breaking off. Beside him, Elle screamed and pressed in close, and he pulled an arm around her.

All that bullshit in the Wending and they were going to die *here*, lost in the in-between of the in-between, a timeless and spaceless void.

Maybe he shouldn't have smashed that stupid thing.

His arm slipped on Elle, dipping, like she had ducked under to get away. The movement made him open his eyes despite the chaos. Sparks rained around him, the lights of the car flickering like some underground club's strobe; handrails and wiring had dislodged from their proper places, swinging; glass cracked and shivered. Edie and Satara had taken seats despite the filth, gripping the side rails for dear life.

Adam glanced to the side, trying to make sense of what Elle was doing. His heart dropped.

She, too, was flickering. Her desaturated form was turning more translucent at intervals, and Adam found he could move his arm through her.

She covered her face with her hands. "No, no, no!"

The Genesis flashed brightly, and in the back of Adam's head, Mikey's voice echoed: *"Adam ... I don't feel so hot."*

Adam's whole body shook once before a strange stillness overtook him. His emotions clenched into a hard ball, his brow furrowing. He secured his arm around Elle again, the other holding the Genesis close, focusing as closely as he could on them. Mikey and Elle were real. They weren't lost anymore; they were here.

He wasn't going to lose them again.

The oppressive silence outside the train gave way to thundering. Below them, Adam could feel more than the crashing of a dissolving train —he felt the grinding of tracks. When he raised his head to peer out the windows, he saw dimly lit bricks and cement rushing past them.

Before his pounding head could register what was happening, they were slowing. Then, with one final screech, the train came to a stop in the dingy station they had left behind.

If nothing else, the smell was familiar. New York City.

Shakily, Adam stood, pulling a still-fading Elle up with him. She had pressed her head to his shoulder, and he murmured into her hair. "It's okay. We're home. It's okay."

He couldn't hold onto her for long, and he knew it. He could feel her energy beginning to slip through his fingers, searching for a place to belong, to make sense of itself. Basile better be ready to catch her soul the second those doors slid open.

Edie and Satara had already stood, but thankfully they let Adam go first, shuffling out with Elle held tightly to him. By the time they stepped onto the platform, she was only a periwinkle mist in the vague shape of a human.

He kept his eyes on her, trying to will her to stay with him just a few moments longer. In his periphery, he could see that a few people sat on the concrete floor of the platform, but when he finally spared a glance, they were not what he expected.

It was Basile, Marius, and a woman he had never met before. But Basile had dropped all pretense of priestliness, instead wearing a turtleneck with the sleeves rolled up. His glamour looked tired, worn, the hair mussed, and his eyes were pits of black with small points of blue light. Marius looked much the same: exhausted, his usually styled hair a crown of cherubic curls, the scruffy beginnings of a beard on his jaw and cheeks. His street clothes were rumpled, obviously slept in.

They were sitting on two sleeping bags heaped with blankets, a large electric lantern between them. The woman, her own dark curls spiraling from beneath a winter hat, held two paper grocery bags in her arms. If Adam didn't know any better, he'd have thought they'd interrupted a few homeless people hanging out.

The three of them stared at the train with awe. But on seeing Elle, Basile stood, holding something up: a crystal, just like the one he'd used to trap their souls. His mouth moved rapidly, reciting some spell too quiet for Adam to hear over the ringing in his ears.

The mist that was Elle glowed in Adam's arms. He shivered as she slipped from his grasp and formed a streak of light that shot toward Basile's hand. There was a flash, and the crystal filled with a hazy, roiling purplish glow.

He lowered his arm and held the crystal tight in his fist, the light reflecting off his glasses. "Gotcha."

"Edie!"

Marius had stood and was jogging forward with such purpose that Adam naturally made way for him. He watched with fast, anxious breaths as Marius pulled Edie into a fervent, crushing hug, hand at the nape of her neck. They lingered for a moment before he broke away.

"*Whoa*," said Mikey, thankfully still in the Genesis, Adam realized with sagging relief. "*Someone's got a crush.*"

The paladin—Adam had taken to thinking of Marius that way—turned and looked them over with disbelief. "By the Wolfbinder, you're actually alive..."

Edie reached out, her fingers awkward and hesitant as she too-briefly touched Marius's jaw. "What ... what the hell happened? You look like you haven't shaved in—" Her tone shifted, darkening. "What happened?"

Adam turned in time to see Basile glaring at him as he tucked the glowing crystal into his pocket. "Just as I thought, your little *stunt* had consequences. You're a real rebel, Frankenstein. We're all very impressed."

"What are you talking about?" Adam breathed.

"I hope you're proud of yourself. You lot have been gone for three weeks."

CHAPTER TWENTY-THREE

BASILE'S WORDS dropped like an anchor in the silence, and Edie felt her heart drop along with them. Three weeks? It felt like they had been gone for a day, max.

Still, Marius's beard didn't lie. The sleeping bags, the lantern, the fact that Yuval—who was now staring at them with tears in her eyes—was bringing them food... It was bitterly cold, when it had only been unseasonably chilly before. Time had passed, and the priest and vivid had been living here all that time, waiting for them. But why—

Edie's train of thought was cut off by a cry of pain behind her. She turned to see Satara standing at the edge of the platform, her wings visible. They shuddered close around her shoulders, and feathers rained from them, coming to rest around the shieldmaiden's feet. They left behind bare patches and slick blood clinging to the remaining feathers. It pattered onto the subway floor.

The change was so sudden that Edie found herself looking around for the enemy who had done it. "Satara!"

She brushed past Marius to go to her, but Satara held out her hands, shaking like a leaf. Her chest rose and fell quickly. "Don't— don't touch me, please..."

"What's happening?" Edie's voice sounded quiet in her own ears, far away. "What's happening to them?"

"You were gone for three weeks," Basile said grimly. "The fledgling curse is catching up to her."

Satara loosed a choking sob and covered her face. Her knees shook as she struggled to stay upright. Edie reached out, careful to avoid her wings, and tried to steady her. The cloying, coppery scent of blood and rotting flesh filled her nostrils. Angry, pulsing purple veins crawled up Satara's arms and throat. How could this have happened so quickly?

"We have to get her to the other valkyir," Marius said abruptly, turning to Basile. "Whatever we need to do, let's do it at once."

The priest simply nodded and set to work drawing a translocation circle. Decidedly less attitude than Edie had anticipated, considering Marius's demanding tone.

The vivid's hand began to glow brightly, and he took a few steps closer to Satara, catching her eyes. "Can I try to heal you?"

Her only response was a nod and a miserable groan. The pain radiating from her almost made Edie's body ache, too.

Marius touched Satara's arm gently, and her skin glowed a warm brown as the magic melted into her. But there was no improvement to the shaking—if anything, it got worse. A second later, she yelped sharply and jerked away from him.

"I wouldn't do that if I were you," Basile said, looking up from his work. "Edie, you might be able to stop the bleeding. Yuval, you could try to wash the wounds. But healing will only make things worse."

Marius turned on him and snapped, "Why?"

"It's not the gods' will."

"Fuck the gods!"

Edie looked at him, goosebumps raising along her arms. Her heart jumped strangely. Fuck the gods, *Marius*? What had happened in these past three weeks?

Basile didn't argue, simply finished the translocation spell and empowered it. "Let's take care of the spirit ... then I'll tell you the next step."

Yuval and Edie flanked Satara, carefully helping her toward the glowing circle of runes that would get them the hell out of here. As they went, followed by Marius and Adam, Edie reached out with her mind, blood magic touching every open wound she could feel on Satara's wings. With practiced haste, she bade the magic to flow into them, slowly stopping what bleeding she could.

They huddled into the circle of runes, and the etchings flashed. The world swam, flickering, then they were standing in the living room of the Manhattan apartment.

Yuval and Marius moved away first, helping Satara to the couch. The stream of feathers she left behind was diminishing, but she still shook, barely able to regulate her breathing. Yuval murmured something in Hebrew, sucking water droplets from the air to sluice over Satara's worst wounds.

Edie stepped out of the circle and glanced back to see Adam gazing around the stylish apartment. "Where are we?" he asked, moving toward the drawn curtains.

"This is the apartment we've been staying in."

The hellerune leveled a glare at Basile. "What about my place? Where's Elle?"

"We had to evacuate," the priest said dismissively. "The Gloaming were catching on. Elle and Cal are here now."

"You didn't think maybe you should tell me that?"

Basile rolled his eyes. "You'll be able to get back to your anime figurines and your PlayStation soon enough, my friend. Try not to sprain something crying."

"What's your *problem*?" Adam demanded.

"What's my problem?" The priest turned. "My problem is you went and broke an entire *plane*, Adam! And the consequences of breaking that plane? *You* broke time, *you* did this!" He flung an arm toward Satara.

"That engine thing was hurting Elle," Adam replied hotly. "It was hurting all of those people."

"You still can't just ... do whatever you want! This is how our universe operates. Nature doesn't have morals, Adam. These things are essential, even if—"

"That's a bullshit excuse for not trying. No, no—that's a bullshit excuse for you to do whatever the hell *you* want." Adam pointed at him. "The universe doesn't have to operate on suffering just because that's the way it's always been."

"Elle is just one soul! You went and cocked everything up because of one person. You were selfish."

"Saving someone isn't selfish. Just because you don't give a shit about anybody doesn't mean everyone else should feel that way, too."

"*Look at Satara!*" The priest was shouting now, and Edie shrank away from them. "You did that. You screwed with the universe and *she's* being punished for it!"

"I— I didn't—"

"You think I don't give a shit?" Basile raged. "I do! I give too much of a shit, about everything, about every*one*, and I'm old as dirt, Adam. Do you know how many people I've watched die? How many goddamn atrocities I've seen committed? It's too much. That's the problem!" He let his hands fall against his thighs, and his voice dropped to just above speaking volume. "But neither you nor I can ever change the way things are, so why try? Why suffer the consequences?"

There was a moment of silence as he stared at Adam expectantly. Finally, Adam replied, exasperation straining his voice, "Because what else can we do?"

"Uh ... hello?"

Edie's heart soared when she recognized Cal's voice. She jumped out from behind Basile and Adam to see him standing in the doorway, arms crossed. His eyes lit up when he saw her. She felt him prodding at their connection with his mind, and she responded in kind, grinning despite the tense air in the room.

His gaze snapped back to the two men, then to Satara. "What in the sideways fuck is happening in here?"

Satara raised her head, nails digging into her upper arms as she hugged herself. She squirmed, apparently unable to sit still. "I ... I can barely think."

"She's in a lot of pain," Yuval said evenly, still tending to the wounds. "If I had to guess, it's probably weeks of pain all at once."

"I'm sorry," Adam whispered. "I didn't know—"

"Wait, wait, wait. Explain this to me." Cal drifted to stand next to Satara, glancing between Yuval and Marius. It only took a few sentences to convey the situation to him, and when he understood, he looked at Adam. "Jesus Christ, bro."

"I'm sorry," he mumbled again.

"Well, standing around feeling sorry for her isn't going to cure her," Basile said, taking the full keeper paragon from his pocket. "The only thing we can do is end this and move on."

Cal squeezed Satara's shoulder briefly, then followed Basile and Adam as they left the living room. Edie looked back at the three on the couch. "Will you be all right here?"

Yuval nodded, but Satara didn't respond, forehead pressed to her knees. Marius simply sighed, clenching and unclenching his fist. She could tell he was itching to heal Satara, upset that he could do nothing to help.

"It's going to be okay," Edie said, in what she hoped was a reassuring tone. "I'll be right back."

By the time she entered the master bedroom, Adam, Basile, and Cal were already crowded by the head of the bed. The curtains were drawn here, too, and they were all looking down at Elle's body. At some point in the past three weeks, someone had dressed her in pajamas, but otherwise, she looked just the same as she had before—gray and seemingly asleep. The sight still made Edie shudder.

Nonetheless, she stood at the foot of the bed, listening to Basile's chanting. His spell was similar to the one he had first cast, when he'd extracted her from the guitar. Edie could only hope this time would be different. She wasn't going into the Wending a second time ... if there was still a Wending to go to.

She watched anxiously as the light within the paragon glowed brighter and began to leak from it, feeling its way almost cautiously into the open air. Sweat beaded on Basile's forehead as he concentrated on the flow of spirit energy, trying to keep a tight hold on it. Slowly, he guided it—with his hand, this time—from the crystal to Elle's body.

There was a moment of resistance, where the energy jerked and tried to wiggle from his hand. A collective sharp inhale broke over the priest's chanting for a moment, but he held fast, his voice never wavering.

Suddenly, with an impossibly quick movement, the spirit fled his grip. Edie's pulse jumped, her body lurching forward as if she could catch it—

It darted forward and stuck to Elle. Then, it spread, and for a split second, her entire form was covered with a periwinkle film.

Then, finally, it sank into her, becoming one with her.

Edie released a breath.

But even as relief washed over her, she knew there was something wrong. She came closer and noticed that, even though the soul had clearly made its home in Elle's body, her skin color hadn't changed. It stayed the same death-gray, and her chest was still, no breath entering her lungs.

For a moment, Edie wondered if it hadn't worked, if all that pain had been for nothing. Maybe people *couldn't* be resurrected. Basile *had* said that he wasn't sure what would happen.

Then, Elle opened her eyes.

They weren't the dark brown eyes that Edie had expected, though. They were milky and greenish. Dead. And in the pits of her pupils, at the back of her skull, blue light coiled like a snake.

Reality hit Edie with enough force that it knocked the wind from her. They hadn't resurrected her at all.

Elle was a revenant.

Slowly and with a groan, the dead girl sat up, looking around. "Adam...?"

He hesitated before reaching out to cup her face. His grimace told Edie it must be freezing to the touch. "I'm here. How do you ... feel?"

She blinked her milky eyes, considering. "I ... I feel really weird."

Edie looked at Basile. "What happened? She's—"

"She's a revenant," Cal cut in, crossing his arms. "I can feel it."

"Revenant?" Elle squeaked, looking between them. "Like a zombie? But you said you could make me alive again!"

The priest shifted uncomfortably, but his expression remained impassive. "I never promised anything. I wasn't sure what might happen."

"Whose revenant?" Edie asked.

"Adam's, I assume."

Adam said nothing for a moment, seemingly concentrating on Elle. Then, his brows tilted helplessly. "It feels ... different. Like I can almost hear your thoughts. But"—he glared at Basile—"you did the ritual. If anything, wouldn't she be connected to you?"

"I'm draugborn. There's no soul for her to connect to." He gestured to the Genesis still on Adam's back. "You must have marked her as your own or something when you trapped her spirit. I don't know. I've never seen anything quite like this before."

Cal huffed and took out a cigarette, putting it between his lips without lighting it. His leg bounced quickly. "That don't sit right. Revenants are made with human sacrifice and shit. You can't just ... steal someone's soul and put it in their own damn body."

"And yet." Basile motioned to Elle.

She'd pulled Adam onto the bed with her and was huddled in his arms. The sight made Edie's heart ache. Usually, she was able to compartmentalize the feelings, but every once in a while, she missed her own dad so much she wanted to cry.

"But," the priest continued, "we could sit around all day wondering why. The reality is staring us in the face; we just deal with it now and figure it out later."

Adam laughed humorlessly. "That's easy for you to say. Just deal with it. My kid is an undead *thrall*."

"Listen, lunatic, you got what you wanted. She's back, so don't cry to me about—"

"Can you two go three fucking minutes without fighting like little pissbabies?" Cal rasped, then looked at Adam sternly. "She's only as much of a thrall as you make her."

"She doesn't have freedom," he returned. "She can't be alone with her thoughts. She's open to suggestion from me. It's not all the way freedom, anyway. That matters."

His words seemed to irk Cal, who squirmed like he had an itch between his shoulders that he couldn't get to. He looked at Elle instead. "I'll teach you to build a wall around your brain." He paused. "I better teach you a couple other things while we're at it. Anti-decomp charms, glamour, what you can eat—"

"What I can *eat*?" Elle burst out. "Do you mean I can't eat food?!"

"Uh ... not unless it's a reeeeally rare steak."

She stared at him for a moment before her face crumpled, sobs bubbling up from her chest. She tucked her face against Adam's shoulder and wept, though there were only a few small tears and no crying blush to be seen.

It was unsettling to see her looking so lifeless and yet moving around. No wonder her dad was upset. Edie would almost have preferred a rotting zombie.

Cal met Edie's eyes. "Let's give 'er some time."

She nodded and gave Adam and his daughter one last look before stepping out into the hall, followed shortly by Cal and Basile. She peeled her jacket from her sweat-coated torso and realized for the first time how desperately she needed a shower. "Well, that was traumatic."

"Yes," Basile murmured, adjusting his glasses. "But he can't be mad at me. I did what he asked; I put her back in there."

"He can probably do whatever the hell he wants," Cal said with a shrug, taking the unlit cigarette from his lips. "I barely remember when I first woke up, but I can tell you it wasn't fun. I didn't exactly have the luxury of workin' through it, so I'm not about to tell a little girl to buck up and shut the fuck up."

"She's only a year younger than me," Edie said with a hint of amusement.

"Little girl."

"All right." Basile sighed heavily. "I get it. I'll leave it be. It's not like either of them are going to be much help for the coming trials."

"Right. Let's get Satara."

Edie threw her jacket over one shoulder and started down the hall. When she entered the living room, the curtains had been opened, revealing the city below. The brightness of the light stabbed Edie's eyes, and it took her a moment to adjust. Her heart dropped when she realized the streets and rooftops were blanketed with a foot of snow, as if it was January and not July.

"Edie?" Yuval's voice caught her attention, and she realized she'd been still and staring for more than a few seconds.

She tore her gaze from the window to look at their hostess, then Marius, then Satara, who still sat curled up on the couch. Her shaking had diminished, though, and her eyes were more focused. She even managed a smile as Edie came to sit on the coffee table across from her.

"How are you feeling?" Edie asked gently.

"Better, thanks to Yuval ... and you." The shieldmaiden glanced between them, looking more exhausted, now, than pained. "I think she was right and the pain was just catching up to me. It still feels ... awful, but nothing I can't handle."

Edie nodded, gaze flicking over the still-visible wings. They were naked in places, bruised, a subtle scent of rot drifting from them. Seeing them as they were now, Edie had no trouble imagining that this process could poison Satara's blood.

She glanced up as Basile and Cal entered the room.

"So?" Marius urged. "Elle?"

"Back in her body, though not quite as we'd hoped." The priest sighed and explained the revenant situation, and puzzlement filled the room all over again.

"That ... shouldn't be possible, right?" Satara asked.

He shrugged. "Evidently, it is. No idea on the why. But that's the reality, so we'll just have to work with it."

Yuval stood. "I should go check on them. New Yorkers gotta look out for each other." She smiled and touched Satara's shoulder briefly before hurrying past Cal.

As she did, Basile peered pointedly at Satara. "Anyway, all the questions can come later. There's a more pressing matter at the moment, isn't there?"

The shieldmaiden's wings twitched, and a shudder ran through her. "Yes," was all she managed.

Basile took off his glasses, cleaning them on the hem of his turtleneck. "All right. First things first, in order to transition to a valkyrie, you'll have to be vested by other valkyir—as you probably know. For this ... you'll have to go to Asgard."

Edie blinked. The World of the gods? *That* Asgard?

She turned to look at Satara, but the shieldmaiden didn't seem surprised, or perhaps she was too drained to react. On her left, Marius glanced between her and Basile with intensity.

"Now," the priest continued, "there's obviously not a heimdyrr to get into Asgard. They're technically always at war with the jötnar—the giants —and don't want to be besieged. We'll have to go as close as we can to the edge of Midgard to cross over."

Cal huffed. "I didn't know you were a flat-earther, Father."

"Shut up. Once we're there, we'll have to call messengers to let us across Bifrost."

"What's Bifrost?" Edie asked.

"It's when Mercy gets a brain freeze," Cal replied helpfully.

Basile rubbed his brow. "All right. You guys have lost your Latinization privileges. In Old Norse it's pronounced more like 'beef-roast.' So now we're calling the gods' interdimensional bridge of pure light Beef-roast, because you couldn't behave, Cal."

"Way to go, Cal," Edie mumbled. "And I guess that answers my question."

"You've probably even seen it before. You might know it as the rainbow."

Cal spread his arms to shrug innocently. "See, that doesn't *sound* very straight to *me*."

"What do we use to call the messengers?" Marius cut in. "To make the bridge appear?"

Basile looked at Satara. "Astrid should have a horn. Runed, bronze, probably kept in a place of honor. Do you know of anything like that?"

Her face shifted, undeniable realization filling her eyes as she straightened from her weary posture. "That ... that's what the horn is for? Why didn't she—" She stopped and held her head.

"What happened?" Edie pressed.

"Someone tried to steal it." Satara glanced between them all. "Just before her death. A ljósálfr thief—a light elf—part of an organization called the Shadowborne. She and I were able to take it back, but she never looked into the matter, and when I did, I couldn't find much information. I still have no idea why they wanted it." She paused and said more quietly, "She said she would tell me what the horn was for some other time."

Images of Astrid's torture and death flashed through Edie's mind, and she had to blink hard to make them go away. Astrid had never gotten the chance—and she never would. She didn't exist anymore, anywhere, in any world.

"So the thing is safe." Basile's shoulders relaxed slightly. "Where is it?"

"It's safe so far as I know. It's in Shipshaven. I didn't bring any of her things with me." Satara looked down at her hands. "I knew there was a reason the thief wanted it, even if I didn't know its significance. So I hid it."

"Well, then, that's easy," Cal said, beginning to pace. "We just go there and we get it and then head on over to Beef-roast."

"I doubt it will be that easy. I'm sure the Gloaming are watching the shop. It's entirely possible that the second we teleport in, they'll know and come after us." She sighed. "But if this is what I need to do, then it's got to be done."

Cal had already gone to the coat rack and was donning his denim shearling jacket. "I'm in. Let's leave."

"Not now," Satara said, shuddering. "Basile needs to replace our souls. I need to eat. And rest. So does Edie." She glanced toward the frost-edged window. "But first thing tomorrow morning, you two can come with me."

Marius stood and added, "I'll come, too."

Satara shook her head. "I don't want to bring a large force. We'll just be in and out, and fewer people will raise less alarm."

The vivid didn't look thrilled. In fact, he looked almost devastated, though he usually took rejection quietly. For a moment, it seemed as though he might argue. Then, his expression closed, and he nodded. "Fine."

If Edie was honest, she wouldn't have minded Marius taking her place. There was no question there would be danger, and at the end of it all, they'd be summoning a celestial bridge and going to the city of the gods. The literal *gods*. She'd been way more comfortable as a nobody in a go-nowhere band, working then sleeping, barely able to live off her wages just like everybody else. She wasn't cut out for a life like this.

She wasn't cut out for anything. Not to wield her magic, not to navigate the world around her ... and certainly not to be the Reacher.

What had Astrid been thinking?

CHAPTER TWENTY-FOUR

The night stretched on and on without mercy. Pain seared through Satara's body with every small movement, but her half-awake restlessness never let her lie in one position for very long. When sleep came to take the pain away, it was only for twenty minutes at a time at most, her rest inevitably broken by her aching body. It felt almost like she was in purgatory—like her afterlife of punishment had come early.

Punishment. What a farce.

She had done a respectable job of holding together for the afternoon, but now, after hours of relentless agony, her resolve was rapidly crumbling. She sat up in bed abruptly, and a sob escaped her lips.

Why couldn't she just *go to sleep?*

Satara knew, though, that all the hoping and begging in the world wouldn't bring sleep to her. The suffering was in more than just her body; thoughts and memories whirled in her head like a viscous slurry that stuck to the inside of her skull.

Hopeless. Broken and hopeless.

It all led back to Astrid, and then further to Darras. It always did. If Satara could have seen ... if she could have been big enough or strong enough to save them...

But look at her now. She couldn't even save herself.

She choked on her remaining sobs, standing from the bed. There was no use sitting and waiting for sleep to come when all that would come were those memories, those thoughts of all the things she had to do, all the obligations she still needed to fulfill. That was an exercise in self-harm, and she didn't have the strength for it tonight.

Wrapping her robe around herself, she headed instead for the living room, sinking into a cozy chair near the window. With two fingers she drew the curtains back a little, enough to see the night—so much brighter than any she had ever seen, between the snow and the city lights. It was as bright as an overcast afternoon in Shipshaven.

Shipshaven. In just a handful of hours, she would be back in her seaside town, her home for over a decade. She wasn't sure she had the strength for that either.

Satara pushed the thought from her mind and reached for the book she had left on the coffee table. If she was honest, she'd been putting off finishing Aevana and Commander Coldheart's story. The author had stopped publishing a century ago, so there would be no follow-up, just a cliffhanger and disappointment. And at the moment, *Throne of Ice* was the one bright spot in her life; she didn't want it to end.

She supposed there was no point in putting it off now, though. After all, there was a chance she could die in a matter of a week, if not quicker. She might as well finish her book.

With a yawn, she rubbed her tired eyes and flipped to her bookmarked page.

Coldheart watched from the wings as the Crown Prince whisked Aevana around the dance floor. His hand rested just below her waist, cradling her hips to his as they spun in time to the delicate music. Her dress trailed behind her like a river of stars, white and sheer but for the blanket of crystals encrusting it. She glowed in the ballroom like a beacon.

Coldheart could almost swear he felt his dead heart beat at the sight of her.

But the hollow in his chest yawned, empty as a chasm. She was smiling, her dark eyes twinkling. Though it had been long since he had felt warmth, it was almost as though fire surged through his veins. He had crossed oceans to reunite with her. He had given up everything for her. And in the end, just like all the others, she had forsaken him.

He couldn't look any longer. He should have known. She would be so much happier without him. Why would she risk everything to be with a monster?

Splitting from the crowd, he stepped out onto one of the many balconies lining the ballroom. Just over the horizon, he could see them: a sea of tiny, tiny blue lights blending together to form a hazy rivulet down the mountainside. The army of undeath. It seemed the Dark Lord had finally given the orders to march on the Court of Stars.

Something in him ached. When they came, everything would be swept up in their tide. Including Aevana.

He could return to the army, could be their commander as before. His master had said as much. *When you are done with the girl, you will come back, and you will take your place at my right hand once again.* No worry, no conscience, no love.

Love. What a terrible, painful mistake.

Satara sat with her face almost fully in the book, scanning the paragraphs frantically. *No.* Coldheart had come to *warn* Aevana and the others about the encroaching undead army, and now he wouldn't just because she was dancing with the Crown Prince? She didn't even *want* to be dancing with the Crown Prince; she was only trying to forget Coldheart. Surely he couldn't do this. He'd changed! She'd changed him!

She was so consumed in the tense scene that when someone cleared their throat in the living room archway, she nearly jumped from her chair. She looked up to see Marius leaned against the door frame, watching her with a strange mix of amusement and concern.

"Something troubling?" he asked, nodding to the book as he came closer.

Satara hesitated before quickly marking her page and snapping the book shut. "No ... just thinking."

Marius stopped by the end of the couch and craned his neck slightly to read the book's title. "*Throne of Ice, a Court of Stars series*." He peered at her, smirking. "You never struck me as a lover of pulp romance."

She splayed a hand over the cover, hiding the name, and pulled the book to her chest protectively. "And you never struck me as one to follow a woman around like a lovesick puppy, but people surprise you." When he seemed confused, she added, "I've seen the way you look at Edie."

That shut him up. He shuttered his expression and sighed, then sat down on the couch. She relaxed in turn, feeling a little guilty, and for a moment, it seemed like he would change the subject.

"What makes you say that?" he asked carefully.

"It's obvious." Satara shrugged. "You hang on her every word, watch her wherever we go ... when we came back, you hugged her so tight you could have broken her spine."

Marius's expression darkened. "You were gone for three weeks. I thought that you had all died. That you had left us behind, here, in this mess..."

Satara looked at him, knitting her brow. The way his eyes ghosted over her, not really seeing her, she could tell that he was thinking of it. Whatever had happened, whatever doubts he had, haunted him.

"But I still waited," he continued more softly. "I waited for you—for all of you. I couldn't move on until I knew what had happened." A pause. "I kept thinking ... I should have gone, I should have gone with them. Given the priest my soul, whatever I needed to do." Marius shook his head. "Or maybe I was meant to stay here and bear witness to everything that happened while you were gone."

Dread licked the shieldmaiden's back. Neither Marius nor Basile had said a word about what had happened during those three weeks. None of them had even thought to ask, as tired and frantic to help both her and Elle as they had been.

Now, Satara burned with an immediate need to know. So much could happen in three weeks, and from the look on his face, none of it had been for the better.

"What happened, exactly?" she asked gently.

Marius looked past her and inclined his chin at the drawn curtains. "You've seen the streets. The snow falls often since you left. It comes every few days, the rain washes it away, the sun comes out ... but it returns soon after, heavier than before."

"A fluke of the weather?" Satara concluded hopefully, nervously. But too much was happening at once for it to be a coincidence.

Marius knew this; she knew he did. Still, kindly, he said, "Perhaps."

"What else?"

He paused in thought. "The Blood Eagles hold their rallies in the morning, nearly every morning now. When they were met with protesters originally, things were tense, but ... it's escalated. The protesters disrupt, the police move forward and crush the protesters, the protesters fight back ... the Blood Eagles are escorted out and get to go home freely. There have been a few riots. One per week, more or less, when the sun sets. No one's sure who's actually starting them, but Basile thinks it's undercover Blood Eagles."

Satara fiddled with the collar of her robe, goosebumps raising on her skin. "Has anyone been killed?"

"One or two people, in the chaos. Some hospitalized. None by the Blood Eagles, yet. Usually, once the Eagles disperse, the police come out in force. They have tear gas, rubber bullets ... whatever." Marius sighed and glared at his feet. "It was just mindless retaliation at first. Now *any* gathering is seen as a protest and dealt with accordingly. Not the Blood Eagles' gatherings, though," he added quietly.

Satara pinched the bridge of her nose. "What else?"

"Anster..." He paused, running a hand over his hair, and pain bloomed on his face. "It's fallen. The local government, the Aurora"—his voice became weaker—"have fled. It's in complete chaos."

Satara's heart nearly stopped. She stuttered for a second before managing, "No one is there to stop it? To at least protect people? Is the rest of the Reach okay?"

"As far as anyone knows, the Anster Police Department has been entirely disbanded. It started with a strike over their safety, and now they're gone. And no Aurora." Marius stopped for a moment to hold his head in one hand, and Satara said nothing, simply letting him breathe. Eventually, "Word from Mercy and Matilda is that our safe houses are doing fine. The Reach is taking in anyone they can find; they're getting by. And small militias are beginning to form, Reach and unattuned alike. But the New Gloaming and whoever else takes advantage of the chaos are a constant threat."

"I'm so sorry," Satara whispered, without further explanation.

No explanation was required. The vivid simply closed his eyes for a moment before opening them again to continue. "Things have started to get restless southward, too. Philadelphia, D.C. Basile believes the Gloaming's on a route, that they're trying to take the entire East Coast. That the same thing is going to happen in New York that happened in Anster, and so on."

"And how long do we have until New York falls, too?"

Marius sighed, his face growing ashen. "In Anster, it began with riots —not protesters but Gloaming. They spread closer to the West End, toward City Hall and the Statehouse. Everything was shut down. The National Guard never came; the people governing the city simply ... left. There were raids on the municipal buildings, empty and otherwise." He paused at length. "The Temple of the Rising Divine was hollowed out. Anster is still on fire."

Satara slipped from her seat and went to his side. She wasn't usually an overly touchy person—she was private, enjoyed her personal space— but she placed a hand on his shoulder, squeezing it gently. Her next question would not be an easy one for him. "And what about the Aurora here? What are they doing?"

"Nothing," he ground out, flexing his fist open and closed. "Nothing. They're retreating into their shells just like the Rising Divine did. Protecting themselves."

The words that first came to Satara's mind weren't exactly kind, but Marius didn't need to be told her opinion of the Aurora. Judging from the way he was grinding his teeth, he probably shared it. "Is it possible this Radiant is being blackmailed like your father was?"

"I don't know. Radiant Oddfreyr isn't ... like my father. His pride is tempered by nothing." Marius's eyes flickered, light swelling in them, but he closed his lids against it. "Someone should ask him. Someone should—"

He cut himself off, and silence stood between them for a while. Satara let her hand fall from his shoulder and twine anxiously in her lap.

At length, he raised his head again, brows drawn in pain. "Thank Odin and Tyr and all the gods that you all came back. I wondered many times if that *thing* in the subway had taken me and I was living in some sort of nightmare."

"We came back," Satara affirmed with a nod, then tilted her head. She chose her next words carefully. "I would've expected you to be ... angrier at Basile, not knowing what had happened to us ... not knowing that it wasn't his fault. But you spoke to each other like equals yesterday."

"He's a good man. For a Christian." A grim smile graced Marius's face for a moment before his usual earnestness returned. "The first day, he was flippant as ever. But as the days came and went and you never returned, he ... changed. Odin wouldn't answer his calls. I could see the way he worked trying to understand what had gone wrong. He tried to follow you in once or twice, but nothing came of it—he couldn't." Marius sighed. "In the middle of the second week, he told me I could kill him, that it would be restitution."

Satara's brows rose. "Was he just calling your bluff?"

"No ... I think he meant it. But by then, I had no desire to. Besides..."

Marius looked at her. "If there was a chance you *would* come back, he was the only one who would know how to help you to your investiture."

The investiture. Satara looked away as an intense mixture of emotions warred within her: relief that she would transition soon, that she wouldn't go to Náströnd; anger that she was going through this at all, and that Astrid had left her with no recourse; sorrow and grief at the loss of her battlemother; fear of the ritual itself, not knowing what to expect...

She said nothing in response to Marius. The silence felt like a thousand eyes on her, watching for her next move. Idly, she wondered if Coldheart and Aevana felt this scrutinized when she read their story.

Finally, Marius spoke. "Do you have any idea what it might entail, even if Astrid didn't prepare you?"

"I know a bit. Astrid told me once that it was a relatively short ritual for something so important. This life will end. I'm ... not sure if you could call what will happen *dying*, but I will change. The valkyir will give me a piece of their consciousness; I'll become a spirit of Odin and Freyja."

The vivid looked at her seriously. "Do you think you're ready for that? If you are to become less of an individual and more a part of one whole..."

Fear gripped Satara, but she swallowed it down. "I'll still be myself, just as Astrid was. I'll have free will like any other valkyrie."

"But ... are you ready for it?"

She stared at him blankly for a moment before looking at her hands. "I'm ready to do whatever I can to avoid Náströnd. This outcome was always a possibility, however small that possibility felt. Even if it's not what I had hoped for."

Marius searched her face for a minute, and Satara couldn't help but feel a little irritated at his examination. She was barely dealing with this on a mental level. If she wasn't handling it with the reverence and grace and deference to the gods he preferred, he would have to excuse her.

But his next words surprised her. "There were times when I felt the same way, growing up, before Tyr's Rite."

"You?" she asked skeptically. "I was under the impression you were something of an overachiever."

"I was a child, once. And a teenager," he added with a snort. "I don't think any teenager likes to be told what to do. Not that I was particularly rebellious. My father was all I had, I wanted to please him. Still ... every expectation people had for me—my entire life—was laid out from the beginning. Of course there were times I dreaded it all."

Satara frowned. "Then what exactly changed your mind? Not to put too fine a point on it, Marius, but you've historically been a bit of a zealot."

To his credit, he took the comment in stride, only huffing. "The Rite was what changed my mind."

"The Rite itself?"

"Yes. As the ritual changed me, it changed everything else, too." He closed his eyes as if trying to recall the feeling. "My hand was gone, and for a few seconds afterward, I thought I might die of the pain. And then ... something filled me. I can't even begin to describe the power, the light. It was like a second soul entered me—a piece I had been missing all along but didn't know I needed. Any apprehension or doubt I had was gone at once." He opened his eyes, irises rings of bright gold. "Everything suddenly felt ... right."

Satara watched the ghost of a smile appear on his face, but it was gone soon after, his gaze falling to the carpet and darkening. Her heart ached for him. To believe so deeply, to have such strong convictions, and to see the other Aurora failing so miserably ... it couldn't be easy.

A moment later, he sighed and stood. "I did not expect it, but after the Rite, I felt ... more like myself. In a way I hadn't known was possible. I hope you can have that."

Satara swallowed, her throat burning almost as badly as her wings. She hoped so, too.

CHAPTER TWENTY-FIVE

EDIE FINISHED DRAWING the last rune in her first translocation circle and stepped back, assessing her work.

It could have been more even. Basile's were always perfect circles with just the right amount of space between runes. But he'd assured her that looks didn't matter, so thank the gods for that. He'd also assured her that the ink would disappear from Yuval's carpet once they teleported. Thank the gods for that, too.

She looked over her shoulder at Cal and Satara, who were ready to go, standing at the edge of the circle, then at those gathered to send them off. An ever-exhausted-looking Adam watched with interest from the doorway, while Basile stood in front of Edie, having coached her through drawing the circle.

Elle sat curled up in the comfy chair nearby, flipping through one of the books Satara had brought. Though Cal had taught her how to use a glamour, her focus wasn't practiced, and it would fade away from time to time. At the moment, she was gray, her pupils glowing, but she was lively as ever, chewing some bubblegum.

She glanced around the room and tucked the gum into her cheek. "Is Mr. Sunshine not coming with you?"

"He wasn't going to," Edie replied, assuming she meant Marius. "I haven't seen him this morning..." With a frown, she looked to Basile for an explanation.

The priest seemed unconcerned; it was Adam who answered, leaning against the door frame: "He said he was going to check on Yuval and her girlfriend. And Klein, who I still haven't met," he added with a tired smile.

Edie attempted to smile back. "Maybe when we get a free second where people aren't trying to murder us."

"I'll be waiting forever, then." He sighed and rested his head against the door frame like he might fall asleep right there.

Cal peered at him, then at Elle. "Make sure your pop takes a nap, okay?"

"I'll try," she replied dubiously, going back to chewing her gum.

"Now..." Basile gestured to their translocation circle. "Whenever you're ready, step into the center, all three of you. Once you're all in, Edie, you need to empower the circle with your magic, and then the runes will do the legwork. You know how to do that?"

She sighed. "Is it going to be one of those 'you'll just know how to do it' things?"

"Kinda."

"Great. My favorite." But how hard could it be? She hated the concept of magic you *just felt*, but as long as it worked...

Without further complaint, she stepped into the center of the circle, and Satara and Cal crowded in tightly after her.

Lo and behold, Basile was right. Standing in the center, she felt like she was standing on top of many intersecting lines, all buzzing with energy. Their power pushed against her in greeting, like a house pet, and she found that pushing back with her own magic was almost an instinct. As she did, the runes glowed a soft silver, brightening until they were blazing fire.

Edie hugged her messenger bag tighter to her stomach and looked at the people they were leaving behind. "We'll be back ASAP!" she said quickly, before the room wobbled and blurred around her. Her stomach sank, pulse racing as her consciousness tilted.

The next thing she knew, they were in Harbinger Trinket & Tome.

She could smell dust and the shop's cedar beams, the lingering, familiar incense of the place. Her vision steadied after a moment, granting her a view of the back hall. It was closed up, the shudders and curtains drawn. Only a few feet in front of her, the ancient wooden door to the shop proper stood latched closed. An orange glow seeping through the crack under the door helped her see in the darkness.

Everything looked just as it had the last time she'd been here.

But there was something wrong.

It wasn't immediately apparent, but the longer they stood in the hall, the more the familiar scent of the shop was overpowered by something ... else. The unpleasant smell of something burning.

As Satara turned to open the door behind them, the door to Astrid's apartment, it became clear that the roar Edie heard distantly wasn't just the sound of blood in her ears. In the back of her mind, she wondered if they had landed in the wrong place somehow, but following Satara into Astrid's old hearth room, she saw that everything was exactly as it should be.

A flicker of movement—something bright orange—in one of the small windows caught her eye, and she snapped her attention to it. The glass was much cloudier and dingier than she remembered it being. And there was...

All at once, she realized what was happening. The distant roar was joined with crackling, shouts, the crash of something collapsing. The smell was overpowering.

Fire, somewhere outside.

Almost at the same second, she and Satara made eye contact and rushed for the windows. But there was little to see besides fire in the distance—the window faced an alley, not the main street.

"Come on." Satara's tone was sharp as she pulled away from the window and hurried toward the shop door.

"What in the Sam Hill is going on out there?" Cal whispered as Edie passed him, his sawed-off already drawn by his thigh.

Her answer was cut off by a *thud* as Satara threw the latch and burst into the shop.

Frenzied orange glared through the large front windows of the shop, washing over them. Smoke hung in the air and crept in through the cracks of the old wood, filling Edie's nostrils and making her cough. Whooping and hollering sounded outside, punctuated by gunshots and the squeal of tires.

Shipshaven was burning.

Almost immediately, a clattering at the front of the shop, near the register, drew Edie's attention. Her heart whaled against her ribs as she realized they weren't alone.

"What was that?" A man's voice; an American accent. A New Yorker, in fact, if she had to guess.

"What?" Another man.

"That slamming."

"Did that come from inside the shop?"

There was a moment of silence, shuffling. Satara backed up, trying to retreat into the hallway and nearly bumping into Edie in the process, but the intruders were upon them in mere moments. There was no time to hide.

The men, though they had sounded about as average as you could get, looked anything but. They were dressed in red robes—brilliant scarlet, finely made although they didn't fit quite right—the hem of which came just below the knee, touching shiny boots. Along with the robes, they wore red hoods, which draped along the shoulders. And in the pit of the hood, where Edie would have expected to see a face...

Skulls. Masks the color of bone, with skeletal cheekbones and bared teeth, silver filigree crawling up the sides. But the eye sockets weren't empty hollows; human eyes, their whites stark against the black greasepaint ringing them, glared out.

They already had guns drawn—handguns, but one of them had a

semi-automatic rifle slung across his back—and in an instant, the man in front raised and fired. The shot went wide and ricocheted, but even as Edie and the others were ducking behind tables and bookcases for cover, he was firing another one. And another.

Edie's ears rang, the smell of gunpowder filling her nostrils. With a shout—"Hlíf!"—Satara summoned a strong, faintly blue barrier around them, but Edie wasn't sure how it would hold up against bullets.

Cal didn't seem to care if he was protected or not. He leaned out from this hiding place behind a shelf and fired his shotgun, opening the chest of the man with the semi-automatic.

The other one had still not ceased firing, and in fact squeezed the trigger *more* in the panicked wake of the shotgun blast. His shots swung toward Cal, punching holes in the shelf and nearby bookcases. Dust, fragments of knickknacks, and scraps of books exploded through the air. Edie heard a few wet thuds and a harsh grunt and knew Cal had been hit.

Then, suddenly, the shots stopped coming. Edie peered past the table under which she and Satara hid. The man's hands shook as he abandoned his pistol rather than reload it and turned to his dying friend, wrestling the strap of the rifle from across his gaping chest.

Almost at the same time, she and Satara unfurled from their crouched position, surging toward the man. Edie straightened a half second too quickly, and the table above them tipped, hitting the floor with a loud crash as books and writing implements sprawled across the wood.

Satara's silver spear was through the man's lower back before he had time to turn around, and with a weak wail, he and his pilfered rifle dropped to the ground.

A second later, the shop's front door slammed open, and two more red-robed figures entered, already aiming their own weapons.

Edie gasped and threw her hand out on instinct, flinging a bolt of death magic past Satara and hitting one of the men in the center of his chest. The red robes dimmed and decayed there, and the rot spread from the epicenter in the blink of an eye, swallowing his form until he was only a gray, lifeless husk.

As his eyes glassed over and he dropped to the floor, Satara threw her shield, knocking the tactical shotgun out of his partner's hands. With a shout, he ducked to pick it back up, and Satara followed through with a lunge, spearing him through the head.

By the time the last man slumped to the floor, Cal had already appeared beside Edie. "Grab something," he mumbled. "One of the rifles. Just in case."

She looked at him assessingly. Getting shot didn't seem to have fazed him in the least, though his jacket and jeans were now bloodied. "Like hell I know how to use a freaking assault weapon, Cal."

"Just point and press. You might wanna grab any magazines you see, too." He nudged her shoulder, pushing her forward slightly. "Come on, we don't know when more of 'em will show up."

Edie sighed and crossed to the first two men. The one Cal had shot wasn't breathing, and the one Satara had impaled lay shaking in a puddle of his own blood. The stink of it invaded Edie's nose, the smell of the battlefield once again making her extremities numb, her breath shallower. Gently, she separated the man from the semi-auto and slung it around her own shoulder.

"Looks like a SIG 556. That'll do ya." Cal whistled through his teeth, half taking it from her to examine it. With a flick, he turned the safety on. "Look at the scope on this thing. Jesus." He looked down at the dying man. "You bastards really think you're something else, huh?"

"I'm not sure he can hear you," Satara murmured.

"Sorry son of a bitch." Cal drew his revolver and shot the man in the head, stilling his movements. Though Edie knew it was to put him out of his misery, her stomach revolted, and she fought to keep her breakfast down.

Satara came closer, crouching to look at the men. She plucked the skull mask from the first one Cal had shot, revealing a man in his thirties, white, unremarkable in every way save for his braided beard and the greasepaint around his eyes.

"Blood Eagles," she said, turning the mask over in her hands.

"What the fuck are they doing here?" Cal approached the windows and looked out at the world of blazing orange.

The shieldmaiden pursed her lips, swallowing hard. "The horn ... I couldn't put it together before I knew what it was for."

"All this because of that horn?" Edie adjusted her hold on the rifle, brows drawing inward.

"Because of me. They're here because of me." Tears pricked Satara's eyes, gilded in the orange light. Her face twisted. "They were trying to prevent me from becoming a valkyrie—first by thievery and now by force. Killing Astrid and letting my wings rot were planned from the start. They planned to let me die." Suddenly, she stood, discarding the mask in the pool of blood at her feet.

"But ... why?" Edie murmured. "Indriði already killed Astrid. Wasn't that her goal?"

"*Cattle die, kinsmen die, you yourself will also die. I know one thing that never dies: the reputation of each one dead.*" The shieldmaiden looked around the shop, gesturing vaguely. "We are never truly gone as long as those who held us in regard keep on living. Obliterating Astrid from this universe wasn't enough. Indriði wanted to destroy her legacy beyond repair, so that she could never be remembered again. That includes me."

"Why not destroy her reputation in some other way? Spread rumors about her or frame her for a crime or something? Why hurt you in the process?"

"Kolya. It was always about Kolya." Satara ran her hands down her face. "Indriði wanted—"

A boom from outside the shop drowned out her next few words. Edie watched as the building across from them—unrecognizable as anything beyond the skeleton of a storefront—erupted in renewed flame. Gouts of fire spat from the windows, and the resulting breeze blew the shop door open again. The heat was blistering even from where they stood.

Cal backed up from the windows and looked over. "It's only a matter of time before sparks float over here. Let's grab the horn and blow this burning popsicle stand."

"Where in the shop is it?" Edie asked, turning back to Satara.

"It's not in the shop," she replied softly. "Even when I had no idea what it was for, I knew it was important. I couldn't just leave it with the rest of Astrid's things, but ... it felt wrong to bring it with me, too. I knew if they sent another thief after it, the shop would be the first place they would look. They would tear this building apart looking for it. So I hid it somewhere else." She rubbed her hands together anxiously. "It's in one of the chest tombs in the old burying ground."

Cal huffed. "Let's do some grave-robbing, then."

They left the men behind, slipping through the front door and onto the burning street. Anything resembling a town had been devoured by flame; the sky was filled with thick, dark gray smoke that choked the air from Edie's lungs and made her eyes water fiercely. With renewed horror, she wondered where the residents of Shipshaven were—if they had made it somewhere safe before the Blood Eagles had arrived.

Satara looked up and down the street, eyes wide and horrified, before going left. They passed the husk of a car overturned in the road. The smell of it was unlike anything Edie had ever experienced, the bitter stench of burning fuel and melting rubber. She pulled the collar of her shirt up over her nose and prayed to whatever gods were listening that the thing had already blown up and wasn't in danger of doing so again.

The town was a maze of smoke and flame, but Edie could still hear whooping and chanting nearby. She squinted through the flickering wall of fire before her and could just barely make out the figures of men down the street, destroying what was left of a burning home. They had dragged something out into the middle of the road and were beating on it with batons. Her stomach dipped. Please let that be an inanimate object.

Besides the Blood Eagles, though, Edie couldn't see any people. She felt a little glimmer of hope that any civilians had made it to safety.

"Hey, boys! Over here!" The shout came from behind them, and Edie's breath caught in her throat as she turned to look—but another wall of flame greeted her. There was only the faint outline, rendered blurry by the heat, of a Blood Eagle coming down the street toward them.

Hoping he hadn't noticed them, Edie followed Satara as she ducked into the shadow of a brick building.

The bricks were cold compared to the sweltering air around her, and she rested a sweating palm to them, trying to catch her breath. The man was already passing, and the crackling fire hid her voice as she breathed, "Where's the cemetery?"

Satara nodded wordlessly and slipped down a side street, leading them away from the main thoroughfare. The smoke loomed heavy over the whole of the town, but as they left the small downtown area behind, the fires diminished until they were a distant roar.

As they hopped over someone's backyard fence and started up a small hill, the predawn twilight around them looked blue against the encroaching orange. Light slanted across the grass even from here, but they kept to the shadows.

Eventually, at the top of the hill, Edie could make out a wrought-iron fence and rows of stone monuments. The old burying ground.

From what she could see, it was a typical New England Colonial cemetery. Lots of grave markers, some monuments, and chest tombs, but no mausoleums. A gnarled oak tree loomed over it, covering half the yard in a black shadow.

Everything was still as they crept past the gate. Looking back at Shipshaven was like looking into another world. What was the fire World called? Edie could sort of remember it from her research. Muspelheim?

"Over here."

She turned away from the burning town to look where Satara indicated. Toward the back of the cemetery, there was a row of nearly identical chest tombs. They were better taken care of than most Edie had seen, with no cracks or chunks missing from them. She could even make out the writing. Shipshaven took pride in its historic burial ground, evidently.

This tomb was unadorned and labeled simply as *Ingeborg Einarsdóttir, beloved friend and mentor*. Satara ran her fingers along lip of the slab on top before pushing it aside with some effort. Edie's heart beat a little faster. In all her years wandering graveyards, she'd never thought those things could actually be removed. But there couldn't be someone inside, could there?

She came a little closer and peered in, but there was only an empty space. And at the bottom, a large ball of fabric.

Satara picked up the ball, unwrapping it to reveal a sturdy leather satchel. She unbuckled it, peeked in, then quickly closed it again. "Let's go."

Edie's shoulders nearly sagged with relief. They had the horn.

She wished she could say it had been a simple or safe excursion, but there was still the matter of the burning town behind her and the dead bodies they'd left in their wake.

"Let's draw the circle here," Edie said, reaching into her own satchel to find the instructions Basile had written down for her. The chances of Harbinger Trinket & Tome being engulfed in flame by the time they got back were pretty good.

As she began looking for a place to start drawing, though, a faint squeal reached her ears. Her heart leapt into her throat, mouth immediately going dry.

The sound of the cemetery gates opening … and a familiar voice.

CHAPTER TWENTY-SIX

EDIE FROZE, exchanging looks with the others. That voice was unmistakable. Her blood turned to ice in her veins.

Had Indriði followed them into the cemetery or was their luck just that bad?

"Hide," Satara mouthed, and slunk into a crouch behind the chest tomb. Edie followed suit, shifting her rifle into a low ready position and double-checking the location of the safety lever. She glanced up in time to see Cal flatten himself against the thick trunk of the oak tree, his own weapons at the ready.

She breathed shallowly, listening to the footfalls of people—certainly more than just Indriði—entering and walking up the burying ground's central path. After a moment of hesitation, trying to determine how close the intruders were, she peered around the side of the tomb.

Immediately, her gaze narrowed on Indriði. She stood in front of an obelisk almost thirty feet away, looking businesslike as always in a black-and-tan color block dress. She was smiling, and Edie wasn't prepared for the white-hot hatred that lanced her heart at the sight of it. This was the first time she had seen Indriði since she'd thrown them back into the dungeon. Since she'd killed Astrid.

Would one bullet to the head end it all? Her finger trembled over the safety for a moment. No doubt Indriði deserved to die, but would ambushing her with a gun even work, given her power? And if it did, would it actually change anything, or were the wheels of whatever godsforsaken bus they were on already in motion?

Slowly, Edie released her breath and took her finger off the safety. Not now. Not yet.

She watched the lesser Norn for another moment before moving on to the people surrounding her.

Immediately, she recognized one of the women with her: Daschla. She had discarded her business casual clothes and was wearing a white gown trimmed with brown fur and draped in red cloth, her hair braided tightly down her back. The second woman was wearing a cloak, but when she pulled the hood down, Edie recognized her at once, too. Scarlet.

Her gaze flicked over to Cal, who was leaned to peek out from behind the tree. His face twisted into a terrifying mask of fury—more than his perpetual grumpiness, more than even the usual anger he displayed when someone brought Scarlet up.

For a moment, Edie wondered if he would jump out from behind the tree and shoot her now. But no; he simply kept his gaze trained ahead, his body still as the tombs around them.

There were a few other people with them. A light elf, Edie guessed based on the buggy appearance, and three armed Blood Eagles. Unlike the ones they had run into in the shop, these ones wore more elaborate, well-tailored robes. Generals, maybe? One of them even had a capotain hat, like a seventeenth-century witchfinder or *V For Vendetta* or some shit. Their terrible fashion choices would have been funny if they weren't so terrifying.

"We haven't found anything, my lady," the one in the witchfinder hat said. Edie glanced between the Blood Eagle general and the others, expecting him to be addressing Indriði, but ... he wasn't. He spoke to Daschla.

So much for Daschla being a pawn in the Gloaming's plot.

"We'll keep the search up through the day and night." Daschla crossed her arms. "If we have to turn this entire town into ash, so be it. The horn won't melt."

The generals nodded, and Witchfinder said, "We'll keep the men searching, my lady." After a few moments, he shifted and asked, "If we had more people, we could search faster. Where is the rest of the Gloaming? I thought we had their support."

Daschla blinked for just a second too long and lowered her arms. "Because you're special," she said quietly. "You don't need the rest of the New Gloaming. You are an elite force."

Witchfinder swelled visibly, and when he spoke, Edie heard the renewed vigor in his voice. "Thank you, my lady."

Daschla smiled, though Edie couldn't make out how genuine it was, and held a pale hand out for him. "You can do this job for me," she almost cooed. "You can fight for me. I can't do it alone."

He reached forward, closing her hand in one of his thick black gloves for a moment before returning it to the body of his rifle. "We'll protect you, my queen."

Queen? Edie screamed internally.

"And when you're through with this," Indriði added, "you still have your big rally coming up." She made little cheering hands, a plastic grin pasted on her face. "Seeing that will more than prove your worth to the rest of the Gloaming. I'm certain of it."

"They'll be sorry they doubted us," Witchfinder said firmly.

Edie frowned, focusing once more on Indriði. It seemed out of character—her true character, anyway—for her to humor humans, whether that was Daschla or her Blood Eagles. Letting Daschla lead these people, encouraging them … there must be some ulterior motive. Just like using Edie to get to Astrid. Either Daschla hadn't outworn her usefulness, or…

Or Daschla wasn't human.

But that didn't make any sense. She looked like a human.

Shieldmaidens had some magic attached to their title, but they were still *human.*

"What's wrong?"

Daschla's words caught Edie's attention. Her tone was slightly sharper, addressing one of the generals. He had said nothing the entire meeting, and was standing stiffly at the back of the pack, slightly set apart from the others. Now, he shifted uncomfortably under their gazes. "It's nothing, my lady."

"Speak freely," she prompted.

He cleared his throat. "It's just … I'm not sure we're ready for the rally. I mean, I have some … doubts about our effectiveness."

Witchfinder turned to look at him and pointed toward the town. "Looks to me like we're plenty effective, General."

"Yeah. I mean, we can start fires." He paused. "But our ranks … not all of the men are ready for what we need to do. They're not all on board yet. If we waited, we could get more—"

"Why," Daschla interrupted, "exactly are they not on board? Haven't I made it very clear what we have to do? Didn't they pledge to lay down their lives if necessary?" After a moment, she added, "Just who are these cowardly men, who would turn away from the chance to go to Valhalla?"

"I—" The general shifted. "It's just sort of a … feeling I get. I don't think it's about the rally, my—"

"What is it about, then?" she snapped in a hot tone that seemed to turn off even Witchfinder.

The third general cleared this throat to chime in. "There's, um … okay, frankly, there's a question about leadership, my lady. Some of us are wondering when we're going to serve under the Wounded, or … another warlord." He tittered nervously. "You are our queen, but … someone needs to be in charge."

Ouch. Even Edie, who felt less than zero sympathy for Daschla, could feel the impact of the statement. It hung in the air as the "queen" took a few steps toward him.

"Someone needs to be in charge," she repeated bitterly. "Someone needs to be in charge." She repeated it once more, her voice rising: "Someone needs to be in charge?"

She threw her arms out, and suddenly, the graveyard was bathed in purple-white light. Edie gasped and pulled back as the glare washed over the tomb, temporarily blinding her. Within a few moments, it receded slightly, but it was still surrounding Daschla, throwing stark shadows.

She checked that Cal and Satara were still under cover before peering, with much more care than before, around the edge of the tomb.

Her stomach dropped into her knees.

Where Daschla had been standing now hovered a winged woman, seven feet tall. The same white gown draped over her toned, athletic frame, and thick, intricate lavender braids were wound into buns on either side of her head. A dark winged helmet adorned her head, a matching gorget around her collar and cuffs at her wrists.

She beat her wings—enormous, void-black, pointed like knives— once, twice before her bare feet touched the dirt. Still, she towered over the men.

A valkyrie.

Beside her, Edie heard Satara choke.

But Daschla was not like the unveiled valkyir she had seen before. They had all had more or less the same color palette: their ghostly bodies were always surrounded by blue and white light, their wings and armor monochrome. Their skin, whether it was pale as the moon or as dark as obsidian, always seemed to glow with an inner light, and the surface was always unbroken.

Daschla's skin, however, was as dull and dead-looking as the underbelly of a fish. There was no inner light, only paleness, shot through with small gray veins. The glow that came off her now was coming through fractures in her body. The breakages snaked over her entire form as though she was made of cracked china, one move away from shattering completely. Her dark purple armor shimmered in the light.

"You swore fealty to *me*." Her voice echoed like it was coming from another realm, but it was definitely the same woman. "Did the Wounded choose you? Has the Wounded trained you? Has the Wounded, time and time again, defended you, provided for you, put—"

She cut herself off with a shriek of fury, pressing her fists to her forehead. Her wings shuddered and beat the air, lifting her again so she was practically above them.

"I'm more than just your damn queen. I am the aspect of death! Do you idiots understand that?" Her next hiss slid through the graveyard like a cold fog: "I am the closest to Odin you will ever get."

The men were silent, though the two without hats took a noticeable step back, clutching their weapons tighter to their chests. From here, Edie could see all three shivering, and she had to clench her jaw shut to keep her own teeth from chattering, too. The temperature had dropped at least ten degrees.

At length, Witchfinder said quietly, "Yes, my queen," and the others followed his example in mumbles.

Daschla hovered for a few more moments before lowering herself to the packed earth again and pointing toward the cemetery gates. "Now go do your fucking job."

The Blood Eagles left in short order, heads down. They said nothing, but Edie could practically feel the bitterness rolling off them. Admonishing them hadn't made them more obedient.

Indriði, at least, seemed to notice this. As Daschla's human form returned to her, the lesser Norn crossed her arms and said flatly, "We need to move the rally closer."

Daschla huffed, tearing the red drape from her body and casting it into the grass. Her gown followed soon after, revealing an undershirt and leggings. "This wasn't how it was supposed to be. They were supposed to be willing to do anything for me."

"Men are fickle." Indriði gestured for the light elf to fetch the discarded clothing, and he scrambled to do so. "I told you they would never follow a woman."

"But I'm not a woman," Daschla snapped back. "I'm not a damn human. I'm more now!"

"Honey, I never said they would let you be their leader. You're worth fighting for: something to protect and be won. Their maiden queen." The Norn huffed a laugh. "I'm surprised they've tolerated you for so long without a male present. I guess one of them was hoping to be the lucky guy?"

"You *promised*." The younger woman's voice cracked. "You said that once I was a valkyrie, everything would be fixed."

"It will be," Indriði said, coming forward to place her hands on Daschla's shoulders. Daschla was of average height in her human form, but the Norn still had to reach up. "We'll move the rally to tomorrow afternoon, before any of them have time to change their minds. Once it's done, everything will be different. You'll be a queen, or jarl, or warlord, or whatever you want, babygirl." She released her shoulders and spread her hands. "You just need to wait a handful of hours."

Daschla's jaw worked slowly. She swallowed hard. Finally, she muttered, "Like the chickens."

"Like the chickens," Indriði agreed with a nod.

Chickens? If Edie hadn't been lost before, she was certainly lost now.

The New Gloaming group said little else. There were a few whispers to Scarlet and the light elf—giving orders, Edie assumed—but then they dispersed, leaving the old burying ground as empty and silent as before they had entered it.

No one dared move until their retreating forms were no longer visible. Then, Cal slipped from behind the oak tree to crouch in front of Edie and Satara.

"Welp," he said, taking out a cigarette and lighting it, his eye still on the cemetery gates, "guess that eliminates the valkyries from our list of allies."

Satara frowned and sat forward. "No, it doesn't. Something isn't right here. Whatever she is, she is not a valkyrie."

"She certainly seems to fuckin' think so."

Edie rifled through her satchel to get the translocation spell instructions again. "Valkyir serve Odin, right? They're connected to him?" she said as she smoothed out the paper.

"They're connected to both Odin and Freyja—they made the valkyir together," Satara answered. "Freyja is their Mother, their general. But they're practically aspects of Odin. Imbued with his magic."

"Then we'll ask Basile." Edie stood and looked around for a good place to start painting, eventually deciding on the packed earth of the central path. "I mean, he's a priest of Odin. So he'll know. Right?"

Satara winced as she stood. "Either way, we need to move fast. That rally they were speaking about ... it must be the one Basile has been predicting. Marius said the rallies have gotten more and more violent, and this one might be the culmination of those..." She trailed off, reaching a hand back to gently rub her shoulder blade.

The sight of her in pain spurred Edie to paint more quickly, focusing on the runes. Their priority had to be getting out of here and figuring out how to stop Satara's wings from poisoning her.

But if they could no longer rely on the valkyir to do it, they were well and truly fucked.

"Daschla is a *what?*"

It was about the reaction Edie had expected, but she hadn't expected Basile to look as skeptical as he did—like she might have been making it all up to embellish their adventure or something.

"She's a valkyrie," she repeated, more firmly.

"Like those hot babes from *God of War?*" Elle chimed in from the chair. It seemed she was camped out there for the day, curled up in a blanket with her phone.

Edie glanced but ignored her, focusing instead on Basile's judgmental gaze. "Satara can vouch for me."

"Oh?" The priest raised his brows and looked over her shoulder at Satara, who lingered in the dining area, eyeing the easel Yuval had left in front of the large windows.

She didn't answer, her fingertips ghosting over the unfinished canvas. Her wings had come unfurled and were sagging down her back, trembling slightly.

Edie watched for another moment before approaching. "Satara?" She kept her voice soft. "Are you okay?"

The shieldmaiden opened her mouth, then closed it again. She nodded to the painting—an acrylic of an overcast field, dotted with wildflowers here and there. "This … it just looks like the field Astrid used to take me for training. Inland a few miles."

"It's pretty," Edie replied, unsure of what else to say.

"It's not exactly the same, but the trees…" Satara traced the treeline. "Astrid used to say it reminded her of Fólkvangr, Freyja's meadow. It always reminded me more of home."

She said nothing else, and Edie shifted from foot to foot, searching for words. Finally, she settled on, "Everyone brings their own point of view to things, I guess." *Or baggage*, she added internally. "Basile isn't gonna believe me about the valkyrie thing unless you tell him."

Satara's shoulders relaxed slightly, and after a few more moments, she turned to look at Basile. "She was a valkyrie. But she was wrong. Almost as though she was broken. And you should listen when Edie tells you something," she added curtly.

The priest had already waved a dismissive hand. "But that's impossible. That's *impossible*. As you know"—he nodded to her—"you can't just become a valkyrie. You have to be inducted by other valkyir. One of Skuld's Riders, specifically—one of the first six valkyir. Or Odin or Freyja themselves."

"So they got one of them to do it," Cal said from the couch, where he was gnawing stubbornly on an unlit cigarette. "Paid 'em off or something."

Next to him, Adam pulled a face and snorted. "With what, Cal? Bitcoin?"

"I dunno, gold? Treasure? The satisfaction of a job well done? I'm not a fuckin' valkyrie."

"That's a shame. You'd look good in a metal bra."

Elle cleared her throat. "Wooow."

"If you two could stop flirting," Basile snapped, "we have some more important things at hand. And no, Cal, they didn't pay them off. These are ancient spirits of Fate, not the Sopranos."

Cal held his hands up, glaring. "Hey! Don't bitch to *me*. You're supposed to be the priest of Odin. So did one of these Rider chicks turn her or not?"

"I doubt it. First of all, Satara said she's, what, broken somehow? Well, they'd have done a better job. And second, there's no way this ... conspiracy or whatever it is goes up that far. Odin or Freyja would know. I don't get a ton of communication from the big cheese, but *that* would be on my radar. And Odin's working against whatever's going on, so he'd have no part of it."

"We'll just have to ask the Riders what's going on when we see them," Edie mumbled, looking back at Satara.

She had eased herself into a dining room chair. Her wings were still down, trembling. The feathers had grown even sparser, and the skin and muscle below was withered and necrotic. Edie shivered at the sight of exposed tendons—or maybe that was bone?

They had no choice but to use the horn now. They were out of time.

"We need to head out," she said a little louder, looking back over at Basile. "Let's get everything we need together and go to Asgard."

The priest glanced at Satara, then back. "Fine. I'll have everything ready within an hour."

Edie allowed tentative relief to soothe her panic slightly. But ... there was one more thing. Something missing. Or, rather, someone. "Is Marius not back from checking on Yuval yet?"

Basile sighed, and Adam winced. Her moment of relief was over before it really started, cold seeping into her limbs.

"We were going to say something," Elle said, wiggling uncomfortably, "you know, before you dropped the valkyrie plot twist. We called Yuval earlier to ask where he was."

She paused, so Edie prompted, with a measure of irritation, "And?"

"She said he was never there."

CHAPTER TWENTY-SEVEN

As Marius exited the subway station into West Harlem, the wintry wind bit into him, stinging his face—but even the unnatural cold could do nothing to cool the anger and anxiety washing through his body.

Three weeks. For three weeks, he had barely left that subway platform, waiting and watching. When he hadn't been pacing back and forth or arguing with Basile, he had slept in fits and starts, always interrupted by nightmares. In the dreams, there was always a pervasive sense of dread, a certainty that his friends were slowly dying. Sometimes, he watched them be swallowed up and dissolved by darkness; others, he found himself unable to move as he heard their screams of agony, cries for help.

In all of them, he could do nothing. And when he woke on that dingy cement floor, sweating through his sleeping bag, he always found the same thing: The nightmares were real. There was nothing he could do.

He'd had the option to go with them. It had been his choice, in the end, to stay behind. He had never regretted a decision so much. And all because he had been too proud to let the priest handle his soul.

Idiot. Useless. Useless to the Aurora, useless to the Reach … useless to Edie and Satara.

He was holding them back. Just as he had held his father back. It was because he'd been protecting Marius's "secret" that Radiant Eirik had betrayed the Aurora. If it hadn't been for his dead weight, could all the resulting betrayal and death have been avoided? If it hadn't been for his stubbornness, could he have helped his allies come home sooner?

He knew the path ahead. He needed to stop the Gloaming. And yet at every turn, he felt powerless to do so. He kept falling down. The loss of his former life, flush against the grief, stacked on top of the helplessness...

Fuck it.

The thought of wasting another second, of failing again, choked him. Suffocated him. He would not sit idle any longer.

There was one thing he knew he could do.

With a shiver, Marius closed his coat against the cold air, shoving his hand in his pocket. It was better than the wind tunnels of Central Manhattan, at least; the buildings here didn't loom quite as tall. Most of them were made of brick, gorgeous and old. It made sense to him that the Temple of the Mid-Atlantic Divine would be in such a neighborhood.

He had been in New York City for a month now, and not once had he seen Radiant Oddfreyr's Aurora. Granted, the Blood Eagles seemed to be harassing the city more than anyone identifiable as the Gloaming—perhaps the Radiant had not yet realized that they were connected.

Still, he had never known the Aurora to stick their heads in the sand while chaos overtook their city. Even his father had mitigated the damage as much as he'd been able. So where were the Blades of Tyr now? What were they waiting for?

Marius intended to find out. From the Radiant himself, if possible.

Of course, the last time he had been in an Auroran temple, he'd been confined to his room, awaiting trial by the Divine Assembly. The last time he had spoken to Oddfreyr, the Radiant had practically threatened to kill him. But after what Edie and the others had gone through in the Wending, risking his own life seemed only fair.

He'd simply have to keep his face hidden until the right moment. For now, all he had to do was walk toward the golden dome peeking up over the other buildings.

The neighborhood around him was not what he had always envisioned when he heard the name *Harlem*. Though as an Auroran he was bidden to isolate himself from the world around him and worship the old gods, his father had seen to his education in history. Eirik hadn't neglected to teach about American history.

Marius hadn't thought about those lessons in a long time, but they came flooding back to him now. If he remembered correctly, through them, his father had revealed a particular fondness for the artists of the Harlem Renaissance. A pang of sadness reverberated through Marius's chest as he recalled that, thinking of his own rogue copy of *Rolling Stone*.

The Aurora had been their whole lives. They had never been allowed normality. Now, with all that expectation pulled out from under him...

He wished more than anything that he could speak to his father now, wherever he was.

But the Harlem reflected in those lessons was not the one he saw now. Its streets were lined with gastropubs and pricey shops. There were more white pedestrians than he had imagined there would be, too, crossing from the college campus into condominiums. He hadn't been expecting to see Cab Calloway dancing down the street toward him, but it didn't seem like the same neighborhood.

It wasn't long before the temple came into view. With its gray bricks, white trim, and Gothic Revival architecture, it looked like it belonged in Westminster more than New York. It blended into the area around it, simply a large complex of buildings that he was sure the average pedestrian assumed was part of the City College campus. In the dawn's light, the dome of the main building glowed like a small sun, almost impossible to look at dead-on.

Now to get in.

Marius had the disadvantage of not having grown up in this temple; he had no idea where the secret entrances were, where guards were stationed, what the quickest route to the Radiant's office would be. But he knew—and saw, as he approached the front doors—that he had come at the right time.

With the sun's rays just beginning to touch the temple, Aurorans were streaming in for morning prayers. The crowd was thick enough that Marius was sure he could join them unnoticed, and so without hesitation, he crossed the street and inserted himself into the throng in time to slip into the vestibule hall.

At once, the familiar smell of freshly baked bread and the heady scent of beer washed over him, so familiar and comforting that he had to remind himself to stay on his guard. After morning prayers, an offering to the gods and ancestors, there was usually a breakfast. His stomach grumbled at the thought, but he wouldn't be attending.

In fact, he already had his eye on his target. As the crowd hurried from the vestibule into the nave, his gaze locked on the golden figure standing before the altar ahead and didn't waver even as he slipped onto one of the backmost benches.

Tall and puffed up, Oddfreyr wasn't wearing his helmet. Marius swore he could see the piercing blue of his eyes even from where he stood. His unsettling gaze scanned over the Aurorans as they took their seats, and quickly, Marius ducked his head as if in prayer. It would be unwise to reveal himself here; he would wait and shadow him.

After a few more minutes of the crowd milling, talking and laughing, the doors to the inner sanctum were closed, and all eyes turned to the Radiant.

As Oddfreyr began his prayers, Marius found himself critiquing his style. There were certainly things his father did differently, and better, though everyone around him seemed content. The words weren't that much different, but the tone was ... off.

He'd had no idea how foreign a temple could feel. He couldn't help but wonder if it was due to a distinction in culture or if, after nearly two months away from his people, he was already starting to think like an outsider.

But now was not the time to dwell on that. He pushed it from his mind and moved his lips along with the others, fudging the words as best he could, pretending to know what he was doing. When the prayers finally came to a close, he rose with the crowd and watched as Oddfreyr and a couple of his vivids exited using the side entrance.

While the rest of the Aurorans began filing out toward the mead hall, Marius diverged just short of the sanctum doors, skirting the wall to the side entrance. It was set in an alcove, with a couple stairs up, and slowly, he leaned to peer into the corridor beyond.

To his left, Radiant Oddfreyr was retreating toward a set of open double doors leading to a large green area. As he and the vivids flanking him crossed over the threshold, Marius slipped into the hallway and followed.

He was surprised at how naturally sneaking came to him, his feet silent against the floor, the cold darkness around him strangely comforting. He was not used to that feeling; he'd lived his whole life in the sun. But however surprising, it was a boon now, and he would take what he could get.

When he stepped into the large courtyard, the comfort of the shadow fled. Dread tickled his spine. Looking around hastily, he could only see a few other people in street clothes, and would likely see fewer and fewer the deeper he was led into the temple. But it was too late to turn back now. He would just have to hope he wasn't spotted or, if he was, that no one asked questions.

The Radiant disappeared through a smaller entrance on the far side of the courtyard, and Marius followed at a distance. Again, cool darkness washed over him. The layout of this temple wasn't the same as the one he was used to, but the cathedral-like stone walls were the closest thing to home he had seen in weeks.

A curved staircase took them up to an empty second-floor corridor, at the end of which stood ornately carved wooden doors. Marius didn't have to be an expert on the layout of this place to guess that those were the doors to the Radiant's office, and more than likely, the vivids with him would end up guarding it.

Heart thumping, he glanced around for somewhere to hide before slipping into a room to his left. An administrative office, it looked like. It was empty for now, but with morning prayers ended, who knew how long that would last? He had to act fast.

Peering from his hiding place, he confirmed his suspicions. The Radiant had disappeared into his office and the two vivids now stood flanking the doors. He would need to get rid of them before anything else. And without his armor, best to try and take one at a time.

He backed into the office, glancing around the room before grabbing a stack of papers from a desk and pretending to riffle through them. "Hey, can someone help me in here?" he called out, and braced himself.

The sound of shifting armor reached him, and after a pause, he heard one of the vivids say under their breath, "Did you hear that?"

"Must be one of the staff."

"Should I...?"

Another pause. "Go ahead. Better they bother *us* than the Radiant."

Marius set the papers down and flattened himself against the wall by the door, summoning a shield of light over his right forearm. He was able to track the vivid by the sound of their chainmail, and he held his breath as they entered and scanned the room in confusion.

He leapt from his hiding place, tearing the vivid's helmet off with his left hand and striking them across the back of the head with the shield in one smooth motion. They dropped to the floor with a loud clatter, and Marius knew their friend wouldn't be far behind.

"Ronnow?" A frantic voice. As more chainmail clinked toward Marius's position, he heard the soft hum of a light blade being summoned.

Marius flexed his fingers and summoned his own in response. His glowing shield dissolved, the light flowing down his arm in a helix before coalescing into a ball of energy at the end of his wrist. He raised it like a cannon just as the second vivid appeared in the doorway, and the light shot forward, exploding in his face.

The vivid barely had time to shout before Marius darted forward, yanking him to his knees and striking him in the back of the head. He collapsed next to his partner.

Marius slid into the hallway quickly, locking the door from the inside before closing it. There was no need to kill them—he'd killed enough vivids to last him a lifetime—but he had to delay them, at least for a little bit, should they wake up.

Brushing off his clothes, he looked down the hall. The door to the Radiant's office stood unguarded before him.

He inhaled deeply, slowly. Who knew what fate lay beyond that threshold? This was for the Reach, and for what was left of the Aurora's honor ... and for himself.

Before he was quite aware of it, he had darted to the doors and thrown them open.

Oddfreyr's office wasn't like his father's. His father's had been situated on a balcony overlooking a beautiful library. This one was smaller and more typical, with wood paneling, a coffered ceiling, and a fireplace. A desk stood as the focal point, with leather chairs opposite. And behind the desk, abruptly standing from his seat, the Radiant himself.

His eyes locked on Marius, and he froze. Recognition bloomed on his face like a fever, changing every inch of his expression, twisting it. "You."

Marius kept an eye on the Radiant as he closed the doors behind him. "So, you're still in the city. I was beginning to wonder if you were here at all."

Oddfreyr scowled. "Never doubt that, *oathbreaker.*" When he saw that the word made Marius flinch, he sneered. "Did you come here to turn yourself in, or did you think you might try to kill me?"

"Your guards made it easy enough," Marius said with a shrug. Though he tried to remain impassive, he couldn't hide his own burning anger at seeing Oddfreyr again; he could feel all his muscles tense, his jaw clench, his brow furrow tightly. "But I don't want to kill you ... if I don't have to."

Oddfreyr relaxed back slightly but didn't sit. "I would ask what you want, then, boy, but it doesn't make any difference to me. Either way, you won't be leaving this place."

Those words chilled Marius, but he held fast to his calm. "I didn't come here for glory. I want answers."

The Radiant said nothing, simply crossing his arms, and so Marius took a few steps closer, poised to defend himself at any moment.

"The Gloaming is infesting the city. Those 'Blood Eagles' are sowing chaos. Everything is falling apart. And here sits the Radiant of the Mid-Atlantic Divine in his ivory tower"—Marius gestured around the well-appointed office—"not sending aid to anyone and standing for nothing. *Why?*"

"I see no Gloaming," Oddfreyr scoffed. "And it is not my job to deal with the unattuned. They have their own institutions for that."

"Those institutions are failing." Marius shook his head, trying to school the disgust and loathing from his voice but not fully succeeding. "How can you not see the Gloaming? You think the Blood Eagles just popped up overnight on their own?"

"Humans have their own free will, apart from the attuned."

"Not usually with such impeccable timing." He frowned, unsure of what he should reveal. After a moment, he settled on, "The Reach has gathered evidence that the two are connected. The poster child of the Blood Eagles is Gloaming."

Oddfreyr curled his lip. "And what do you want me to do about it? You're not in a position to tell me how to do my job, coward," he added, face becoming redder.

"Stop them!" Marius snapped. "I want you to stop them. Use the army of Tyr at your disposal and *stop* them."

"I haven't seen them doing anything worth that reaction."

"The rallies? The *riots?*"

Oddfreyr barked a laugh. "I haven't seen them start any riots. Only the people 'protesting' them."

"Yes," Marius breathed. "How convenient that the riot gear only comes out once the Blood Eagles are done with their business."

The Radiant was unmoved, waving a hand dismissively. "The affairs of the unattuned have nothing to do with me. My duty is to the Aurora alone. I'll hardly put our temple and our way of life on the line for something we have no stake in."

Icy numbness bled into Marius's limbs. "So, what? You're going to let the world fall around us? You'll let the Gloaming take this city just as they took Anster? Then *nothing* would be left for us to protect. Would Tyr—"

"*Don't,*" the Radiant exploded suddenly, slamming his hand on the desk, "presume to tell me what *Tyr* would want. My ancestors have worshiped him for thousands of years, Marius. How long have *your* ancestors been worshiping?"

Another jolt of numbness. "That isn't relevant."

"Your father failed," Oddfreyr spat. "He wasn't suited for his station, and he stretched himself too thin, and he *failed* and *died* as a traitor."

Marius grit his teeth. "I thought the official story was that he was exiled, Your *Grace*. But we both know neither of those stories are true. What else has the Aurora lied about? Who else have we demonized?"

"There is no 'we,'" the Radiant hissed. "You are nothing."

Marius ignored the stinging in his chest. "Call me what you will. I came to demand that you do the right thing. Before Tyr, on your honor, you have refused to do your duty."

"I am doing my duty!" Oddfreyr's face was red, his posture swelling, jaw flexing. "I am protecting the Aurora. More than you or your oathbreaker father ever did."

"There are more important things to protect than the Aurora!"

Marius felt breathless once the words had left his mouth, like his lungs might collapse, and all at once, his body felt drained. A deep sorrow washed over him as he realized the truth of those words. Though he opened his mouth to say more, to qualify his statement, he couldn't muster the energy.

There was no point. Oddfreyr wasn't lost; he was hiding. And it was too late for Marius to go back.

Without ceremony, the vivid turned away, opening one of the office doors. Loss weighed heavily in his chest, dragging his gaze down to the floor, but immediately, he knew something was wrong. As he jerked his head up, his breath caught in his throat.

A squad of nine vivids filled the hall in front of him, in a three-by-three formation. Their weapons were summoned and at the ready, humming with warm energy.

He looked back at Oddfreyr and found the man smirking darkly. "Did you really think that you could just walk out, Marius?"

No. I suppose I didn't.

Marius slammed the door, grabbing a chair and swiftly wedging it under the knobs. By the time he turned back, Oddfreyr had already rounded his desk, a longsword of plasma summoned in his grip. They locked eyes for a half second before the Radiant slashed, aiming for Marius's neck.

He barely dodged out of the way, backing up toward the far side of the room. But the office was tiny, and the vivids were already pounding at the doors. The chair would barely impede them. He was a talented fighter, but he could not take ten warriors in close quarters.

The teachings of his mentors raged in his head. He knew what would be honorable, what the Aurora and the ancients would want of him. Stay. Fight. Die. Accept his fate.

Forget it. He wouldn't make his death easy for them.

Oddfreyr lunged for another strike, and Marius summoned a shield of light just in time, sending orange sparks hissing to the polished wood floors. He sent a pulse of energy through his shield that surged with a *pop*, knocking the Radiant back a few steps.

The chair dug into the floor, then slipped. The doors burst open, vivids pouring into the room.

At the same moment, Marius turned, sprinting toward the window. Without breaking stride, he dove forward, enveloping himself in a bubble of light as he crashed through the pane in a shower of glass and splinters.

And then he was falling.

The office was higher up than he had realized, but the fall would still only take a few seconds. More than enough time.

With a shout, he called his lightsteed. In the sunbeams streaking across the courtyard, the winged horse materialized, rocketing beneath him.

The glowing beast dipped slightly as Marius fell into place in the saddle, but it never faltered, skimming the grass for a moment before swinging back up.

Solar arrows whizzed past Marius. A few managed to strike the lightsteed, but they did nothing to stop the ascent, only causing little bursts of flame.

Soon, they were out of reach, soaring through the gray sky toward Manhattan.

"We need to get that motherfucker a phone."

Edie didn't respond to Cal's grumblings, hurriedly tying her boots. She hadn't had them off for more than a few minutes before another crisis reared its freaking head.

To be completely honest, she wasn't sure where they should start looking for Marius. New York was huge. But the thought of sitting around the apartment and waiting while he could be in danger was unbearable. It would be just her and Cal searching initially; Basile and Satara were busy preparing for the valkyrie situation in the other room anyway.

If they needed more … well, that was a bad fucking sign.

She stood and considered the semi-automatic rifle she'd left on the coffee table, then picked up Mercy's machete instead, clipping it to her belt.

Cal was armed to the teeth as always. "Ready?" He jerked his head toward the apartment door.

"As ready as I'll ever be." With a sigh, she went to open it.

Before she could, the knob turned quickly under her hand, and she stepped back just in time to avoid getting hit as the door swung inward.

Marius crossed the threshold, golden eyes wide and furious.

So much for a daring rescue. Thank the gods.

"Marius!"

Instinctively, Edie reached out with her magic, prodding him, though she had no idea what she was looking for or how she would know when she found it. Somehow, his energy felt tumultuous; the usual seething brightness writhed with something darker, both equally intense.

She wrestled with the feeling for a moment, dazed, before she noticed he was hurt. His coat was torn at the shoulder, and there were a few scratches across his right cheek. "Where were you?"

"Holy shit," Adam said, having just entered the living room. "Man, what happened to you?" On his back, the Genesis chimed in with a warbly moan.

"Oh no, he got all beat up and sexy," Elle mused from her armchair.

"I'm fine." With a huff, Marius glanced around the room before settling on Edie. "I was at the Temple of the Mid-Atlantic Divine."

Her stomach did a flip. "Did they follow you?"

"No."

"Bummer." Cal sighed heavily and patted the shotgun holstered at his thigh. "Soon, baby. Soon."

Edie ignored him and reached out, touching Marius's wrist. "Let's get you cleaned up." When he frowned in question, she said, "You're hurt. You didn't notice?"

He reached up and brushed his cheek, wincing slightly. "Oh."

"Come on." She gestured for him to follow and kicked her boots off once more before passing Adam, through the kitchen, into the bedroom hall. As they walked by Satara's room, they were afforded a peek of her

and Basile chatting as he drew a complicated circle. Only a door down
and they reached Edie's room.

She tried not to think of how awkward it was to have Marius here as
she approached the bathroom. The last time he'd been in here, it had
been after that godawful nightmare … and that had been dicey enough.
At least they were both fully dressed this time.

Once in the bathroom, she flipped the toilet lid down and gestured
for him to sit. As he did, his entire body sagged tiredly. The righteous
fury was draining from him somewhat, though she could see in his face
that he was clinging to it bitterly, trying to keep himself going.

"You should take off your coat," she suggested, opening the linen
cabinet and taking out a washcloth.

By the time she had wet it with soapy water, Marius was in his T-
shirt and jeans. Edie had to admit she still wasn't used to seeing him in
anything other than shiny Auroran armor. It was kind of nice to see him
be more human.

Aside from the scratches, there was a deep gash on his cheekbone,
and gently, he brushed his fingers against it. Light warmed his skin, but
the gash didn't close. It took her a moment to realize he must be
sterilizing it.

"Here, let me." Edie came closer, brushing some hair from his face
without thinking. Her ears began to burn a second later. "You can't heal it
if there's crud in it."

There wasn't really any dirt in the wound, but might as well put the
soapy washcloth to good use. After a few good passes and some wincing
from Marius, she balled it up and chucked it into the dirty laundry basket.

"What are Satara and Basile doing?" he finally asked, following her
movements closely with his eyes.

Edie took a deep breath. She was starting to wish he had come with
them. "We got the horn."

He frowned, searching her face. "But something happened. What?"

"I could ask you the same question. You lied about where you were
and ran off to see the Aurora … and apparently got hurt."

"You first," he pressed with a grimace.

She leaned against the side of the tub and recounted what had happened that morning: the fires, the Blood Eagles, the graveyard, how they had had to hide … seeing Indriði, watching Daschla unveil. She couldn't help the goosebumps that sprang up on her arms when she thought about it. "There was just something … wrong with her. Satara said she didn't feel like a normal valkyrie."

Marius's brow had furrowed, his gaze almost glowing in its intensity. "So there is going to be a rally."

"It doesn't sound good."

"No." He scrubbed his hand across his face, careful to avoid the scratches. "We need to get moving."

Edie jerked her chin in the direction of Satara's room. "We're leaving in around an hour to do whatever it is we need to do for Satara's wings. Then … I guess we'll have to figure out how to take on a whole army of crazy people with guns."

She looked over at him and realized, suddenly, that he wasn't healing himself; he simply sat patiently, expectantly.

"Did you … want me to use blood magic on you?" she asked slowly, in disbelief.

Marius faltered. "Should I not?" A pause. "I could do it myself, I'm just a bit tired."

Tired was an understatement. "I just assumed you wouldn't want me to heal you with, you know, ebon magic or whatever."

He hesitated. "It's fine."

Edie peered at him for a moment before pushing off the tub and standing in front of him. Again, she brushed some curls from his face, trying not to notice how warm the skin of his jaw became when she cupped it.

She focused on the smaller cuts first, calling to the blood and flesh, and soon, they were completely healed. The gash on his cheekbone took more concentration, but within a silent minute, it, too, knit together as if with invisible thread.

When she pulled away, his warmth left her, sending a shiver through her body. He had felt it, too, if his earnest expression was any indication. But she had no hope of parsing that expression. She still wasn't one hundred percent certain where they stood, even after that ... moment ... in the subway.

His wounds hadn't been serious enough to exhaust her, but with a bit of her energy depleted, she lost whatever resolve had been keeping her together before. She sighed and rubbed her forehead, voice just above a whisper. "What are we going to do?"

"I don't know." Marius's intense gaze searched hers again. "But we can't rely on the Aurora. The Radiant is pulling them all off the streets. They won't be there to help, no matter how bad it gets."

Edie blinked. "But why? Isn't his whole job to care about what the Gloaming is doing?"

"I don't know exactly. Perhaps he's just too proud to put the Aurora in harm's way. Perhaps he just doesn't believe they're a threat." He paused, then gave a hopeless shrug. "Or perhaps he agrees with the Blood Eagles' ideals. Perhaps he likes what they're saying so much that he's willing to look the other way for as long as he can."

"And no one is stopping him."

Another hopeless shrug. "What can the Aurora do?"

"*Better.*" The word left her like a curse.

"I'm sure there are those who would like to see him replaced. Or dead," Marius added with a humorless chuckle. "But I wouldn't know who those people are. And we have no time or means of finding out."

For a moment, they were silent, both turning their heads to watch the rain melt the snow outside the bathroom window. Then Marius spoke again, so quietly that Edie almost didn't catch it.

"Gods help us."

CHAPTER TWENTY-EIGHT

SATARA TRIED to suppress her queasiness as the world rippled and shifted around her—in vain, it seemed for a moment. But then, the brisk sea air hit her face, filled her lungs, and she managed to hold on.

Just a little longer. If she could just keep her body from failing for just a little longer...

The place they had landed was nothing like the Manhattan apartment they'd left. They were near the edge of a sea cliff jutting out into frozen water, with a sheer drop to the ocean about thirty feet ahead. Icy grass glittered around them, gentle sunlight rendering it practically glowing as it twitched in the salty breeze. It was late morning, so they must have left the US. The smell of ozone was thick in the air.

Despite the beauty of the isolated landscape, Satara felt her stomach dip, waves of nausea threatening the back of her throat again. She shuddered violently, making her breastplate clink against her gorget. Every inch of her skin was hot. Her vision swam at intervals. Her muscles felt so weak she could barely hold her spear. And *gods*, how her wings ached.

She held the means to her salvation—the horn—in her left hand, but she was hardly reassured. Her limbs were numb, her torso tingling with anxiety. She could barely think, but through the haze of pain, panic showed its face.

However this ended, her mortal life was about to come to an end. It was only a matter of whether she would go on to serve the gods for eternity or if she would languish in agony in Náströnd.

It was obvious which path was better, but she couldn't shake the overwhelming, warring feelings she had about this fate.

Glancing over one shoulder, she counted her companions: Edie, Marius, Cal, Basile, Adam, and Elle. The latter two were a bit more wide-eyed than the rest, but they were all on edge. It wasn't every day you called on heavenly messengers to take you to the city of the gods.

Edie and Basile were the first ones to follow Satara out of the translocation circle, and as Edie came to stand beside her, the necromancer looked her over. "You're not wearing ceremonial armor."

Satara glanced down at herself. "No. As you can see."

Edie tilted her head. "When you and Astrid came to see Indriði..." She trailed off, her gaze darkening. "Before— Well ... she said something about making a good impression."

Satara sighed. She had considered mending her ceremonial armor to wear it. This was supposed to be the most important day of her life, after all. But every time she took it out to start patching up the holes, or to launder the stains that had transferred from Indriði's dungeon, she thought about that night; she saw Astrid dissolving into oblivion again and again, as clear as if she were reliving it.

Donning the armor had been Astrid's great gesture, a show of strength. She had come dressed for war and, by the gods, she had found one. Satara couldn't bring herself to do the same.

"It's not my ... style," she said quietly, gazing out onto the rolling sea. A shock of anxiety numbed her stomach and legs. "That was Astrid's path. If I'm going to do this, I have to find my own."

She glanced back to see Basile looking at her steadily. Then he turned away, going to stand near the edge of the cliff.

"Fair enough," Edie said simply.

"Windy as a bastard up here," Cal complained from a few yards behind. "So where's the pot of gold at the end of the rainbow?" He looked over at Marius in his gilded Auroran armor. "Oh, shit, found it."

Marius rolled his eyes, but Elle gaped. "I can never tell if you're just being an asshole or if you flirt with everyone you see, Cal."

"I think a little of both," Adam mumbled, smirking.

The revenant shrugged. "What can I say? I'm a rovin' cowboy. I got horny mojo."

Marius pulled a face. "You're *dead*."

"Then why do I feel so alive when we're together?"

"Oh, brother," Basile mumbled, though his voice was carried away on the wind before it reached the others. He motioned Satara forward. "Let's get this over with."

She sighed, approaching. Usually, Cal's antics made her smile, but today … she wasn't sure anyone could soothe her today.

Once she stood by his side, Basile indicated a spot near the edge of the cliff, then the horn. "Face the horizon and blow the horn," he said, adjusting his glasses. "Like this: da-daaaa, da-daaaa."

She planted her feet where he'd instructed, frozen grass crunching under her boots. With a deep breath, she raised the horn. The pain in her wings lanced her arms, sending bolts of heat up and down them. There was no delaying this any longer.

She pressed it to her lips, staring out onto the horizon. Then…

Da-daaaa. Da-daaaa. The rich, keening notes echoed over the sea like sorrowful wails.

For a few moments, nothing happened. Bifrost didn't appear. Satara's stomach dipped in terror. Was she too late? Had the horn not worked? Was it not the right one?

She was about to raise it and blow again when she heard Adam's voice from behind her: "Whoa, what the fuck is that?"

The clouds over the sun had parted, and its blazing glow stabbed her eyes. She shaded them with a hand but could still see nothing. It wasn't until Basile pointed just above the sun that she could make out the change.

A seething, shimmering ribbon of light had struck out of the sky like a giant snake. The head of it slithered closer to them, and as it did, its colors became more vibrant—red, blue-green, purple, all writhing together. If not for the time of day, Satara would have thought she was looking at an aurora borealis.

But no aurora moved this quickly. She fought the urge to back up as the lights touched the edge of the cliff with a shrill hum like a saber being drawn. Each color shivered and burned like fire, and indeed, she could feel heat coming off the strip of red; she could hear the crackling of flames. The air around them went from freezing to warm in a second, and the frost on the grass began to melt away.

Then, distantly, the sound of beating wings reached her ears. She raised her head and spotted three figures gliding down the band of light. As they approached, she could tell they were armed, their skin glowing with an inner light and their hair twisting in the air around their helmeted heads. Valkyir.

They soon came to stand at the end of Bifrost, hovering just off the ground. All three were tall, much taller than even Cal, holding bloody shields and spears. Their eyes weren't visible from under their winged helmets, but Satara could feel all three gazes burning into her. Instinctively, in greeting, she spread her tattered wings as wide as she could.

"Satara," the one in the middle said, her voice rich and somehow silvery against the skin, "shieldmaiden of Astrid. Faithful of Freyja. You have blown the horn and called us three messengers to Midgard." There was a pause as her voice echoed over the cliffs. The sky seemed to have gotten darker around her and her sisters. "Are you prepared to step into the realm of the gods and accept your trial?"

A jolt of fear ran up her spine at those words. "I am."

"Then come."

"Ah-ah"—Basile's voice came from over Satara's shoulder, and she turned to frown at him—"not so fast, sister."

It took her a moment to realize he was speaking to the valkyrie. The valkyrie's face remained impassive, but her tone held an undercurrent of annoyance: "What is it, priest?"

"I think there are a few people who'd like to see this thing through to its end." He jerked a thumb at Edie and the others. "I'm sure the big guy won't mind if you let them in for a bit."

The valkyrie scanned the group, mouth pressed into a line. Satara shivered as her gaze swept the cliff top—she could *feel* that this being saw more than any human's eyes could. Eventually, she raised her chin and motioned for them all to follow her.

Satara stepped forward, though she hesitated at the edge of the bridge. The colors were nearly opaque, but the way they seethed made the whole thing seem insubstantial. Still, she found it held her as any other bridge would, the misty jade of the center strip winding around her ankles. She avoided the hot red at the far end, though its heat didn't seem to affect the valkyir at all.

As she trudged forward, pushing through her fever, she began to wonder how long it would take to walk the cosmos. Would they actually be climbing the World Tree? Would they climb higher and higher until they breached the atmosphere? How would that affect her human friends?

But she hadn't taken five steps before she could no longer feel the bridge under her; indeed, she could no longer feel her feet, or her legs moving.

Suddenly, she was moving much faster than anyone could ever walk. Instead of the sea and the cloudy sky, her vision was filled with prismatic light, twirling and coruscating like a kaleidoscope. Within a few seconds, past those bright colors, she could see stars. Galaxies. A trillion planets and suns that, at this distance, at this speed, looked as insignificant as a smudge against a black canvas.

Then, just as suddenly, they slowed. Satara wasn't sure where they were, but the skies were the color of a ruddy sunset. The bridge was a visible structure again, and far in the distance, she could make out the walls of an enormous, golden city. It was floating on air, Bifrost its only connection to anything else.

Ásgarðr. Asgard. The realm of the Aesir.

To her right, still far away but significantly closer, was another floating structure. Its placement reminded her of a waycastle, a fortress to watch and protect the one route to the city. She realized that this must be the home of Heimdallr, the watchman god.

Though their travel across the bridge had slowed, they were still moving quite fast. They only lingered by the waycastle for a few moments. Looking up, Satara could barely make out a horned figure that was, in all likelihood, Heimdallr himself. Then they were speeding off in the direction of Asgard again.

The thought of being watched by a god chilled her to the bone.

Even traveling quickly along Bifrost, it took what felt like forty-five minutes to reach the walls of the city. As they did, without warning, the soles of her boots made contact with the light bridge, and Satara was able to feel her legs again. Glancing down, she could see her body properly, and glancing behind her, she watched her friends materialize near the end of the bridge, too.

The lot of them marveled at the golden walls before them, Marius most of all, expression so earnest as to be almost pained. Satara watched as the pair of jewel-studded ivory gates, taller than she could see, slowly opened for them.

A gasp caught in her throat. Before them, Asgard rolled on for what seemed like an eternity. The lower city held a thousand dwellings, ranging from cozy to large, their beams and eaves intricately carved, their roofs thatched with glittering golden straw. Shields bearing family crests and paintings or carvings of the gods' deeds decorated the outer walls. To and from these dwellings, beings of tall stature walked, very few of them in any hurry; they spoke and laughed and drank, a cluster gathering in what looked like a city square in the distance.

Though apart from their height most of them were indistinguishable from humans, Satara realized with her heart in her stomach that these were lesser Aesir. They were in the presence of enough gods to fill a celestial city.

And they hadn't slipped under the radar. The gates of Asgard opening must not be a common occurrence, because as the valkyir led them through, many of the Aesir turned to look at the newcomers. Satara was sure the valkyir had been expecting *her*, but confusion crossed most of the Aesir's faces when they saw the size of the party following her.

"Come," the middle valkyrie said, turning sharply to the right, in eerie lockstep with her sisters. "Mortals aren't meant to linger in this place."

Satara glanced at her friends as they followed the valkyir. Most of them looked on the verge of panic, all for different reasons, she was sure. Except for Cal, who only looked vaguely uncomfortable, and Basile, who looked no more concerned than if he was strolling through Midtown. Satara herself couldn't deny that she was overwhelmed, especially when she felt hundreds of gazes shift to her damaged wings.

But soon, mercifully, the valkyir showed them to a ramp with parapets. It looked to be made of limestone, but its surface shifted, oddly iridescent. Following it with her eyes, Satara saw that it climbed upward in lazy circles before evening out above the city.

Her entire body seized, waves of pain and nausea crashing into her. Exactly what she needed when she was on death's door: a test of cardio.

"This path will lead us to the Hall of the Riders," the valkyrie announced, mounting the ramp. The bloodied gray shroud around her waist, falling down past her feet, whispered against the stone as she climbed quickly; and just as quickly, the two valkyir flanking her took to the skies, soaring ahead of the group.

Satara longed to spread her own wings, however injured they were, and expedite her journey. But, aside from the fact that the pain of flying might kill her at this juncture, she was almost certain this was part of her test. Looking back, she exchanged glances with Edie, then mounted the ramp herself.

The first few turns weren't so bad. The last was nearly torture. As they reached the heights and the path became straight, though, the breeze hit her—an oddly honeyed breeze, as if scented by mead—rejuvenating her trembling muscles, if only a little.

She could do this. One foot in front of the other.

And if she couldn't, she could feel Edie at her back, so close she was nearly touching her. The necromancer would figure out something, even if it meant *carrying* Satara into the Riders' hall. Of that, the shieldmaiden was absolutely certain.

A blessed numbness sank through her muscles at that thought. It was nice to be certain of something.

It wasn't long until the Hall of the Riders loomed before them, covering them in shadow. Satara was sure they could see the whole city below them from the glimmering catwalk. Behind her, she could hear Marius speaking softly to Adam and Elle, pointing out the halls of the gods in the distance—the starry tower of Breiðablik, Baldur's hall; a speck on the horizon that was apparently supposed to be Thor's Bilskirnir; nearer and to the east, the walls of Odin's Valhalla keep. The handful of others must be farther away, spread out within this seemingly endless realm.

She could only focus on the building bearing down on her: an enormous stone barrow, every inch engraved with staves, runes, or images of death. Moss grew on the domed roof, hanging off the edges—though it was more red than green, painted with blood that sluiced down the sides of the hall. The tops of the largest support stones had been carved with snarling wolf heads, and dozens of ravens perched on each. Standing stones etched with tales of the valkyir flanked either side of the approaching walkway like sentinels.

The formidable circular doorway was blocked by nine intersecting spears in the shape of the Web of Wyrd, but as they reached it, their guide held out a hand, and the spears retracted into the stone. With a great bone-shaking roar, the door lifted.

Satara stepped over the threshold, and all at once, the sunny civilization of Asgard melted away. The familiar cold of death embraced her—usually an oddly comforting feeling. The feeling of being a child, venturing into her clan's barrow to help her father prepare and tend to the dead, or to watch her mother ward against wights and draugar.

But, as their guide led them further down a hall lit with blue sconces, she could tell that this place was not the same. The sharp, distinct scent of blood filled her nose, sticking to the back of her throat. It smelled like war here.

The dread of what was about to happen, what she was about to become, filled her again.

Almost as if reading her mind, Basile said, "Psst," and pulled up beside her. "Remember what we talked about."

Before she could answer, their guide threw open the doors at the end of the passage and ushered them in.

What awaited them beyond was a strange combination of a meeting hall and a burial chamber. It was a long room, its walls decorated with gore-crusted weapons and shields. Six pillars, carved to look like nude valkyir in the midst of reaping souls, held up the roof, and carrion birds crowed among the crossbeams.

A quiet river of conversation flowed from the actual valkyir, all unveiled, who filled tiered rows of benches on either side of the hall. Each one was armored, their skin with that unearthly inner glow—all strong, though their physiques ranged from lean and toned to full and powerfully thick.

At the end of the hall, a large fire pit stretched lengthwise before a dais, the blue flames crackling steadily. Atop the dais were six thrones, all occupied save for one. The valkyir lining the room were awe-inspiring enough; as Satara approached the beings in the thrones, she had to fight to keep from shaking. The power emanating from them was so ancient that it was nearly primordial.

There was no doubt—these were Skuld's Riders, Freyja's elite captains, the first and most powerful valkyir ever created.

In the back of her mind, she wondered why the sixth throne was empty.

Their guide motioned for Satara to stand in the center of the room, facing the Riders with the fire separating them. She could feel her wings folding in, half-cradling her, but she couldn't stop them. Hopefully that was the only indication that she was barely keeping it together. Was this really happening?

All eyes turned to her, a hush falling over the valkyir. Silence reigned as one of the Riders pushed up from her crystal throne and stepped off the dais.

Like all her sisters, she was much taller than an average human, her pure black skin shimmering with that same ethereal glow. But it was clear that she was not just any valkyrie. Her raven wings were etched with faintly glowing coils and runes, making them look more like a magical text than feathers. Aside from her silver helmet—featuring not wings but an elegant rack of antlers—and breastplate, she wore no other armor; an intricate, layered silk dress poured from her waist and shoulders like water. Jewelry of silver and bone glinted on her wrists, her fingers, her chest. In one hand, she held a wand with a pear-shaped head like a distaff.

The jaw-hugging collar of her dress shifted as she raised her chin. Though her helmet obscured the top half of her face, with seemingly no eye slits, her gaze penetrated the entire room.

She raised her distaff diagonally across her chest, idly drumming the fingers of her free hand against the head of it. "Welcome, Satara, shieldmaiden of Astrid. Welcome, priest of the Blind. Hellerunan, again-walkers, Blade of Tyr. Welcome to our hall."

Satara bowed her head and didn't dare to look back at the others. Considering the wand, she was relatively certain she knew which Rider she spoke to—the one whose name meant *wand-wielder*, of course. "Göndul, my lady, thank you."

She felt Basile step up, not quite at her side but close. "Göndul. I don't believe we've properly met before."

If nothing else, Basile had the nerve.

Göndul leveled her gaze, and a smile crept across her dark-painted lips. "No, draugborn, we have not. It pleases me to meet one about whom I have heard so much."

"All good things, I hope," he said half-heartedly. Satara was able to tear her gaze away from the Riders for a moment to see that his expression was tinged with confusion. "Are there not supposed to be six of you?" He scanned the thrones and frowned deeper. "Where is Skuld?"

His words were met with eerie silence. Even the dignified Göndul tensed and stilled.

Satara's blood turned to ice. Something was wrong.

CHAPTER TWENTY-NINE

WHEN NO ONE answered promptly enough for him, Basile's tone became harsher, more urgent. "Where is Skuld? Where is your General?"

Perhaps unhappy with his attitude, another of the Riders rose from a throne covered in thick, opaque icicles. This being towered over even the other valkyir, her armor apparently made of shards of ice. Frost clung to her deathly blue skin and hair the color of dead straw. "Skuld is not here, little priest. She is missing."

"Excuse me, *what?*"

"What Skögul says is true," Göndul said evenly. "Skuld has been missing for two of your Midgardian months."

Satara shivered, dread spreading like poison. Missing? What were the chances that a Rider—the only beings besides Freyja and Odin who could create a valkyrie—would go missing around the same time Daschla showed up?

She wasn't sure she could speak even if she found the words, but there *were* no words for this weightless feeling.

Thankfully, her words weren't required. Of their party, only a few fully understood the gravity of the situation, and of those few, it seemed only Basile was bold or stupid enough to sass these godly beings.

"What the hell do you mean, *missing?*" He sputtered. "She's a Norn; where the *fuck* could she have gone?"

One of the other Riders growled, though she didn't rise from her throne of icy spears. She was similar in appearance to Skögul, though not as tall. Satara assumed this was her twin, Geirskögul. "Watch how you speak, soulless one. You are unwise to have no fear of us."

Göndul held up a long hand. "Fear is the snarling wolf that lashes out. Is that not so, Gunnr?"

The leftmost Rider, whose throne and body were both draped with pelts, reached down to scratch the withers of the horse-sized timber wolf curled up at her side. "Aye, so it is." She looked at Basile, her eyes laser-point blue dots boring into him from the hollows of her wolf's skull helmet. "He fears much."

The priest rolled his eyes. "I didn't ask to be psychoanalyzed, ladies. There are *apparently* more important matters at hand." To Göndul, "Skuld?"

"Freyja and Odin have been informed," she said curtly. "I have been communing and scrying with our Mother Valkyrie since we became aware of the General's disappearance."

"*And?*"

"We have reached the conclusion that she was abducted." Before he could open his mouth, Göndul added, "By whom, we have no idea. We are without a Rider-General."

As the wand-wielder confirmed abduction, Satara could practically hear the gears clicking in her friends' heads. A few whispered curses reached her ears. Now they were beginning to understand. A missing Rider was bad enough. A missing Rider *now?*

What had the Gloaming done?

Fuzzy numbness began to crawl up the back of Satara's neck. Her mouth and chest felt unbearably hot and dry, her veins pulsing.

"And Odin didn't think he should maybe bring this up with me?" Basile spread his hands. "Perhaps just *mention* the Rider-General, one of the *Mother Norns*, was missing so I could keep my eyes peeled?"

The last Rider—Hildr, Satara thought vaguely through her numbness —hissed from her throne of skulls. She was a thin, deathly pale creature in black armor and a shadowy cloak, her face obscured by the hood. Smoke, or perhaps steam, like what curls off a battlefield of freshly dead men, shrouded her so that only her head, shoulders, and hands were fully discernible. "Let's have done with this man, sisters; we asked for no meddling priest. It is the fledgling's right alone to speak with us now."

No sooner had she said it than pain ripped through Satara's body, exploding across her shoulders and down her back—brighter than anything she had felt so far, even worse than when she'd exited the Wending. A scream tore the room, accompanied by the sound of weapons clattering to the floor. Suddenly, she was on her hands and knees, her palms and wrists stinging as the cold stone floor bit her flesh. Another keening scream. Her head was too foggy to tell whose.

She smelled the blood and heard it pattering to the floor before she could focus enough to see it. It fell around her like rain, along with feathers and bits of flesh. She raised her trembling hands and saw that the purple burn in her veins had spread, nearly reaching her fingers now. Her wings seized violently around her for a few moments, exposed sinew twisting ... then her entire body slumped to the ground.

They were killing her. They were so heavy, and sick, and they were killing her. Astrid had died, and now she would die, too; she could already feel the cold seeping in.

Clinging to her last shred of consciousness, she could feel bodies crouching next to her, warmer hands trying to lift her. Male voices— "Satara!" "Wolfbinder! Is she all right?" "Can you hear me, kid?"—and one stern female voice she vaguely recognized as Edie. "Whatever happened to Skuld, we need to do something for Satara *now*. We can't do anything either way until she's better."

"I agree." This voice was clearer, like a pool of water. Göndul. "Keep her still."

If whoever was holding Satara held her tighter, it barely registered compared to the pain. She panted against the stones as the air around her became colder and colder. She was dying. She must be. The mists of Niflhel were already coming to swallow her.

Then she managed to look up, and saw despite her darkening vision that Göndul had crouched before her. The Rider's aura was as frigid and magical as a silent winter's morning.

With a few whispered words, the Rider reached out, touching one of Satara's shoulders with the freezing head of her wand.

Suddenly, the crystal ice water of Göndul's voice was in her. It burst through her veins in less than a second, chasing the burning poison that seared her body. With a shock of cold and a gasp, she felt her wings go rigid, quaking with the force of the magic.

And then, the ice receded, leaving a cool balm lingering where pain had been. Satara felt like she was floating, nearly delirious from the sudden relief. She was rejuvenated, body and soul, and almost smiled as her wings—fluffy once more—cradled her shoulders.

"Rise, fledgling," Göndul said softly, offering a hand to her.

Satara didn't hesitate to place her hand in the Rider's, but as she rose, she noticed something new. A pattern across her skin. Where the poison had irritated her veins, she now had a matrix of scars, slightly lighter than the deep umber of the rest of her skin. They sliced up her arms like lightning, looking more faded than fresh scars should.

She waited for grief to stab her heart. Already, this ordeal had changed her body. But she found, unexpectedly, that she hardly cared. She was alive and safe from eternal torment.

Despite the best efforts of those who would see her shamed and broken, she had arrived at her trial.

"Satara," Göndul said, still holding her hand as if they were already sisters. "I am pleased that you were able to find your way to us. When Astrid was unwoven, we worried for your future. We all felt the disturbance."

"In the force?" came Adam's murmur from somewhere behind her, followed by a sharp wheeze as someone elbowed him.

Göndul either didn't hear him or didn't care. "You must complete a trial. When you have proven yourself, you will return here for our ritual and join our sisterhood."

Behind her, Hildr's billowing form shifted. "If you fail, you will remain as you are."

"Your wings will rot once more," Gunnr said, still scratching her wolf. "Your soul will journey to the Corpse Shore, and you will forever feast on decaying flesh in the hall of vipers."

Satara suppressed a grimace and bowed her head.

The next voice was Skögul's. "You will be allowed one champion from among our ranks to accompany you to Odin's hunting grounds."

"There," continued her twin, voice smooth and sharp, "you will feed Odin's dogs."

"Great," Cal said. "Where's the Alpo?"

Satara raised a hand to rub the center of her forehead. Of course it was too much to ask for her friends to be reverent for more than a few minutes at a time.

From her throne, Gunnr sneered. "The Allfather's hounds are ravenous and greedy. They must be fed with a glorious hunt."

"You will need to track a great beast and slay it," Göndul said. "It will be a difficult task. And even then, the finding of the beast will be simple compared to the killing of it. Do you see, fledgling?"

"I understand."

The Rider lowered her wand, chin lifting a bit. "Along with your chosen champion, you will be granted another boon. Odin's hunting grounds are vast; you will need a guide to lead you through. Someone who knows them very well indeed."

She motioned to the entrance of the hall, and Satara turned away from the Riders, unable to quell her curiosity. When the double doors opened, her stomach leapt at the sight of him.

He was tall, broad, and imposing, and the moment he entered the hall, Satara knew she was in the presence of a god. The dark iron helm that obscured his face was shaped like a skull with the face of a wolf and the antlers of a stag. He wore a fur overcoat, covering the majority of his armor, but the motif of snarling jaws and hungry eyes was carried through the pieces still visible, trimmed with fur and carved with glowing runes.

What drew Satara's eyes more, however, was his bottom half. Instead of boots on both feet, his armor was asymmetrical; his right leg was encased in thick, intricately molded iron, from his hip all the way down to his toes. Lively fire glowed within the details carved into the metal, almost as if she were looking at a forge and not someone's leg. The armor extended so high up that it felt strange to call it a boot, but somehow, she knew that was what it was—all one piece, a part of him. She would be surprised if he actually had a leg of flesh under it at all.

Göndul didn't need to announce him. There was only one god who would wear such a boot.

"Lord Vidarr." The words left Marius almost on accident, it seemed, a reflex of shock. He bowed his head, fist over his heart, and Satara followed suit, as did most of the valkyir. As Vidarr strode closer, the rest of the party seemed to take the hint as well. Even Cal had the sense to avert his eyes.

They parted to clear the god's path to Satara, and he stopped in front of her, looking down. He must have been over seven feet tall. The scent of campfire, pine, and furs encircled him, mixed with the strange metallic smell of his magic. Her heart hammered against her rib cage.

Slowly, he raised his hands and removed his helmet, shaking out chin-length dirty-blond hair. His eyes were the same fiery orange as the glow of his armor, glaring out from beneath a perpetually furrowed brow. She had to imagine his lips were set into a harsh line, but she couldn't see them properly. Across his mouth, along the bridge of his nose and hugging his jaw, was a metal mask that reminded her of a grate or a cage. The sight of it chilled her.

It took a few moments for Satara to find her voice. She had spoken with plenty of beings most would consider strange and powerful and had rarely been at a loss for words. A god, however ... felt different. "You honor me with your presence, Wolfslayer," she finally said. "You have my thanks for your guidance."

He said nothing, only looked at her, searching her face.

She'd expected as much, but beside her, Cal bristled. Despite Satara's internal begging and Vidarr's intimidating air, the revenant grumbled, "What, you too fuckin' good to talk to a mortal? Can't even muster a 'you're welcome'?"

Vidarr's attention snapped to Cal, but again, he said nothing.

"Cal," Marius said through clenched teeth, eyes nearly glowing. "Vidarr is the god of vengeance. A vow of silence binds him until he kicks Fenrir's jaws open and pierces his heart at Ragnarok. He can't speak." After a pause, the vivid added grumpily, "Even if you were worth speaking to."

To his credit, the revenant averted his eyes. He looked like he wanted to sink into the floor—an expression Satara had never seen on him.

With a huff, Vidarr raised his hands over the group, and for a second, Satara thought he meant to attack them with a spell. Instead, as though someone had struck a smoldering log, orange sparks rained down on them. When they hit Satara's skin, there was no heat—only a strange sense of awareness that she couldn't quite explain, like someone had turned a radio dial in her brain.

Vidarr scanned the party, lowering his hands. Then, after a few moments of silence, he began to move them, and a shiver went through Satara as his magic took hold. With every precise, complex hand signal, she found that words bloomed in her mind. A unique sign language.

She could read the signs fluently, his spell translating them into a sentence structure she recognized. «With my father Odin's blessing, your trial will be brief. What is your name?»

"Satara," she managed, trying to suppress the embarrassment of finding herself so breathless.

«S-A-T-A-R-A. Choose your champion and we will begin.» The god's eyes roved over each of the valkyir in the wings, sizing them up, as if he was trying to guess which she would pick.

Satara, too, turned her attention to them, but she couldn't help the pit of dread in her stomach. She was sure they were all more than capable in combat, and any of them would have insight for her, having gone through similar trials. But the thought of working with a stranger, in a situation that was more pressing even than life or death, made her nearly nauseous.

She took a few steps toward the benches, scrutinizing her choices. Some looked stronger, others faster. But how they looked had little to do with how they acted, or how much help they would really be to an orphaned fledgling valkyrie. The longer she looked, the more anxious she was.

With every second that passed, she became more certain of her true answer. It was just a matter of whether the Riders would accept it.

There was only one way to find out. She ignored the gnawing in her gut, turning back to the Riders and the Silent God.

"Have you made your decision?" Göndul asked.

"I have." Satara glanced around the room one more time before looking at her small party. "I choose Edith Holloway as my champion."

There was a moment of cold shock. Edie herself tensed, wide-eyed. The valkyir exchanged confused glances. Vidarr gazed at Satara, slowly tilting his head.

Geirskögul broke the silence. "You choose … a mortal," she said, leaning back in her seat. "One whose presence here is already unorthodox."

Göndul stopped her with a raised hand. "There is no rule that states the champion must be one of our own. The choice was hers."

"To bring a hellerune over your own sisters," Hildr crooned. "How intriguing."

Satara stood a little straighter. "My friend has proven herself to me many times. She was there when my battlemother was obliterated. If you're worried about balance, she won't give me any advantage over bringing a valkyrie; she's mortal, and the lord Wolfslayer will be there to watch us."

Göndul exchanged glances with Skögul, then Vidarr, almost as if they were communicating without speaking. Finally, she looked to Edie. "Do you accept, hellerune?"

There was a pause. Then, Edie spread her palms, glancing from the Rider to Satara. "Well ... yeah. Of course."

"Are you sure?" Marius cut in, looking at her sharply. "It's Odin's hunting ground. You have no idea what you might find there."

Cal grunted. "Sparky's right. Could be only gods and valkyries even have a chance of surviving there."

Vidarr's gaze lingered on Marius, then turned to Edie. «Keep your wits about you and you will live.»

Edie nodded, clearly trying to swallow her own uncertainty. "As long as Satara is sure, I'm sure. Let's go."

Basile, who hadn't spoken since he'd been dismissed by the Riders, crossed his arms and glanced at Göndul. "Go on ahead. I have a few things I should fill these ladies in on anyway. Who knows, maybe we'll be able to help each other."

"Perhaps," the Rider mused, then addressed Satara. "When you return, the ritual will commence." She bowed her head briefly. "Blessings to you, Satara."

Satara bowed back, then turned in time to see Vidarr draw a dagger. With it, he traced an oval in the air before him. A faint golden glow split the room where he had traced, and as the glow spread, Satara could make out the hazy image of a landscape on the other side. Trees and grass.

The god stepped back and gestured for Satara to enter first. Her body buzzed with anxiety as well as anticipation. Only a few steps forward. Her entire existence would be defined by what happened in the realm beyond.

She took a deep breath, held her spear tightly, and walked through.

CHAPTER THIRTY

Vidarr's hot metallic power washed over Satara as she stepped through the portal. Something about the god's magic was antsy, and she found herself relieved when a cool breeze kissed her skin on the other side of the portal.

At first, her vision was unfocused, almost like her brain couldn't process what she was seeing; then, Edie and Vidarr came through the portal behind her, and things sharpened slowly.

Odin's hunting grounds were lush and rolling, a land of seemingly infinite space from the wooded hill where she stood. They had landed in a grove of golden trees, their trunks a shimmering alabaster, but she could see brushwood and tall grasses in the distance, as well as denser forest, an active river, and even what looked like tundra in the far northeastern mountains. Just on the western horizon, the smoke of what might be an encampment floated lazily into the sky.

It seemed these hunting grounds were meant to be all-purpose; Satara had never seen so many varied terrains in one place before. After weeks in cities, it felt good to be somewhere green again. Her guts ached with the realization that she couldn't return to Shipshaven—not for a while, at least. Perhaps her parents would come to celebrate her trial and welcome her home ... but she wasn't sure what she'd say to them.

She only had a few moments, however, to take in the hunting grounds. Vidarr started down the hill without ceremony, and she and Edie had to trot to catch up to his long strides.

In short order, he had crested another hill, planting his boot on a boulder as he loomed over whatever spread out before him. He glanced back at the two women, signed, «Your hunt,» and gestured downward.

When Satara joined him, she found herself looking down into a hill pass, a stretch of golden grass with few trees. A tributary of the river ran down the center, the water white as it rushed over rocks, and alongside it, several figures were locked in pursuit. Six of these were men, humans, but the last—ahead of the pack by an appreciable margin—was a creature Satara had never heard of, let alone seen, before.

It was enormous, at least the size of a draft horse, with silky sapphire fur. With the head of a hare, the body of a buck, and the tail of a fluffy dog, it was unlike any other beast. An intricate, spiraling rack of antlers crowned its head, and they seemed to glow and drip with little points of white light, like tiny stars. Satara had no idea what to call it besides a stag.

Though it was strange looking, she felt an odd draw to it. Her heart ached at its unfamiliar, undefinable beauty, at how gracefully and effortlessly it bounded away from the party hunting it.

This must be the great beast she'd been sent to kill. It was certainly game fit for a god.

She turned to look up at Vidarr and noticed he had been watching her intently with those orange eyes. An embarrassing chill ran through her. He was her guide, and a *god*, but she was still a woman. Chills like these were reserved for her favorite romance novels.

Wordlessly, he took his boot off the boulder and slid his helmet back on, gaze never wavering. Her turn.

The trial had begun.

Trying her hardest to ignore the Silent God's stare, Satara motioned for Edie and turned back to the hill pass. Together, they watched as the stag turned sharply right and ran up the hill, disappearing into a dense wood near where the river diverged. The hunters gave chase for another minute or so, but as they reached the treeline, they stopped and doubled back to regroup.

Edie brushed some windblown hair from her mouth and shaded her eyes against the noon sun. "Looks like they gave up. Maybe we should go talk to them? Y'know, as long as they're not going to use us as target practice."

"They may have more information on the beast," Satara agreed quietly, "depending on how long they've been hunting it."

Edie glanced back at Vidarr, as though in question, and Satara followed her gaze. But the god was stoic as ever, arms crossed.

"Let's go down there, then, I guess." The necromancer turned and zipped up her leather jacket, shoving her hands into the pockets. "Maybe they'll let us join them, even."

Satara wasn't sure how that would affect her trial, but surely there was no harm in asking questions. Using her spear as a walking stick, she started down the hill, Edie at her side, Vidarr trailing behind. It was around a quarter mile before they reached the hunters, who were arguing among themselves as Satara approached.

Now that she was closer, she could see that they were all white Norsemen, ages lingering around their prime, complexions tanned from being outdoors. They were draped in furs, and their weapons—spears and bows, mostly—were well kept, lovingly decorated, the fletching of their arrows colorful, their quivers embroidered. These were proud hunters. Hopefully, they were cooperative ones, too.

As a few of them took notice of the approaching small party, she felt heavy gazes on her. One of the men wore an oversized bear pelt mantle. Probably the leader. When he turned, his eyes crawled up her body painfully slowly, and she knew they were about to have a problem.

"Well met," she said as she came to a stop before him, mustering a pleasant tone.

"Well met." His tone was more reserved, almost wary. He stared more briefly at Edie, then bowed his head to Vidarr. "My lord."

The god said nothing, and the man's guarded gaze shifted back to Satara.

"We weren't expecting anyone to come interrupt us ... let alone two does toting an Aesir." A few of the men snickered behind him, and he grunted. "Who are you? What are you doing here?"

"My name is Satara. This is Edie," she said with a gesture. "I could ask you the same thing, my friend. What is a party of humans doing hunting in Odin's territory?"

"I am Siggi; these are my men. We are faithful of Mighty Thor." The hunter tipped his chin up. "He invited us to hunt here, in his father's forest, in his name. What game we bring back will be our blót."

Satara turned her head, taking in their surroundings. From where they stood, she could see a pack of wild boars snuffling at the treeline; just on the brow of the hill she'd left behind, there was a family of mottled deer. Even the river was so overflowing with fish that she watched five jump from the water in quick succession.

With a frown, she looked back at Siggi. "The valley is plentiful. Why waste time chasing after one stag when you could be bringing in all this?"

For the first time, the man broke into a smile. The ferocity of it threw up a red flag for Satara. "Because I want it. Imagine how nice a trophy like that would look on a mantel."

"And all of your men have agreed to this?" She addressed the others: "You'd help one man get one trophy? Don't you have families to feed?"

One of the men, who was sitting on the ground restringing his bow, looked up. His gaze clung to her body in a way that made Satara want to grow a hard shell to retreat into. "There are plenty of other trophies in this realm, if you know where to look. And free for the taking."

She tore her eyes from him. It was easier to pretend he hadn't spoken. "And how goes your hunt so far?" she asked. "What do you know about the stag?"

"It's a buck," Siggi offered readily, apparently unconcerned that these two women might take his quarry. "Seems to be in his rut, with the way he's roving around."

"They're in season," one of the men rasped behind them, his eyes glued to Edie. "Twenty does to a buck and every doe will still get bred."

The necromancer blinked slowly. "Think I just threw up a little in my mouth, to be honest."

Satara pressed, speaking directly to Siggi this time: "Where does he usually roam?"

"He does something of a circuit. Prefers those areas in the sun when he stops to rest. Follows the day and beds down in the west. We've seen him enter the thicket, but haven't been able to track him there. Yet."

"How long have you been tracking him?"

Siggi paused, then raised his chin again. His gaze had turned slightly colder; his tone was controlled, projecting what Satara could tell was false confidence as he answered, "A few days."

Though she tried with all her might to suppress it, Satara could feel a wobbly smile start to spread on her face. "Ah. He must be ... very elusive indeed."

"He is," Siggi returned sharply. "Has an uncanny knack for dodging arrows, hearing so keen it takes ten times as long to approach him, stride so great and quick he's near impossible to chase down." He planted his spear in the dirt and closed the distance between them. When he stopped, he loomed over Satara, so near that she could smell him. "But how does any of that concern you, girl?"

"You still haven't said what you're here for," one of the others said, a bit more timidly. "With the Wolfslayer, no less."

Siggi filled Satara's vision such that she couldn't see his men, but she refused to break eye contact with him anyway. "I have been sent by Skuld's Riders to track and slay a beast. Your stag."

"Is that right?" he sneered. "You think two females can track that thing better than six veteran hunters?"

"More efficiently, certainly." She planted her spear between them and leaned against it, hand over hand. He could scowl all he wanted; she wasn't cowering.

Behind her, Edie spoke up. "There's more than enough animals to hunt in this place. Some of them are so close you could literally kill them without moving from your spot, and there'd be enough for all six of you to do whatever you want with them."

"I don't care," Siggi said, still staring into Satara's eyes. "The stag is mine."

"Yeah, well, she needs it more than you." Edie stepped up to stand next to Satara, shoulders squared. "So back the fuck off."

Cal was beginning to rub off on her.

"Edie." Satara held up a hand. Her head felt cool, focused, each thought lining up neatly behind the previous one. A strategy was beginning to form. She smiled thinly at Siggi. "You're free to do whatever you wish, of course. But I'll also be tracking the stag. May the best hunter win."

He snarled. "Stay away from it. Your stink will scare it off."

Her chest burned with a white-hot heat. It took everything within her to keep her wings veiled. "It's not my stink that's been scaring it off these past three days, O Mighty Nimrod."

Siggi took a step closer, seeming to swell as he raised his arm. Satara braced herself, ready to jump away, but in the blink of an eye, the hunter stilled with a gasp.

A wave of heat washed over her, and she was all at once aware of Vidarr standing next to her, his magic tickling her skin.

He had grabbed Siggi's wrist in a crushing grip, fiery gaze boring into him. The hunter's jaw worked soundlessly, pain making his eyes bulge. A moment later, the Silent God released him, shoving him into the arms of his men.

Vidarr didn't need words to make his message clear. The men glared and Siggi sputtered, his face red as blood. He thrashed, pushing the other men away and pulling himself properly to his feet, but all he could muster was a pitiful, "May the best Norseman win," before he stormed off. His men shot Satara and the others glances and glares over their shoulders as they followed.

Once they were out of earshot, Edie blew her bangs from her face. "Screw those guys." Then, looking at Satara, "That was a pretty sick Bugs Bunny diss, though."

"It was more biblical," she responded wearily, casting her gaze to the sky. She couldn't let that confrontation shake her; they still had plenty of sunlight. "This hunt sounds difficult. It's been a while since I hunted deer, and I don't have a bow."

"I'll see what I can do." Edie wiggled her fingers. "Um, how much of this beast do they need intact, exactly?"

There was a swell of magic, and both women looked in time to see Vidarr sign, «You must sever the head and present it to the Riders.»

Edie shrugged. "The head? I can just try not to aim for the head. Maybe … rot its legs so it can't run, then you can get the killing blow?"

Satara cringed and bowed her head. Edie could sometimes be a bit more ruthless than she gave herself credit for. Perhaps it was an unwitting trait of hellerunan, or perhaps she was more like her father than she realized.

Either way, Satara had felt something when she'd looked at that stag, something that had made it hard to be quite as pragmatic about the situation. The way its strange beauty had compelled her had been almost heartbreaking; it was a supernaturally pure, simple being of magic. Had Edie not felt it?

"Satara?" She looked up to see Edie watching her closely. "You okay?"

"I'm fine." She started toward the treeline, giving the boars a wide berth. If this was what the Riders wanted—if this hunt was the only thing that could save her life—then she would do it. But it felt unnatural in a way hunting never had before.

Holding a hand up, she checked the direction of the wind, relieved to find that it was blowing to the east. Hopefully, with their scent covered, they would be able to sneak up on the stag. Regular deer had the most sensitive sense of smell in the animal kingdom and could be frightened away by the smallest change; Satara had to imagine that a creature such as this would be even more attuned.

As they entered the forest, she spread her awareness. It was something she'd learned to do from a young age, growing up surrounded by woods. Most people went through life with blinders on, only looking straight ahead. But to thrive in the wilderness, you had to be aware of all directions at once, for fear of animals as well as some of the forest's more malevolent denizens. There were forces out here, where you could only rely on your own perception to hold reality together, that didn't abide by the laws of humans. Satara assumed that was doubly true for a god's hunting lands.

Spreading her awareness was also necessary in tracking the stag. Every out-of-place twig, every depression in the pine-needle-and-leaf-blanketed forest floor, every scuff on the deadfall painted a picture of the beast's route through the wood. Occasionally, she would glance behind her to make sure Edie and Vidarr were following comfortably. Out of the three of them, Edie was easily the loudest; the Silent God, true to his name, moved as quietly as mist.

They continued to follow the stag's path. A few times, Satara was even sure she saw it between the trees, darting swiftly and quietly despite its truly massive size. It wasn't until hours later, when the sun was drooping toward the horizon, that they followed it out the opposite end of the forest.

It had led them into a plain of long grasses that swayed in the breeze, covering the sound of their approach. She crouched slightly, praying that the direction of the wind wouldn't turn against them. The creature was a mere thirty yards from them, now, where she could finally get a clear look at it.

Despite having been hunted for days and surely shot at, it didn't seem to be wounded, though she could see a few gnarled scars peering through the silky fur of its haunch. She got the sense that this was an ancient beast, that it had lived to see hundreds if not thousands of mating seasons. She almost felt like she was looking at something she wasn't supposed to—like she was looking at a god, despite an actual god looming just behind her.

She crept forward, trying to ignore the sickening feeling that pierced the base of her neck when she readied her spear. She could throw it an appreciable distance if she had to, perhaps hit something vital that way.

She glanced behind her, and Edie slid closer, weaving a death spell between her fingers as gently and quietly as she could. Vidarr stood at his full height, as if he wasn't even trying to hide, but he was so still the beast didn't seem to notice him.

Satara closed her eyes briefly before motioning to Edie, holding up three fingers. Now was as good a time as any. It wouldn't be long before sunset.

She tried to ignore the apprehension prickling the back of her neck.

"On three," she mouthed. "One … two…"

The beast stilled.

Satara signaled forward, giving the command, and Edie loosed a bolt of hissing-cold magic aimed at the stag's back legs.

But before the spell even left her fingertips, the stag had raised its leporine head, the twinkling lights around its antlers bobbing. When it saw the bolt of blue light rocketing toward it, it darted to the side with a fearful bellow and began to sprint westward.

Adrenaline screamed through Satara's veins as she jumped out of the grasses, reeling back and hurling the spear as hard as she could at the beast's retreating form.

The stag was preternaturally fast. Instead of piercing it, the spear pierced the ground, quivering, the silver shaft gleaming yellow in the waning day.

With a curse, Satara pursued, wrenching her spear from the ground. Her feet pounded the earth as she ran. She could hear Edie close at her heels. For every yard they gained, however, the stag gained three, and as they followed it over the brow of a hill, it became obvious where it was heading. Far in the distance lay the thicket the hunters had mentioned.

Almost without conscious thought, Satara spread her wings, beating the air. In a moment, she was soaring over the plain, fast approaching her quarry. It was just a matter of who would reach the thicket first—her or the stag.

She was gliding above it now, feet poised forward like a falcon swooping for its prey. All she had to do was descend, hurl the spear one more time. She had a clear shot at the heart if she struck now.

She raised her spear.

CHAPTER THIRTY-ONE

AND SHE FROZE. And watched as the stag became only a streak of blue between brambles.

By the time Edie and Vidarr caught up to her, Satara had landed at the edge of the thicket and was staring in.

"You had him," Edie panted, doubling over to rest her hands on her knees for a few moments. Her nose was wrinkled in confusion. "You had him…"

"I…" Satara shook her head, casting her gaze back over the plain. "I didn't have a clear shot," she lied after a moment. "I wanted to be sure I hit something vital."

Edie huffed. "Should we follow him in?"

"It's too dark. The sun's beginning to set. It would be a fool's errand." Satara brushed her braids over her shoulders and fixed Vidarr with a cautious gaze. "Are we allowed to make camp?"

«Do whatever suits,» he signed back. «You have as long as your wings will last.»

She shifted her wings slightly and realized there was an ache in them she hadn't noticed before. Göndul's healing spell was already beginning to wear off, though the scars on her veins remained. Her mouth dry, she looked to Edie. "Let's build a fire and make camp. We can go back to tracking it tomorrow. Maybe from here we'll be able to see it leave the thicket in the morning."

"Here?" the necromancer murmured, looking around. "We don't have any equipment. Tents and stuff."

"Right. We would be sleeping around the fire."

Her dark brows shot up. "Right next to these creepy-as-shit woods. Without so much as a sleeping bag."

Satara shrugged, suppressing a smile.

"You know I've lived my entire life in the city, right? I've only been inside an actual forest, like, three or four times." Edie gestured into the thicket, then let her hand smack against her leg. "What if there's, like, I dunno, Slenderman in there?"

Vidarr peered into the trees like he might be looking for the slender man she spoke of.

"A fire should keep away most of the animals." Satara stepped away from the thicket, searching for a good place to set up. "As for anything else, perhaps an elf prince will beckon you into the forest."

Edie trudged after her. "And I'll say, 'Nice try, Slenderman, but I'd prefer someone with eyes.'"

"Especially pretty gold ones," Satara added under her breath. She managed a smirk over her shoulder and was met with a stormy scowl and bright pink cheeks.

"Or maybe orange ones?" Edie tilted her head an infinitesimal amount toward Vidarr, who was following them at a distance, and raised her brows.

Satara flushed. She must have given Edie a look, because the necromancer hurried to fall into step with her, lowering her voice.

"*Yes?*"

"Edie." Satara averted her eyes, shoulders tense. "We've just met, and he's a god. And I have a million more important things to be thinking about right now."

"So? I mean, I assume it's okay to just look."

She suppressed the urge to glance back at him, sighing heavily. "I'm not immune. And he's always ... smoldering."

"Literally!" Edie added.

Satara shook her head, finally stopping. The ground here was relatively soft, free of roots, and afforded a nice view of where the stag had disappeared. "We'll set up here ... I'll figure out something for us to eat. There's certainly no shortage of game here."

"I'll look for firewood and stuff, I guess," Edie said, scratching the back of her head as she turned to the thicket. Awkwardly, she peered at Vidarr and asked, "Can you start a fire so I don't have to be rubbing two sticks together like a caveman?"

He stared at her for a moment before looking at Satara, as if to say *This is who you chose as your champion?*

Satara frowned at him. "Just go with her. Trust her." Normally, she wouldn't make demands of a god, but she took exception to his skepticism. Edie was braver than he could ever imagine. Turning away, she mumbled more softly, "I'll be over here. I need to think."

She had to think about the stag, about how she would bring herself to kill it. And how she would quell the guilt and dread filling her body with every moment.

A trial indeed.

It got dark much quicker than Satara had anticipated, but Edie and Vidarr had managed to get a large fire lit by the time she returned with food. They'd even dragged some dead logs from the forest and set them up like benches—or maybe barricades, considering Edie's wariness.

Edie offered up her machete and watched with fascination as Satara dressed the rabbit and gutted the fish, but they sat roasting them in relative silence. Crows clung to the treetops like black clouds, calling to one another until they were a roar of voices. It felt wrong to interrupt them, somehow.

But soon, they cleared out, and the cold night became oppressive around them.

Vidarr had rejected food. Satara wasn't sure how often gods needed to eat, but she suspected that removing the grille mask from the lower half of his face was an ordeal of which this particular meal was not worthy. That was fine; she doubted the one rabbit she'd managed to trap and a few fish would be enough to feed a man his size anyway.

It did bring to mind the million questions she had about him, however. Though he could communicate with them when he needed to, it seemed he preferred to be nonverbal. Or perhaps he was simply used to it.

Either way, it was obvious there was a lot more going on than what he said. Satara could practically hear his thoughts racing as he stared into the fire.

She wanted to know more about him. Beyond whatever base attraction she had to him, he was a *god*, a son of Odin, and one she knew only a little about. When the food was gone and it seemed she and Edie had exhausted all possible topics of conversation to fill the creeping dark, she peered up at him.

"Wolfslayer..."

His gaze snapped to her at once, almost as though he'd anticipated her speaking.

"I'm ignorant. You're our guide, and yet I know very little about you." She tilted her head. "Is that by design, that there is so little information to be found?"

Vidarr considered for a moment before taking off his helmet. Satara's heart thudded a bit harder. «There is not much to say. I serve my father and our clan when they need me. Otherwise, I reflect on my oath, and I wait.»

"Marius said something about your oath," Edie said, poking at the fire idly with a stick. "A vow of silence until...?"

Vidarr huffed in her direction, as if he resented being forced to communicate. Nonetheless, he signed, «When Ragnarok comes, it is told, the Ravener, the World-Eater, Fenrir, will break from his chains, and the gods will ride into battle to defeat him and the Army of the Twilight. The Wolf will overtake Odin, my father, in battle and devour him. With my boot, I will pry the Ravener's jaw open and tear him apart. When I avenge the Father of All, then speech will return to me.»

Edie blinked. "Okay, fair enough." Motioning downward, "It must have taken a pretty badass blacksmith to make you such a badass boot."

«Yes. All of them.»

"All of— Every blacksmith?" She raised her brows, glancing at Satara. "That's a hell of a collaboration."

«Every excess scrap of metal shaven or hammered in the forge, every bit of leather trimmed from the heel, is for me.»

Now that Satara was looking more closely at the boot, in firelight, she noticed that it wasn't one homogeneous piece of metal—it was all fitted together expertly, but there were slightly different colors, different textures. But as awe-inspiring as the boot was, she was more interested in his vow. "You have a brother, don't you?"

He huffed again. «Odin is my father. Our chieftain, and a wanderer. I have many siblings.»

"A brother who made an oath similar to yours," Satara clarified. "Váli, if I'm not mistaken?"

«Yes. When my blind brother Hodur killed my younger brother Baldur, Odin enchanted the goddess Rindr and forced her to conceive Váli. Váli grew to adulthood within hours and vowed not to wash his hands nor brush his hair until Baldur was avenged.»

Edie stared at him for a moment. "There is ... a lot to unpack there. At least you can wash your hands, but, like, the bar is low."

«Váli killed Hodur eons ago now. He is free.»

He is free. Satara's stomach knotted at those words. She knew the need for vengeance. She had wanted vengeance for Darras. She wanted vengeance for Astrid—of course she did. But to be bound by an event that hadn't even happened yet...

"Could you ever speak?" she asked, watching his face carefully.

His expression didn't waver, though he now searched her face in return. «A very long time ago. Longer than memory.»

"What were you like before?"

It took him a moment of thought. «I understand I was an energetic child. I remember my growth into adulthood being a joyful time.» He paused. «Everything was more joyful when Baldur was alive.»

Sadness rang through Satara's chest. She wasn't sure what she had been expecting, but for a brief moment, Vidarr's expression was truly sorrowful. The gods seemed so powerful, so untouchable. Their dealings in death and war had always been stories and lessons for her.

To see one of them before her, genuinely mourning the death of his brother, served as an abrupt reminder that these things had really happened. That, gods though they might be, they felt pain and loss just as humans did.

"I know how you feel," Satara said softly. "I lost my brother when I was young. Things were never quite the same."

Realization overcame Edie's face as she gazed into the fire, but she said nothing.

Vidarr turned more fully toward Satara. «Your battlemother was slain as well.»

Satara swallowed. "Obliterated, actually."

The god's brow twitched. «The wounds run deep.»

That was certainly true. When Satara tried to recall the person she had been before losing Darras, there was nothing but an empty void. A child's memories buried by grief. Even when she tried to recall who she had been a mere month ago, it felt like that life belonged to another person.

As though he had read her mind, Vidarr signed, «Who we were before matters little. Vengeance awaits. We must remain ever-focused.»

He was right that she wasn't the same person. But an existence given fully over to an all-consuming lust for vengeance didn't sound appealing either. No doubt Indriði deserved to die for what she had done, but

Satara knew her life was worth more than the damage she could do to an enemy.

Or ... she hoped it was.

Her heart sank. Of course, she had still given her existence over to something. Grief. Perhaps she had always been a little melancholy, ever since she was that little girl hiding in the woods, but this—this grief was different. It was heavy and dark like a rain cloud. It poisoned her.

She didn't know how to shed it any better than Vidarr knew how to shed his duty.

It wasn't long before Vidarr bade them to rest, and the two women curled up by the fire. Satara had to admit she felt much more secure under the watchful eye of a god. She fell into the dreamless sleep of exhaustion despite everything going on in her head.

When she woke, it was to the smell of smoke—blearily at first, and then all at once, with a sudden jolt.

The world around them was cold and bright in the morning sun, dew gleaming on the tall grasses like crystal. The fire had gone out recently enough that there was still thick smoke rising from the charred remnants. A cool breeze skimmed across her skin, and for some reason, it chilled her to the bone.

With dawning horror, Satara realized that the wind was blowing the smoke—and their scents—directly into the thicket.

She sat up quickly, loosing a small noise of defeat. Across the fire, Edie stirred and cracked open her eyes.

A swell of magic drew both their gazes to Vidarr. He sat on a log, exactly where he'd been sitting before, elbows resting on his knees. At some point in the night, he had shed his coat. «Your stag left an hour ago.»

Edie sat bolt upright and glared, reaching to pick twigs and grass from her bun. "That would have been nice to know an hour ago."

The god remained impassive. «Tracking the stag is part of Satara's trial. If I interfere, she will be punished.»

"It's fine," Satara murmured, dragging herself to her feet. Sleeping on the ground with only the fire and the clothes on her back to warm her was not ideal. Her body ached like she'd been hit by a truck. "Which direction did it go?"

The Silent God pointed to the northeast, and once they were sure the fire was properly doused, they began marching that way.

Satara cursed herself internally as she searched for tracks and scat. She shouldn't have gone to sleep. It wasn't as though it would make a difference at this point. One way or the other, soon, she wouldn't need sleep at all. She'd rather be tired but assured safety from Náströnd.

Tracking the stag through the valley by prints alone proved nearly impossible, but soon, they reached the wood they'd passed through the day previous, and its marks mercifully started showing again.

Unfortunately, so, too, did the marks of the men stalking it. An unpleasant reminder that Satara wasn't the only one hunting the beast.

She was beginning to wonder how far ahead of her they were when the dense trees parted for a clearing and she nearly ran into Siggi. She stopped just short, barely suppressing a squawk of surprise as she looked up into his snarling face.

He looked worse for wear this time, his shaggy reddish-brown hair threaded with twigs and broken leaves, his bear pelt covered with dirt and grasses. Dark circles ringed his eyes. The five other men were in similar condition, some expressions agitated, others hollow. She knew without being told that they had been lying in wait all night for the stag.

"Where is the beast?" Siggi demanded immediately.

Satara attempted to close her expression, gesturing forward. "Up ahead, I assume. I'm tracking it that way."

"Your tramping around has scared it off its usual path." He looked back at his men. "We haven't seen hide or tail of it since you showed up."

She wasn't sure what to say in response to such an accusation—that her mere presence could change nature's course. "What do you think I did? Bewitched it?"

He began to turn pink at the collar and the tips of his ears. "Don't speak to me like I'm stupid, girl. You've been chasing it off on purpose so we wouldn't be able to find it."

Before she could respond to that ridiculous charge, his posture shifted. He tilted his head, eyes suddenly sparkling, a vicious grin spreading across his face.

"You're a test, aren't you? A test sent by the gods to try my patience. An extra layer to challenge me."

Satara's shoulders tensed. He reminded her of a coiled snake about to strike, and she didn't want to take her eyes off him for a second. She barely registered as one of his friends slunk, wolflike, to the side to get closer to Edie.

"Or maybe a gift from Mighty Thor," the man said, his reedy voice shaking with a mixture of overexhaustion and adrenaline. "Two women between the six of us isn't so bad. We've made do with worse."

Edie crowded in closer, and Satara could feel the breeze of her icy death magic as she summoned it. "You can make do with my foot up your a—"

"We're not a test." Satara struggled to keep her voice even. "Or a gift. Just fellow hunters."

"Then forget the stag," Siggi growled. "It's mine."

As the hunter spoke, Vidarr's heat washed over her skin. Her spirits lifted slightly, emboldened. Siggi might have been invited to this hunting ground by a god, but she had that god's brother on her side. Tipping her chin up, she responded, "Nothing in this forest belongs to you. And judging by the pathetic skill with which you hunt, it never will."

Siggi raised his hand. If Satara was honest, the jolt of fear that struck her heart hurt more than the smack itself, but the blow echoed through the forest, along with the sharp words: "Know your place!"

She staggered back and collided with another body; a moment later, Edie gripped her arm. "Are you okay?" the necromancer asked feverishly.

Satara didn't answer. Being struck had momentarily dazed her, but as her vision came into focus again, Vidarr stepped out of the treeline. In two long strides, he made it to the hunting party.

He made no move to draw his weapon, but the way he was looming over them, hands working at his sides, it was clear he was fighting the urge.

Satara held up a hand and murmured, "Don't. Stop."

Vidarr looked over his shoulder, burning gaze bemused. Still, he eased back slightly, taking a step away from the men now practically cowering in fear. Not taking his eyes off the hunters, the god stabbed a finger at the other end of the clearing, and without so much as a word, they turned and left.

While he watched them go, Edie put her arms gently around Satara, trying to swallow the shaking in her voice. "Fucking monsters."

Satara kept her gaze on Vidarr and the treeline as the hunters disappeared. She couldn't help but feel a twinge of envy when she thought about how easily he'd intimidated the men. Her face stung, her heart stung. If only she could make herself terrifying like him, no one would ever hurt her again.

She inhaled deeply, closing her eyes. Such a sudden, intense desire. Was it wrong to want that?

When she opened her eyes, Vidarr had turned, and Edie had released her. She shifted, easing her vise grip on her spear, trying to find new resolve. The hunt had to continue. "Let's just move on. I'm not letting *them* steal my kill."

"What's our next move?" Edie asked cautiously, keeping step with her as they crossed the clearing. Vidarr followed a couple paces behind, as always.

It was nearing midday, and the sun was climbing higher, beaming through gaps in the forest canopy. Satara watched how the shadows moved against the underbrush, easily picking out disturbed branches and deadfall marking the stag's path. "The beast will need to stop to drink. If we find water, I think we'll find it."

The party fell silent as they wove through the trees. Edie had become more practiced at walking quietly, or perhaps Satara was so focused on the noises of the forest that she had tuned out anything else. As they walked, every once in a while, faintly, she could hear a whisper of what she was looking for—then she would step in the wrong direction and lose it.

But soon, the occasional whisper turned into a distant hissing, then a faint roar, until she could almost feel the water rushing against her skin. She walked more quickly in the direction of the noise. Suddenly, she realized she was thirsty, too, and the sound was only making her mouth drier, spurring her on.

Less than a minute of walking later, the forest became less dense. The sound of rushing water surrounded them, filling Satara's ears and making the ground vibrate in a way that made her think this was more than just a stream.

When she peered around a thick, mossy tree and into the glade beyond, her suspicions were confirmed. The area ahead of them wasn't a clearing in the true sense; the old trees were spaced out, their winding roots overtaking the forest floor and their branches creating a green canopy. Shafts of light illuminated a lush waterfall. The water she had heard cascaded from a rocky outcropping into a seemingly self-contained basin, glittering in the sun. It was so perfect and green it almost looked more like a fixture than a natural feature.

And standing by the edge, its head bowed to lap at the churning white water, was the stag.

CHAPTER THIRTY-TWO

SATARA HELD HER ARM OUT, signaling the others to stop moving and keep silent. They were lucky the creature hadn't heard them approaching over the rushing water.

She watched it closely, in awe at its size and majesty, admiring the small balls of light that swayed from its antlers. Little droplets of mist from the falls clung to its coat, rendering the silky fur even more gemlike than before. The simple act of stopping by the waterfall and having a drink seemed to relax the beast, its large eyes closing in bliss.

Again, something about the creature wrenched her heart. It was almost as if there was some kind of enchantment, a defense mechanism against hunting, but Satara sensed no magic. Witnessing the beauty and innocence of this creature felt like a gift from the gods. The thought of killing it was abhorrent—and the knowledge that she had to made her feel ill.

The air next to her shifted, human warmth and the cold of death mingling, and she knew without having to look that Edie had sidled up to her. The necromancer whispered almost in her ear: "Same plan as before? I take out the legs?"

Satara balked, face twisting as she looked at her. Could Edie really not feel whatever pull this creature had? Or was she just that brutal?

"I ... I don't know." When Edie raised her brows in question, Satara sighed. "This feels wrong."

"Wrong? Haven't you hunted before?"

"Of course. Plenty of times." She scrubbed a hand across her face. "The act of taking another creature's life is a sacred honor. It's always solemn, but this ... feels different."

Edie peered at the stag, perhaps trying to see what Satara saw. "How?"

"I don't know. It's just ... wrong. It's all wrong." Satara clenched her teeth, hand tightening around her spear. The closer they got to their kill, the more she felt like she was on the wrong path. She knew it was more than her apprehension over her investiture, and yet Edie didn't seem to feel it.

As she tried to puzzle out what she was feeling, the stag barely moved, simply lapping at the crystal water.

Then, suddenly, it lifted its head, staring into the forest somewhere off to Satara's right. Its entire body was tense now, still as stone. Its ears swiveled rapidly, then its head turned as if trying to locate something Satara couldn't sense.

By the time she heard it, it was too late.

A great rustling and a whoop echoed through the forest as Siggi came crashing from the trees, spear raised. The stag immediately bolted, but Siggi's cry was answered by others elsewhere around the glade.

Satara's heart jumped as the stag fled through a narrow passage leading to a greater clearing, dodging hunters that leapt from the bushes. It was fast as ever, but no doubt there were more men waiting for it. It was flanked now, surrounded. They were closing in quickly.

"Fuck!" Edie cried.

An angry heat surged through Satara's veins, filling her heart until she thought it might burst. *Siggi.* The arrogance. The entitlement. The reckless, grasping selfishness. And the stag wasn't the only one who would fall in the wake of these things—if he succeeded in this, if he stole her hunt, she would have nothing. She would die and be sent to rot in Náströnd for eternity. An eternity of torture and pain, all so one hunter could have something pretty on his mantel.

But, of course, it didn't matter to him. Even if she had decided to tell the truth, to tell him of her trial, he wouldn't care. When people like him *wanted* something, gods help anyone who stood in their way. They would put their desires above the lives of others every time. And no one would stop them.

But I will.

She leapt into the glade. The blood rushing in her ears rivaled the waterfall; she sensed rather than heard Edie and Vidarr following closely as she gave chase, boots beating the forest floor.

They sped through the narrow passage and almost immediately burst into a larger, more open clearing. There was no canopy here, only an overcast sun in a steely sky. And just under a hundred yards ahead, a sight that stopped her in her tracks.

Sprawled on the grass, pinned down by hunters bearing weighted nets, was the stag. It bellowed and bucked, trying to struggle its way to freedom, but the men had descended like a pack of wolves, a few of them even sticking it with their spears to keep it in place.

They roared and grinned, and Satara's heart clutched. This ferocity was unlike the first time she'd seen them chasing it; this was almost animal. The difference was, an animal didn't hunt for glory.

Siggi stood by, watching, until the stag's struggling died down. Its torso heaved with fear and exhaustion, eyes wide and terrified, as the hunter approached it and sat heavily on its chest like one might collapse into a chair after a long day's work.

He looked down into the animal's face and smiled. "Good work, my friend, but you can stop running now. I always get my kill."

The beast honked as if to reply, and that strange mixture of boiling hot anger and cold, dull sorrow surged through Satara again, making her bones ache. To be so willing to crush something so beautiful, and to do it with such glee...

He was worse than an animal. He was a monster. A *beast*.

The thought struck her, and a moment later, the answer to her puzzle was revealed with surprising clarity.

Feed Odin's dogs. That was her task, as the Riders had presented it; to provide meat for Geri and Freki, the Allfather's insatiable war hounds. But Odin's dogs didn't eat venison, did they?

Satara, along with every other warrior, knew very well what Odin's dogs ate.

The stag had never been her quarry.

Her head spun, thinking of how close she had come to killing it. She turned and looked at Vidarr, opening her mouth to say something—but there were no words. His fiery gaze was knowing. He simply crossed his arms.

"Edie," she said softly, "the men. Kill the men."

The necromancer stared at her. "I can't say that's not an idea I can get behind, but what about the stag?"

"Forget about the stag. Let it run."

Satara turned back to the clearing, tightened her grip on her spear, and stalked forward. She was only about twenty feet from the hunting party when Siggi noticed her striding purposefully toward him.

He seemed unconcerned, knees spread on his grisly throne, one boot lodged in the stag's ribs. Satara stopped her advance a couple feet in front of him, and he smiled. "I told you the best Norseman would win, did I not?"

"You did," she said icily. "And I suppose your theory was that you had the advantage because I am neither Nordic nor a man."

Siggi tutted. "Neither of which are your fault. How about a kiss for a job well done? It's only fair now that I've beaten you."

She ignored his request. "I may not be *Nordic*—or whatever euphemism you'd like to use—but I am more Norse than you or your friends will ever be."

The men fell quiet. Even in their adrenaline-fueled boisterousness, they were speechless.

"And," Satara continued, "how can you be so dismissive of *females* when it was a woman who birthed you, a woman who wove your fate, and a woman who will decide when you die?"

Siggi sputtered. Then his expression darkened. "You're no valkyrie, bitch."

"I don't have to be."

With a quick motion, she shifted her spear under her arm and thrust forward.

The spear pierced Siggi's chest with a sickening pop and a squelch. Pain bloomed on his face for a moment before his expression went slack. He slumped to the side, his eyes glassy, and Satara yanked the spear from him.

A second later, the heretofore silent men sprang into action. Two nocked arrows, two pulled their spears out of the stag to face Satara, and the final hunter drew a dagger.

Her final test began.

"Archers," Satara barked, stomping a foot and summoning a magical shield in front of them.

Edie replied swiftly, "On it!" as a globe of bone-chilling death magic shot past Satara, hitting one of the archers in the hip. The magic spidered across his form in an instant, withering the skin of his right side and turning it ashen. With a shuddering gasp, he collapsed to one knee, and his bow and arrow along with him.

His partner loosed an arrow in the same moment, aiming for Satara's head, and she raised her wooden shield. Her shielding magic would only mitigate some of the momentum and damage, and frankly, she'd rather not have an arrow in her skull at all. She was barely able to block it, the shaft splitting against the edge.

As she threw her arm up, she was exposed, and the man with the dagger lunged forward, stabbing between the buckles of her breastplate.

He was only able to tear the gambeson beneath, but pain radiated through her ribs and up and down her right arm and leg.

With a shout, she lashed out using her shield. It whiffed past the dagger-wielder, but she recovered quickly and jumped backward, putting distance between herself and the advancing spearmen.

Five trained men against one shieldmaiden and a hellerune just coming into her powers ... it wasn't an even fight. She wondered for a half second if Vidarr could intervene, but there was no time to plead with him either way. Another shout bolstered her magical shield, staggering the dagger-wielder and the spearmen.

In a haze of fluid smoke, Edie materialized within one of the spearmen's shadows. Without hesitation, she jumped up, wrapping her arms tightly around his neck. A mixture of death and shadow magic burst from her, and the spearman began to scream, swinging his weapon sightlessly as his body withered. After a few moments, he collapsed under her weight, and she jumped to the next spearman.

This one was ready for her, spinning as she appeared behind him. She was too close for him to stab, but he punched her hard in the chest, sending her sprawling across the blood-speckled grass. She hit it rolling. An instant later, the head of his spear sank into the dirt where she'd been lying.

Satara's heart leapt at the sight, but Edie could get away, and she was holding the dagger-wielder at bay with her spear. It was the remaining archer she was more worried about.

In all the commotion, the stag had managed to struggle to its feet, bellowing. The weighted net still ensnared it, but it bucked wildly. Once it got free, it would stampede anything in its path—the men would scramble to get out of its way. The perfect time for a distracted archer.

Despite the pain, she raised her right arm. When the stag finally freed itself and shot for the horizon, her spear shot forward, too, arcing through the air.

She couldn't be sure what part of the archer she hit, though she heard him howl in pain. She spun immediately to address the dagger-wielder trying to sneak up behind her, throwing her shield and cracking him across the jaw. He fell to the ground like a bag of sand.

His falling body revealed Vidarr, standing a few yards back, watching intently. Briefly, Satara was transfixed.

Grunts of pain pulled her out of her reverie—female grunts.

Edie. She spun again.

The remaining spearman had not fled far from the stag's unpredictable stampede. He'd brought Edie to her knees, a fist clutched in her raven hair. In his other hand, he held his spear, poised to impale her.

Through heavy breaths, he managed, "Let me go and your friend lives."

Satara shuddered, gaze locked with the man's. These were her options? Let him go and fail her trial or watch Edie die, just as she had watched Astrid die?

Slowly, she spoke. "You have to know that, if you release her, there's nothing stopping me from killing you after."

"Your word." He jerked his chin at her. "Or would you be an oathbreaker as well as a murderer?"

Her fists tightened at her side. Was this another test? Valkyir were supposed to choose who lived and who died in battle—was this some sort of sick play on that? But she had already determined that the hunters had to die. What did the Riders want from her? To let Edie die, too?

The necromancer was struggling in the hunter's grasp, but he had bent her back at an awkward angle. It seemed like she was having a hard time keeping upright, let alone fighting. Even if she did, that spear was inches from her chest. One move and it was over. Her eyes glinted like polished stone, alight with fear.

Satara's heart fractured. How could she let a friend die in fear?

If that was what the Riders wanted her to do, it was too much to ask. Investiture be damned.

"Release her," she said solemnly. "I swear I'll let you go."

The man stared at her for a beat. Then he pushed Edie onto all fours, turned on his heel, and started sprinting across the field.

But Satara felt little relief. In fact, all she felt was a strange, cold focus enter her body. Her vision narrowed, zeroing in on the man's retreating form; everything else seemed to fade away. Every fiber of her being said to *go after him*. To kill him.

Hot metallic magic washed over her. She felt the chilled metal of her spear against one palm, the grip of her shield against the other ... someone giving her her weapons. Her hands closed around them. A buzzing sensation at the base of her neck said *go*.

She spread her wings, beating the air until her feet left the ground. Wind seemed to jump under her wings readily, ferrying her across the field like an old friend.

Looking down, she was shocked when the terrain below her wasn't the green, dew-covered glen she had seen at ground level. It was dark, the grass a muted blue under the heavy fog crawling across it. Eviscerated, dismembered bodies littered the landscape, their armor and weapons sticking haphazardly out of the mud, rusting.

Carrion birds circled and landed, their cries filling the air. She felt one with them; she, too, was a carrion bird.

How she was seeing this battlefield now, when all she had seen was a grassy field before, she had no idea. But in the center of it all, one running figure stood out, his soul outlined in blue and red. Her body and mind filled with certainty.

A cosmic dirge echoed through the glen as she descended, spear first, and thrust into that blue-and-red glow.

A moment later, the light flickered and died. She looked below her and found she was standing with one foot on the hunter's head, her spear sticking from his torso. She took a step back, wrenching the spear from him. The fog began to creep over him like it was a hungry beast itself.

An eerie feeling beckoned her gaze upward, and she tore it away from the fog to look ahead. At first, she didn't notice anything different. Then, she saw the tops of the pines swaying, the trees parting closer and closer. Something enormous was moving through the forest.

Soon, they emerged: two giant dogs, charcoal gray with blazing white eyes. They frothed and scented the air and watched from the treeline, waiting.

Suddenly, Satara felt an immense warmth behind her, and the smell of copper intensified. She glanced back as Vidarr wrapped an enormous hand around her upper arm.

«Quickly.» He struggled to sign with one hand. «Behead him.»

There was an edge of urgency to his movements. She got the feeling she shouldn't keep Odin's dogs waiting.

Dropping to one knee, she felt along the ground until she found an abandoned sword. It was rusted, but she didn't have time to look for anything better. She gripped the hunter by the hair and drew the blade along his throat, hacking to sever the spine, until his head came loose in her hand.

It was a grisly sight … and yet it filled her with a sense of righteousness, and she knew she had chosen correctly.

Vidarr had released her arm, but as she rose, he motioned for her to follow him. They trotted back toward Edie and the other bodies, and Satara was surprised to find that the gruesome battlefield didn't fade back to normal—and it wasn't all in her head, if Edie's gray complexion was any indication. Had she changed it somehow, or had it been the arrival of the wolves?

Speaking of the wolves, they had advanced into the battlefield, hunched over with their muzzles in the fog. Making a meal of the freshly dead hunter, Satara guessed. She turned quickly to the task at hand, kneeling and raising the rusty sword again.

"Here." Edie fumbled at her hip for a moment before handing Satara the dagger of truth. "It's sharp as hell; it'll go faster."

Satara hesitated a moment—it seemed disrespectful to use a holy artifact for something like this—but then swiftly set to her solemn work. By the time the heads of the other five men were severed, the dogs were prowling closer, their hulking shadows black in the low light.

"I need someone to help me carry these." She held two in one fist, offering them out to Edie.

To her credit, the necromancer took them without hesitation. Once they were in her hands, though, she gagged and shuddered all over.

Vidarr grunted and cracked a smile beneath his mask—something Satara could already tell was a rare thing. «You will only have to hold them for a minute.»

"I'm fine," Edie said. "This is just … a *lot* grosser than I thought it would be. And, uh, their hair is very, very unwashed," she added more quietly.

Satara handed Edie a third, then rose with her own three and nodded to Vidarr. The dogs were less than a hundred yards from them now. "Let's go."

Vidarr turned, drew his dagger again, and carved their portal in the air.

CHAPTER THIRTY-THREE

THE RIDERS' hall was almost exactly as they had left it, although Basile had switched sides so that he now stood next to Göndul. As Satara, Edie, and Vidarr emerged from the rift, all heads turned toward them. There was a long silence as they lined up side by side to face the Riders.

Then, the silence was broken with a whistle and a "Woo-hoo! Hell fuckin' yeah, bro!" Distinctly Cal.

His cheer was followed by others; Elle first, then Adam joined in, then a triumphant Marius. Then, the benches on either side of them erupted into applause and shouts. Even Basile managed a genuine smile and a golf clap.

The praise filled Satara's body with something like electricity. She could barely keep herself from shaking. It almost made her forget about the ache still radiating through her outstretched wings.

Göndul raised a hand to quiet the cheers. When all fell silent again, she spoke. "Satara, you completed your trial with determination and cleverness. You identified your goal by following your instincts and did not let your focus waver from what Fate had decreed—even when the alternative was perjury."

"I beg forgiveness for breaking an oath," Satara said softly, fists tightening in the hair of the heads she carried.

"Your oath, first and foremost, is to Fate, and to the Allfather and Mother Valkyrie."

She relaxed slightly, raising the severed heads. Beside her, Edie followed suit. "Then I present you with these. Proof that I carried out Fate's will."

Göndul smiled. "And may they weight the Lady's loom."

"And may they."

Göndul stepped forward, and the blue fire between the thrones and the rest of the hall blazed higher. Behind her, the other Riders rose from their seats.

"You have done well. Your battlemother would be proud."

For the first time, Satara felt hot tears prick her eyes. She bowed her head.

"Satara Izem, it is time to complete the ritual. It is time to vest in you the power of the valkyir. Will you accept and become our sister?"

Satara tried to slow her heart, her breathing, the dizziness. "I accept. I will become a valkyrie."

Göndul bowed her head and spread her palms, beginning to chant softly under her breath. The other Riders did the same, their voices slithering over Satara's skin with an ancient, primordial power—a power she imagined one would feel in the deepest cavern, the loneliest forest, atop the highest mountain. Though the valkyir still whispered, their voices became louder somehow, until they were filling the entire hall.

Slowly, as they chanted, the blue fire in the pit spread outward, crawling into channels carved in the floor. Once in the channels, it spread more quickly, shooting up the walls and along the ceiling in spiraling patterns. Within only a few seconds, the ducts curving around her lit up.

She was surrounded by the spectral fire, and as it raged, so did her emotions. Fear, relief, apprehension, grief, acceptance, excitement—all mixed together in a nauseating slurry. She knew she could do this. She had made it through; her wings had not killed her, in the end. But she had hoped she would be more ready for this when the time came.

The Riders had all closed their eyes. Göndul, in particular, had her face tipped up to the ceiling, her body swaying slightly as she chanted. Slowly, she opened her eyes and leveled her gaze at Satara. Her irises were blazing pale blue; magic seemed to cling to her ebony skin, shimmering like starlight.

"Cast your trophies into the fire. Tie the threads of Fate. Send the souls of your chosen dead to their destinies."

Satara's limbs felt weightless as she threw the heads into the fire and watched it jump higher. She took the other half from Edie and did it again. The flames ate at the hunters' flesh, but she couldn't look away; blue filled her vision, sickly-sweet copper filled her nose, and impossibly loud whispers filled her ears.

Then, without warning, darkness enveloped her.

Satara wasn't certain how long it was before she regained consciousness. It could have been a minute or days. But she got the sense that that didn't matter anymore; she was no longer bound by time.

At first, there was nothing but blackness—a void that felt endlessly deep despite there being no light to create depth. By all rights, she should have panicked. The threat of floating through infinite space, untethered, completely alone for longer than the universe would exist, should terrify her. It should cause her to go instantly mad. But to her bones, she felt nothing but calm, even restfulness.

She wasn't alone. Slowly, as she floated through the cool darkness, she began to sense and then eventually *see* things. Things that *felt* like what she was now, somehow. Little points of light in the distance. Only a few at first, then more and more, until she realized she was passing them. She was moving through the void at an unimaginable speed, though she felt no wind or friction.

Just as quickly, she came to an abrupt but gentle stop—a stop that defied the laws of earthly physics, given her momentum a split second ago.

As she looked out into an endless field of these little lights, she suddenly realized what they were. Stars.

Seeing them felt like seeing family members she had never met. They were so unfamiliar as to be foreign, and yet she felt a deep kinship. They were the same.

Most of the stars were fixed in position, still as sentinels. One of them, however, swayed slightly in the darkness. It became larger and larger until Satara realized it was *walking closer*, part of some massive form she couldn't see.

It was hard to tell with little depth perception, but after a few minutes, it seemed to be very near. She could smell pine and ozone and could hear a steady *thump ... thump ... thump ...* as though someone was using a walking stick.

She realized with a shock who was approaching, but whatever form she was in now did not allow her to react. She simply watched in awe as the form of a hooded man bearing a spear was outlined in stardust. Nebulas bloomed from his sole eye, filling the outline, and then—

White light burst from his chest and enveloped Satara, washing out every sight or thought. Thousands of millions of voices flooded past her, rushing over her soul, most in languages she couldn't understand. Even if she could have understood them, they were so numerous they'd be incomprehensible. Blinding images of impossible geometry and runes no human could ever conceive of burned themselves into her vision, leaving behind dark, blurry ghosts in their wake.

The images and the voices came faster, faster, until she was sure she was on the brink of madness. Her consciousness expanded until it was long and stretched like a rope of taffy. She was a lattice of nine intersecting lines; she was nine spheres all colliding with each other at the same moment; she was stretching to the heavens, nine holes carved in her trunk, each pouring light and darkness into the others.

Satara.

This voice stood out over the others, the most beautiful voice she had ever heard. A woman's voice, she thought. It had a sharp edge, glaring with magic and power, but the waxing, softer part of the sound felt like a caress against her cheek. And then ... she was sure she felt an *actual* caress on her cheek, feverishly warm against her death-cold skin.

Satara, the voice said again. *You are a child of many mothers ... just as all humans are. Now, you have one more.*

With a snap, her consciousness took a more condensed shape, and the light receded. When she looked at the field of stars now, she found she could reach out with her mind and touch every single one. There was a tether connecting her to all of them, a million vibrating threads linked in infinite space.

Some of the threads vibrated differently, faster—she knew that these connected her to the valkyir. Some slower, less steadily, their presence hitching now and again—she knew that these threads connected her to every living thing. And some were still or stilling, their threads not as taut as the others—she knew that these were the dead things, still an inextricable part of the weave, but stagnant.

The Web existed. Of course, she had known, but to see it herself ... she could feel the very presence of Fate, the primordial connection of everything that had existed, did exist, and would exist.

Except for Astrid.

And, like a stone, grief dropped into her chest. Even here, perfectly at peace, given the absolute certain knowledge that the dead were still a part of the living, she could not forget this loss.

She understood now, seeing the truth of the universe, how Astrid had been obliterated. Energy couldn't be destroyed. But it could be severed from every other thing and cast adrift.

The thought of that profound loneliness made her want to wail, and to her surprise, she found she could. She loosed a mournful scream into the void, her trillions of threads throbbing with sorrow.

She had thought that Indriði had merely destroyed Astrid, expunged her from existence entirely. It was worse. She had *unanchored* her from existence, sent her careening off into Nothing. Connected to no one, living or dead, past or present.

A lesser Norn would know that. *It had been on purpose.*

Satara threw her head back and loosed another wail, staring into open space. Pain sliced her heart open, but still she stared. And the longer she did, the more clearly she could see ... something above her.

An incomprehensibly large shape, as dark as the void but velvety, its curves shimmering slightly. Some long, bent part of this object arced over her, a thousand miles overhead. A leg, gingerly stepping along the threads. She counted three ... no, four others on this side...

Light split her chest and engulfed her.

The next thing she knew, she was in the Hall of the Riders again. Her consciousness was not squarely in her body. She sensed that she somehow existed outside of herself for the moment.

Before her stood an unveiled valkyrie bursting with pale blue light. She wore a drape-neck gown made of what appeared to be tiny linked flecks of silver, as well as a gorget, tasset, and pauldrons. The highly polished armor lay stark against her luminous umber skin. Her eyes were aflame with ultraviolet light, and her braids fluttered in a phantom wind. Along her chest, down her exposed back, onto her hands, lightning scars blazed like bioluminescent markings.

The scars Göndul's healing had given her.

As soon as Satara recognized herself in this valkyrie, her consciousness snapped back to her body. All the pain was gone, replaced with a profound strength. She spread her wings—sharper, longer, more responsive—and looked at the Riders. Waves of thoughts and emotions from every corner of the room ebbed and flowed over her—shared sensations from every valkyrie, including the Riders.

"Satara?"

She turned when she heard Edie's voice. Her friends all stood looking up at her, and she realized she towered above them, nearly seven feet tall. With a bit of concentration, she could sense the emotions vibrating from each of them: Edie wavered between relief and concern, Cal was terrified,

Marius was awed and proud, Adam was so overwhelmed he might shake out of his skin, Elle was excited...

The only one she couldn't feel was Basile. She looked at him and frowned, and he seemed to understand what she was asking. He replied with a resigned shrug.

To her right, fiery magic collided with her new, wintry aura, and she turned again to face Vidarr—the only being here besides the Riders that she could still look up at. Son of Odin ... she felt she could comprehend his existence so much more easily now. His smoldering gaze held hers. He didn't even have to move his hands for her to sense his *Well done.*

"Satara ... you feel okay?" Edie ventured, grabbing her attention again.

She wasn't sure how to veil herself. She wasn't certain she wanted to. The awareness she had gained seeing the Web was the only thing keeping the horror and sorrow over Astrid at bay—would that awareness go away if she took the form of a human again?

"I feel ... different," she answered honestly. Even her voice had changed, silkier and more echoey. "I ... went somewhere." Instinctively, she knew she shouldn't divulge anything more.

Edie's brows tilted uncertainly. "You collapsed. You don't remember? You..." She hesitated. "Died."

Satara bowed her head. Perhaps she had died, in a way, but it didn't feel like death. The threads connecting her to the dead were still and dull; her own threads weren't anything like that. If anything, she felt more *alive*, vibrating at a faster frequency than the humans.

Either way, something had certainly changed. "I'm sorry I scared you."

"That's really you, right?" Cal asked, voice rougher than usual. "They didn't pour some asshole's soul into your body or something?"

"My soul ... doesn't feel alone." She chose her words carefully, watching the revenant's reaction. He wouldn't show it, but he was scared for her. "I feel more open. Something changed ... but I'm still me. I have all my old memories."

Elle brought her hands to cup her own chin. "You went from, like, five-alarm-fire, Themyscira hot to, like ... level eleven, actual living goddess, Queen-Serenity-eat-your-heart-out hot." She looked at Adam. "Maybe *I* need to become a valkyrie."

"I'm sure it's not that easy," he mumbled, even as Mikey in the Genesis squealed his approval.

"Satara." She turned her head when Göndul addressed her. "A surprise has been prepared for you."

"A surprise?" She couldn't hide the confusion in her voice.

The Rider smiled. "Of course. A feast in your honor. It is only proper to mark such an important occasion."

"A feast? My thanks ... sister."

"Do not thank me," Göndul said, raising a hand. "Save your thanks for the people who arranged it."

Satara turned to her friends, but they all looked as clueless as she felt. A mixture of excitement and anxiety roiled through her gut. Could Göndul be suggesting what she thought—what she hoped, and yet what she dreaded?

Vidarr took a few steps back and carved a portal. She could just barely see, on the other side, a familiar island. Mare Isle.

Home.

CHAPTER THIRTY-FOUR

VIDARR'S PORTAL led to the docks of Mare Isle, and as Satara stepped onto the sun-bleached wooden planks, her heart soared.

What she could see of the village looked just as she remembered. Fishing boats lined the shores, tied for the evening to jetties. Lobster cages were stacked nearby, and Satara could smell them from here—a reek she had never thought she'd miss.

Though the paint was slightly more worn and cracked, the general store sat facing the shore, greeting visitors. Adjacent to it, with a dirt road separating them, was the post office. Trees encircled the area despite its closeness to the ocean, tall and dense enough that she could only catch glimpses of the rest of the village beyond and the very top of the distant lighthouse.

She moved forward like a ghost, nearly hovering, forgetting that her friends would soon be behind her. The scent of pine surrounded her as she floated from the dock, down the dirt road, and through the trees. Her wings relaxed; her movements were silent save for the whisper of her gown over the gravel.

The beating of her heart had been replaced by an electric thrumming that became more and more intense. She could feel *everything*, from the trees to the smallest bug. And it became all the more overwhelming when she finally stepped into the village proper.

The center of the town was an open space, unpaved, with paths branching from it. The muddy season had come early because of the snow, but the townspeople had placed rough-sawn planks over the roads and the worst places of the square, just as they did every year. It was worth it to smell sunbaked dirt instead of pavement every summer. Along these wooden avenues, people bustled back and forth, some leading their animals or carts. Cats roamed freely from house to house, blessings from the goddess herself.

With her gaze and her soul, Satara touched each person and building she recognized: the blacksmith's forge, cold for the evening, and the blacksmith himself, helping two other men move a large table; the huntmaster and the herbalist leaving the bakery together with armloads of baskets; deeper into the village, partially obscured by trees, the footbridge, and the river, and the mill and its mossy wheel. In the center, in pride of place, the heart of Mare Isle: the temple, standing tall with its tiered roof, freshly painted and decorated with colorful designs.

Satara blinked tears from her eyes as she watched the comings and goings. She could feel each of these people, their threads singing with excitement or stress or nervousness. Some had begun to notice her, striking as her new image was, but others were too busy to glance over at the trees.

She recognized another one of these busy people. Rushing from the temple to the mead hall to the bakery in a hurried circuit was High Priestess Eniola, her cornrows piled on her head, her flowing purple-gray dress tied up around her knees to keep it clean. As she went, stopping people and inspecting their baskets and giving instructions, she was still putting on her amber necklace and earrings.

Eniola was an anxious person, fussy at times. She was in her element here, managing everyone in a panic. The last time Satara had seen the high priestess, they had fought—about her education, her duty, her going to live with Astrid—but seeing her now, her heart swelled with fondness.

Satara took a few steps forward, barely suppressing her magic. She wanted to let it flow from her like water, wanted the people—*her* people —to look at her and be proud. But she didn't want to halt their preparations. The sight of her alone had already stopped a few people in their tracks, and they whispered to their companions, smiling and pointing.

Eventually, enough people stopped that the high priestess paused to look back at the path. Her eyes widened.

"Satara!" The name left Eniola's lips in a joyful cry, and she leapt forward along the planks to meet her. She had been middle-aged the last time they'd met, and now she was a decade older, but still just as energetic. She stopped short of hugging Satara and clasped her hands to her chest. "You're here at last!"

Satara bowed her head, dipping in a curtsy that did little to change their new height difference. "High Priestess. I'm honored to be home."

Eniola stood on her tiptoes, and Satara bent so that she could cup her face. "Gorgeous," she breathed. "Absolutely beautiful."

"Thank you."

What else was there to say? For a few moments, Satara was speechless; then she straightened and squinted farther into the village, past the mill.

"Where are my mother and father?"

"Resting," Eniola said, wringing her hands despite her grin. "At home. I told them to let us take care of everything today. It's their daughter being honored, after all."

Satara stepped to the side. "Would you excuse me? I'm going to see them."

The high priestess's grin faded slightly, and she glanced behind Satara. "Oh, but who is this?"

She already knew to whom Eniola was referring, but she turned anyway, looking at her friends. With a frown, she counted faces. "Where is Lord Vidarr?" she asked Edie.

"I asked him if he wouldn't mind grabbing a few extra friends," Edie replied with a sly smile. "I know some people who'll want to be here for this." Before Satara could ask who she meant, Edie came forward, extending her hand to Eniola. "Hi. Edie Holloway."

The high priestess glanced at her hand before shaking it. "Satara's friends? Well, welcome to Mare Isle." Her tone held a note of skepticism Edie was probably used to by now.

"Thanks." Cal put his hands on his hips, scanning the busy village. "You guys need help?"

Eniola fixed him, then Edie, with a look. "We can do our own work, thank you very much."

"He's offering freely," Satara said, motioning. "Cal and Elle are both free revenants."

Elle was already rolling up the sleeves of her skater dress. "Yeah! Put us to work!" To Marius and Edie, she added, "I can bench like three hundred now. May as well put it to good use."

The high priestess still looked a little wary, but Satara squeezed her shoulder. "They've taken care of me," she said softly; then, more firmly, "I'm going to see my mother and father."

She turned and left before Eniola could stop her. People parted as she walked through the center of the village, over the footbridge, and past the mill.

At the top of a small hill, surrounded by trees, she could see her childhood home: a cottage within a small wilderness, its thatched roof covered in moss, its front door carved with a parade of wild horses. She could almost hear her mother and brother laughing in the side garden, could almost smell her father's special venison stew.

She walked up the hill, not bothering with the house. They wouldn't be there. Instead, she took a narrow path nearly hidden between the trees. The farther she walked, the more clearly she could hear a drum and a faint voice—a voice she recognized.

Her pace slowed a bit. Seeing the rest of the village had made her so eager to see her parents, but now, anxiety was setting in. It had been so long since they'd spoken to each other in person. She had been a child when she'd left; her entire adulthood had been spent away from them.

She had changed.

They didn't know her anymore. There was only so much that could be conveyed through letters and postcards. They had no idea that she was learning to paint ... that she devoured beautifully overwrought romance series, that her favorite action movie was *Live Free or Die Hard*, that peanut butter cup was her favorite ice cream, that she hated coffee and couldn't have tea without cookies.

She had never gotten to share with them her down-to-a-science system of watering her plants or doing dishes. They didn't know that her best friends were a compassionate necromancer and an outrageous dead man; they didn't know how many people she had killed since she'd left them; they didn't know that she woke up screaming, some nights, dreaming of Darras.

Then again, even if they knew, would they care? Last time she'd checked, they had cared about her being a *warrior*, serving the goddess—and here she was.

What if they saw her like this and it still wasn't enough?

Worse, what if it was? What if their reunion only confirmed her fear that they would only be proud of their daughter if she was a valkyrie?

Finally, the trees parted, revealing a wide-open field of emerald grass. Centuries ago, the area had been cleared of trees to give the people of Mare Isle space to create barrows. The burial mounds resembled rolling hills in an otherwise flat stretch of land, each surrounded by rune-marked stones.

As she walked among them, the drum became louder, the words of the song clearer:

"*Deyr fé, deyja frændr,*

deyr sjalfr it sama,
ek veit einn, at aldrei deyr:
dómr um dauðan hvern."

Cattle die, kinsmen die,
You yourself will also die,
I know one thing that never dies:
The reputation of each one dead.

Those words had been echoing in her head for weeks now. How funny that her mother had been thinking the same thing.

She emerged from behind one of the barrows and finally saw them.

Her mother was standing before another mound, tapping on a hand drum, the breeze tangling her rose-colored gown around her bare ankles. Locs fell down her back, over a foot longer than when Satara had last seen them, and her skin took on a faint silver lining under the overcast sky. Father was nearby, sitting in the grass and gazing up at her as she sang. He wore a tunic to match her gown, and his smile was so bright, they didn't really need the sun anyway.

An unexpected sob escaped Satara's throat. She broke into a run. "Mama! Papa!"

Her mother turned and dropped the drum in time to open her arms, welcoming the creature of death without hesitation. The valkyrie sagged into her mother's arms, palms pressed to her back, reaching to brush the ends of her locs. She smelled the same, like strawberries and honey. Her heartbeat sounded the same.

Tears flowed, boiling hot against Satara's grave-cold cheeks. She pressed her face into her mother's shoulder, drying them on her gown. Not a moment later, her father's warmth joined the embrace, and the smell of sweetgrass washed over her, mingling with the strawberries and honey. He always kept a braid of it on his belt or in his vest pocket...

There was no telling how long they stayed like that, huddled, weeping together; time washed away in a wave of bliss. It was as if, in this place, in this long moment, Darras's death, Astrid, the last decade apart hadn't happened at all.

When Satara finally pulled away—slightly—she was surprised to find herself eye to eye with her mother, looking up at her father. She glanced down to find that she was wearing her old armor. The life had returned to her skin, though Göndul's scar was still there. Her braids were their standard length.

Quickly, she unveiled herself again. The valkyrie was what her parents wanted to see. A gentle bloom of white light and she towered over them again.

"Satara," was all her mother could say, face twisted with emotion.

"Mama." She looked at her father, her hand still shaking in his. "Papa." Then she gazed behind them, at the barrow. "Darras."

She closed her eyes for a moment, feeling the threads that extended from her bright star. Two of them, quite close, sang with joy; the third was still, but at the end, she could feel a star almost as bright as hers. Perhaps it was simply wishful thinking, but she thought she felt a little swell of ... something coming from that point of light.

When she opened her eyes again, she eased back a step. "Eniola said she told you to rest."

Her mother quirked a brow. "She can tell me anything she wants, but I'm grown."

Satara felt a smile tugging her lips as she nodded at her father. "At least he was sitting down."

"I was enjoying the view," he said. Her mother reached up to rub his bald head, then kissed his bearded face.

"I was told there was going to be a feast," Satara ventured. "Is that what everyone is setting up for? For me?"

"Of course." Her mother tipped her head. "And why shouldn't they? It's not every day a girl from our village becomes a valkyrie."

She noted a change in Mama's face, felt her joyous vibration mellow slightly, but she wasn't sure how to read it. "I'm thankful."

Beside them, her father chuckled and opened his mouth to speak. Before he could, his attention was caught by something behind Satara, and his brows drew as he looked narrowly at the treeline.

Satara turned, too, and was surprised to see Vidarr emerging from the woods. With long strides, he reached the family in only a handful of seconds, then stood awkwardly about ten feet away.

Mama curtsied to him, and Papa bowed in time, so Satara followed suit. "It's an honor to host you on our island, Wolfbinder," Mama said, "even if for a little while."

Vidarr bowed stiffly back and signed to Satara, «I have summoned your guests, and the preparations are nearly complete. The sun will set soon.»

Mama squeezed Satara's hand. "Our loved ones await."

She took one look back at the barrow, then turned and focused ahead. "They certainly do."

The sun was low in the sky by the time Satara and her parents entered the field. It was one she had played in plenty of times as a child, but it looked different now.

Trees that had been saplings when she'd left towered above her. The villagers had set up several long tables heavy with food and drink, and in the center of it all was a large bonfire waiting to be lit. Gentle music, flute and drums, wafted through the air even as people cheered at Satara's arrival.

From where she stood, she was sure she could see the whole population of the village. As she scanned it, she recognized more familiar faces. Some faces were new; some of the old faces she searched for were missing. People who had been children when she'd left now had children of their own, chasing each other around the field.

Thinking of how much she'd missed made her heart ache. But she'd known she wasn't wanted here. They had sent her away.

She searched for Edie and Cal, and when she found them, she felt her brows jump up. Standing there with Edie, Cal, Adam, Elle, and Marius were none other than Mercy, Fisk, and Sissel.

Her hand slipped from her mother's, and she went quickly to them. "I didn't expect you to come!"

Mercy released her grip on one of her crutches briefly to wave, grinning ear-to-ear. "We wouldn't miss this! Wow, look at you! You look ... different!"

"You mean all edgy and dead and hot?" Elle asked, eyes glinting with mischief.

"You look like Albedo from *Overlord*." Sissel's voice was muffled by bread she'd snagged from the table behind her. "Also, hi!"

"Oh." Adam peered up to consider Satara again. "I guess she kind of does."

Satara huffed a laugh. For all their sakes, she'd pretend to know what they were talking about.

She was eye level with Fisk, now, as he swaggered up and thumped his fist against his chest. "Daughter of Freyja, this vættr would present you with an offering."

"That really isn't necessary, Fisk," she said, unable to suppress a smile.

Fisk hesitated and looked back at Mercy, who was already grimacing apologetically. "Maybe you can show her la—"

But it seemed the sea spirit's excitement wouldn't keep. He turned quickly and produced something that had been leaning on a chair behind them: a large scroll tied with red ribbon.

Satara untied it carefully and opened it. It took a few moments for her to realize it was a watercolor, created with materials pilfered from her own collection, and another few moments to realize that she was looking at a gruesome, bloody battle scene. Standing above the carnage was a very poor rendering of what she assumed was supposed to be her.

"Wow ... Fisk ... I don't know what to say."

He bared his teeth, chuffing happily, then came closer to point at something on the canvas. "See the warriors violating their opponents' corpses?"

"Yes, I do. Wow." She rolled it up quickly and handed it back to him. "Why don't you keep it safe at home for me?"

"Not to worry, my dear friend. I will frame it properly and hang it in your room." He put his fist to his chest again and went back to Mercy, who still wore that apologetic grimace.

She patted his arm but spoke to Satara. "Matilda's sorry she couldn't make it, but something came up with the safe house committee that she had to deal with. She said to send her congratulations!"

"Tch." Cal crossed his arms. "Probably just busy with her twiggy boytoy."

"I understand." There was still a face missing, however. "Where is Basile?"

"He stayed behind," Edie said. "He and the Riders were still discussing the whole Skuld thing."

Satara sensed her mother and father approaching before she heard them, and turned slightly to welcome them into the conversation. She was surprised to feel her mother's hand slip back into hers the second they were close enough.

"Mama, Papa, these are my friends." She nodded to each. "Mercy, Fiskbein, Sissel, Adam, Elle, Marius, Cal, and Edie." When the Genesis protested with a squeal, she added quickly, "And ... Mikey inhabits this guitar. Friends, my parents, Galib and Amat."

"Hello." Her mother looked them over assessingly, never a woman of many words.

Papa said what she was probably thinking: "What a motley crew!"

Cal shrugged. "Eh, I prefer Bon Jovi."

"You're certainly welcome on Mare Isle," Mama said. "Satara's friends are ours." She glanced over one shoulder, then let go of Satara's hand to gesture to the table behind the group. "Please, sit. The sun is about to set; I think Eniola is going to give her speech soon."

Satara turned slightly to run her gaze over the tables. In the center was the elders' table, but directly on the right was a table reserved for her family, and next to that, one big enough to accommodate her friends.

Both were draped with tablecloths bearing her family's coat of arms, the chairs tied with ribbons in their colors: blue, red, and silver.

Before she could ask where she should sit, her mother led her around the table, sitting her rather firmly in the largest high-backed chair. "You sit in the middle. Galib, you sit on the left."

"As you wish, wife." Papa chuckled and sank down with an exaggerated groan, reaching over to pat Satara's forearm. "Your old man has only gotten older."

Satara tried to smile despite the painful twinge in her heart. Mama sat at her right side, smoothing out her gown, and the others settled a table over, chatting among themselves.

She wished she was with them, but ... they looked so happy without her. The pit of fear and insecurity that had started to bloom in her stomach the moment she'd stepped onto the island was only getting worse. Was this a trend, that everyone could take or leave her? Would it get worse now that she wasn't human—an outsider?

She sat in silence, watching the horizon as the sun crawled slowly down the sky and the clouds bled peach. This was supposed to be the happiest day of her life. She had reunited with her family and was surrounded by friends. Why, then, did she feel so alone?

It wasn't long before the villagers who had been milling and playing in the field took their seats. All the elders had sat, with Eniola seated among them. The high priestess scanned the crowd before giving a decisive, satisfied nod and standing.

"Evening, everyone!" she called out, her voice filling the field. If nothing else, she could project. "Tonight we celebrate the investiture of our beloved Satara. A blessed valkyrie sits among us!"

Applause rippled through the crowd, along with shouts and whistles.

Once they settled down, she continued: "Like day into night, Satara's transformation is not an end or a beginning; it is simply one transition in a cycle. As she takes on his new phase of her life, let us hope that her conviction impassions us to serve Lady Freyja with even more fervor."

Again, the crowd erupted in agreement, and Satara shivered as the praise washed over her. What a strange feeling.

As the last rays of light disappeared under the horizon and the sky turned to steel, High Priestess Eniola raised her hands. "Her trials were many, but she met them all with readiness and love in her heart. Let that be a reminder to us, friends, as we face our own trials, as we carry out our own cycles. Our pride in Satara will strengthen us, too. We transition, too."

As the heavens darkened, tiny lights began to appear in the trees around her—not electric lights, but a trivial illusion spell—as if the branches bore all the stars in the night sky. They were enough to light the feasting area and the field, where the villagers would soon be making merry.

"Now—eat, dance, and be well. In honor of our daughter and our protector, and of the Lady herself, make the night your own!" With a gesture, Eniola struck up the small band, and cheerful flute and drum filled the air.

Several people left their tables behind to dance at once, arm in arm, smiling, eyes shining. Satara watched as Mercy and Fisk left, too; then Edie crept out of her seat, gazing around the field in wonder, and Marius stood to linger by her; finally, Elle dragged her father from his seat. She could vaguely hear them quarreling as they left: "Elle, I haven't eaten in like a day and a half." "I wanna dance!" "Can't you dance with people your own age? That's what teenagers do, right?" "I'm twenty-two!"

Under the table, Mama slipped a hand over hers, making Satara jump. Her touch was so immensely warm against the valkyrie's icy skin. "Are you going to dance with your friends, my love?"

Satara hesitated. Looking around, she spotted Vidarr, who was being circled by a chain of dancing children. She mustered a small smile but, after a moment, pulled her hand from under her mother's. "I ... I don't know. I might step away for a few minutes." Even as she said it, she rose from her seat, sweeping her gown around her and averting her eyes from Mama's disappointed frown.

"Come back soon," she said softly, not quite concealing the mix of concern and suspicion in her voice.

"I will." Satara planted a kiss on her father's head before gliding behind the elders' table and back to the path, through the trees. She tried to ignore the gazes on her back as she did—of course the retreating form of the guest of honor, standing at seven feet, would draw some attention. She just hoped no one would follow her.

Or perhaps, secretly, she did. She wasn't even sure anymore.

She left the music and the laughter of the clearing behind and, as soon as she was somewhere clear of trees, spread her new, permanent wings. Lifting into the air came as naturally as breathing now. In a moment, she was soaring above Mare Isle, every detail keenly visible despite the twilight.

She flew over the barrows, then the deeper parts of the forest; when she came too close to Darras's death place, she circled back around and passed the lighthouse. The village came back into view, her childhood home peeking between the pines, but she kept going, swooping east and following a familiar beach path.

Soon, she reached a steep pebbled shore and a dock of her father's make, only big enough to moor the one rowboat that was tied to it. As she landed, the dock bobbed slightly, sending ripples through the purple water. Somewhere nearby, a loon wailed: a mournful, lonely sound. Someone trying to find their friend or family member. Satara crouched on the dock and held her face in her hands, trying to deny the tightness in her throat.

What was this feeling? Was this what Astrid had felt all those years? Was this why she'd isolated herself like she had? Was this part of the process or was she, like Daschla, a fraud—broken, just in a different way?

Even if this was preferable to the Shore of Corpses, it seemed like she had traded hell for solitude. How could she be so apart from life when she could literally *feel* it, all around her, humming through her being from every angle?

She wasn't sure how long she stayed crouched. Time felt so different now. So arbitrary. But when she sensed one of those brilliant living threads vibrating faster and closer, she raised her head to see that the twilight was gone, the sea before her like a black mirror.

"Satara?"

She spun quickly and faced a figure carrying a lantern, framed by the trees around the beach path. Even in the low light, she knew at once who it was.

"Mama." Slowly, she stood, turning toward her mother's approaching form. "I'm fine. I'll be right back."

Mama didn't falter in her path, nor did she take her eyes from her daughter's. She set her lantern on the shore in front of the dock and came closer, lifting her gown around her ankles. "You've been out here half an hour, my love." After a pause, she cocked a brow. "You didn't even realize, did you?"

Satara exhaled. "Things have changed, Mama."

"Of course they have." Her mother's brow remained raised as she flanked Satara, craning her neck to look up at her. After a moment, Mama let go of her gown and wrapped an arm around the valkyrie's middle, squeezing their sides together in a gentle hug. "We can all see that well enough."

"*I've* changed."

"I know."

"No, you don't." The words escaped Satara in a breath as she carefully extracted herself from her mother's embrace. *How could you know?* she thought. *You don't even know who I was before.*

Mama's brow knit tightly, lips pursed. "What is this? What is this about, Satara?"

Satara crushed ten years of pain and uncertainty down, down, down, until it was a condensed ball of sour hatred. As usual, she pushed it down and tried to address the matter at hand. "I'm scared," she admitted quietly, unable to keep herself from shaking despite her indifference to the cold.

"Scared?" her mother repeated in that tone Satara knew well, the one that asked for more without asking.

"I..." A trembling breath filled the air between them. A breath Satara didn't really need; another reminder that she was no longer human. "This ... being this way feels so different. Nothing is how I remember it ... every sensation is strange. Time and life and my body and how I perceive you and the living and the dead..." Her voice turned into a croak, and she brought both hands to her forehead now, smoothing them over her braids.

Her mother said nothing, simply listening.

"But I'm tired of being different, Mama." Satara blinked, and freezing tears rolled down her freezing cheeks. "I'm tired of being alone and ... sad. And most of all, I'm tired of others making decisions about my life. I'm tired of being forced into one role, onto one path. And—" Her breath hitched. "And if that's what my existence is going to be from now on, I don't know if I want to exist at all."

Silence fell between them, Satara's shaky breath melting into the sound of the water rippling around them. Another loon wailed. From far in the distance, the sound of laughter and music wafted to the shore, very faint.

When the silence became too much, Satara whispered, "I'm sorry. I shouldn't cry, but—"

That strikingly warm hand against her back made her words run dry. "Cry," her mother said. "Cry. From your first day on this earth, it's always been how you've told me what you need. Why would I ridicule you for that?"

Satara couldn't deny the wave of bitterness that washed over her at those words. She had cried the day they'd told her she was to leave Mare Isle. She had cried the day they'd put her on the boat to the mainland. Her mother had answered with a stiff chin and a distant gaze. Satara raised a hand to wipe at her tears, taking another deep breath.

"When you were born," Mama continued, "you cried. Transition is difficult—from death into life, life into death, and every transition between. You are still being born, through every change. Becoming something new. And becoming is still scary. So why shouldn't you cry? That's what children do."

Stubbornly, Satara murmured, "But I'm not a child."

"You're my child." Mama spread an arm, gesturing back toward the island. "And I'm my mother's child, and she was her mother's child. We are all Freyja's children. We are all children of Midgard. *Everyone* is someone's child."

With a tearful grimace, Satara turned, jerking herself out of her mother's reach. "Then why did you send me away? If I was so precious to you, why did you make me leave you?"

She was surprised at the volume of her own voice, raw with emotion. Mama was similarly alarmed, simply staring as if she'd been slapped.

Satara spread entreating hands toward her mother. "Were you punishing me for what happened to Darras? Do you *blame* me for it?"

"Of course not," Mama returned firmly, her gaze a warning.

"Then why? Why did you hate me enough to send me away from you? All I ever wanted was to be here, be home, with you and Papa. I don't need to be Mother Valkyrie's warrior; I don't need honor. *This*"— she gestured around wildly—"was all I needed."

"Satara!"

The way her mother said her name was enough to bring her to tears again. She could have sworn they felt hotter this time. "If I wasn't good enough for you then, I never will be. As long as I'm your daughter, I will remain as worthless to you as I ever was. Sending me away couldn't change—"

"Satara." Mama took a long step forward and grabbed one of her wrists, pulling her close, and then down—down to her knees, low enough that her mother could cradle her head against her breast.

Her hold was shockingly strong, but Satara didn't attempt to fight it, simply surrendering to the warmth of the embrace. As she sobbed, her mother's nails combed gently between her braids; she stroked each plait, fingering the ends. No matter how many breaths she took, Satara found she couldn't stop trembling.

Then, as she shifted, she realized she wasn't trembling at all.

Mama was. Mama was crying.

Satara looked up to search her face. Rarely had she seen her mother's expression twisted like this, in anguish. Pain lanced Satara's heart. Speech failed her, and she reached to grip her mother's upper arm, wordlessly begging her not to cry.

Mama's voice was thick, shaking slightly as she spoke: "Satara, how could you say that?"

Satara closed her eyes briefly, another wave of sadness washing over her. When she answered, her speech was thin as smoke: "I want to be sorry. I don't want you to cry. But I can't apologize for my feelings."

She opened her eyes, watching her mother take a few deep, grounding breaths. Mama swallowed, wiped her tears, and took her hands from Satara's shoulders to cover her own face for a few moments. "Lady give me strength."

After another deep breath, she lowered her hands to gaze sadly down at her daughter.

"We wanted you with us," she began softly. "Of course we did. Your father and I love you more than anything." She paused at length, the ocean wind whipping her rose gown around her. Satara watched goosebumps raise on her skin, and a moment later, Mama wrapped her arms around herself. "But there is a secret we've been keeping from you. We thought it would serve you best never to find out. I see now ... that we were wrong."

"What?" Satara breathed. She had never had any inkling of a secret.

Her mother sighed and covered her face again before composing herself enough to continue. "Satara ... when your brother died ... you remember that day, don't you?"

She nodded.

Another deep breath. "The way we live ... it's a very tenuous balance, Satara. A majority-Black island off the coast of New England, a small community acknowledging the sovereignty of the Wabenaki, a group of peaceful pagans ... for centuries, outsiders have wanted to destroy us.

They've tried through unspeakable means, with forces you could not imagine. In the past few decades, it's become less likely that we will lose our very lives than it was a century or two or three ago. People are far less likely to take up arms against us when they can try to displace us other ways." She bowed her head, her eyes shining with grief and rage. "But not always.

"Those men—those beasts. Raiders. Vikings. Whatever you would call them. They approached our island by way of the forest, thinking we would never see them coming. They found your brother first, and..." She shivered against the night air. "You know what happened next. But your escape gave us forewarning—enough that we were able to gather the priestesses together to call on Freyja for her protection. But we are bound by an ancient pact. An oath.

"The pact decreed that, in exchange for protection like this, the reweaving of Fate, Freyja demanded a sacrifice: one of our daughters must go to serve one of her daughters when she came of age. When the danger had passed, the parents in the village drew lots." Mama's voice became thick again. "You were chosen."

Slowly, Satara rose to her feet, towering over her mother. Mama looked so small now, hugging herself, head ducked against the cold air and bitter memories. She searched for words, but Mama continued first:

"I'm so sorry I never told you. I ... I never meant to hurt you. To make a young woman doubt her worth directly opposes Freyja." She met her gaze, tears rolling down her cheeks. "I've failed. As a follower and as your mother."

"No..." Satara reached out, drawing Mama close, cradling her head this time. "But ... if you had just told me, I wouldn't have thought you hated me. I would have come home for feast days. I never would have alienated myself from you."

Mama laughed miserably into the strange fabric of her daughter's gown. "You thought that we hated you, and I thought that you hated us. Oh, Satara."

"I don't hate you," Satara whispered softly, running her hand over her mother's locs. "But I never wanted to be a warrior."

"Just like your brother."

She nodded. "Darras wasn't a warrior. He always said so."

Mama was quiet for a while; then, at length, she peered into Satara's face. Slowly, she reached up, cupping the angel of death's cheeks as though she were still a baby. "My love ... no one can force you to become something you aren't. Not for very long, anyway. You *are* just like your brother ... you are not a warrior. You are a defender."

"Mama—"

"If you had not fled the forest and told us what happened, we might all be dead. You stand strong for your friends." Mama gave a wobbly smile, letting her hands fall. "Even against your own mother, you defend yourself."

Satara sighed and shook her head. "You say that ... Basile says that ... that as a valkyrie, I can be whatever I like. That I could care for the dead like I've always wanted, that I could keep myself. I could still be Satara." She raised a hand to grip her mother's wrist lightly, eyes misting again. "But even my *trial* was warlike. I had to kill six men. Was it six? See, I can't even remember."

Mama's brow furrowed, but she simply asked, "Why?"

"There was a stag," Satara began quietly. "I'm not sure what else to call it. It had the body of one, but the head of a hare, and a tail like a dog. Its fur was sapphire, and its antlers looked like they were dripping starlight. It was so ... strange, but it was breathtaking. One of the most beautiful things I've ever seen. Looking at it made me almost cry, and I..." She closed her eyes. "The men were hunting it. But I hunted them instead. I killed them all, Mama—that was my task. The Riders were *pleased* with me." Grimacing, she hung her head again. "No matter what I try to make of myself, I will always be going to war."

"My darling..." Mama cupped one of her cheeks again, stroking with her thumb. "Even for those of us who aren't warriors, some things are worth going to war for."

The impact of her words stunned Satara for a moment, such that she could do nothing but watch as her mother drew away and started back up the dock, retrieving her lantern as she went. She was about halfway up the beach path when she stopped and turned her head, not quite looking over her shoulder.

"Lady Freyja would never hold you against your will, Satara. I should think that if you truly want your life back, you have but to ask."

CHAPTER THIRTY-FIVE

As Edie staggered out of the Hall of the Riders, the bright light of Asgard might as well have been knives in her corneas. She shielded her eyes, but was nonetheless temporarily blinded, drawing a groan from the back of her throat.

Last night had been the first time in a long time she'd actually let go and had fun. It was a shame she couldn't remember it, especially now that Fisk, Mercy, and Sissel were back home. She wasn't a stranger to drinking, especially considering her stint at Nocturnem, but Norse alcohol hit totally different.

Unfortunately, it had also left her with a bastard of a hangover, which had made it nearly impossible to pay attention to the important meeting they'd just left.

She ventured a bleary look over at Cal, who looked back with a knowing smirk. Suppressing another groan, she mumbled, "Sorry I was so useless back there."

Basile answered instead: "Eh, don't worry about it. It's not the first time, and it probably won't be the last."

"Whatever, man." She was too tired to banter with him. Instead, she turned to watch Satara, veiled now, speaking to High Priestess Eniola and one of the Mare Isle elders. Beside Satara, Vidarr stood, silent as ever but watching the valkyrie intently. She didn't seem to notice his stare, or perhaps she was politely ignoring it.

They talked for another minute or so before parting ways, Satara hugging her people and bowing to Vidarr; then she joined them on the catwalk above the gods' city, looking much more resolute than she had lately. "We should go back to Midgard as soon as possible."

"Don't have to tell me twice," Cal murmured around a cigarette that had somehow found its way between his lips. "This place gives me the heebie-jeebies."

Basile had already started walking. "The Blood Eagles' rally is tomorrow. You better believe I'm going back." Under his breath, he added, "I don't plan to miss this."

Edie attempted to walk as fast as the three supernatural beings at her side, pushing through her headache, but their journey back to the gates of Asgard was mostly a blur to her hungover brain. Before she knew it, they were rocketing across Bifrost toward their own World. A half hour later, frigid wind hit her face, and she opened her eyes to find that they had returned to the sea cliffs. The freezing air sharpened her focus, at least.

Basile busied himself with drawing a translocation circle, and soon, they were standing in the living room of their Manhattan apartment.

As the spell's magic dissipated, the first thing Edie could make out was Marius sprawled across the couch, an arm covering his eyes and a water bottle in his hand. Apparently, she wasn't the only one with a hangover. She tried not to notice that his shirt was riding up his toned stomach. If she remembered correctly, they'd danced together last night. A lot.

The group shuffled out of the translocation circle, and Marius jumped to his feet with a start, his palm already glowing hotly. A moment later, he realized it was just them, and relief melted most of his grimace. "Oh. You're back."

"They're back?" came Adam's voice from the kitchen, and he and Elle appeared a moment later, looking far better than Marius did. It took a lot to get a revenant drunk, and Adam had spent all night politely declining alcohol. "How'd it go?"

"Same thing as always," Cal said, crossing his arms. "Buncha old-ass fairytale creatures standing in a room, using fancy words to talk about, what else? Politics. Sparky, did you just fuckin' melt that bottle?"

Marius turned the now malformed plastic over in his hand. "I ... did, yes." He set it on the coffee table. "I suppose I shouldn't drink it now."

Edie dragged herself into one of the comfy chairs, rubbing the space between her brows. Her brain was screaming at her—screaming a lot of things, but mostly to close her eyes. She kept them cracked long enough to see Satara hurry toward her bedroom and Adam hesitate, watching her go, before deciding not to follow her.

Instead, he came to sit on the floor between the coffee table and the chair, and Elle followed, perching on the arm beside Edie. She was wearing some kind of sweet perfume, bubble gum or something, but the smell was making Edie's headache even worse.

"I guess one good thing about the *torture* of not being able to get wasted is no more hangovers. So?" she prompted, offering Edie a mug of something. A cursory sniff said strong black coffee. "What did the old-ass fairytale creatures have to say? Wait, what were we asking them in the first place? Not to be a stereotypical blond bimbo, but a lot's happened in the past couple days and I'm lost."

Edie waited until the coffee hit her brain to answer, her voice coming out soft and scratchy. "We wanted more information about Skuld's disappearance."

"That's the leader of the Riders, right?"

"She's also one of the Mother Norns," Basile cut in, already pacing in front of the large windows. Outside, snow was beginning to fall again. "The three most powerful Norns in all existence ... the ones who weave the fate of the universe."

Elle grimaced. "Okay, so really not good that she's missing."

"Even less good when she happened to go missing the same time a weird, fucked-up valkyrie appeared." Edie took another sip of coffee. "I've never seen a valkyrie that looked like Daschla did, and at this point, I've seen a lot of freaking valkyries."

"There are only a handful of beings in this universe that can make someone a valkyrie," Basile explained, "and Skuld is one of them."

"So what's the deal with Daschla, then?" Adam asked. "Whoever she's working for—the Gloaming, I guess—they kidnapped Skuld and forced her to turn Nazi Barbie into a valkyrie?"

"Exactly so," Basile said. "But there are certain ways you have to do things. Like you saw. Satara had to go through a whole process, do a trial, honor Odin and Freyja and get their blessing. Daschla didn't do any of that."

"That's why she looked all broken and purple." Edie took another sip of coffee, relishing the warmth and the hit of caffeine, then looked up at Elle. "Actually, even if you were a blond bimbo, you'd understand this analogy: you know how you can jailbreak an iPhone?"

"Oh!" Elle grinned and took her phone from the front pocket of her skirt, showing off her cartoon pig phone case. "I totally used to do that so I could delete apps and get cute emojis! I actually have this thing that lets me personalize my theme now." She unlocked the screen and showed Edie. "I can change the layout and icons and stuff, see?"

Edie waved the bright phone light out of her face with a grunt. "You broke the phone's operating system so you could do whatever you want with it."

"Well, yeah, but look at how cute my clock app is now. It's a duckie, Edie."

"Daschla and Indriði and whoever else enabled them sort of did the same thing. The gods didn't even know she existed."

"They wanted all the power of a valkyrie without having to uphold the oaths associated," Marius said, glowering as he pieced what she was saying together. "And Odin or Freyja wouldn't have given their blessing to her anyway. So they cheated."

Cal sank onto the couch, taking out a cigarette and twirling it between his fingers. "And now they got a bargain-brand valkyrie runnin' around tellin' people, 'Gun someone down in the street! That'll solve your problems!' Holloway, kid, we gotta stop ending up in smoking-free places."

Edie sighed and glanced down at Adam, intending to check to see how he was taking all of this. She was surprised to find him with a thoughtful expression on his face, like he was on the verge of solving some huge puzzle. "You good, Frankenstein?"

"What? Oh." He looked up and shook his head. "It's stupid."

Edie noticed Basile opening his mouth and cut him off before he could quip. "No, what?"

"I was just ... I worked as a drone processing payments for this bank for a while. They were big on security and stuff like that, obviously. Really hard-asses about what you did with your personal tech, too—we had guidelines and stuff." Adam shrugged. "I was just thinking ... there are downsides to jailbreaking your phone, too. Every operating system has barriers in place to keep your info safe, but when you fuck around with the OS, you fuck around with those, too, and you're more vulnerable to viruses, or worse, hackers. You could totally brick your phone. It'd be unusable."

Marius lowered his eyes. "So you're saying that, without the blessing of the gods ... there's nothing protecting her. She could be killed in battle?"

"Without us having to go through the process of taking and killing her fylgja," Edie muttered, sipping enough coffee to burn her mouth. Anything to chase away the memories of Astrid's death.

Basile's stance shifted. "Why didn't I think of that?" He looked between Edie and Cal accusingly. "Why the hell didn't I think of that?"

"Try not to sprain something crying about it," Adam sneered.

Basile grimaced and waved a dismissive hand. "All right, you've made your point. *If* you're right, this is good news ... it means we can take her down, and her little movement with her. But let's not get carried away. We still need to confront her."

"We talked about the Blood Eagles rally, too," Edie said.

"It's tomorrow." The priest adjusted his glasses, looking at each one of them. "We're going to be there, and we should be ready for a fight."

Adam frowned. "How exactly are we supposed to fight against hundreds of armed people? There are only a handful of us."

"We took care of that. Plenty of cavalry to call in. You'll see. But don't think that means this is going to be easy. You're right, there will be hundreds of people, armed to the teeth. If they're not decked out in their weird cosplay, they're going to be in tactical gear. And even then, you don't need tactical gear or a gun to break a window or beat someone to death."

"You really think they're going to do that?"

"If they have anything," Cal mumbled, "they have the balls. They burned Shipshaven to the fucking ground."

Basile turned to look out the window again. "That was just a warm-up. They were testing to see how much they could get away with ... and the answer was murder. The ashes are barely cold and people are already making excuses for why none of them have been arrested. Plus, with those masks, most of them aren't exactly identifiable." He shook his head. "The feds are trying to weed them out, but it's too late. The damage is done, and another rally is tomorrow. You're kidding yourself if you don't think it's going to be worse, and it's gonna be the Bronx, it's gonna be Brooklyn, it's gonna be Queens or Harlem."

Marius scrubbed his hand across his face, groaning. "If I had to guess, I would say Harlem first. It's where the Auroran temple is." His golden eyes glowed from behind the shadow of his hand, his tone heating. "I tried to warn them, but Radiant Oddfreyr seemed perfectly content to sit back and watch it happen."

"Well, I assume the trouble won't reach him for a while," Basile said. "For the people on high, violence is only a pressing concern when it's suddenly coming for them."

Adam stood to linger in the archway between the living room and kitchen again, glancing toward the bedroom hall. "I think I'm gonna check on Satara. What, uh ... what should we do to get ready for this thing?"

The priest shrugged. "Feed yourself, rest until morning, warm up your magic ... pray? It's been a while since I was in a proper battle, I have to admit."

"Shit, it'll be fine," Cal said, cracking his neck nonchalantly. "Just do what we do and wing it."

Edie snorted. "At least we have backup this time. Usually we have to go in guns blazing with, like, six of us tops."

"Ooh, that's right." He grinned. "We have *cavalry* now."

Adam breathed a laugh and flashed a half-hearted thumbs-up. "I'll keep that in mind."

"Keep it cool, Frankenstein. You probably won't die. Now, if you'll all excuse me"—Cal stood, stretching with a sigh—"I have to go shine my Nazi-stompin' boots."

Thin sunlight was just peeking over the river when Edie woke up to raised voices in the apartment.

As she pried herself from her pillow and checked the time on her phone, she got the sense that she had woken from another of her reoccurring dreams, but the details were already becoming fuzzy. The same as before, she was pretty sure—the same as it was every few nights, with the spine-tingling river of souls.

For a moment, she wondered if she was hearing the TV, or maybe Cal and Elle were having a spirited conversation and had forgotten that the other people in this apartment had to sleep. But no, a second later she heard Marius's voice, rising hotly, clashing with Satara's and Cal's.

What the hell?

Quickly, she swung her feet over the edge of the bed and shuffled to the door, poking her head into the hall. The heated argument was louder, but she could barely make out what they were saying in her sleepy haze. Without thinking twice, she hurried down the hall into the dining room.

French doors on the far side of the dining room led to a terrace, and they were open. Cal stood half in, half out, hands thrown up in frustration; Elle lingered in the living room archway, watching with crossed arms. Marius and Satara, however, were both outside, the vivid with his back facing Edie and the valkyrie battle-ready with her spear. She was backed up against the parapet, glaring at him.

Finally, Edie was close enough—and awake enough—to understand what was being said. Marius was shaking his head, fist clenched at his side. "No. This is a terrible idea."

"You only think so 'cause that bitch didn't take anything from you, Sunshine," Cal said, stabbing an accusing finger at him. Then, to Satara, "At least give me a sec to get ready so I can come with you."

Satara's expression was set and determined, her wings unveiled behind her. "Without the others, you'd be in danger, and I'd be responsible. I'm not putting you in danger."

"So you're putting yourself in danger?" Marius pressed.

"If I have to go alone, so be it, but I'm going."

He shook his head again. "You're going to regret this."

"Maybe," she murmured. "But I'll regret not doing anything more."

With that, before Edie or anyone else could stop her, Satara spread her wings and lifted off the terrace. She beat the air a few times, whipping up flurries of snow from the parapet, before she veered to the side and swept behind a building.

Marius pulled back from the terrace, cursing. When he turned and saw Edie standing there, he stopped. "Edie. I—"

"What was that?" Panic buzzed up her spine, souring her stomach. "Where is Satara going?"

"The Baccarat," Cal cut in, leaning against the door frame and crossing his arms. "Not for high tea, either. Indriði's there."

Marius sighed heavily, running his hand through his curls. "I tried to tell her not to go." His brows drew tightly. "She wants Astrid's spear and shield back, before we confront Daschla. Indriði fled once and she thinks she's going to try again. Satara wants to kill her first. I tried to tell her vengeance is too risky, we should err on the side of caution, but she thought we had the resources to do both things."

"If not now, when, Sparky?" Cal demanded. "We've got the time, we've got the manpower, and she's gonna do it with or without us."

Shooting a glare at Cal, Marius added, "Yes—*Cal* was supposed to help in talking her down, but she mentioned Scarlet would be there, so now he's all gung-ho about throwing our lives away."

"Hell yeah I wanna wring that vampire bitch's neck! But she made some good points besides." The revenant rolled his eyes. "What am I s'posed to do, tell 'er she's wrong?"

Edie rubbed the bridge of her nose. "I guess Vidarr had a little more influence on her than I thought. Marius, you realize shutting her down probably just made her run off quicker? If you'd all *waited* until I was awake to have this life-altering conversation, we could have gotten a plan together." She gestured to the terrace. "Now she's gone."

Marius looked away, cursing under his breath again and pacing to the other side of the room. Elle, still silent, offered him a stick of bubblegum, and he stared at her a moment before taking it.

Edie considered the terrace and the snow flurries beyond, mind racing. They could probably get everyone together to help Satara, but Marius was right; it was a risk. They had no idea what kind of situation they were walking into in terms of security, but Edie had to believe it would be just as bad if not worse than when they'd stormed Indriði's townhouse. And if Satara was already heading there now, there wasn't much time to prepare.

At length, Edie asked, "How does she know where Indriði's staying?"

Marius glared, grinding out, "Basile."

"What? How the hell did he know?"

"What doesn't that irreverent asshole know?"

Edie still wasn't used to hearing Marius curse, but she had to say, she didn't mind it. She wasn't sure how someone could make the word *asshole* sound so appealing, but … *Okay, getting off track here. Satara is in trouble.*

"I'll text her," Edie said, already backing up toward her room. "She's upset, but she's not irrational. She'll listen to me."

Before they could respond, she headed down the hall and collapsed onto the soft bedspread with a groan. It was starting to seem like being exhausted while battling for her life was going to be the norm.

She crawled her way across the bed and flicked on the lamp, then grabbed her phone from the bedside table. She had a few texts from ChatsApp—Mercy and Sissel talking in the group chat about some stupid meme. Swiping away the notification, she opened her conversation with Satara. The chances of the valkyrie even *having* her phone weren't good, but she had to try.

She tapped the message field ... and froze.

What was it Satara wanted, anyway? Weeks ago, she'd wanted vengeance. She had been willing to wait for it, but they'd all known that her end goal was to take Indriði down, avenge Astrid, and get her spear and shield back.

Edie had seen her struggle with that desire for vengeance. Satara, better than anyone, knew the price of constantly waging war ... what that did to the people around you. She'd watched her juggle doing her duty and protecting people with her need for justice. Edie knew her better than to think she'd put herself or them in danger for no good reason.

And if she was being honest with herself, she wanted vengeance, too. She hadn't been very close to Astrid, but watching her die, knowing she had been obliterated from existence entirely, not even a spirit left ... Astrid could have been a stranger and Edie would still want to see Indriði suffer for what she'd done.

Besides, it wasn't just Astrid who had been hurt. Edie doubted she would ever be able to scrub those images from her mind, and she was sure the same was true for Satara.

Still, the urgency in Satara's voice, her unwillingness to wait even a second longer to carry out justice—that wasn't just a thirst for revenge. She *wasn't* irrational. Becoming a valkyrie had changed Satara, given her domain over life and death.

She *knew* something. Something that made Indriði's crime that much more heinous. Something that had made her unwilling to wait for even one more day.

Edie didn't know what it was, but understanding and accepting were two different things. She felt that fire. There were no words she could say to Satara to change her mind. And if she was going to do this thing, they better be there to back her.

She tapped the message field again and typed the only thing she could think of.

[Edith Holloway]: We're with you.

Seen: 5:20 AM

CHAPTER THIRTY-SIX

THE BACCARAT LOOMED fifty floors above Edie, a tower of crystal that shone even under the overcast morning sky. The first twenty floors were wider than the gleaming shaft of the remaining thirty, making it look like the throne of some celestial being—a beautiful but unfeeling god, glittering and framed by black steel armor.

She was sure she looked like a tourist, staring up at it, but that was the least of her worries. The building was more window than anything else; she'd be surprised if the Gloaming hadn't seen them coming. As she stared, she patted herself down, double-checking her weapons. Trusty machete at her thigh, dagger of truth in her coat. Marius still hadn't asked for it back, and she wouldn't argue. Gods knew she needed it more than he did.

Beside her, Adam stood with the Genesis slung across his back, peering at the Baccarat with obvious suspicion. "I just wish we had more people," he said quietly, repeating what he'd been saying for hours now.

Edie sighed. She'd already explained why infiltrating a place like this with a few people was better than bringing an army. If there was one mistake the Gloaming kept making time and time again, it was underestimating the Reach. But she couldn't blame him for being anxious; she was shivering with anxiety herself.

All she said was, "I know."

They were far from alone, though, even if it was just her and Adam going through the front entrance. Cal and Marius would enter through the kitchen, and Elle and Basile were coming from the back service entrance. Satara would join them from the roof. They'd done more dangerous things with fewer people before and survived.

"The Blood Eagles are loyal to Daschla, not Indriði, so they won't be guarding her," Edie said, echoing what Basile had told her earlier. "But we can expect to fight through New Gloaming agents."

"What do they usually use? Guns?"

"Worse. Magic." She glanced over at him. "Melee weapons, too." Then she turned her gaze to the roaring fireplace set within the hotel entrance. *Now or never.* "Ready?"

Adam shifted, pulling the Genesis into his hands. The frets shimmered, and it trilled softly, drawing a weak chuckle from Adam. "I guess we have to be."

"That's the spirit." Edie gathered herself for another moment before walking forward and pushing into the vestibule.

It was as though she had walked into a cave. Despite the enormous chandelier hanging over it and the weird light fixture taking up one of the walls, the vestibule was dim and small. It was like she really was entering a super villain's lair. She stepped in, looking ahead at the elevator—

Something slammed into her from the left, and she crashed against the crystal light wall.

As soon as she touched the marble floor, she was back up again, lashing out with a wild blast of magic. When she turned fully, a man dressed in black and silver lay at her feet, his body withered from the death energy she'd sent his way.

Adam appeared a second later, looking down at the body. "New Gloaming?"

"Yeah. They're not too hard to spot." Edie reached back to rub her already aching shoulder. "Black-and-silver armor, raven feathers ... usually trying to kill you. That sort of thing."

She turned her attention to the elevator again, its standard silver doors and red floor indicator almost comically out of place next to the richly carved dark wood walls.

Their bootsteps echoed as they approached it. Above the elevator lobby were yet more chandeliers; to either side, candelabras twinkled against two mirror walls, giving the illusion of an endless hallway getting darker the deeper it went. With a shiver, Edie pressed the call button and waited.

"There's probably usually a—" Before she could finish her thought, the doors opened, and the business end of a sword passed less than an inch from her face.

She jumped back, and two New Gloaming—a woman with a sword and a man with fire magic wreathing his hands—rushed after her.

The woman dove and knocked Edie to the ground, and she hit the marble tiles hard, all the air leaving her lungs. Breath-starved weakness entered her body as the woman raised her sword, poised to plunge it through her neck.

With a shout, Edie jerked her hips as hard as she could to the side, toppling them both over. A burst of pain filled her, and though it numbed immediately, her body reacted before she could process what had happened. A burst of blue magic sent the woman sailing back. She hit the wall next to the elevator like a rag doll, more skeleton than flesh.

Beside her, Adam was standing over the crumpled fire mage, taking slow, ragged breaths. It looked like he hadn't had time to get a note of his magic out, instead holding the guitar by its neck like a bat. With a shaking hand, he wiped blood and hair from the base of it.

Edie glanced at the mage. She could tell without having to check his pulse that he was dead. Officially the first living person Adam had killed, as far as she knew. An image of her own first kill, the witchwolf who'd attacked her and Cal on their way to Maine, flashed through her mind.

"Come on," she said, pulling her aching body from the floor and stepping into the elevator. He joined her silently as she pressed the lobby button, and remained quiet as they ascended a floor.

When the doors opened, they were in a hall much brighter than the one they had just left behind. Down the corridor to the right was a door to the stairwell, and to the left, a glitzy concierge desk. At the other end of the short hall in front of them gleamed what must be the grand salon, though Edie couldn't make out much more than parquet floors and white seats.

She stepped forward slowly, trying to keep quiet. Faintly, she could hear the sounds of fighting—shouting, swords clashing, magic hissing, a gunshot—but she wasn't sure where it was coming from. The hall leading to the sunny room was like a hall of mirrors, both walls and ceiling made of crystal squares. It was oddly claustrophobic, like she was a reptile in a glass display case, and she was happy to squeeze into the larger room.

And to be honest, she felt like she'd just walked into an imaginary world. Everything shone and glittered, from the silk walls to the gilt display cases. What must have been millions of dollars of Baccarat crystal adorned every surface. It was like a movie set version of what a fancy French hotel should look like. Yet it was modern—the sort of luxury she imagined an ultrarich person would call *subdued* or *elegant*, maybe even *understated*. Uniform. Polished. Distinctly corporate. All one color, save for the vibrant red roses on every table.

The one thing that made it unique was the windows, made of thousands of shafts of crystal side by side, prisms that sliced the light into a rainbow of dancing color even under an overcast sky. It was beautiful.

But there was no time to linger. Here and there, priceless artifacts of crystal had shattered across the floor; a few chairs were knocked over, tables jerked out of place, lampshades lopsided. The sounds of fighting had stopped. Edie was willing to bet the others had blown through this room while taking their opponents down. She and Adam just had to find their way to the bar and meet up with them.

Edie went to the left first, peering into the adjacent room, but found only a smaller lounge filled with dark wood and an obnoxiously large chandelier. The bar must be the other way. She turned to cross the main room again but paused when she saw Adam.

He stood in the middle of the salon, arms limp at his sides, face tipped up as he took in the room. Slowly, he turned where he stood until Edie could see his expression. Something like heartbreak, she thought. Maybe anger.

She took another few steps forward. "Everything all right?"

Adam was silent for a second, but even as he spoke, his gaze was stuck on the room. "I've just..."

Edie glanced around the salon, wondering if she was missing something.

"I've been living on my own since I was seventeen," he started again. "I slept on a bare mattress in a room I shared with two other guys. My friends and I would split a slice of pizza in half for meals. There were times in our squat we had no water for weeks, or the heat would break all winter, or the cops would come destroy our shit just to make our lives a little more miserable. We had to take materials from buildings being torn down around us just to keep ours from giving out under our fucking feet." Finally, he looked at Edie. "And twenty years later, less than halfway across Manhattan, they build this."

She shifted, unsure of what to say.

"Hell, fuck the twenty years. Same shit, different year, different neighborhood." He gestured upward, and the Genesis whined lowly over his shoulder. For a second, it looked like he'd continue. Then, he exhaled and simply said, "People are going hungry, man."

Edie scanned the room again, slower this time, seeing more than the undeniable beauty. Her gaze touched the globes of roses on one of the tables, the red crystals in the chandeliers, the red foot stools ... the red streak across the parquet floor. She did a double take and stopped, and as she reached out with her magic, she recognized it as blood—like someone had been dragged through the room.

Wordlessly, she followed it to a glass door, through which she could see white chairs and a checkerboard floor. When she opened it, the smell of copper and gunpowder washed over her.

Along with familiar voices.

"Give 'er a few minutes, Mr. Golden Sun," Cal was saying. "I think she's got it together enough to open a door and take an elevator."

"There were more of them. You know there have to be more of them. And what about Satara? What if she—"

Another gunshot cut Marius's voice off, and Edie rushed into the room with Adam on her heels. A wall cutting the seating area in half obscured her view at first, but when she rounded the corner, she watched a black-and-silver-clad man slump against the far wall.

Behind the bar stood Cal, glass of Scotch in one hand and smoking gun in the other. Sensing her movement, he turned his head, then relaxed. "See? Told ya." With a smirk, he heaved a massive binder of cocktail recipes onto the counter, flipping through it. "Hey, kid, you want a Corpse Reviver? Twenty-six bucks."

"I think I'm all set on the corpse reviving." Edie surveyed the scene before her, no longer wondering where the blood had come from. Honestly, she was surprised there wasn't more of it.

At least seven dead Gloaming agents lay scattered across the checkered floor. Huddled against the front of the bar, several humans in pressed shirts and staff vests were clutching their friends or their wounds, which Marius was working overtime to heal. The sight and smell of the injured and dead made Edie's heart pound harder, her vision sharpen. Every noise echoed off the high ceilings and amplified in her skull.

"Are you hurt?" Adam asked, slipping from behind her to go to Elle, who was pouting on one of the barstools.

"I'm *fine*, Dad." She sighed and showed him her blood-bathed hands. "I tore a guy's head in half. But I ripped my freaking stockings."

Edie crouched by Marius without a word and gently moved aside a woman's arm, beginning to weave blood magic into a laceration in her side.

"Are *you* hurt?" Marius asked, stopping for a moment to look Edie over. His eyes widened, and he reached forward, stopping just short of brushing her face with his thumb. "You're bleeding."

"Am I?" She patted her face with her other hand and was surprised to find a deep cut on her chin. Of course, once she noticed it, the pain bloomed brightly. The New Gloaming agent must have scraped her when they'd rolled.

"It looks deep."

"I'm fine." Addressing the woman, she tried to sound braver than she felt. "When I'm finished with this, do you know a safe way out?"

"The kitchen," a man in a red tie answered readily, clearly not sure whose side he should be on yet. "We could go out through the kitchen."

"Okay." Edie took her hands off the woman, satisfied that she had at least stopped the bleeding. "You need to go out through the kitchen and get to a hospital as soon as possible. Some of you are hurt. Got it?"

The woman nodded numbly, strands of chestnut hair sticking to her lip balm. Edie almost wanted to cry, seeing how pale she was.

Edie and Marius stood, and the staff followed suit, some of them running and some of them moving more slowly to support their friends. As they cleared out, Cal called after them, tapping his glass with the barrel of his pistol, "Oh, and put this on my tab!"

Marius crouched again to begin searching the Gloaming bodies, and Edie felt the back of her neck burning, hairs standing on end as they usually did when someone was staring at her intently. She turned to find Basile boring a hole into her.

After a moment, she ventured, "What?"

"Oh." He blinked, broke eye contact, and adjusted his glasses as if he had been in a trance. "It's nothing, nothing. Find anything, Marius?"

"Nothing of significance," he mumbled, tugging on a silver chain around one of the bodies' necks. "Except these necklaces. They're all wearing them." When he finally freed the necklace from the agent's shirt, he lifted it for Basile to see—a silver pendant with a white opal stone.

Recognition shocked Edie, nearly making her jump. "I've seen those!"

The memories were so strong, they almost took her breath away: choking, betrayal, her friends being hauled away.

Marius frowned. "You have? Where?"

"At Indriði's townhouse, when she first trapped us. All the Gloaming there wore them, too." Chills ran up and down her arms. "It seemed to protect them against her time magic ... they were able to grab Satara and Astrid while we were suspended in time, anyway. Maybe we could use them. Unless there's some spell to make them work."

Cal snorted. "Considering the, uh, *turnover* of these New Gloaming bastards"—he grinned at the one he'd just shot—"chances are good using 'em's a no-brainer."

"Ha!" Basile grinned and gestured for Marius to hand him the pendant. "Don't you just love it when the villain's own stupid henchmen are his downfall?"

Marius handed it over, then began to search the bodies for more. "There should be enough for each of us to have one." Not thirty seconds later, he had a fistful of silver chains. "Try to conceal them with your clothes. It might help give us an element of surprise."

"Ooh," Elle said as she clasped hers, tilting the stone to admire it. "It's kinda super pretty? Yeah, I like this."

Cal set his gun and Scotch down to slip the necklace over his head with a grimace. "Christ, I look like one o' those LA moms with my stupid statement necklace."

The younger revenant grinned goofily and blew a blond curl out of her face. "Just pretend it's a gift from a sexy lady. Imagine it between two perfectly round boobs!"

He scoffed and waved her off, but glancing down at the necklace again, he looked like he felt a little better.

"So that leaves us with the question of the hour," Basile announced, gesturing widely at the bar. "Where is Satara?"

"She was supposed to come from the roof and meet us here." Edie pulled out her phone, but there were no new messages.

The priest grunted. "This new lone wolf, loose cannon thing she's doing is really cramping my style. Perhaps we should've, I don't know, *planned* a bit better before throwing ourselves at the mercy of a Norn."

"It's not like you throwing us into the Wending was planned," Adam cut in defensively. "You'd want to take Indriði down if she wronged *you*. Or is it only irrational when Satara does it?"

Basile rolled his eyes. "Frankly, Mr. White Knight, all that matters at this point is stopping the Blood Eagles from burning New York City to the ground. The only reason I'm even here is because, against my better judgment, I care what happens to you people."

"That's enough," Edie snapped, shoving her phone back into her pocket. "I'm fucking tired of hearing you bicker. Adam, I know I'm one to talk, but quit it with the whining. Basile, maybe you could endeavor to be less of an unmitigated asshole? I'm twenty-three years old, I shouldn't have to be telling middle-aged men how to behave." She sighed sharply, rubbing her temples. "What matters right now is making sure Satara is safe. So?"

Elle raised her hand, twinkling her fingers. "*I* think she might have gotten caught on one of the residential floors on her way down. Me and Basile tried to take the residential elevator while we were looking for the bar, but it wouldn't call. The lights were just blinking, like something was jamming it up."

"Okay, how do we get to the residential floors?"

"We used the stairs off the lobby to get up here, so there must be more."

Edie had already crossed to the glass door of the bar, holding it open. "I think I saw the stairwell down the hall to the right of the elevator. We need to move now."

One by one, the others filed out of the room and headed in the direction she indicated. As Marius crossed the threshold into the next room, Edie looked over at the bar, where Cal was still casually sipping his Scotch.

"You coming?"

He sucked his teeth. "Ya know what, I'm gonna stay here. Enjoy my four-hundred-buck glass of Scotch while I have the chance. Watch 'n' see if they send any backup. I don't think Scarlet's here," he added in a mumble.

Edie paused before taking a few steps toward the bar. "What about Indriði?"

"No way they haven't evacuated by now. If there's one thing the Gloaming are good at, it's scattering like cockroaches. But hell, maybe they left the spear and shield behind. That's one fuckin' thing outta the way." Idly, he paged through the binder of cocktails still sitting on the bar. "Go ahead. I'll be peachy."

"Are you sure?"

"What are they gonna do, kill me? Hey, if they do, you can just mix me a Corpse Reviver." He flashed a yellowed grin and waved her off.

She watched him reluctantly for a few more moments before leaving the bar. He'd already survived the unthinkable, and if he was outnumbered, he wasn't stupid—he'd run, or get to her and the others, or something. She just had to trust him.

She ran through the grand salon and to the stairwell, sprinting to catch up with the others. Who knew how much time they had to save Satara?

As the Reach thundered through the Baccarat, killing goons as they went, Edie prayed Cal was wrong about one thing. She hoped Indriði *was* here, so they could end this once and for all.

For Astrid, for Satara, for herself, and all the people Indriði had hurt in her too-long life.

CHAPTER THIRTY-SEVEN

I<small>T WAS EERILY</small> quiet in here, Cal thought. Even the noise from the traffic outside seemed far away.

Which was really saying something. There wasn't much in this world that an undead guy could rightfully find eerie, but maybe a couple weeks of sitting alone in a room with a young lady's corpse had put "eerie" into perspective a little. There were still things that could make him shudder after all.

And he didn't like the quiet. Especially this kind—quiet in a place that shouldn't be. Like the universe was holding its breath, waiting for something to happen. It was creepy as shit, and it made it that much harder to enjoy his The John Walker.

Idly, he turned the crystal flask it came in, watching the light play in the topaz liquid. Over three thousand bucks for a bottle barely bigger than his palm. It was damn good Scotch, but he wouldn't pay that if Johnnie Walker himself rose from the grave and did a jig. Good thing he wasn't planning on paying for it. When in Rome...

He finished his current glass and poured another couple ounces. The sound of the Scotch hitting the crystal was deafening in the silent room. There was only one thing that'd make this moment better, though he'd probably have to break about a dozen laws to do it. Then again, the tiles were smeared with blood, and he'd already put bullets in most of the walls. To say nothing of the stiffs scattered around the bar.

Eh, fuck it. He drew out a pack of Newports and lit one up, taking a drag. As he exhaled, it was like he was pushing all the tension out of his body, too, relishing the familiar bite of the menthol at the back of his throat and in his nose. Such as it was.

Cal allowed himself to relax for the time being, taking his eyes off the bar's entrance and instead gazing around the room. Chances were, if backup actually came, he'd hear them long before he saw them.

It was a nice place. Way too fancy for his tastes, obviously; too much modern art on the walls, not enough neon and chicks on hot rods. The wine-colored paint and the blood-red crystals in the chandeliers were right up the Gloaming's alley—or the Old Gloaming's alley, at least—but the checkered floor, the white leather seats, and the quirky art reminded him of someone else.

He spent an awful lot of energy trying *not* to think about her. Usually, it wasn't so hard. But when Edie had disappeared those couple weeks, he'd been on the horn with her almost every day, giving her updates, listening to what she was working on over in Anster. All her committees and coalitions and private fundraisers to bring the Reach back to the old shithole of a city...

If there was one thing that could be said for Tilly, it was that she knew how to charm rich people into giving their money away. Cal had no idea why Edie didn't want to be the Reacher, considering. Most of the work was already being done for her.

But Tilly was a rare breed. She bled money almost compulsively when she was pointed at a cause. And you wouldn't see her enjoying no four-hundred-dollar Scotch either.

Cal shook his head. Who'd have thought the Baccarat would make Matilda Ardelean look down-to-earth? He wasn't sure he'd ever understand that woman.

And, well, shit. He had to accept that. Most times, he was sure he had. Then other times, he couldn't stop seeing her everywhere.

Must be that vampire magic. They could compel people if they were strong enough. Just usually not people a stretch of interstate away.

Cal shook his head. That was enough stewing about her. Lord knew he had a dozen more important things to think about, including the fact that he was sitting in the belly of the Gloaming beast having a drink.

Did he honestly think Indriði or Scarlet was here? Hell no. If he really thought Scarlet was here, he'd be the first one racing up those fucking stairs. She still owed him for rooting around in his head, and he intended to make her give back whatever memories she'd stolen, the little leech. But running away with their tails between their legs had always been Indriði, Scarlet, and Zaedicus's MO. Why would it change now?

What would happen was they'd rush up there, find Satara tearing Indriði's empty apartment to shreds looking for Astrid's shield and spear, and try to get out before more Gloaming—

As Cal raised his glass to drain the last of his Scotch, a gunshot rang through the bar. Before he even registered what had happened, the crystal exploded in his hand, whiskey raining to the polished floor.

Shit.

He raised his pistol, firing the same moment he saw the gunman— one of two New Gloaming agents who had just walked in, cloaks shrouding their faces. Quickly, he pivoted and put a second bullet through the other's face as they tried to zig to the left.

The smells of smoke and Scotch mingled together. Gunshots rang against the high ceilings, and Cal shook the liquid off his hand. "Watch where you're pointing that thing," he said to the air. "If I was payin' for this, you woulda cost me half a grand."

A second later, a third figure stepped out from behind the wall partitioning the room, the stupid wall that had caused his blind spot in the first place.

She wore a white satin slip dress, her jet hair falling long over her shoulders. When her black eyes met his, she stopped midstride, staring.

Scarlet. And about as surprised to see him as he was to see her.

Cal had daydreamed about what he might say to her when they finally went mano a mano, but right now? All those cowboy one-liners left his head as surely as if she'd stolen them from him, too.

Her eyes glittered. A wide smile filled with deadly canines parted her lips. Then, she crouched like a tiger and pounced.

Revenant reflexes were almost as keen as wight reflexes, but she was quicker. She hit him with what felt like a few tons of force, and they slammed into the back wall of the bar, cracking the wooden shelf and sending thousands of dollars' worth of glass and booze crashing to the floor.

Beneath the explosion, another distinct sound reached his ears: his pistol clattering to the floor beside them. His sawed-off was still holstered at his thigh, but a frantic, instinctual thrill told him *get the damn Colt!*

Fury surged up his arms, and he grabbed Scarlet around her waist, throwing her as hard as he could to the side.

She flew from his grip and crashed against the mirror wall at the far end of the room, cracking it on impact. Cal dove forward, grabbing his pistol and standing with it already aimed head-height.

But as he rose over the bar, she was nowhere to be seen. Only the body of the guy he'd shot earlier slumped against the bench below the mirrors.

A bit of dark blood oozed from a cut in Cal's cheek now, and he raised a wrist to wipe it as he crept forward, leading with the barrel of his pistol. "Better come out from wherever you are. I'll find you eventually."

In response, her voice rang out all around him. He turned quickly, but it didn't seem to come from any one place. "Perhaps I should be flattered you want to kill me so badly ... but then, I guess mindless violence comes naturally to worm-shells like you."

"Flattered? Don't be." As he checked behind the partition wall and found nothing, he reached for his Bear Claw, then stopped. A slug to the face wouldn't do. "Who says I wanna kill ya?"

"Oh, Calcifer. That's pathetic, even for you. But I suppose there aren't any better ways of getting ladies at your disposal."

"Do you ever shut up?" he ground out, turning toward the mirror again.

A peal of laughter rang through the room, making him wince. "Maybe I'm right behind you and you just can't see my reflection. Or are you not quite stupid enough to believe that myth?"

Before he could answer, something tinkled above him. He barely had time to glance up and notice the track lights above him before the full force of her weight came crashing down on top him.

He swung his arm blindly as he fell, and the pistol discharged. The bullet missed her, but one of the light fixtures above them popped and rained sparks. The sparks mingled in Scarlet's hair as she wrapped her cold fingers around his throat, squeezing tightly, her grin just as white and horrible as ever.

Fuck that. She wanted to fight dirty? He didn't need a gun to beat wholesale ass.

Her grip on him was uncomfortable, but given he didn't need to breathe, that was all it was. He jerked to the side, catching her with a left hook that sent her tumbling into the barstools. As she picked herself up, he did the same, holstering his pistol and cracking his neck.

He was ready for her when she lunged at him, her claws slashing through the air. With a grunt, he planted his boot in the center of her chest, causing her to stagger back against the bar. It was only when she dodged to the side that he noticed she was barefoot; as she pranced toward the balcony, she tracked New Gloaming blood across the tile.

Oh no you don't. He took off after her, diving and catching her by the waist before she could reach the balcony doors. As they hit the floor, she rolled from his arms but was up a second later and bearing down on him, bracing against his shoulders, pinning him down.

With a hiss, she opened her mouth wide, her teeth turning to spikes. Claws dug into his shoulders, sending dull pain through his body. He went for another left hook, but she turned in time, wrapping his wrist in a crushing grip.

"Someday," she breathed, looking down her nose at him, "you're going to come up against something you can't shoot or punch. And what will you do then?"

He searched her pale, grinning face as he considered his options. Some revenants could shapeshift into animals, change their size to become giant, sink through the earth to escape, even control the weather. Magic coursed through his veins like adrenaline—he, just like every other necromancer's zombie, was made of it. But it had never come easy to him.

"What will you do once your bullets are gone and your finger bones are dust, thrall trash?" she asked again in a whisper, grin widening.

Best to just stick to basics. He bucked, jostling her partially off him, and kneed her hard in the stomach. She doubled over, and he pushed her to the side, sending her sprawling across the tile.

"Probably something like that."

Cal dragged himself up off the floor, snatching a handful of her hair before she could recover. He pulled hard and transferred the hold to her throat, planting a foot on the other side of her and leaning down. She'd have to fight him if she wanted to stand up.

With his free hand, he drew the sawed-off, pressing the barrel against her forehead.

"You know," he mused, tone casual, "I hate your guts, but I expected more from ya. Nazis, really?"

Scarlet bared her teeth. "You wouldn't understand the purpose of Daschla's little exercise. The Wounded didn't understand either, but he let her continue. Power is power, I suppose. You should know that."

The only thing he knew was *better than to humor whatever crazy shit she was talking about.* "I'll make this simple. If you want to live, you'll have to give back what you took from me. I want my memories."

"Why?" She smirked. "It's not as if you were using them."

Cal shook his head, moving the shotgun to her stomach and firing.

The *boom* echoed deeply through the room. Wooden shrapnel exploded, eddying through the air. Chunks of flesh, shards of bone, and bloody mist blew out her back.

She gasped in pain. He could see clean through her middle now. Her satin dress hung in singed tatters around the massive hole, but she was still just as alive as she'd been a moment ago. "Creature," she hissed.

"Now you know I mean business. So start talking."

Her glare sharpened. "As if I would ever give anything to a man holding me by the throat."

"This ain't about that—power. Not everyone is like you, you evil bitch." Cal set his jaw, moving the barrel back to her forehead. "This is your day in court. So testify. If you can't *give* me what you stole, then *tell* me it. Now!"

Beneath the still-hot steel of the barrel, her black eyes sparkled. A slow realization seemed to come over her face, and along with it, a genuine smile. "You really don't know about them, do you?"

Cal could feel his brow twitching. "Them? Who the fuck is *them*?"

A real, gleeful laugh echoed through the bar, and she dug her claws deeper into the meat of his forearm. "You've been dead for so long, they probably hardly remember you. But they're better off anyway."

Something tickled the back of his mind. He was overcome with the feeling that he *should* know who she was talking about—that if he'd really dug, the memories had still been there, just deep and buried. But not anymore.

Suddenly, he felt their absence freshly. A piece of him missing. Again, he was choking down the smell of that alley she'd dumped him in. He could hear broken glass shifting, feel the bite of cement against his skin. That filthy, violated feeling was creeping back in.

And she was laughing. That was real—she was laughing at him now. It was almost deafening in his ears, echoing in his skull. The only thing he could think was *shut up*, over and over and over again.

Fury came in like a boiling wave to wash away all other emotions. His vision was red. He could feel her larynx collapse as he crushed it, cutting off that ungodly sound.

He'd never squeezed a more satisfying trigger.

She slipped from his grip into a pile at his feet. There wasn't much of her head left. Finding all her pieces would be a hell of a job, but he wasn't about to leave that open as a possibility. He leaned over the bar to grab one of the few bottles that had survived their fight and poured it out over her, then reached into his back pocket and flipped open his lighter.

Cal lit a cigarette for himself, then tossed the lighter onto the remains of the vampire. Wights burned like kindling.

As the flames climbed, engulfing her, he didn't move, taking a long drag. She was dead—for good this time—but she'd left him with more questions than answers. Answers were what he needed.

He glanced down at himself. Answers and a long shower.

As Edie flung open the door to the forty-seventh floor, a wave of blue-white light filled the hallway beyond, blinding her momentarily.

When the light faded, Satara stood there, brandishing her weapons, unveiled with her braids writhing—amethyst blood streaming from her wounds but still very much alive.

Thank the gods she was okay. Edie was beginning to have her doubts.

Her relief was short-lived, however, when she saw what the valkyrie was facing off against.

At the end of the hall, two hulking forms were recovering from her burst of energy: half man and half spider, in the style of centaurs. Their human chests were bare down the center, but a shiny, sticky substance crawled across their ribs and pectorals, like a living organism trying to pretend to be clothes. Their faces were handsome, but their eight spindly legs did them no favors.

The one in front was armed with a spear. The other, standing before the door to the apartment, held a staff, and Edie could see him beginning to conjure a spell in the form of a shadowy ball.

Before she could react, an opaque black shadow streaked across the floor from somewhere behind her. It stopped behind the witch-spider and grew vertically, adopting the form of a man's silhouette. It took Edie a moment to recognize the length of the silhouette's hair and the cut of its jacket, but by the time she realized it was supposed to be Adam, it had already knocked the staff out of the witch-spider's claws.

"Watch out," came Adam's voice from behind her. A high note keened from the Genesis, and a blast of purple-edged shadow magic flew past, slamming into the spear-spider.

It was only then that she realized the silhouette wasn't the actual Adam but a copy.

Could *she* do that?

She'd have to test it out later. Instead, she called on her familiar death magic, blue flames engulfing her fists.

Beside her, Marius's weapons burst to life, and he followed Adam's blast of magic closely, throwing himself into the fray with his typical fervor. He batted the spear-spider's weapon away with his shield as if it was a mere nuisance, letting it glide across the lucent surface with a sizzle before swinging onto the creature's back.

Satara kept her eyes on the man-spiders, shield up, but she shouted across the hall at Edie, "You came!"

"Why didn't you meet us?" she shouted back, firing a blast of magic that hissed between Basile and Elle as they surged forward. Elle picked up the witch-spider's staff and snapped it in half, but it didn't seem to need it, shadow magic crawling up its arms like a second skin.

"I got caught up." Satara paused to deflect a bolt of purple magic. "They jammed the elevator, so I've been fighting my way down the stairs, but there were too many."

"Here, take this!" Edie tossed one of the opal necklaces to her. "You'll need it!"

Suddenly, an inhuman screech tore her attention away from the conversation. She looked over just in time to see Marius plunge his sword into the spear-spider's thorax, slicing through him like butter. The spider bucked violently, sending Marius tumbling across the floor and, in the relatively tight hallway, right under the witch-spider's feet.

He summoned a shield to protect his head and tried to roll the other way, but the witch-spider boxed him in with his many legs. Edie's heart raced watching him struggle to get out from under the powerful body, but she couldn't unleash the full strength of her magic here—there wasn't enough room, she'd hit the others.

A moment later, Elle crashed into the witch-spider's flank with enough force to knock him onto his side, eight legs skittering as they tried to find purchase.

Marius ducked and jumped up, curls falling in his face. He didn't miss a beat, turning back to help Elle in her new endeavor of dismantling the spider leg by leg. A loud sizzle and another inhuman shriek cut the air as Marius's blade sliced through the shiny exoskeleton.

Meanwhile, Basile, his human glamour gone, was using his wispy spirit magic against the wounded spear-spider. He was too close to be struck effectively with the spear, so the spider had attempted to back up, and they fought in a corner now.

Edie jumped in, calculating how she'd have to move to avoid the reach of the spear, but as the spider raised it, a wintry frost enveloped his arm, slowing the movement. Thanking Satara internally, she dove under the spear and slammed into the spider's human torso with a death-magic-fueled punch.

The spear-spider crumpled under the assault from both her and Basile. Dark purple blood spattered Edie's pants and boots as the witch-spider's head was severed. She hardly knew who was doing what anymore, lost in the heat of battle.

All she knew was, seconds later, both man-spiders were curled, dead, on the tile, a large pool of blood forming beneath them.

And the way to Indriði was clear.

Without further ado, smearing the crystal handles with blood, Edie threw open the doors to the queen's ivory tower.

CHAPTER THIRTY-EIGHT

THE INSIDE of the apartment was creepily silent, like a tomb after the loud, hot battle in the hall.

As Edie crept from the entryway into the living area, she wasn't surprised to see it was ultramodern and chic, in Indriði's typical style. The Baccarat residence made Matilda's place look like a grandma's cluttered cottage. Even the Norn's old townhouse paled in comparison. Leather, chrome, and furs decorated the room. White shelves displayed artifacts of great wealth but, to Indriði, these things were commonplace. Afterthoughts.

It was Indriði herself, however, who drew the most attention, cutting a commanding figure—despite her short stature—in a screaming-red fitted blazer, pencil skirt, and pumps. Her throat and ears dripped with diamonds and rubies, and her voice dripped with venom as she said, "Great, you've finally arrived."

She raised her hands, and that familiar sizzling clap cut the air.

Edie braced herself for the horrible feeling of time skipping in frames ... but the skip never came. The time magic washed over her, tickling her skin unpleasantly but otherwise rolling off like nothing.

So the opal pendants worked. Good.

Watching Indriði's expression shift as she realized what had happened was almost worth all the pain it had taken to get here. Her pale eyes widened, face slack and innocent for a moment before it screwed up in annoyance.

Quickly, she schooled her expression into one of unconcerned smugness, lowering her hands. "Bravo," she said as she clapped mockingly. "Or *brava*. So you stole some jewelry. It really won't make a difference once the Wounded shows up." A pause. "You know, I'm surprised you're here instead of at the rally. Everyone there's expecting you, after all."

"I'm here for my rightful property," Satara replied, veiled now but giving off an icy light. "And for vengeance."

Indriði quirked a brow. "How special." She pursed her lips and glanced to the side, at a tall, skinny light elf Edie hadn't noticed before. The one from the old burying ground, if she wasn't mistaken. "Ilphas, be a dear and mix me a Manhattan."

The ljósálfr snapped to attention, dark eyes so wide the whites of them could be seen. His antennae flattened against his head, and he hurried to the sleek bar not far from them. While he busied himself with the bottles and glasses, Indriði sprawled out on the pure white sectional, loosing a sharp whistle. A soft skittering came from the hall leading to the bedrooms, then a familiar fuzzy sapphire-and-orange body appeared.

Percy!

The Norn lifted her feet and, when Percy shuffled under them, rested them on his back. The poor little spider shifted uncomfortably, but Indriði didn't seem to notice or care.

With a smirk, she drew a knife seemingly from thin air, testing the point and twirling it between her fingers idly. A blade of dark metal, etched with runes. Edie recognized it immediately. The knife she'd used to torture Astrid.

"I'm guessing by the guitar that you must be Adam." She nodded to him, eyes glinting. "I heard you made quite a splash in the realm of lost souls. It's good to finally put a face to a name. Too bad you ended up being such a disappointing investment. And that EP you put out last summer sucked."

The Genesis vibrated hard in Adam's hands as Mikey's spirit vented his displeasure with a few angry chords.

"Oh, shut up, you hunk of junk," Indriði sneered. "As if I need a lecture from a gender-confused ghost trapped in a piece of furniture." With a chuckle, she addressed Elle: "You know, if your dear old dad had just agreed to join the Gloaming, you would be alive right now, instead of stuck inside a rotting corpse. All the cheeseburgers your fat ass could eat."

Elle scoffed. "At least I *have* an ass, unlike whatever that washboard on your back is."

The elf, Ilphas, emerged from behind the bar to deliver Indriði's Manhattan into her waiting hand. The Norn sighed happily and took a long sip, ignoring Elle in favor of sizing up Basile. He hadn't replaced his glamour, still a grinning skeleton in a cassock, but cold loathing rolled off him in waves.

It was as though she smelled it in the air—like a shark scenting blood. "And of course, how could I forget the *un-child*. Father Bolet, the lich prince, desperately searching for meaning to his pathetic existence without his mommy." She tilted her head, cooing mockingly. "But what will happen when the sarcophagus opens and Her Majesty inevitably joins the Gloaming?"

"Frankly, ma'am," Basile deadpanned, "fuck you."

"Who even asked for this lame-ass roast session?" Elle said.

"What about you, Edie, babe?" Indriði continued, undaunted. "Funny, you're usually inseparable from your slave. Did you finally get tired of the big stupid zombie, or is he running your errands?"

Before Edie could open her mouth, *Marius* jumped to Cal's defense. "His name is Cal, and he's not a slave."

"Nice comeback, vivid. Oh, wait..." A smarmy smirk spread across her face. "I guess I can't call you that anymore. Tell me, does the armor feel a little heavier when you have no right to wear it?"

A blade sprang from Marius's hand in a helix of light, but he held back, jaw working as Indriði laughed at him.

Finally, her gaze rested on Satara, icing over with genuine hatred. Her lip curled, parting, showing brilliant white teeth as her first word began to form. "Astrid—"

With one swift movement, Satara launched her silver spear, nailing Indriði in the center of her chest with a wet crunch. Blood burst, staining her shirt the same color as her blazer, soaking the sectional and pattering to the rug in bright, vivid blooms.

The Norn's eyes widened, the whites veined with pink. Percy scrambled out from under her feet to hide behind the couch, and Ilphas followed suit, folding himself in half with his pointy knees to his chest.

"Don't say her name." Satara's voice was steady. "You don't deserve to have that name on your lips."

Edie's heart flipped as she watched Indriði struggle there like a pinned insect, the color draining from her face and into the couch cushions. To finally see the same fear and pain in her eyes that she'd seen in Astrid's...

The satisfaction was short-lived. With a growl, Indriði raised her hands, grinding her teeth in concentration. Rapidly, the blood that had soaked into the sectional began to recede; the pink returned to her face, and a moment later, the spear was launched backward, out of her chest. It landed at Satara's feet with a deep clang.

"Did you honestly think that would work?" The Norn rose to her feet, seething. "Do you know who I *am*? What I possess?"

Elle stuck her tongue out. "Uh-oh, I think she wants to talk to our manager."

"I know what you possess," Satara replied. "Give me my battlemother's shield and spear. Now."

"Your *battlemother* was a murderer!" Indriði spat, her smug mask slipping. Strands fell from the white lock of her cropped red hair into her face. "And you will be, too."

Edie's cheeks and ears were suddenly hot, her vision throbbing. "Get a fucking grip. Soldiers *die* in *war*, it happens *all* the goddamn time. I'm pretty sure most moms don't go on murderous rampages because of that, and your son wasn't more important than any of theirs. And by the way, your kid got ferried to fucking *Valhalla*, you psycho. What more do you want?"

"You should be honored," Marius ground out.

"*Honored?*" Indriði's face was almost as red as her hair now, and her eyes flew wide as she laughed. "Do you even know what Valhalla *is?* In Odin's hall, warriors tear each other apart in battle like animals. They maim and torture and rape each other, for hours—and then, the next day, they do it all again. And again. And again. In perpetuity, until Ragnarok comes and they're called to battle one last time before they're *finally.* Fucking. Set. Free."

No one spoke as she paced to the window, but Edie stepped forward, thinking to corner her, and the others followed suit.

"And I'm supposed to be *honored* that my son is there, fighting and dying over and over again? My baby suffering a thousand deaths is supposed to be a *comfort* to me?" Turning toward them once more, she bared her teeth. "Honor is to be remembered after death, yeah? Well, Astrid spent every waking moment trying to forget our son. She wouldn't even speak Kolya's name."

"You already got your revenge on Astrid," Edie said, balling her fists against the magic thrumming in her palms. "You tortured and killed her. So what the hell is all this?"

"This is..." Indriði gestured vaguely, her smirk returning. "A little revolution, you might say. Fate decreed that Kolya and hundreds of millions like him should die. Maybe Fate is outdated."

Edie blinked. *What?* From what she'd been told, Fate was what held the universe together—they were all tied up in one big tapestry. Pulling one thread could undo the whole shebang. A lesser Norn, of all people, would be aware of that. "You're willing to destroy the universe over one man?"

Indriði inclined her chin. "If that's what it takes."

"You're insane," Basile said flatly.

"Am I? Because in the grand scheme of th—"

"Enough." Satara surged forward, close enough that Indriði was pressed up against the glass. "No more monologuing."

"Fine, valkyrie," Indriði sneered. "Do your worst. There's nothing you can—"

Without ceremony, Satara kicked Indriði hard, boot hitting her in the center of her stomach. Her back cracked against the window, but Satara followed through. Shards of glass fell like rain, and Indriði screamed, pinwheeling her arms as she teetered on the window frame.

Then gravity caught up with her, and she went sailing over the edge like a sack of potatoes.

Satara was still, chest rising and falling quickly, and silence fell over the apartment. It was as though time stopped. Everyone held their breaths.

After a few moments, she planted her foot on the window frame and unhooked the horn from her belt—the same horn she'd used to summon Bifrost—blowing into the steely morning sky.

Da-daaaaa, da-daaaaa, da-daaaaa.

Edie started and cringed when the resonance broke the rest of the windows on that wall, the tempered glass piling in its frame like a snowdrift.

Before their eyes, the sky changed. The gray veil began to glow, as though lightning was flashing beyond it. The clouds roiled, swirling. Edie was reminded of the night of Zaedicus's party, after the Wounded and his army had retreated, when valkyir had swarmed the sky. Like they had then, they rode the gloom on spectral wolves, ravens, and horses, their wings outstretched and hair flying.

An uproar of honking and squealing tires rose from the street as the small ghostly army approached the Baccarat. A handful of them dismounted and stepped into the apartment through the broken windows, while the others remained levitating outside.

As Satara spoke to the other valkyir and the group began to assess themselves and each other for any injuries, Edie drifted toward the sectional.

Her limbs barely consulted her; she moved as though in a fugue as she ran a hand over where Indriði had been sitting. Dry. No blood. It was hard to imagine someone could be so powerful that they could reverse time in a bubble like that.

It was also hard to imagine that a fall from a skyscraper had killed such a person. She glanced over at the valkyir, who were embroiled in a heated discussion as they peered over the edge of the building. A horrible suspicion that they hadn't seen the last of Indriði crept up her back, and she looked away.

How the hell were they supposed to kill the bitch, then?

As Edie continued examining the sectional, something caught her eye. Something flat and dark, sandwiched between two cushions. She plucked it out, wrapping her hand around the grip. The dagger's runes flashed purple briefly, then faded to regular etchings.

If Indriði wasn't dead, Edie might as well get something out of this. It also meant she could give Marius back his dagger of truth. She traced the runes with one finger, shivering, before tucking the dagger away in her coat. For now, an extra weapon certainly wouldn't hurt.

Movement in her periphery caught her attention. She turned her head, cocking a brow as she noticed that the blanket thrown over the back of the sectional was trembling slightly. She approached, looking behind the couch. The hem of the blanket led her gaze down. A pair of long, thin green feet and four hairy blue legs poked out from under it, shuffling. Soft prayers in Old Norse were muffled by the gray cashmere.

With a sigh, Edie pulled the blanket off Ilphas and Percy.

The spider pivoted to look at her, pedipalps working anxiously. The light elf cowered, holding his hands up in supplication. "*Ah*! Hellerune! It — It's you!"

"Hi," she said slowly. "Ilphas, right?"

"Ilphas Miravn, at— at your service." He bowed his head, long ears pinning back. "I— I really had nothing to do with Indriði's plans! I was simply sent here by my master to work, I swear to you. A replacement for her old steward!"

"Roggvi," Marius said as he came to stand beside Edie.

"That's him!" The elf nodded vehemently. "He was killed. H-How did you know?"

Marius crossed his arms. "Because I'm the one who killed him."

The blood drained from Ilphas's face, big brown eyes going wide again. In a second, he was prostrate before them, every inch of him shaking. "Please, spare me! All I knew was that it was a personal assistant job!" He sat up, spreading his hands pleadingly. The shadows of the valkyir searching through the apartment crossed his face. "I can tell you all I know. Give you information! I can prove I'm loyal!"

"Clearly not to your mistress," Marius mumbled. "So why would you be loyal to us?"

The elf's ears flattened against his head again. "This is different. Indriði was a cruel woman. The Reach—that's what you are, aren't you? You're supposed to help people with no other place to go. That's me!"

Edie sighed and looked over at Basile. "The spider is a friend. Do you have somewhere they can stay until we can get them to Anster?"

"I can arrange something." The priest nodded and flagged down a valkyrie, pointing at the two as he chatted. At least Sissel would be happy to see Percy again.

Suddenly, the apartment doors flew open with a bang. Edie jumped, magic shooting up her arms as she reached for one of her daggers—but relaxed when she saw it was Cal.

He was harried, covered in blood. Her heart pumped harder. "Are you okay? What happened?"

"I'm fine," he said, jogging in. He took a quick look around the room. "Indriði?"

"She's gone," Satara answered, emerging from the bedroom hall. In her hands were two weapons of wood and iron, deceptively simple looking for what they were. Astrid's heirlooms. Armed with them, Satara looked ready to take on anything. "But I got what I came for, and she can't run forever."

"Right on!" Cal took a step to the side and leaned to fist-bump Satara. "Now, not to put a damper on the mood, but we got a, uh, problem."

Adam frowned and tugged on his guitar strap. "What's up?"

"Reinforcements, that's what. Right on my ass, if we don't get on top of it." He jerked his thumb back toward the hall. "More'n I could ever hope to take on."

"The Wounded is here." Edie wasn't sure how, but she was absolutely certain of it. She looked at Satara. "We need to get to the rally, but I don't think the Gloaming is going to let us slip out. Can you fly us?"

She glanced at the other valkyir. "We can."

There was a *boom* several floors below them—an explosion. Every muscle in Edie's body tightened. "Sounds like our cue."

CHAPTER THIRTY-NINE

"Here," Marius said as the others paired off with the dozen or so valkyir who'd volunteered to help, "you can ride with me."

Edie tilted her head, watching as he summoned a horse of light from the thin shafts of sun coming through the clouds. It was gold, slightly translucent, and seethed with plasma just like his weapons did.

When the horse came level with the window, Marius mounted swiftly, apparently unafraid of falling fifty floors to his death. Then he leaned and extended his hand, gripping Edie's forearm.

With his help, she was in the saddle before she had time to psych herself out about floating six-hundred feet above street level.

She was surprised to find herself sitting in front of him, cradled by his arms as he reached forward to grab the horse's glittering rein. His warmth was certainly welcome in the frigid air, but with all the blood rushing to her face, she wasn't sure she'd need it.

"Hang on," he murmured, practically in her ear as he waited for the others to settle in with their valkyir.

Edie shivered and peered over the side of the horse, holding on to the saddle for dear life. The street was a long way down, but it looked like her suspicions had been correct—no sign of Indriði's body. There was, however, one hell of a traffic jam, and a crowd gathering around the base of the Baccarat, staring up at them.

Finally, the valkyir took off, and Marius followed them. Edie squinted against the harsh wind, hardly able to see for her watering eyes.

Above the overwhelming roar of air in her ears, she shouted, "Where is this thing happening, anyway?" Marius must know—he'd spent three weeks with Basile—but she'd never thought to ask.

"No one was sure until a few days ago," Marius shouted back. "We only knew it would be in Central Park. But they've chosen the Bethesda Terrace. Are you familiar?"

She snorted. "I barely know the names of stuff in Anster."

"Well, it isn't exactly a rally venue. They probably don't have a permit to be there."

Edie gritted her teeth. "I guess they figure, who's going to stop them?"

"We are."

And with that, they were flying over Central Park, much faster than Edie had anticipated. Though green prevailed here and there, it was mostly an expanse of white. Some of the trees were bare, and as they careened toward the ground, she could see a mostly frozen lake over the tops of the trees.

She heard the rally first: a woman's voice shouting into a microphone, though the feedback and echo this far away were too bad to make out what she was saying; the thunder of a crowd shouting a muffled chant.

Then, as they sailed over the treetops, she saw it.

In front of the frozen lake, there must have been a stone terrace and a pair of staircases, but at the moment, it was hardly visible. Every available space was swallowed by a sea of red. Armed Blood Eagles paving it treeline to treeline. On the upper terrace, Daschla was set up with a microphone and speakers, dressed in the warrior queen garb she'd worn at Shipshaven.

She was surrounded by people. There must have been a thousand bodies, give or take a hundred, but no police to be seen. The only part of the terrace that was clear was the large fountain. In the center, an angel spouted murky green water.

As they soared over, a roar climbed from the mob. People turned their heads and pointed. Edie wasn't sure where the valkyir intended to land, but as Marius followed them, circling in for a landing, she caught some of what Daschla was saying:

"Your ideas have *power*. And power is what we need to put our ideas into *action*. The world is ending, but an end is also a new beginning. A farmer scorches his earth to make the soil richer for the next harvest. We will scorch the earth! And our children and our grandchildren will say that this was the place where the revolution began. This was the place where our warriors took back our country and our lives and our world!"

Edie's spine felt like ice. Her instinct was to dismiss those words as insanity. But Daschla wasn't insane, and there was no way every one of these thousand people was either. They knew what they were doing. They were just evil. Greedy and hateful and selfish and hungry and evil.

The horse finally touched down, and it took her a moment to realize that they were standing on the frozen lake. With a sweeping breath, one of the valkyir leading the charge blew winter onto the ice below them, strengthening it. As Edie and Marius dismounted, she was surprised to find that it wasn't even slippery, pitted and snow-crusted as it was.

She raised her head, crunching across the ice quickly to join Satara and Basile at the front line. The Blood Eagles had turned to them, a tumultuous sea of red, shaking their signs and banners and shouting things she wouldn't dream of saying to her worst enemy. The valkyir and the Reach stayed still.

Edie shielded her eyes with one hand, hair whipping around her head as she gazed at the upper terrace. Daschla had handed her microphone off to one of her aides, and with a burst of purple light, her true form was revealed—that dull, cracked, imperfect form.

Apparently, there were those in the crowd who had never seen it before; a large portion of them turned their attention from the Reach to their queen, shouting their awe, cheering for her. She spread her wings and swept over the horde, touching down just in front of the fountain, closer to the lake but still surrounded by her followers. She towered over the men, whose body language said they were ready and willing to kill for her.

"There are so many of them," Elle whispered, her voice nearly lost in the wind.

"Yeah." Cal grinned around his lit cigarette. "But we got cavalry, 'member?"

Before Daschla could speak, Satara raised her horn to her lips and blew, the sound trumpeting richly through the park.

Again, the clouds lit up, and the ghostly forms of valkyir charged in a line toward the earth. Riding behind every one of them were human women, their armor trimmed with feathers and fur. Shieldmaidens. In all, there had to have been a hundred valkyir, with a shieldmaiden for each.

Satara blew the horn a second time, and the air behind them sizzled, a faint golden outline appearing as if someone had cut through reality with a hot knife. The glow spread, taking the form of an oval portal. The image of a blue sky and grass swam in the oval for a second; then the image rippled, and a familiar woman stepped into the chilly air.

Amat Izem held an ornate distaff in one hand. Where she didn't wear white padding, she wore silver armor, her locs wound into a tight bun on top of her head. She walked toward Satara, joining the valkyir and their shieldmaidens behind the front line. Following her, a hundred priestesses, defenders, warriors, and archers dressed in blue, red, and silver poured from the portal, filing into place with regimental precision.

High Priestess Eniola stepped through last, dressed in dark blue, and the golden glow closed behind her. She took her place at the front line, beside Satara's mother, and called out an order in Old Norse. The Mare Isle forces began walking forward, spurring Edie and the others to do the same. Her heart pounded harder the closer they came to the terrace and the Blood Eagles. Their slurs and chants became even louder.

Their approach seemed to agitate Daschla. She began to shout, her voice booming over the men around her.

"The time has finally come, Blood Eagles. The Reach is here to wage war against us. To kill you and your families and take what you've earned." She spread her arms, looking around at them. "My warriors, didn't I tell you how deep this poison had spread through our very own faith? People attacking those with actual claims, actual European ancestry, and pushing you out? They think they can take whatever they want, but it's time to say enough is enough! It's time for the old ways to return, for the world to be ours again. The battle has always been yours, Odin's chosen!"

Edie's heart thundered in her rib cage. "Why would you think Odin chose you for anything when we're standing here with ten dozen valkyir behind us?"

Cal flicked his cigarette and spat. "Maybe you should give a little speech of your own, Miss Reacher."

She clenched her jaw, glancing at the others. Satara tore her eyes from the Blood Eagles to give a little nod, tightening her grip on her horn. Adam and Elle watched with wide eyes, tense. Basile carefully took off his glasses and tucked them in his breast pocket. The Mare Isle forces looked on, backs straight as they waited for the order to charge.

Performing on stage several times a week had mostly ironed out her stage fright, but Edie was no general. She couldn't give a proper inspirational speech.

Looking back at the mob, their insults echoing in her skull, she felt her face get hotter. If she couldn't speak inspirationally, there was at least one thing she could do—speak angrily.

She raised her voice above the wind, letting words tumble from her mouth. "You freaks carve runes into your guns and kill innocents like you're ancient warriors or whatever, but you're not. You're evil, entitled bastards. Look at you! The crap you do doesn't mean what you think it does. Spraying forty-five rounds a minute into an unarmed crowd because you're angry people look different than you isn't honor! Setting a religious building on fire and running away isn't battle. Killing a girl because she won't sleep with you won't land you in the gods' halls when you die.

"The Vikings did horrible things. A lot of people did. They're called the Dark Ages for a reason. But they were still *horrible*! Trying to absolve yourself of doing evil garbage by saying 'This aligns with the old ways' isn't fooling anybody. We don't live in 800 AD anymore!"

She turned to the small army behind her, her fast breath fogging the air.

"The old Reach is gone. Okay? I can promise you that. We don't *need* to be Switzerland, and we don't need to do what the Aurora does to protect innocent people. If we remake the Reach, it'll be based on compassion ... and justice. No more slavery. No more slaughter." Edie looked back at the Blood Eagles. "And no more of *this* bullshit."

Beside her, Satara raised her horn and blew one last time into the sky, longer and louder than before. The sound made the earth rumble, the fullness of it filling the air with a wavering, antsy energy.

For a moment, nothing happened. The air was still, a light snow beginning to fall around them.

Then, directly in front of the Blood Eagles, sparks flew, like someone had taken a grinder to a sheet of metal. Before Edie could even comprehend what was happening, the sparks burst into the shape of a doorway, and a large, fiery form shot out, crashing into the Blood Eagles' front line.

She watched in shock as Vidarr picked up the nearest human and tore him in half like a phonebook.

Gallons of blood exploded, painting the snow and the other Blood Eagles nearby, and chaos erupted.

Daschla looked just as shocked as Edie was, watching her men attack Vidarr. Some of them neglected their weapons to try and dogpile him. Some were able to squeeze off a few panicked rounds, but they learned their lesson quickly as the bullets ricocheted off him and became friendly fire instead.

The Silent God was unmoved. One by one, he tore the humans off him like they were mere nuisances, crushing several skulls in the process. The Mare Isle defenders pushed through the front line to slam down their massive shields, but the scuffle was surprisingly short. The god of vengeance stepped onto the ice and turned toward the Blood Eagles, but only a few lackluster rounds followed him.

Edie raised her head a bit, squinting over one of the defenders' shields to look at the mob. It swam with discord, louder than ever. Toward the back, she could see a handful of men scattering and fleeing toward the Mall.

"Seems your Blood Eagles aren't as brave or loyal as you thought they were," Satara said, her voice carrying over the din despite her steady tone.

Daschla turned, whipping her head back and forth as she scanned the terrace, watching her men desert one by one. When she turned back, her eyes were blown wide, her teeth gritted, chest rising and falling quickly. If she'd had steam coming out of her ears, she'd have looked like a Looney Tune.

She struggled to hide her expression, holding her hands over her Blood Eagles again. "It's just as well, isn't it, brothers and sisters?" she boomed, not quite convincing in her breathlessness. "Those of you left are the true warriors. You're the real chosen ones. You would never see one of your brothers slaughtered and run away! You're the ones who actually deserve the gift I'm going to give you! Shall I give you the gift?"

The crowd's enthusiasm had been waning dramatically, but her words rallied them. They screamed for her, those who weren't wearing the skull masks practically foaming at the mouth.

"When I was a little girl," Daschla began, beginning to weave a sickly blue magic between her fingers, "we owned chickens. Every spring, the chicks would hatch, and every autumn, we culled them. It could hardly be called cruelty ... we used the meat to feed ourselves and sustain our village. But their entire existence, before they were even born, was already decided. They were born to be fed from."

She stretched her wings out, beating the air until she was hovering several feet above their heads. The magic in her hands was growing larger the more she wove it, resembling a scarf as it wound around her body.

"Of course, to a child, these things seemed so unfair—that the animals I cultivated had to be killed on my behalf. But you learn the facts of life quickly as a farm girl. The chickens were livestock, not friends. They had served me well, and they'd continue to do so after death. Their deaths allowed me to thrive..."

The magic flowed out from her now, like tendrils, reaching across the entire crowd. She raised her arms, and the energy floated higher into the air, the flows reminding Edie of a spider's web. The web began to settle gently over the blood-red mob.

Her heart thudded hard, then skipped a beat in her chest as she realized what was about to happen.

"You want to fight for me," Daschla said, looking down at them. "But the truth is ... you're simply not good enough. You have so little power, and glory comes at a very, very high price." She leveled her gaze at the Reach. Edie felt like she was staring straight into her soul. "All the living are prisoners of Fate. And so, I release you."

She raised a hand swiftly toward the sky, spreading her fingers. The web jerked, trying to follow her movement, but it was as though it was stuck to the crowd of Blood Eagles. In fact, the more she tugged, the lower it seemed to sink over them like a hazy blue net.

Still, she continued, chanting softly, closing her eyes. As the web closed in on the mob, cries of pain and terror surged, a wave of misery that washed over the terrace and the lake and shook Edie to her core. But the Blood Eagles couldn't move—they seemed bound where they stood.

"Autumn is here; the twilight's so close," Daschla cried earnestly, face screwing up as she concentrated on pulling her web. "It's time for the harvest. I *have to feed*. I have to be strong..."

The screams rose and rose until they were practically deafening—and then, nearly all at once, they stopped. One by one, the Blood Eagles collapsed under the weight of the psychic net, falling like marionettes whose strings had been cut. Their masks, weapons, and banners clattered to the brick of the terrace.

A darker part of Edie might have been thankful Daschla did their work for them, but there was no moment of relief, only mounting horror. Standing where the Blood Eagles had once stood, one for every fallen body, were ghostly apparitions.

They looked like they had stepped out of a movie, dressed head to toe in lamellar armor and chainmail. The visors of their helmets were fashioned into human likenesses, but the eyes were hollow and empty. They stood with shields at the ready, prepared to kill for their queen.

When Daschla grinned, it hit Edie like a ton of bricks. This had always been the Blood Eagles' purpose. From the first moment they had started supporting this movement, the Gloaming had had ulterior plans for these people.

Their purpose had always been to die and create an army of unholy, unstoppable warriors.

But ... *I have to feed. I have to be strong.* What did that part mean?

"My god," Basile whispered, reaching to grab Edie's shoulder. "My god. She's going to—"

Before he could finish his thought, Daschla unleashed a bone-shaking shriek. Her body burst with purple light, braids flying in an unearthly wind.

The unholy army roared in response and drove forward, charging the Reach's front line.

CHAPTER FORTY

As THE UNHOLY warriors sprinted forward with preternatural speed, the Mare Isle defenders dug their heels and their shields into the icy snow.

For a second, Edie wondered if they would even hold the spirits back —the spirits seemed too insubstantial, like spiders' silk in the wind. The next moment, she got her answer: they hit the shields with force, just as any solid man would.

They crashed into the ranks, some of them managing to breach the line and lash out with their unearthly weapons. Necrotic fire raged up Edie's arms as she watched a few Reach fall to them.

"Flank them!" Satara called out.

A squad of valkyir lifted off with shieldmaidens in tow, soaring over the ghostly mob, narrowly dodging flying spears and arrows.

"People on this side, press them! Get off the ice!"

A war cry erupted in front of Edie, and she ducked just in time to avoid the blade of a spectral fighter's axe. The ice coating the lake was strong, bolstered as it was with the valkyrie frost, but the heat of battle would melt it. If there was one thing Edie had learned about battles, it was that they always turned unbearably hot.

Having Vidarr here, who seemed to constantly be spitting sparks, didn't help matters. As Satara and Eniola shouted orders, he was the first one to tear through the crowd, carving swaths through the spirit army with his sword.

Edie and the rest of the Reach followed suit with a roar, rushing off the ice and toward the terrace. Daschla had disappeared, but the Blood Eagles' fresh corpses still steamed in the wintry air.

The Reach pushed the offensive, swords and axes passing through the spirits and making them explode into eddies of white wisps. But as Edie reached the terrace, an uproar turned her attention back to the ice.

Her heart sank. There was no trail of bodies in their wake. The fallen spirits simply re-formed, howling and screaming like gales, angrier and more bloodthirsty than before. They charged forward again.

"Great," Cal shouted, emptying his shells and speed-loading with a practiced movement. "So they can hit us as hard as they want, but we're fucked!"

"This way," Satara called, flying over the defenders. "Flank them, push them toward the Mall!"

Edie drew her dagger, clutching it tight in a clammy hand as she raced past the angel fountain, leaping over fallen bodies. *At least the ghosts don't have guns*, she thought. But a slight loss in execution efficiency was a small price to pay for the invincibility they'd just demonstrated.

Somehow, they needed to contain this army in Central Park, here and now. If they got into the city, New York would end up like Anster.

When she climbed the grand staircase to the upper terrace and looked across at the Mall, she understood why Satara wanted them to move there—much more room, room they could get creative with.

If she knew Satara, the valkyrie's gears were spinning a million miles a minute trying to come up with how they were going to kill a deathless army. Hell, Edie's wheels were spinning just wondering how she was going to make it out alive.

The Reach fighters retreated across the narrow street, following

Satara's order to lure the spirits into the wider area. Edie was about to follow suit when she caught a flash of familiar armor.

She froze and turned to watch Marius climb the staircase to the first landing, then jump and scale a sandstone pillar to the upper terrace. "Marius!" she cried out, running a couple steps toward him. The spirits were closing in fast, barely slowed by the flank. "We need to go!"

"I want to try something." Without taking his eyes off the mob of spirits, he stood on the parapet and wrestled something from the pouch on his belt, throwing it like a pitcher into the center of the crowd. Whatever he'd thrown exploded with brilliant yellow light, leaving a crater in the spirits' ranks.

Edie held her breath, waiting for them to reform ... but they didn't. It was like the light had stunned them out of existence.

"I knew it," Marius breathed, jumping from the parapet and taking off running next to Edie. The spirits were right on their heels, so close she could feel their deathly chill. Marius summoned a shield at their backs and raised his voice. "Satara! They're evil spirits. Use holy magic. Use holy magic!"

The valkyrie circled above their heads, squinting as if straining to hear him—but once she understood, she was off like a shot again, spreading the message: "Eniola, use the magic of the Aesir!"

"Spirit magic will work, too," Basile said, pulling up beside them, his glamour still intact for now.

Edie spared a glance over her shoulder as they continued to jog. Her heart leapt when she saw that the flanking Reach had managed to push the unholy army across the street. "So anyone who doesn't have holy or spirit magic is just shit out of luck," she said breathlessly, looking back at Basile.

"Just corral them toward someone who can kill them for you. Oh, and try not to die."

"Thanks! Great strategy!"

The remainder of the choice words she had for him were cut off when a spectral spear pierced the icy snow just inches to her side. Edie turned her head in time to see another soaring squarely toward Marius's back.

With a squawk, she grabbed his arm and tugged him roughly to the side, pulling them both behind a tree.

It was a temporary respite, but the unholy army was so single-minded in their advance that they charged right past them, chasing after the others.

Marius gazed across the frosty Mall, then looked at Edie. "Thank you."

"No problem. So what's the plan?"

"I'll try to stay near. You can lure whoever comes after you to me, and I'll kill them with blessed sunlight." He dug in his belt pouch and pressed something into her hand—something metal, and hot, nearly unbearably so.

She opened her palm to examine it. The object looked almost like a tea ball: an orb with tiny holes punched through it. The cap of the object was gilt, and from each hole streamed a brilliant shaft of light. This must have been what he'd thrown earlier. "What is it?"

"A holy boon. Use it in an emergency. Just throw it with force, or break it otherwise ... but be careful." Marius scanned the area and pointed to the main thoroughfare of the Mall, a paved esplanade. "I'll try to stay along this road, but who knows where the battle will travel."

Edie shoved the boon in her jacket pocket, then exchanged her newly acquired dagger for the Puretongue's blade instead. It caught Marius's eye, and she smiled. "Now I'm glad I didn't give this back."

He looked seriously at her, golden gaze seething. "We're outnumbered by nearly seven hundred, and not all of our combatants can kill the enemy. People are going to die. Brutally. Please be careful."

"Satara and the other valkyir will come up with a strategy. We'll save as many people as we can."

Edie glanced back toward the battlefield, glowing dagger at the ready. The fighting had spilled into the Mall proper now, some of the valkyir and shieldmaidens flanking the Blood Eagles on the side nearest to Edie, the Mare Isle forces pushing them on the other. From where she stood, she thought she understood Satara's strategy—to sandwich all the unholy warriors so the valkyir could rain spirit magic from above.

But having to funnel the spirits to the priestesses and valkyir was breaking the formation. Edie watched as multiple Mare Isle soldiers attempted to shepherd the spirits and fall to the mob in the process. The sight made her blood heat, adrenaline kicking through her system. With every ally that fell, the enemy was able to chip away at the line just a little more. Before they knew it, the battlefield would be chaos.

As Marius followed her gaze, his weapons blazed to life, and he leapt into battle, driving his glittering shield into the enemy. "Hold the line! Edie, go!"

She ran a few more feet, then stopped again to assess the battlefield, heart beating frantically. She'd never been in a battle like this before. The fight at Zaedicus's party had been more of a slaughter—a culling, as Sárr had called it—and she'd spent most of her time running and trying not to die. The battle in the Auroran chapterhouse had been close-quarters chaos, basically a slugfest.

This? This was calculated warfare, and she was surrounded by veterans of this sort of thing. Where did she even jump in?

Before she could find her place in the battle, the battle found her. A war cry erupted above her and she looked just in time to see a spirit flying down from one of the trees, his blade poised to sink into her neck.

Edie pitched herself to the side, rolling across the ground. The *clang* of steel striking pavement, as though the spirit wielded a real sword, reached her ears. She jumped to her feet, reorienting so she could face her attacker.

The shock of his blade hitting pavement seemed to have stunned him for a moment, and a voice at the back of her skull whispered, ***Don't hesitate. Kill.***

On instinct, she obeyed instantly, darting forward. Death magic raged up her left arm, and she fired a blast of blue flame at the warrior. He burst into a flurry of white magic but, just like before, the magic soon coalesced back into the shape of a man. If nothing else, it stunned him for a few seconds ... *but stunned is not what I need. Death is what I need. Power. Kill.*

The spirit roared as he reformed, even more berserk than before, and brought his sword down. Again, Edie dodged to the side, but she gave him no time to recover. With a vicious, quick movement, she sank the dagger of truth into one of the eyeholes of his helmet.

The silver blade penetrated his translucent form, and with a yowl, he disintegrated, light eating him away from the edges like a melting snowflake.

Edie's heart lifted, but there was no time to celebrate the victory. Another wispy shape charged her flank. She was able to dodge the spirit's weapon, but his shield slammed into her, knocking her over one of the fences separating the esplanade from the green.

She struggled among the gnarled roots of a tree to pick herself up. The fence had staggered her, but she assumed it would be nothing to the spirit—they could fly and phase through things when they wanted to.

Without looking back to confirm her suspicions, she instead looked forward, gaze catching on the first shadow she saw: the shadow of a tree about twenty feet ahead, lined up perfectly.

There.

The next moment, she was. She turned as the shadows cleared from her vision and saw that the spirit who had been mere inches from running her through wasn't alone; there were three others with him, all charging for her. No way a tiny dagger could save her from four at once.

With a bit of effort, she pushed out a wave of death magic that crashed into the four forms, dispelling them momentarily. They reformed after a few seconds, their bodies pulsing with murderous energy, and she darted to the side, jumping the fence. The second her boots hit the pavement, she took off, pumping her arms.

All around her, weapons flew, people cried out and fell. The heat of battle she was used to wasn't as prominent as she thought it might be—no, it was rent with a bone-deep cold. It emanated from each of the spirits as she charged through a corner of their formation on her way to Marius, cutting their ranks with a sweep of death magic.

Those warriors re-formed, too, of course, and joined the mob chasing her, so close the hairs at the back of her neck stood on end. She ducked and wove through the valkyir flank to avoid their spectral spears and arrows.

By the time she finally reached Marius, some of her *admirers* had been picked off by the valkyir and their shieldmaidens, but there was still a crowd of perhaps fifteen at her back.

"Marius!" As he turned, she slid past him on black ice, then wheeled around and drew the Puretongue's dagger again.

Marius reacted immediately, his blade and shield reshaping into a greatsword. The pommel slotted into his wolf's head vambrace as he took the grip into his left hand and swept outward, then down, slicing through several spirits in just a few movements.

One escaped his blows and charged toward Edie, but she was ready with a blast of stunning magic and another dagger to the eye. A few others followed him, but Marius spun and shot a beam of light through their chests. What remained of them flurried toward the sky.

"Like that?" Edie said between heavy breaths, scanning their surroundings as she stepped closer to him.

"Yes." Marius's breath came harshly, too. "Though I'm not sure a sane person would have baited quite that many."

"If I was ever sane, I don't think I'd have survived this long." She opened her mouth to say more, but a flash of movement over his shoulder caught her eye. A spirit was diving straight for him, spear extended, mouth open in a roar. "Behind you!"

Marius began to turn, but the spirit warrior was practically on top of him now. Time slowed to a crawl as the tip of the spear rocketed toward his head.

Then, at the last second, it stopped. The spirit was tugged back midflight, and its body was sundered in half before exploding, white flecks mingling with molten orange ones. On the other side stood a now-familiar, fiery visage.

Vidarr had traded his regular sword for one that looked to be made of flames, though Edie knew without having to be told it was holy fire. He was an Aesir, after all.

"Lord Vidarr," Marius said, switching his weapons back to a blade and shield. "My thanks."

The god said nothing, simply turned away and lashed out at another large group of spirits, destroying them in one fell swoop.

As Edie shadow jumped back into the fray, her heart lifted. Marius was right; this was dangerous, and people were going to die. But having a god and this many valkyir on their side meant they couldn't lose.

...Right?

As Adam skidded across the icy pavement, asphalt biting into his leather jacket, he realized he was probably going to die here.

The thought was as startlingly clear and harsh as the noon light reflecting off the snow. Obvious. People were dying all around him; the stench of the battlefield overpowered the senses. He wasn't any different from them. He wasn't special.

Dragging himself to his feet, he faced the spirit who had thrown him and ground out a riff on the Genesis that punched a bolt of shadow straight through its chest. The shadow was chased closely by a lance of spirit magic thrown by a valkyrie circling above, and Adam spun, looking for the next threat.

There was no time to think. There was no time to do anything but fight or die. And yet as his gaze swept over the Mall—a place he'd been a hundred times, so different now—he felt compelled to stand still for an extended moment and admire the scene. Blood, viscera, death, misery...

Ain't it pretty?

Adam blinked and shook his head hard. That voice kept creeping up in his mind, but it didn't feel like his own. It wasn't the first time he had felt a buried-deep presence surface, but until recently, he'd never heard it in the back of his head like that. Thinking for him.

Can't live if you're afraid to die. Get them. Chase them. Kill them.

When he'd heard it before, the voice had disturbed him, even terrified him. But in that moment, as the feeling washed through his body, the anxiety of the battle melted away; he felt energized, excited, like that buried part of himself was vindicated by the violence. Leaning into it, he felt like he could think and react faster. His senses felt sharpened; his magic felt less like a tool and more like it was *him*.

Kill them. It'll feel good. You won't even get in trouble ... people'll thank you. Prey. Prey. They're all prey.

Hell, whatever it took to stay alive at this point.

His boots against the pavement and the strain in his legs barely registered as he swooped into battle. The shadows came to life around him, saturated voids of magic. He darted in and out, zigzagging from tree to cement to grass, stalking his prey. Silhouettes fled from him in droves, weaving through the skirmish as he picked out weaknesses.

Before he knew it, he found himself in front of the Literary Walk, standing between the statues of Robert Burns and Walter Scott.

The bulk of the battle was nearly a hundred feet away now. He could tell from the thrumming in his fingers that he'd been playing the Genesis, riffing spells as he swept down the promenade, but he could hardly remember it. It was like he'd blacked out.

But he'd survived. And, surprisingly, he felt amazing. Alive. Electric.

"*Adam?*" Mikey's tentative whisper wound around his brain, and the guitar vibrated in his hands. "*Are you okay, man? What was that whole thing?*"

"I'm fine." He clenched and unclenched his jaw. "I'm just ... trying to learn to use these powers ... and trying not to die. Some of us make that a priority."

The Genesis went quiet.

Adam turned around, poised to channel more shadow through his strings. He'd race up and down the esplanade, luring as many spirits to their deaths as he could, for as long as he could. Then—

A ghostly roar interrupted his train of thought, and he ducked just in time to dodge something flying toward his head. It landed behind him with a heavy metallic *CLANK*, chilling him to the bone. If it had hit him, he would be dead.

It only took a moment to pinpoint the origin of the roar. A spirit hovered next to the now-decapitated statue of Robert Burns, a maul grasped tightly in both hands. With a shriek, the spirit descended, swinging for Adam.

He ducked and rolled as his attacker swooped low. The maul whistled past his shoulder. Adam turned, picking himself up quickly, and summoned a spike of shadow with a whip-quick sequence of notes.

But the spirit didn't even try to move. He simply let himself be impaled—and when his form reshaped, he was stalking toward Adam, pale eyes burning with hatred.

Adam's fingers froze over his frets. He knew those eyes. He knew that face. It was different now—blueish, translucent, coated with frost—but there was no mistaking it.

"Brian?" Adam whispered.

The spirit didn't reply with words. Maybe he couldn't. He simply growled, a nearly subsonic noise that shook the ground, and raised his maul again.

"*Brain Damage?!*" Mikey cried as Adam shadow jumped to the base of a tree behind the spirit. "*Brian's one of the bad guys?*"

"Are you that surprised?"

"*Aren't you? He was our friend!*"

"Never a very good one, let's be honest." A dark cloud stuck to Adam as he lurked in the shadows of the trees, circling Brian's spirit. "He always treated you and Clottia like shit. I just never thought he'd go this far."

The spirit wheeled around, searching frantically for his opponent. In broad daylight, Adam was only able to escape notice for a few more moments before Brian clocked him and ran full tilt, screaming and swinging his weapon.

Adam ducked behind the Walter Scott statue and rounded it, summoning a shade at Brian's back. It stabbed him in the spine with a spike of shadow, but the attack didn't even dispel him, only slowed him down.

As Brian spun to kill the shade, Adam backed up, casting his eyes to the sky. He'd need to get the attention of a valkyrie or one of the priestesses of Freyja if he wanted to take Brian down.

It felt horrible, thinking that about an old friend. In some ways, he felt responsible. If he'd looked harder, he would have seen it coming. He'd known Brian had shitty, misguided opinions. He'd known he blamed a failing system on people who didn't deserve it. Maybe it was Adam's fault his friend had gone off the deep end. If he'd tried to talk some sense into Brian before it was too late, maybe things would be different—if not for him, for the people he'd hurt.

But no one had forced him to put on a mask and pick up a gun and pledge to kill people. Brian had chosen his side, and they'd used him. And now, in the most literal way, he was too far gone.

Eyes still on the sky, Adam took off running, hoping to slip past Brian. He thought he remembered seeing a few priestesses and their defenders holding the line not far from here, or maybe a valkyrie would notice them—

As he ran, he sent out another shade to distract Brian. It appeared behind the spirit and attempted to put him in a headlock, but he simply shook it off, barreling forward.

Adam staggered to a halt as his former friend blocked his way, maul gripped in both hands and malice burning in his eyes.

"Brian," Adam muttered, gripping the Genesis close to his chest. "Brian, are you in there? Can you understand me?"

The spirit responded with another subsonic growl. If Brian was still aware, he wasn't interested in talking.

Adam dodged to the side, hoping to get around him, but Brian lashed out with the maul and only barely missed his right temple. Drawing in a sharp breath, Adam tried the other way, but the spirit was so quick, coiled so tight, ready to react to the slightest movement.

Feint.

Adam obeyed, feinting to the left—then, when Brian lashed out, he jerked to the right, nearly passing him. But the spirit was turning too fast, maul raised above his head now.

Every calculation was made within a nanosecond: almost as soon as Adam dodged right, he realized his mistake. Brian was about to pulverize him, and he'd been knocked out of his zone; there was no time to look for a shadow to jump to.

Instead, as he passed Brian, he turned. What use was an indestructible guitar if you didn't hit shit with it?

The maul came down so quickly that Adam barely raised the Genesis in time, gripping it by the head and body and stopping the maul's momentum neck to shaft. The strength behind the blow was incredible, and it took everything Adam had to keep his arms steady. He stumbled to one knee.

Then he watched in horror as the Genesis splintered and the headstock snapped off.

CHAPTER FORTY-ONE

"*Ow! Fuck!*" The Genesis vibrated discordantly.

As Adam rolled to the side, the maul whistled past his head with a breeze. The pavement shuddered and cracked under him when it was struck.

Headstock in one hand, the rest of the Genesis in the other, Adam jumped to his feet. Dread filled his chest, making him instantly nauseous. That would be an expensive repair, but it hardly even crossed his mind.

"Mikey?" he whispered, keeping his distance from Brian's spirit as they circled one another.

"*I'm still here. That jerkoff cut my motherfucking head off!*"

Relief cooled Adam's heart. "You and Robert Burns both."

"*Screw Robot Burns, Auld-Lang-Syne-ass ... watch out!*"

Adam didn't need to be told to see Brian charging him like a bull again. He shadow jumped quickly behind a statue of Columbus, then looked down at the ruins of the guitar in his hands.

Curses flowed freely as he tried to piece the headstock back onto the neck. Most of the splinters seemed to be there, at least, but that didn't help him now. How was he supposed to channel explosive magic without his focus?

"What the hell happened?" he whispered to Mikey, hidden in the shade for now. "I've hit other stuff and you never broke. I thought your spirit magic or whatever made you invincible."

"Man, I dunno, I just live here."

Adam peeked around the base of the Columbus statue. Brian was moving closer, aided by supernatural senses. "We're gonna have to do a little better than that, Mike."

"He's a spirit ... I'm a spirit ... these guys die when they get hit with spirit magic. I guess his big hammer is spirit magic, so it hurt me."

Brian stopped, fixing Adam with that evil stare, and he knew he'd been spotted. He glanced around him. If he shadow jumped just right, he might be able to make it back to the battle...

He's a spirit, I'm a spirit.

Or he could end this. Right here, right now.

Kill, boy. You need to. You need it. It's in your blood. And anything's a weapon if it ends a life.

With a roar, Adam threw himself from behind the base of the statue. A heavy wave of shadow and death, unrestrained by the Genesis, rolled from him, crashing into everything in the Literary Walk. The huge flowerbed in the center of the roundabout withered to stalks; the lampposts squealed as they were toppled; the elms groaned and bowed under rot. The statue behind him snapped at the ankles and came crashing forward.

He had already rocketed well out of the way by the time it slammed to the cobbles. With the Genesis brandished like a pike, he ran straight into Brian, impaling the spirit with the splintered guitar neck.

Brian's eyes widened, and Adam looked into them, thinking—for just a split second—that he saw some recognition in that gaze.

But it was gone quickly, in an eddy of magic and snow, and all Adam was left with was a bitter end.

He stood there for a few moments, staring at where Brian had been.

Then he looked down at the broken Genesis, and back ahead at the battle.

What now?

His magic was too destructive to use without a focus, and nothing was getting strummed on this guitar.

"Adam! Dad!" Elle trotted off the green toward him. Her stockings and sweater were torn, blond curls caked with dirt and blood. He couldn't see her glamour—he was slowly getting used to seeing her gray as stone with glassy eyes—but he could feel that it had slipped. Her skin was covered in cuts that oozed dark, sluggish fluid.

"Elle." He was still, simply watching as she came closer.

"Oh my god! What happened? Is Mikey okay?"

"He's fine," Adam croaked, looking at her hands. "You're hurt."

She rolled up her sleeves, revealing more cuts. "I'll be okay. Cal says it's real hard to kill a revenant for good."

Adam glanced toward the battle. "I'm not sure what to do without the — Are we winning?"

"I think so," she said, following his gaze. "Between that hunky fire guy and the valkyries, their numbers are dropping like crazy."

He looked down at the Genesis, trying to process this while at the same time puzzling out how he was going to fight now. If he could find Edie or Satara, or even Cal, they would know what to do.

He faced the battle. "Let's go."

Before he could take a step, though, the sky seemed to darken. Something that sounded like thunder rumbled, and he looked up, expecting sudden rain.

"Wait—" Elle gasped, covering her mouth and pointing behind him. "What the fuck is *that*?!"

When he turned and saw, he nearly dropped the Genesis. What looked like a glowing cloud rolled toward them, the apparent source of the thunderous noise. As it came closer, overtaking the entire sky, his heart sank.

It wasn't a glowing cloud—it was another mob of spirits, soaring through the air, toward the Mall. And at their head, voidlike wings cutting the sky, was Daschla.

As Satara swooped in and out of battle, her stomach flipped.

The tides were turning in their favor; there was no doubt of that. Steadily, the Reach and the Mare Isle forces held the line, the flanking valkyir picking away at the unholy army.

But each little victory came at a cost. Many had already died. More would—and at the end of the day, when the dust had settled, it would be her job to take their souls away. That was the way of things. Part of her nature now.

As surely as war raged around her, war raged within her.

Feeding her anxiety was the fact that she'd not seen Daschla since the spirits' initial charge. Whatever that meant, it could not be good.

Satara touched down in the middle of the esplanade, wreathing her spear and shield in spirit magic. Dodging this way, thrusting that way. She threw her shield, and it sliced through several spirits before boomeranging back to her hand.

Every move was calculated, precise. She had been a skilled fighter before, but nothing compared to this. Time seemed to flow around her more smoothly, in her favor. She could feel every living thing in her vicinity, when their souls brightened and when they dimmed. So many threads connected to her, so close, vibrating and shining so vividly...

She would pull back to assess the situation and adjust their strategy soon, but for now, she was in the zone. So much so that she hardly noticed the sky darkening above her.

It wasn't until she heard a familiar voice that she tore her focus from the battle. The voice was frantic, cutting through the din of metal on metal and hissing spells. Satara attempted to pinpoint where it was coming from. A moment later, Adam broke through the crowd.

He was wan, his hair stringy with sweat. Cuts and bruises covered his face, neck, and hands, and his nose was bleeding. With a shock, Satara realized that the guitar slung across his back was snapped at the head, only held together by strings.

But his hazel eyes were bright and wide, and he ran with purpose toward her. She could finally make out his words: "Satara! Auxiliary! Daschla! She brought auxiliary. They're coming!"

Ice lanced her heart. "How many?"

"She must have another thousand more," he said between heavy breaths. Elle appeared next to him a moment later, nodding in agreement.

Satara raised her eyes to see for herself, numbness entering her limbs as spirits blanketed the sky.

She no longer had to wonder where Daschla had gone—there she was, leading the charge. Her discordant vibrations made Satara so acutely uncomfortable, her entire being revolted by the broken valkyrie's very existence.

She must have had more Blood Eagles lying in wait, somewhere away from the rally. They had mere seconds before the new wave of unholy soldiers were upon them.

Pushing off the ground, she flew to one of the other valkyir, relaying orders: "Tell the defenders to continue flanking and holding the line. Have some sisters summon their steeds and enfold them from the air. Now."

The valkyrie nodded. "What of the broken one?"

"Leave Daschla to me."

The valkyrie flew off at once to relay orders. Satara took the air, beating her wings, awestruck at the sheer number of spirits coming toward them. Just as she suspected, they careened toward the battle, trying to take advantage of the Reach from above. But, roars echoing through the Mall, they were met by resistance from mounted valkyir.

Satara expected to see Daschla dive into battle as well, but no ... as the army swooped in, she simply kept flying, clearing the air thirty feet above Satara's head on her way toward the Bethesda Terrace.

You will not run away.

Fire and ice mingled in Satara's chest, compelling her to give chase. She sped after the false valkyrie, unbothered by the cold winds slicing her face. As Daschla angled her path downward and disappeared into the Bethesda Arcade, Satara followed.

They were isolated from the battle here. The sounds of fighting had faded, mere echoes bouncing off the arcade's sandstone arches and intricately tiled ceiling. The cobblestone floor was carpeted with snow, packed down from the thousands of people who traveled through this short tunnel daily. It was odd to think that such a beautiful place was hidden under an ordinary asphalt road.

As she stepped under the arches, deeper into the arcade, the silence struck her. Compared to the heat and cacophony of the battle, this place was like a tomb. Every hair stood on end as she crept farther in, grip tightening on her shield and spear.

Daschla had entered here. Had she been quick enough to reach the other end of the tunnel and escape? Or—

About halfway through the arcade, the arches opened on either side to galleries of a sort. Satara was just coming abreast of them when a shriek rent the air and Daschla lunged from the shadows.

When Satara saw the blur of black and purple headed for her, she raised her weapons. Daschla's blade collided with the rim of the shield but only left a tiny dent in the dwarven-forged metal. Satara jumped back, thrusting her spear at the false valkyrie's heart.

She dodged easily, jumping high, her wings skimming the ceiling of the arcade as she leapt over Satara in one bound. Satara rolled forward and turned, unwilling to show her back.

"So," Daschla said, spinning her sword in one hand, "Astrid's new shieldmaiden. We finally meet face to face."

"I haven't been a shieldmaiden since your mistress killed my battlemother." Satara readied her spear for another thrust.

"Still sore about that?" Daschla lunged again, but Satara slid to the side and lashed out with her shield, knocking her strike aside. "You should be thanking us. Astrid deserved to die."

"All Astrid did was her duty. *Your* only duty is to yourself."

The false valkyrie growled, circling Satara in the blink of an eye and slashing. She had no time to dodge; pain exploded in her arm, flecks of amethyst spraying her and Daschla's armor. With a grunt, she turned, staying defensive with her shield up and her spear ready to fend her opponent off from a distance.

"My duties are different than yours," Daschla said, "that's all."

"Then you'll never be a true valkyrie. You'll always be the malformed, broken, disgusting creature Indriði created."

Daschla wiped her blade on her thigh, eyes shining with hatred. "I'm here to make a difference, not follow warriors to Valhalla and bear them mead." She bared her teeth, slashing again and missing Satara's shield by a hair. "And what will you do, hm? Be a little servant and do as you're told, or seize your own fate? *What are you here to do?*"

Satara ground her teeth. "I'm here to fucking kill you."

She lashed out, and her shield flew from her hand, the runes on its surface glowing as it cracked against Daschla's jaw. The false valkyrie staggered back with a grunt but recovered quickly, rocketing toward Satara with one hand outstretched and sword at the ready.

Satara's shield returned to her hand with barely a second to spare, and she was able to deflect the blade. But a blast of magic materialized in Daschla's palm, hitting her squarely in the face and sending her flying backward. Wind whistled in her ears, then stone cracked, fine dust falling as she collided with one of the arcade arches.

She ignored the ache in her body as she pulled herself up, just in time to dodge another blast of magic. It hissed and sizzled as it hit the wall behind her, death and shadow magic mingling to create a deadly missile.

Deadly to most, at least. Satara didn't know if she could die in Midgard—not by normal means, anyway. Still, Daschla needed to be put down. And if Basile's theory was correct, without Odin's blessing, it could be done.

The more injuries Satara sustained, the harder it would be. The more time she wasted. The closer New York came to chaos under New Gloaming control.

She charged forward again, meeting her opponent. Blade clashed against shield, then against the spear's shaft. It was no wonder Daschla wanted to fight at melee range, in the close quarters of the arcade. It was nearly impossible to hold her at range enough for Satara to use her spear effectively.

With a bolstering shout, Satara knocked her opponent back a few feet, following up with another shield toss. It found its mark in the center of Daschla's chest, then boomeranged past Satara. She gripped her spear with both hands, spreading her feet.

She could feel the magic pulsing through the ancient weapon. She could win this fight. She was a valkyrie. All she had to do was listen to the flow and let it carry her.

Be ready.

Daschla roared and surged forward, the cracks in her skin glowing brightly as she raised her sword. Satara blocked, using the spear like a staff, but Daschla twisted, bearing down until the tip touched the cobbles. She slashed again, and Satara narrowly escaped a beheading, ducking and rolling forward.

In one fluid motion, she unfurled to her feet and turned, blocking another strike. The blade bit into the spear's wooden handle but only left a small notch. Again and again, Daschla lashed out, and Satara blocked her each time, backing up.

"Hit me!" Daschla finally snapped, her voice shaking the arcade. "Hit me, you coward!"

If that was what she wanted...

Satara obliged wordlessly, thrusting forward.

The tip of the spear sank into the chainmail of Daschla's underarm, drawing an unearthly scream. Blood burst from the wound, coating her armor and the spear. As Satara jerked back, Daschla retreated, leaving a dark purple trail in the snow.

The false valkyrie's face twisted, breath coming heavier and fogging the air between them. Her lips pulled back like a wolf's, her pupils shrinking to little white points of light. "You fucking bitch," she rasped.

Keeping her spear in a defensive position, Satara stepped closer. She wasn't about to let Daschla bow out after one good blow. "Your one chance to prove you're worthy of being a valkyrie and I haven't even broken a sweat."

An easy taunt. And, Satara realized as she watched Daschla's face turn purple, a very effective one. She shrieked like a banshee, spreading her wings and shooting forward.

Satara tried to dodge, but Daschla clipped her shoulder, knocking her onto the cobbles. Before she could recover, the false valkyrie was on top of her. Eyes aflame, she discarded her sword and wrapped her hands around Satara's neck.

The pressure was much more intense than expected. Even though Daschla's soul was discordant, her strength matched any other valkyrie's, and Satara struggled to release herself. As she gripped Daschla's wrists, trying to buck her off, the grip tightened. Her vision blurred.

Panic snapped in Satara's mind. It shouldn't be this much of a problem. She didn't need to breathe, but Daschla seemed to be taking something from her that wasn't breath. The spirit magic wreathing her hands was weakening her; she could feel power draining from her into Daschla. As the power transferred, her grip became tighter and tighter.

She was fueling herself. She was using Satara's spirit to become more powerful. Was that what she had meant by *feed*? In that case—

The pain was too much to bear. Satara could feel her throat giving way. Almost nothing in Midgard could kill her ... but could another valkyrie? A valkyrie of equal strength?

Another surge of panic shocked her muscles, and she bucked again, exploding with death magic. It jostled Daschla, loosening her grip momentarily and interrupting her power drain, but it wasn't enough to knock her off completely.

Satara struggled, nails and heels of her boots scrambling and scratching against the cobbles beneath her. Daschla almost seemed to become bigger before her eyes, the cracks in her skin becoming thinner and thinner.

She's killing me...

Picturing the oblivion awaiting her, the one she'd sensed for Astrid, conjured screams in her mind. Alone—so alone, for the rest of eternity. Trillions upon trillions of years and more still. Her sanity slipped at the thought. She struggled harder, harder, desperate to escape that fate.

"The Wounded will come soon," Daschla whispered, her eyes cold, grip steady. "Lord Sárr will bolster my army and help us defeat yours. And when they're all dead, I'm going to feast on your loved ones."

"Like hell you are." A voice rang, rich and powerful, through the arcade. A voice ingrained in Satara's bones, in the grooves of her palms, at the roots of her hair. A voice she had known since the moment her soul had winked into existence.

Daschla went stiff above her, grip on Satara's throat rapidly loosening as a sword—her own sword—grew from her chest, shining and slicked with purple.

A moment later, the blade twisted, and Daschla scrambled off Satara with a wail. The weapon slid from her middle.

Standing there, blade in one hand and staff in the other, was Priestess Amat.

CHAPTER FORTY-TWO

As DASCHLA STAGGERED, Satara jumped to her feet. The world spun, but she grabbed her spear and called for her shield with a whistle. It was in her hand in a second, and she stood between her mother and Daschla, ready to finish this.

Daschla turned to look at them, clutching her middle. Dark purple blood poured from between her fingers, staining her front. She stood there silently, breath labored, for a few moments.

Then she turned, spread her wings, and fled the arcade.

Satara bounded after her, Mama close behind. She felt sluggish. Her body was so much heavier than usual, every step a challenge. Still, she followed Daschla back to the Mall, back to the battle.

She and Mama followed even when it seemed the false valkyrie was running blindly into the fray. As she passed spirits, they abandoned the battles in which they were locked to cling to her. She was drawing them to her somehow.

It wasn't until they reached a small, empty bit of green that Satara could actually see what was happening. Daschla stopped running and opened her arms wide, drawing the spirits—gathering them around her, closer and closer.

One by one, their translucent forms melted into her skin. Each time, she glowed brighter. She seemed to swell with power, the cracks in her skin tightening.

She was devouring them. Feeding. And, Satara realized as she watched her flesh and armor knit back together, healing herself.

When there was nothing left of the spirits but excess mist on the air, Daschla turned on Satara. In a half second, she was upon her. A swift, strong punch to the jaw knocked her back.

And it *hurt*. The world spun again. Satara remembered this feeling from previous battles, when she had been human ... from sparring practice with Astrid. This was the feeling of fighting someone who was much more powerful than you.

More powerful than she had been a few minutes before.

Satara threw her shield and released a bolstering battle cry. As her sister valkyir descended on Daschla, she turned to Mama. "Tell our defenders to corral the spirits away from this area. Daschla has to stand on her own."

"What just happened?" Mama demanded.

Satara gritted her teeth. Saying the truth aloud sent a jolt of ice through her body. "Every spirit she consumes makes her stronger. Soon, we won't be able to stop her."

"Incoming!" Edie shouted. She melted through the shadow of a large elm and rematerialized behind Marius, narrowly escaping the wave of spirits she'd lured toward him.

With a grunt, Marius lashed out with his plasma whip, cutting through a swath of unholy dead. As the whip came back, it curled and formed a shield, and a blade roared to life in Marius's left hand.

Behind his cover, Edie was in charge of crowd control, flinging gouts of death magic left and right.

But the defenders were pushing more spirits this way, like they were trying to separate them from Daschla for some reason, and Edie could feel her strength slowly draining. She'd only learned to control this power in the most basic ways *weeks* ago.

"Why are they coming toward us?" Edie called as she spouted another blast of death.

"It looks like orders from Satara," Marius managed between strikes. "To get them away from Daschla."

"Why?!"

"I don't know!" He spun and slashed again. A cone of sunlight burst from the tip of his blade, scorching the earth in front of him.

Even with his holy powers, though, the push toward them was overwhelming. He retreated, never turning his back on the spirits, and Edie followed suit.

"Can you hold them off for a moment?" he asked without taking his eyes off the mob.

"I can try."

Edie concentrated hard. During the battle in the Temple of the Rising Divine, she had done ... something. She wasn't even sure what to call it. Her death magic had coated the ground as a blazing blue sigil that had felled everything in its vicinity.

She could try to do it again, but it had completely drained her last time. She'd blacked out. If she could just—

A cry of pain drew her attention back to Marius. He sliced through the middle of a spirit in front of him but staggered back as it dispersed, his shield flickering out of existence.

A translucent spirit blade stuck out from between the pauldron and breastplate of his right side, buried in his underarm.

The weapon burst into wisps of spirit magic like its owner had, and Marius began to bleed. Strong, steady spurts of blood stained his alabaster armor.

That *had* to be an artery. With a gasp, Edie grabbed him by the other arm and began to run, searching frantically for somewhere safe to stop the bleeding. He tripped after her, dragging his feet, already weakened. All around them, defenders ran and spirits closed in.

Nowhere was safe.

She darted to the side, pulling him toward the nearest structure, a permanent stone bandstand. As they reached the side, she helped him sit at the base, pressing her hand tightly to his underarm.

"Edie," he whispered, face already ashen.

"Shh. Shut up. Be quiet. You're gonna be okay."

With shaking fingers, she unfastened his pauldron and let it fall to the side, but she couldn't get past the chainmail unless she wanted to undress him fully right here. This would have to do.

She pressed harder, trying to focus on the song his blood sang to her —gods knew there was plenty of it on her hands. It was sharp and warm and strong, and she closed her eyes, trying to become one with the sound, the smell.

By the time the blood stopped flowing, she was shaking. But with all her being, she pushed harder, trying to mend the cut in the artery. His tendon was sliced to shit, too, but it'd have to wait.

"Edie," Marius croaked.

"Relax!"

"No, Edie!"

She heard the spirit first. Its shriek echoed off the stone of the bandstand. When she whipped her head around to look, it was closer than she had anticipated, sword raised high in the air.

Marius grunted and fired a ball of light that hit it square in the chest, but when he lowered his hand, he was panting. She could tell from his eyes and the sweat on his brow that he was barely clinging to consciousness.

"Just rest." She brushed his curls away from his forehead, hand still clamped on his wound.

A moment later, another shriek echoed, and she watched helplessly as a mob of spirits dove for them, their faces twisted with hatred. Marius raised his left arm again, but only a few sparks belched from his palm.

No time to grab the Puretongue's blade. Instinctively, Edie leaned over him, shielding him with her body.

Then, something blotted out the sun.

For a brief second, Edie thought this was the end. She was dying. She couldn't feel the pain, but the world was dimming.

But no—it was a shadow, and a familiar cold aura.

She looked up and saw Satara. Her wings were outstretched, shielding Edie and Marius as she fought off the spirits. Edie grinned, relief flooding her chest.

"Edie..."

For the fourth time, Marius said her name. She turned her attention back to healing him, but she could hardly keep the blood from flowing, let alone use any of it to heal him. He needed every ounce of what he had left.

With her free hand, she unsheathed the blade of truth and drew it across her wrist—not too deep, but deep enough. It was a clean slice; ruby blood welled from her pale skin. As she pressed harder into Marius's armpit, she concentrated on the brightness of it. Vitality. Oxygen. Life.

A chill raced down her arm. Before her eyes, the blood defied gravity, mistlike as it rose from her veins and slithered into Marius's.

Yet again, Marius whispered, "Edie." His golden eyes looked into hers with the urgency of someone who was buckling under heavy weight, weight he was desperate to pass off. This time, she let him continue. "I want to— I have to tell you something."

Edie tried to focus on the call of the blood. "What is it?"

"When we first met," he said quietly, barely audible over the sounds of battle raging just over her shoulder, "I called you an abomination. I believed that was true. But ... over and over, you've proved you're not."

"Marius, it's okay. I know you—"

"Listen." The earnestness with which he looked at her made her uncomfortable. "The people who told me that were wrong. *I* was wrong. More than wrong. I've never known anyone as brave or as kind as you ... recklessly so, more often than not."

He reached out and clumsily grabbed a chunk of hair that had fallen out of her bun.

"Edie—"

"Hey! What's going on over here?"

Edie jerked her head up to see Basile running against the current of the battle, toward them. He'd gone full skeleton, but judging by his tone, she imagined that if he had facial muscles, he'd look very concerned. "Marius?"

It took a moment for Edie to find words. "He's hurt."

Basile looked from Marius to Satara. He raised one hand near where his lips should be, palm up, and opened his jaw. A wispy ball of energy floated from his mouth into his palm, and with a mumble, he released it.

The ball flew toward Satara and wreathed her weapons with more spirit magic, until they were glowing like neon. Her spear and shield cut through the unholy army like butter.

Basile turned back to Marius and Edie, crouching beside them to assess the damage. "You got this under control?"

"I don't know. I'm trying. One of them hit an artery. It'd be easier if I had some water."

The priest raised his head to scan the battlefield. Looking for water, Edie thought at first, though that seemed kind of absurd. But as the seconds passed, she caught on to the heavy hopelessness of his aura.

"What's wrong?" Marius asked, apparently sensing it, too.

Basile hesitated. "Look ... things are, uh ... going south out there."

Edie followed his gaze to where the battle had migrated. There were so many spirits that the Mall looked more like water than pavement. Like the river from her dream. They had barely cut the army in half by the time Daschla arrived with reinforcements, and now...

Vidarr's form was the first to catch her eye, large and fiery as it was. He was trying to disengage from the battle to get to Daschla, but it was as if the spirits knew. They were swarming him, dragging him down to the cement. He was on his knees at the moment, struggling against spectral weapons gouged into his flesh.

Many of the valkyir seemed to be suffering the same fate as they tried to keep the spirits and their queen separate. Some had been pinned down, others mobbed and trapped. As Daschla fought her way through their line, she seemed to be *absorbing souls*, and as she passed, she left a trail of broken valkyir on the ground.

Edie's heart raced. Without Vidarr and the valkyir, they were fucked.

"What the hell is she doing?" Edie asked, tracking Daschla with her eyes as she felled another valkyrie. She seemed to be growing larger and brighter. It almost hurt to look at her.

"Those spirits she's absorbing, she's feeding on them. The more she consumes, the stronger she gets. I assume the idea was for them to destroy the city with her as their leader, in a position where she could feed on them whenever she needed to."

"Now she's cutting her losses," Edie mumbled, touching Marius's forehead again as he slumped against the brick. "Shit. He passed out."

"Even if we're able to bring her down somehow," Basile continued, "the sheer number of these spirits ... if we don't retreat now, every last one of our defenders is going to die."

She looked at him. "If we retreat, they're going to move into the city. They're going to kill a shitload of innocent people."

"I know." His tone was grim, thoughtful.

After a pause, he glanced over his shoulder. Another valkyrie and her shieldmaiden had joined the fight, along with Cal and Elle, and Satara was able to step back for a moment of rest.

"I have an idea," Basile said, looking between her and Edie.

Satara's chest rose and fell quickly despite her not needing to breathe. "Good ... we could use one, and I'm running out."

"To stop her from absorbing the spirits, I could absorb them first. They're just floating around out there. I wouldn't even have to flay them."

Edie thought back to their first meeting in Central Park, when he had devoured the souls of the Watchers chasing them. But that had only been five people. "Is that possible?"

"I think so. Very, very difficult ... but not impossible. But listen." He stood, spreading his bony hands. "You remember when we first met, and I told you the more souls I consume, the bigger the risk?"

"The emptiness inside of you could become bigger, and you could get … hungry," Edie said. "I remember."

"Yeah. Well, if anything does it, two thousand evil souls will." He took a deep breath, looking between them. "I could turn against you. If that happens … I need you to kill me. And then I need you to destroy my mother's sarcophagus."

Satara frowned. "There must be another way. If—"

"Satara, look." He gestured helplessly to the battlefield. "You know there isn't another way. We either retreat, or we all die, or I do this."

"But *you* could die," she pressed.

"If it means saving eight million people and your island, I'm okay with that. Just promise me you'll do what you have to do."

Satara looked between him and the battle still raging, and after a few moments, sighed. "I always do."

Without another word, Basile strode into the battle, pushing through the crowd. Spirits dissolved under his fingers as he brushed past them, their essence clinging to his cassock and the heels of his shoes like flurries of snow.

He stopped at the cobbled area just before the promenade and turned fully, surveying the entire battle.

As he did, Satara joined a group of other valkyir, shouting, "Sound the retreat!"

Moments later, horns filled the air, so close and loud that Edie's teeth chattered. As the defenders began to retreat toward Bethesda Terrace, she stayed where she was, still putting pressure on Marius's wound. She tried to split her attention between him and Basile but could only get glimpses the priest's dark outfit as people raced by her.

"Edie!" Adam emerged from the retreating defenders, looking exhausted and bleeding from a cut across his chest and collar. He jogged toward her, gaze filled with worry. "Is he—?"

"Give me your hand."

"What?"

Edie grabbed him and pulled him into a crouch, replacing her hand with his. "I need you to use your blood to heal him." She tugged at the sleeve of her jacket to show him her sliced wrist. "Just enough that he won't die, but don't leave him."

"But, Edie, they sounded the retreat, there's no way we're gonna— And I don't know—"

"Listen to me. The blood ... I don't know how, but it knows what to do. You'll know. Just listen to it."

She stood, turning to look for Basile. Most of the defenders had made it back to the terrace, and Daschla took to the air to follow them. Yet the spirits weren't following her, and they hadn't turned to attack Edie either.

No ... they seemed much more interested in Basile.

He still stood before the promenade, looking up at the sky. The air around him quivered with power, and a circle of pale periwinkle fire about five feet in diameter surrounded him fully.

Spirits swarmed him, attracted by the immense energy he was giving off, but the circle seemed to keep them at bay. He simply looked up at the gray clouds and the shafts of sunlight that had managed to break through.

Then he raised his hands. Rapidly, the circle of light tightened until it disappeared under his feet, and his body flashed white for a split second. A sudden strong wind ruffled his cassock and made Edie's hair whip around her face.

Not an ordinary gust of wind. Strangely, Edie could feel it inside, like a pulling in her chest. *Oh, shit.*

Quickly, she snapped into action, turning to Adam. "We need to find cover. Can you pick him up?"

"What? I— With all this armor—"

"I'll help." Edie crouched and supported Marius's legs. "Get a move on unless you want your soul flayed from your body."

Silenced, Adam lifted his upper half, and they shuffled behind the bandstand. Once Marius was settled on the ground again, with Adam tending to his wounds, Edie peered around the structure to get another glimpse of Basile.

The wind had picked up, and though she couldn't feel it tugging at her insides anymore, it was strong enough to bite her skin and make her eyes water. The spirits were fighting against it, digging their heels into the pavement and leaning into it stubbornly. Otherworldly screams of anguish filled the Mall, and Edie covered her ears, gritting her teeth at the sound.

Slowly, then faster and faster, the souls were being pulled toward Basile. He leaned back, skeleton face toward the sky, jaw open, arms wide. The wind picked up, quicker, more vicious, and Edie found herself clinging to the bandstand just to keep her footing.

Most of the spirits weren't so lucky. Many of them tripped and were caught up like empty plastic bags, swirling around and around in the air as though they'd been sucked into a twister.

The harder the wind blew, the more souls were sucked in—until eventually Edie couldn't see one unholy warrior with their feet still on the ground. They formed a whirlpool of wispy purple above Basile, swirling down, down into his open jaws.

Edie's chest felt like ice. Just like the river in her dream.

In a matter of seconds, the last of the spirits were flushed through Basile's invisible funnel.

His body flashed white again, the circle of fire enfolded him, and he fell to the ground like a stone.

For a long time, Edie simply stared. The battlefield was silent for the first time in hours. She could hear birds and traffic, police and ambulance sirens coming closer. The stench? Horrific. The sight? Bloody, bodies strewn across the pavement.

But the sound? So calm and normal that it was jarring. Her ears rang.

Creeping out from behind the bandstand, she took a few steps toward Basile. Was he dead? Was he sleeping? Or was this a trick to get her closer so he could kill her?

Before she could get any closer to find out, screaming from the terrace drew her attention. Daschla was standing on the upper terrace, locked in battle with Satara.

Without thinking, Edie darted forward, across the street.

Past the terrace, she could see the frozen lake. Vidarr and the valkyir were forcing the humans through portals, back to Mare Isle. Some of them held their dead or dying friends in their arms; others struggled against the valkyir, refusing to give up the fight. The sight made her heart ache.

They needed to kill Daschla or she'd make more warriors. Basile and everyone else's sacrifice would be for nothing.

As Edie approached the upper terrace, Daschla and Satara were struggling sword to spear, trembling in deadlock.

Edie planted her feet, drawing both the Puretongue's blade and the runed dagger. "Your spirits are gone," she shouted at Daschla. "You don't have anything left to feed on. You fucked up."

Her words caused the false valkyrie to falter in her defense, and Satara shoved hard, knocking her to the ground.

In one swift, fluid movement, Satara twirled her spear and plunged it through Daschla's middle, pinning her to the pavement.

Daschla's face was a mask of horror. Her expression hardly changed as she rasped, "You can't do this to me. The Wounded won't let you do this to me."

"Where is the Wounded?" Satara asked, never breaking eye contact. "I don't see him."

Daschla said nothing, simply opened her mouth in a silent wail. Tears slicked her temples.

"Are you frightened, now that you're as disposable to him as your followers were to you?" Satara pushed her spear further. Dark purple blood coursed across the terrace. "It didn't have to be like this."

She lifted her head and nodded to Edie, beckoning her closer. She stopped near Daschla's head, looking down at her.

The life was already leaving her; she only moved to twitch. She seemed so immobilized that Edie wasn't afraid to crouch down.

A spark of clarity seemed to light Daschla's eyes as she did. "Kill me," she whispered, gazing at the blades Edie held.

Edie looked at Satara. She nodded.

With surprisingly steady hands, Edie grabbed a fistful of Daschla's braids, exposing her throat. She took a deep breath and held it, then exhaled. "This is more than you deserve."

She stabbed the runed blade into the side of her neck, slicing so deeply that metal scraped bone.

Daschla was gone before she even removed her blade. Severing the carotid artery was an instant, painless death. Blood burst and coated Edie's hands, her chest, her face, but it hardly registered.

Everything was still for a moment.

Then it wasn't.

At first, she thought Daschla's corpse was twitching—death throes or something. But a second later, she understood what she was witnessing. The cracks in Daschla's skin were widening, and as they did, her skin seemed to flake away, crumbling like loose dirt into the sickly light growing inside her.

Inch by inch, her body turned to dust, until her form was only a white void. Then a cosmic groan cut the air, and the void blinked out of existence, leaving only a black blotch in Edie's vision.

She looked out over the lake, letting her hair stick to her face. The others were still struggling to get the Mare Isle defenders home, but there was nothing to retreat from now. The bracing wind carried the scent of death away from her.

Satara wiped her spear off on the snow, allowing Edie to stare before breaking the silence. "If you knew what's waiting for her on the other side, you'd know that was exactly what she deserved."

With that, the valkyrie turned and crossed the street.

CHAPTER FORTY-THREE

THE FLOOR of the Baccarat's grand salon was covered in a fine gravel of tempered glass and crystal. The crunch of it underfoot echoed hollowly in Zaedicus's ears, agitation rising in him with every new step.

She was supposed to be waiting. She had told the Wounded she'd be waiting for him. Where was she?

Technically, Zaedicus should be back in Anster. He was the Gloaming Lord of that province, after all. But the title had not been long in his grasp before he'd realized that was all it was—a title.

For all his scheming and ambition, the Gloaming in which he'd longed to gain power was gone. In the Wounded's New Gloaming, the real power was on the ground, not in the high castles with the coffers. Now, he was judged not on his status and estate but by his martial prowess ... and in that, he had come up sorely lacking.

Lords waging wars with iron, like barbarians. How *common*.

He couldn't even throw parties. The Wounded found them frivolous, and Zaedicus couldn't be sure how many more chances he had before he, like Fahraad before him, was assassinated and deposed.

In short, Anster had become frightfully boring. The Gloaming all but ruled it now, the human governments were panicking, but none of that interested Zaedicus.

Oh, he had always been a slave to ambition. He always wanted what he couldn't have. When he got it, he rapidly lost interest. It wasn't something he felt compelled to change in himself. He'd simply move on to the next thing.

First, Anster. Next, Scarlet.

He had it on good authority that she was here, although what he would do once they were together again, he wasn't sure. He hadn't thought of it, had simply traveled here in a white-hot haze of rage and desire.

It was unlikely that she'd come with him willingly. Perhaps he could offer her safety. No one he had asked was sure, at the moment, where Indriði was. Scarlet would need someone to protect her. Or perhaps he would enthrall her. He doubted a lowly human-wight would be able to resist his superior elven power.

But first, he needed to find her.

As he meandered to the other end of the salon, taking in the broken, bland interior, he paused. Ah, yes. His informant had said the plan was for Scarlet and the Wounded to meet in the Baccarat bar after the hellerunan had been captured, to discuss her role in New York City's long-term occupation—and beyond a glass door about ten feet from him, he could see the very end of a bar.

He straightened his posture, smoothing his beaded white doublet. The Wounded, he assumed, was still upstairs, searching the place for the hellerune and her friends. He needed to act quickly before Scarlet's one moment of privacy was snatched away from him.

Zaedicus pushed through the glass door and took a step inside.

He balked at the smell that greeted him. A wall cut the room in half, but the bodies were numerous enough that they nearly carpeted the floor. Disgust tickled the nape of his neck as he stepped over them, passing the wall and beholding the room in its entirety.

Scarlet was clever and fierce. The death in this room meant nothing.

She must be hiding, or perhaps she had escaped to the upper levels ... perhaps she was meeting with the Wounded now.

He took a few more steps in, toward a wall of mirrors, gazing at the chandeliers above the bar. There had once been three, but one now lay in pieces, half-caught on the smashed shelves. There had been quite a battle in here.

Suddenly, the checkered floor beneath his feet was no longer wood. It felt soft, like he was stepping on sand or silt, and immediately, he stepped back, looking down.

He froze. A pile of ash glittered there, in a distinct mound save for where his boot had scuffed it. Had his heart been beating, it would have stopped.

Undead remains, burned to true death.

Gingerly, he knelt on one knee, careful to avoid the ash as well as the blood coating the floor. The gray, slightly shimmery remains were repugnant, and he didn't want to touch them, but he lowered his head for an experimental sniff.

He would know that scent anywhere ... he'd dreamed of smothering himself in it every waking moment for months now.

This was Scarlet.

Unceremoniously, he plunged his fingers into the ash—something he would normally never do, and yet it was as though there was a cloud over his mind, like someone else had possessed his hands. He sifted through the pile with the single-mindedness of a revenant, uncertain what he was looking for. Until he found it.

It felt like minutes before his fingers finally touched the silk, though in reality it was probably only a second or two. From the pile, he pulled the tattered remains of a long white dress, stained brownish-black where ash had clung to blood.

Scarlet. *All that's left of her*. The thought stunned him as he clasped the fabric tightly, staring at it.

An oppressive presence entered the room, and Zaedicus turned his head to see the Wounded standing behind him. The young man looked surprised, for a moment, to see the Gloaming Lord but schooled his expression quickly.

"What are you doing here?"

Zaedicus did not move, only looked at Sárr. "News of your movements travels fast, my lord." He looked back at the ruined silk. "I wanted to witness you taking the city."

The Wounded grunted. "Somehow, I doubt that. Even so, you have your own city to worry about."

"What happened here?" Zaedicus demanded. "Who did this to her?"

When the Wounded didn't answer, the high-wight looked over his shoulder again—in time to see Sárr bend and pick something up off the ground. A shotgun shell, slick with blood from the floor.

He raised it to his nose, then offered it to Zaedicus. "An easy guess."

Scowling, Zaedicus batted the shell away. "That revolting zombie." Quickly, he averted his eyes, hoping he had escaped the Wounded's wrath. If a subordinate ever smacked something out of *his* hand...

But the Wounded didn't flinch. He simply straightened, suddenly looking exhausted. "The hellerunan are not here, so I am leaving."

Zaedicus staggered to his feet, still clutching Scarlet's tatters. A small flare of hope heated his thirst for blood. "The rally," he whispered. "You must be going to Daschla's little rally. The revenant will be there. He must be slain."

The Wounded sighed and half-turned dismissively. "No. I am not going there."

Genuine confusion gave Zaedicus pause. "But Holloway and the other hellerune will be there. Daschla will be expecting the New Gloaming to support her forces."

"I'm sure she will be." The Wounded walked to the terrace windows and looked out. "According to my scouts, her excuse for an army outnumbers the Reach six to one. If she can't overcome them with a thousand deathless warriors ... I won't bother wasting my men on saving her."

Zaedicus, ruthless as he knew himself to be, found himself shocked.

For a noble elf, of course, the dispensability of soldiers' lives was well known, but the Wounded Lord had always valued strategy and strength in numbers.

"My lord, that's two thousand indestructible soldiers lost. The force that was to bring New York to its knees. If they are gone, it will change everything. The whole plan for taking the city will have to be done over."

"Daschla is a failed experiment, Zaedicus. Just a warped little girl desperate for power over others. I don't need her or her evil spirits."

"Power over others," the high-wight repeated, brow furrowing. "My lord, is that not what we all want? To bring the Gloaming back to glory? As our ruler, you'd have power over *everyone*." Another pause, one that felt hollow and stale in his chest. "Is that not what this all has been about?"

The Wounded lowered his gaze to the floor, toeing a fallen warrior's weapon out of the way. Rather than answer the question, he simply said, "When which cities fall won't matter, in the end. They all will, eventually."

Then, he turned and left the bar.

As he disappeared through the glass doors, two black-and-silver-clad New Gloaming agents stepped in to survey the scene. Zaedicus carefully laid the silk shreds on top of the ash pile and turned to them, trying to appear imperious rather than shaken by the conversation.

"You, put these ashes and those scraps in something. I'm taking them back to Anster with me."

CHAPTER FORTY-FOUR

"OKAY, EDIE." Adam steepled his fingers. "Marius is dead. The cleric is running out of spell slots and Cal is on his last healing potion. How do you want to do this?"

With a sigh, Edie looked up from her phone, skimming her character sheet. "Um, I think you should refer to me as my proper name if you're going to address me."

"Okay, Susanne from Finance, the kobold barbarian ... it's your turn and the cyclops is charging toward you. What do you do?"

Edie looked at the others gathered around the apartment's dining room table. "What do you guys think?"

Marius adjusted the sling holding his right arm. Between his own healing and frequent visits from Yuval, he had made a lot of progress in the past week, but he still winced with every movement. *Dungeons & Dragons* would be the only combat he'd be seeing for a while yet. "We've been fighting this thing for over an hour. It's got to be close to dead. I say just hit it."

"You should probably Rage," Satara suggested as she reached across him to grab a corn chip. "Aevana lowers her quarterstaff and shouts to Susanne, 'Use your Rage! It's the only way!'"

Marius smirked, exchanging a glance with Edie. "Ah, right, roleplaying. Zephyr the Lightbringer … lies there limply, gasping out his last."

Edie scratched the back of her neck. "Okay, I shout, 'This better not make me late to the PTA meeting!' and I'm gonna Rage. Um, Adam, which dice is that again?"

"Roll your d20 to hit, then roll damage for your greataxe with the d12, then add your Rage and proficiency mods."

She rolled, peering at the dice. "Sixteen?"

"Okay, that hits. What's your damage?"

"Uh … what's nine plus two plus three?"

"Fourteen," about half of the table, including Cal, replied in unison.

"All right." Adam grinned. "And that's going to kill him. How are you doing it?"

"I bonk him with my axe."

Satara rubbed her forehead. "You could at least try to take this a little seriously. It's the dungeon's final boss."

"Okay, fine … I soar through the air! And, uh … I slice him across the chest, cutting off both nipples in one fell swoop. As he comes crashing to the ground, I jump back."

Over Elle's cackling, Cal grunted. "Would a cyclops have two nipples or one nipple?"

Adam clapped, scribbling a few things down behind his GM screen. "Cool, so he's dead, which means you're free from initiative … and you can plunder his treasure if you like."

"Yay!" Elle pointed across the table at Marius. "I'm going to run over to Zephyr and touch him to cast Revivify."

"Zephyr thanks you," Marius replied.

"*Aaaaand?*"

He sighed. "And gives you a chaste kiss on the hand."

Cal raised a finger. "I blow on the barrels of my pistols all sexy and holster them. Then I run over and start looting the gold pile." He picked up his twenty-sided die and rolled a three. "Ah, shit."

"You don't have to roll for that, I'll just give you treasure." Adam shuffled some papers behind his screen before pointing to each one of them, starting with Elle. "Firbolg cleric Ewelina—"

"Ewelina *what*, Adam?"

He sighed. "Ewelina the Well-Endowed ... you receive ninety gold pieces and a Scroll of Hideous Laughter."

"Hell yes."

"Cal, Bruce Killshot the half-orc gunslinger receives sixty gold pieces and a violet garnet. Zephyr the human paladin, you get sixty gold pieces and a Scroll of Detect Undead."

"A scroll for a spell I already have ... how generous." Marius nodded across the table to Cal. "See, there's one now."

"Don't start with me, Sparky."

"Aevana the high elf sorcerer receives one hundred and fifty gold pieces and a Scroll of Shocking Grasp. And Susanne from Finance receives forty gold and five flasks of acid."

"It begs the question," Edie said, "what was a cyclops doing with all these scrolls?"

Marius frowned. "How insulting. Light reading, obviously."

"Did he just tell a joke?" Cal rasped. "I think you just told a joke."

"All right." Adam looked up from his papers. "So, after plundering the hoard of the cyclops, your adventuring party manages to find its way out of the dark caves. As you exit, you realize you've been in there all day, and you kind of"—he blocked his eyes with a hand—"wince against the sunset. Except for Susanne, of course, who's wearing goggles."

"Cat-eye goggles. Tortoiseshell."

"Right. So, would you like to go back to the village, or ... what would you like to do?"

Cal grunted, scribbling on his character sheet with a pencil that looked comically small in his big, meaty hand. "Let's go back so I can sell all this shit and get some cash. Bruce Killshot wants to woo some tavern wenches."

"Okay, so you journey back to Mako Village. It takes about a day, so remove one day's provisions from your sheet. And, um, as you enter the market, where would you like to go first?"

Elle raised her hand. "Are there any fruit stands nearby?"

"Yes, there's one in the square."

"I would like to steal a watermelon."

Marius sighed. "Do I have to witness this? Stealing breaks my tenets."

"It breaks *your* tenets, not mine!" Elle held up her character sheet, pointing aggressively. "It says right here, my religious tenets are eating pussy and having fun!"

Adam looked at Marius. "Uh, the group can split up and Zephyr can go with someone else."

"I'm going to the jeweler," Satara said, crunching another chip.

"Me, too," Cal chimed in. "Yo, Dungeon Master, if I sell this garnet, can I buy a tattoo?"

"Depends..." Adam raised a brow. "What do you want?"

Cal extended his fists. "Knuck tats. One'll say KILL and the other'll say SHOT."

Edie leaned back in her chair, tuning the others out as they argued about knuckle tattoos and the logistics of illicit melons. Considering the horror of the last few weeks and the exhaustion in her body, it was nice to take a moment to breathe, even if it meant being coerced into playing a tabletop roleplaying game.

She scratched the back of her neck again. It was itchy as hell for some reason.

Sitting at the end of the table, opposite Adam, she was the first to notice the apartment door opening. Her heart sped up a little, but she relaxed once she realized who it was.

Basile stepped in, a book tucked under his arm, his overcoat dusted with snow.

Edie stood from the table. "Hey!"

"Howdy," he said as he entered the dining room. He pushed his glasses up his nose. "What's this?"

"*Dungeons and Dragons*," Adam replied, giving him a once over. "You look good. Feeling better?"

"Not really. But I'll live. Or, continue to exist, I guess."

Satara had twisted around in her chair to face him. "You should rest more. You deserve it—you almost killed yourself barely a week ago."

"Meh." Basile waved a dismissive hand, then beckoned to Edie. "Come here. I need to talk to you."

She glanced at the others. "Uh, keep playing while I'm gone," she said, handing her character sheet to Cal before following Basile into the living room.

With a groan and what she swore was cracking bones, the priest settled onto the sofa, gesturing for her to sit next to him. She faced him with crisscrossed legs.

"So," she began, keeping her voice low. "Are you ... really okay? I was so sure you were gone, then you came to and were alive. Grumpy as always, but alive."

He exhaled slowly, adjusting his glasses again. "I'm ... well, I'll be fine. I've got work to do." He patted the book in his lap. "We've got work to do."

Edie felt any mirth or energy the game had given her draining away when he said that. She scratched the back of her neck.

Basile peered at her. "Something bothering you?"

"It's ... nothing."

"Turn around." He gestured with his chin. "Something's different; I can feel it."

After a moment's hesitation, she did as he said, brushing her ponytail over one shoulder. Behind her, Basile sighed, and she could hear him take a picture with his phone. When she looked over inquisitively, he offered it to her.

Shit. Edie blinked. "A new tattoo. Or mark. Or whatever it is." She turned around, still looking down at the screen. "What is it?"

"It's othala, *the blood*. It represents family. Blood. Birthright. Prosperity within a clan or group. On the other hand, of course, it means

... well, you saw it on the Blood Eagles' banners. Totalitarianism, prejudice ... bondage."

She cringed. "I'm ... not sure I want that tattooed on my body after everything that happened."

"Yeah. Seems like you don't really have a choice, though." With a light sigh, he shrugged and spread his hands. "Try not to worry about it too much. Your actions speak for themselves."

"I guess." Edie wasn't as confident. At least her jacket would mostly cover it. "So, what did you want to talk to me about? You said there was work to do...?"

Basile nodded and adjusted his glasses as he flipped through the leatherbound book in his lap. "The Riders loaned us some of the valkyir, and as you know, some of them died. A couple were unable to be retrieved. So even if we didn't owe them before, we sure as hell do now."

"Right." Everyone always wanted something, but at least this was pretty fair. "What do they want?"

"Well, we did agree to help them find Skuld. I've been doing some research, confirming my suspicions about how Daschla might have been created. If the Gloaming has her somewhere ... well, I know the valkyir are going to make finding their Rider-General a priority, so it should be the Reach's priority, too. Doing anything else first is going to make things, uh, complicated with the Riders, and we could really use the allies."

A bitter taste entered Edie's mouth. "We ... the Reach." She jerked a thumb toward the dining room. "Why are you talking to me about this and not them?"

"Because you're the Reacher. That's what I've gathered, anyway."

"Astrid *wanted* me to be the Reacher. I really— I don't think I'm qualified. I'd be terrible at it. That's what I keep trying to tell everyone."

Basile sighed. "Edie. The world needs the Reach, and the Reach needs a leader. Astrid was part of the Reach for a thousand years, and she chose you. If not Edie Holloway, then who?"

She hesitated, rubbing her hands together. "I've actually been giving it a lot of thought. Astrid thought we needed one leader, but ... I don't think that's true. Why do we only need *one*? Why can't we have more than one? Like a council or something? Then we can all hold each other accountable and everyone has strengths to fill in the others' weaknesses..."

The priest tilted his head. "Who do you have in mind, exactly?"

Rubbing her neck again, she looked toward the dining room. It was a lot to consider, but she'd had plenty of time to mull it over. At this point, the answer to that question seemed so obvious she wondered why it even had to be asked.

Silently, she indicated Cal and Satara. "I could add more people later if I needed to."

"Hm..." Basile peered at her thoughtfully. At length, he spread his hands again. "Well, hey. If you're all serious about this thing, you're going to need a place to set up. Somewhere with lots of room, walls for defense ... somewhere that makes the Reach look important when people visit."

"Yeah," Edie scoffed. "I'll start searching the classifieds and see if I can find a fortress for rent."

"No need." A grin spread across his face, eyes twinkling. "I know a place."

GLOSSARY

I USE a lot of crazy words in this book that you might not know how to pronounce, so here's a small list of all of the Norse words in *Unholy Spirit* and how to say them.

Some things to keep in mind before you read this guide:

1. Some words have been adapted from Old Norse rather than taken from Old Norse, so their pronunciations are different. It's also important to note that any "authentic" Norse pronunciation is reconstructed.

2. Some words are pronounced different contemporarily, so they aren't widely pronounced the way the Norse would have said them. In fact, I mix and match a lot—sometimes I use the legit Old Norse words for things, and sometimes I use the more contemporary forms. In the case of **valkyrie/valkyir**, I literally just made up the plural "valkyir" because it sounded cool.

3. I've had to cobble together words like "**hellerune**," etc., from other languages, so their pronunciation is a little fudged.

As for the full sentences, I'm absolutely fudging vocab and grammar. If you know someone who can hook me up with an authentic Old Norse translation, I'll take all the help I can get.

4. Pronunciation basics: the Norse almost always **rolled their r's**. The letters f and v, when they don't start the word, are pronounced as a v sound and a w sound respectively. The "aw" I've written to express the letter á is a round-mouthed almost-o sound like the au in the English word "**maul**" as opposed to "ow." The letter j is pronounced like y is in English. The letter thorn (Þ, þ) is pronounced like the "th" in "Thor," while the eth (Ð, ð) is pronounced like the "th" in "father" or "this." I've expressed the eth sound as "**dth**" because that's what it sounds like to me.

CHARACTER NAMES:

- Sárr – SAWR (almost "sore.")
- Marius – MAH-ree-us
- Eirik – EY-rick
- Fiskbein – FISK-bane
- Indriði – INDRI-dthee
- Hati – HA-tee
- Sköll – skohl
- Roggvi – ROGG-vee
- Ynga – ING-ga
- Freyja – frey-ya (Or, with reconstructed Norse pronunciation, "FROY-ya.")
- Odin – OH-din (Old Norse "Óðinn" or "OH-dthin.")
- Vidarr – Vih-DAAR (Old Norse "Víðarr," or "Vee-DTHARR)
- Skuld – skoold
- Daschla – DAHsh-la

- Hærfríðr – HAir-free-dthir (with "HA" said like you're starting to say "had," so it's really more like "haaihr.")
- Oddfreyr – ODD-froy-r
- Göndul – GOAN-dool
- Skögul – SKO-gool
- Geirskögul – GAIR-sko-gool
- Gunnr – goon-r (sort of a clipped "oo" sound rather than long)
- Hildr – hill-dr

RUNE NAMES:

- Ingwaz – ING-wahz
- Ehwaz – EH-wahz
- Othala – OATH-a-lah

MISC:

- Ván – vawn
- Hellerune – HELLA-roona
- Hellerunan – HELLA-roonen
- Vættr – vaa-tur (where "æ" is pronounced like the a in "had" or "mad.")
- Wight – white
- Dís – dees (longer "ee" sound than in "griss.")
- Heimdyrr – HAYM-dyur (the y sound makes a rounded "ee" sound like the u in "tune," but it's difficult to say.)
- Valkyrie – VAL-kur-ee (in reconstructed Old Norse, "valkyrja" or "VAUL-keer-ya.")
- Valkyir – VAL-kyeer
- Alfheim – AWLV-hime (Old Norse "Álfheimr" or "AWLV-hay-mur")

- Asgard – AS-gaard or ASS-gaard (Old Norse Ásgarðr, or "OSS-gaar-dthur)
- Aesir – ICE-eer (Old Norse "Æsir" or "ASS-eer," which for obvious reasons doesn't sound as cool...)
- Breiðablik – BREY-dtha-blik
- Bilskirnir – BILL-skeer-neer
- Heimdallr – HAYM-dallr
- Wyrd – weird
- Ragnarok – RAG-nah-rok (also known as Ragnarök or Ragnarøkkr)
- Fenrir – FEN-reer
- Váli – VOLL-e
- Baldr – BALL-dr
- Valhalla – VAL-hal-la or VAHL-hah-lla (Old Norse "Valhöll" or "VAHL-holl.")
- Yngvi – ING-vee
- Fylgja – FYULG-ya (where the y almost makes a rounded "ee" sound like the u in "tune". Plural "fylgjur" or "FYULG-yur.")
- Sjóvættr – SYO-vaa-tur
- Ljósálfr – LYOES-awl-vur
- Náströnd – NAW-strohnd
- Tyr – teer (Old Norse "Týr," where the y makes a rounded "ee" sound like the u in "tune")

NON-NORSE WORDS

(I'm not an expert on any of these languages, so take these with a BIG grain of salt!)

- Zaedicus – ZAY-di-cus and ZAI-di-cus (I made this name up and use both, which I'm sure he'd despise.)
- Izem – EEZ-im (Berber/North African; I always imagined some of Satara's ancestors being from there.)

- Ardelean – ar-DELL-yan (being Matilda's last name, this is Romanian, of course, not Norse.)
- Inuusuttoq – inoo-oo-sutt-ok
- Kolya – COAL-ya
- Ilphas Miravn – ILL-fass Meer-AH-vin
- Eniola – En-YO-la
- Galib – GAH-lihb
- Amat – AH-maht

ABOUT THE AUTHOR

Genevra Black is an author, a video game and movie nerd, horror buff, and lover of all things odd. She lives in Maine with her partner and her pitbull. She has always been enamored with mythology, folklore, and the paranormal. Her favorite pastimes include playing Dungeons & Dragons; gaming; watching slasher films; and designing and creating costumes/cosplay. She loves spending time in epic, exciting worlds, and each and every one of her stories is a personal invitation for readers to join her!

Find her at:

genevrablack.com
fb.me/GenevraBlack
twitter.com/GenevraBlack
instagram.com/authorgenevrablack
genevrablack@gmail.com

And if you join her mailing list at GenevraBlack.com you can download the exclusive short story "Night Vet of the Living Dead"—the tale of exactly what happened to Edie's undead hamster at the emergency vet.